*The earl jade-colored oil on his wrist.*

"Put that down!" Grabbing up a rag, Ciara rushed to his side. "It will burn right through your flesh." She set to wiping off every trace of green.

His touch was surprisingly gentle as he closed his hand around her wrist.

"I haven't finished," she murmured, hoping he didn't hear the odd little catch in her voice.

"Neither have I."

Ciara had every intention of pushing him away but some strange alchemy kept her frozen in place. He kissed her lightly, the brush of his lips feathering across her cheek. Suddenly she was no longer cold, but hot all over. Somewhere in her core a flame licked up. Her flesh began to burn as his palms slid up her arms.

*No. No. No.* This could not be happening.

Dazed, she opened her mouth to protest, only to find it captured in a far more intimate embrace. His tongue traced over her lips, and his teeth nipped her flesh. Then he was inside her, tasting of salt, of smoke, and some earthy spice she could not put a name to.

Her attempt at speech came out as a wordless moan. It had been so long since she had been kissed. So long since she had been desired. So long since she had felt this alive . . .

# To Sin With A Scoundrel

## Cara Elliott

FOREVER

NEW YORK    BOSTON

This book is a work of fiction. Names, characters, places, and incidents are the product of the author's imagination or are used fictitiously. Any resemblance to actual events, locales, or persons, living or dead, is coincidental.

Copyright © 2010 by Andrea DaRif
Excerpt from *To Surrender to a Rogue* copyright © 2010 by Andrea DaRif
All rights reserved. Except as permitted under the U.S. Copyright Act of 1976, no part of this publication may be reproduced, distributed, or transmitted in any form or by any means, or stored in a database or retrieval system, without the prior written permission of the publisher.

*Cover design by Diane Luger*
*Book design by Giorgetta Bell McRee*

Forever
Hachette Book Group
237 Park Avenue
New York, NY 10017
Visit our website at www.HachetteBookGroup.com.

Forever is an imprint of Grand Central Publishing. The Forever name and logo is a trademark of Hachette Book Group, Inc.

Printed in the United States of America

First Printing: March 2010

10 9 8 7 6 5 4 3 2 1

*For my mother,*
*whose incredible artistic talents and creative spirit*
*inspired me to see the magic of giving*
*one's imagination free rein.*

*Thanks, Mom*

# To Sin With A
# Scoundrel

# Chapter One

*M*urder.

The word looked rather ghoulish on the printed page.

Closing her eyes for an instant, Lady Ciara Sheffield reminded herself that it sounded even worse.

"Murder." Though she said it with barely a breath, the echo seemed to shatter the stillness of the room. Seeing that the inquest was officially closed, she had thought the past had finally been laid to rest. But apparently she was gravely mistaken.

She set aside the *Morning Gazette,* yet the flutter of newsprint was a disquieting reminder of the malicious whispers. For months following her husband's sudden collapse, the drawing rooms of Mayfair had been aswirl in *ondits,* each one more outrageous than the last.

At least this morning's article had not called her a witch but instead accorded her the dignity of referring to her work as "scientific."

Her breakfast was now cold, and as the taste of the tea

turned bitter on her tongue, Ciara crumbled a bit of toast between her fingers. Would the *ton* never tire of gnawing on the bones of old scandal? Sighing, she angled another peek at the column of newsprint. By now the rumors and innuendo should have died a natural death.

*Oh, how she hated being fodder for gossip.* But perhaps, with any luck, her story would soon fade from the front pages.

Especially if the infamous Lord Hadley kept up his escapades.

Much as she despised wastrels in general, Ciara found herself almost liking the man for being so utterly, so outrageously debauched. His latest antics could not help but distract the tattlemongers from her own quiet life. When it came to selling newspapers, a reclusive widow was no match for a rakehell earl.

Not that she had any interest in learning the sordid details of this particular incident. Determined to turn a blind eye to the columnist's lurid prose, Ciara reached for her notebooks. And yet she could not quite help catching sight of the next few lines . . .

*Dear God, surely the writer was grossly exaggerating.*

Despite herself, she read on. She was acquainted with the fountain in question—though not with the cyprian who had apparently consented to play Leda to Lord Hadley's Zeus-as-Swan. According to the account, the naked female was a good deal more statuesque than the sculpted marble. And a good deal more vocal. Apparently half of Berkeley Square had been woken by her shrieks when the earl's slip landed both of them chest deep in the frigid water.

That ought to have cooled their ardor, thought Ciara

grimly. Not to speak of inflicting more permanent damage. It was hinted that the earl had suffered several good-sized bruises to a rather sensitive section of his anatomy.

No doubt he was wishing that "brass balls" was not merely a metaphor.

The newsprint suddenly crackled. The coals hissed, and flames licked up to consume the crumpled wad of paper. *To hell with Lord Hadley.* And the rest of London Society, for that matter. Let them play their wicked games. She had witnessed enough malicious intrigue and mindless debauchery to last her a lifetime. It was no longer shocking, just dreadfully dull.

Pushing aside her plate, Ciara gathered up her notebooks and hurried from the breakfast room.

"Bloody hell! Another hit, dead center through the card!"

*Bloody luck.* Lucas Bingham, the Earl of Hadley, squinted in the glare of morning sunlight. He was a damn good shot, but after the three—or was it four?—bottles of port he'd consumed over the last several hours, even the sharpest aim could go astray.

"La, sir." One of the luscious lightskirts he and his friends had hired for the trip slipped her hand beneath his shirt. "Your touch on the trigger is unerring. What say you to reloading and taking a shot at another sort of target?"

Before the earl could answer, Lord Farnam let out a low whistle. "Damnation, Lucas. I swear, you could shoot a farthing off the tip of a man's cock without doing any damage."

"Especially yours, Freddy," called Baron Greeley. "Even Hadley can't hit what he can't see."

Farnam joined in the bawdy laughter before replying, "I, on the other hand, have no trouble spotting your fat arse, Georgie—especially as it's exposed in a rather precarious position right now. So keep a civil tongue in your head unless you wish to feel the full force of my boot."

Greeley's ladybird lay draped over one of the garden statues, and her embrace had angled the baron and his naked posterior into full view. "Come, come, gentlemen," she called. "Let's have no talk of violence, only fun." Her hands inched lower, drawing Greeley's breeches along with them. "After all, we're all here to have a good time."

"I'll drink to that!" Farnam uncorked another bottle of champagne. "A toast to Lucas—our own Mad, Bad Had-ley—for giving us such a *swimmingly* good reason to quit Town for a while. The Season was becoming a bloody bore. Nothing like a country house party to keep us all in good spirits until the prigs have time to forget about your moonlight swan dive."

*Forget.*

Lucas winced as the word cut through the haze of wine.

*Damn.* Up until that moment, his promise to his uncle had completely slipped his mind. It wouldn't be the first time he had left Henry in the lurch. Not by far. Of late, his negligence was becoming such a habit that his failure to show up at the appointed hour was no doubt expected.

A fact that only made the prickling of guilt dig in a little deeper. And not even Marie—or was her name Marguerite?—could caress it away.

The feeling was bloody uncomfortable. Not to speak of inconvenient, seeing as they had arrived at Farnam's estate only at dawn, after carousing half the night in one of the seamier gambling hells in St. Giles. Tossing aside the pistol, Lucas grabbed a fresh bottle and gulped down a swallow, hoping to drown the host of tiny daggers jabbing against his flesh.

Instead, the ruthless little buggers intensified their attack.

"Blast," he muttered, pressing his fingertips to his throbbing temples. "You've just reminded me of a pressing engagement, Freddy. I'm afraid I'm going to have to return to town immediately."

"Put it off, *chéri*." Mademoiselle M began to toy with the fastenings of his breeches. "Along with your buckskins. Why rush off when we can play a bit of slap and tickle right here and now?"

"I can't," he replied, grimacing as he gingerly removed her hand. That particular portion of his anatomy was not feeling very . . . playful at the moment. He vaguely remembered a midnight encounter involving very cold water and very hard stone. "The truth is, my uncle expected me yesterday."

"But *chéri!*" She pursed her lips into a provocative little pout. "If you leave now, it will throw off the numbers."

"Someone will have to double up." Lucas watched Farnam take another swig of wine and then thrust himself between his companion's thighs. "Freddy looks willing to give his pump handle a few extra turns."

The lightskirt narrowed her kohl-rimmed eyes. "That leaves me with the short end of the stick, so to speak. I didn't make the journey out here to sit around and twiddle my thumbs. The deal was that I got *you*."

His headache seemed to be taking a turn for the worse. Fishing a wad of banknotes from his coat, Lucas tossed them over. "Here, perhaps counting these will keep your clever little fingers busy."

"Don't be such a spoilsport, Hadley," called Ingalls. He was lying spread-eagle on the grass, smoking a cheroot. "Surely another day or two will make no difference to your uncle. After all, he isn't likely to be going anywhere."

His other friends found the quip uproariously funny.

"I say, that's a good one, Fitz," said Greeley, wiping the tears of mirth from his cheeks. "Not going anywhere! Ha, ha, ha."

The casual cruelty concerning his uncle's infirmity hit him like a slap in the face. Lucas felt a surge of anger well up inside him, and for an instant he was tempted to lash out and smash the slurred smiles to a pulp. But if anyone deserved to be pummeled, he realized, it was himself. The other three simply followed his example, as they had since their schoolboy days at Eton.

*Mad, Bad Had-ley.* Hell-bent on raising the art of outrageous behavior to a science. The pursuit of pleasure, executed with perfect precision.

He found himself frowning. Was he really such a sodden, self-absorbed sot? A reckless reprobate reeking of spirits and sex?

Lucas shifted his stance, trying to shake off such dark musings. The fall into the fountain must have coshed his wits as well as his whirligigs. He didn't usually subject himself to such soul-searching introspection . . .

"You aren't in any condition to travel," called Greeley. His friend fixed him with a bleary-eyed squint. "Fact is, you look like shite."

"Nonetheless, I mean to leave for London within the hour," he muttered.

"Oh, come on," coaxed Farnam. "It's not like you to leave your friends in the lurch."

"At the very least, have one more round of drinks with us," added Ingalls.

"Well . . ." It was, after all, still early in the morning, thought Lucas. "Maybe just *one* more."

Marguerite smiled and ran a caress up the inside of his thigh.

*Oh, what the hell.*

Her workroom—her sanctuary—afforded a place of refuge from the poison pens and other painful realities of the outside world. Tall, mullioned windows filled the space with a clean-edged light. The leather bindings of her books glowed with the mellow warmth of aged sherry, a rich complement to the gleam of polished glass. The orderly rows of vials and beakers mirrored the precise arrangement of her scientific instruments. Microscopes, calipers, and magnifying lenses . . .

Here the truth was not distorted to suit personal desires. Empirical data could be measured. Rational thought ruled over raw emotion.

And yet, pressing her palms to her cheeks, Ciara was dismayed to find them still burning with indignation.

And perhaps a touch of fear.

"Damn," she muttered, angry with herself for allowing the latest headlines to threaten her peace of mind. What did it matter if her name was splashed across the gossip pages? The inquest into her husband's death was closed, and Sheffield's family would have to live with that fact.

"The danger is over," she added, as if saying it aloud gave the words an extra ring of truth.

*Don't dwell on the past.* With her young son away in the country, this fortnight was supposed to be a pleasant interlude for her, as well. A time to catch up on her scholarly research, not stew over the most recent efforts of her late husband's relatives to blacken her reputation.

As she opened her notebook and began to write, the scent of the simmering herbs and spices filled the room. The original recipe—a potion for relieving the pain of gouty joints—had come from a medieval manuscript she had discovered in the attics of Sheffield Manor. But based on her own knowledge, she was making a few changes.

*Rosemary, essence of juniper, sumac . . .* Ticking off the list, Ciara made a note to mix in myrrh at the next chime of the hour. That would give her just enough time to organize her notes for the weekly meeting of the Circle of Scientific Sibyls.

Her lips quirked in a rueful smile. That was the group's official name, but among themselves they had taken to calling it the 'Circle of Sin.' After all, intellectual pursuits were not considered proper conduct for a lady. But undaunted by public opinion, the five female members were serious scholars who shared a common interest in the natural sciences. And despite their differences in age and background, they had also come to share a special bond of friendship.

Ciara smoothed her papers into a neat pile. Lud, she was not quite sure how she would have survived the last half year without their stalwart support. By her own admission, she had shunned the social swirl of London.

Still, the viciousness of the personal attacks after her husband's sudden death had staggered her.

Drawing in a gulp of air, she forced herself to swallow the memory of terror, of confusion.

Sheffield's relatives had been quick to start the whispers of ugly speculations. As the rumbling of suspicion grew more ominous and the tone of the inquest turned more threatening, her own family had taken cover from the growing storm of scandal, leaving her to stand up to the sharp-tongued magistrates and hatchet-faced coroner on her own.

The law required that the circumstances surrounding a sudden death be looked into. No matter that her husband was a dissolute man who had probably drunk himself into an early grave. By all accounts, he had downed a half-dozen bottles of brandy during the night of his collapse. And yet she had been forced to listen to his family and their cronies offer testimony about her shrewish temper, reclusive habits, and secret lair full of strange potions.

Ciara closed her eyes, trying not to picture the faces of the jury as they listened to the witnesses. She had seen the fear and loathing when their eyes met hers. Indeed, right up until the end, she had been sure they would find her guilty of her husband's death and order her turned over to the authorities for a criminal trial.

Yet somehow she had found the strength to survive the terrible ordeal. Not for herself, but for Peregrine. She would have died a thousand deaths before she let Sheffield's grasping family gain custody of her son. Oh, they had tried, even after the coroner had grudgingly announced that there was not enough evidence to indict her for murder. Even now they continued to spread stories about how

her unnatural interests and unstable mind made her unfit
to be a mother.

*More lies, more innuendos.*

Her hands clenched. She had done her best to protect
Peregrine—first from the fickle moods of his father, then
from the sordid details of the inquest, and now from the
swirl of scandal that still surrounded her name.

But was her best good enough?

Forcing her chin up, Ciara refused to surrender to
despair. While there was still a breath left in her body,
she would not let Sheffield's family beat her down. So
far, they had not been able to offer a shred of proof
to support their allegations. No doubt they would keep
trying, but surely, as time went on, it would become
more and more difficult to claim they had actual evidence of a crime.

Let them continue their campaign of evil whispers. Let
them plant nasty lies in the newspapers. Words were their
only weapons—and words could not hurt her. And yet
Ciara felt her throat constrict. The same could not be said
for Peregrine. He was so young and impressionable . . .

Thank God for friends like Alessandra della Giamatti.

A fellow member of the Circle of Sin, the marchesa
was also a widow and had a daughter the same age as
her son. Having experienced her own share of personal
travails in Italy, Alessandra had gone out of her way to
include Peregrine in the everyday activities that made life
seem . . . normal for a child.

At the moment, the three of them were spending a
fortnight in Bath, where some ancient Roman ruins had
recently been unearthed. Ciara allowed a small smile. An
expert in archeology as well as chemistry, Alessandra had

been eager to observe up close the initial digging. And so had the children.

The fresh air and open fields would do Peregrine a world of good.

As for herself . . .

The chime of the clock roused her from such unsettling reveries. Shoving the past aside, Ciara hurried to mix the last ingredient into the bubbling potion before leaving for the meeting. As she reached for her shawl, her glove grazed a small blood-red notebook lying beneath the fringed silk.

She quickly added it to her reticule.

After all, hadn't Hippocrates written that humor was one of the most potent medicines known to man—or woman? Following the regular agenda of the meeting, her friends might find her latest additions to their other ongoing scholarly research amusing.

It was far more than an hour later when Lucas finally staggered to his feet and refastened his breeches. "I really must be off," he muttered, gathering up his rumpled coat and cravat. Turning for the terrace, he cocked a last salute to his friends. "Enjoy the country. I fear that London is going to be a bore without your company."

"Then stay," called Greeley.

He shook his head. "No, I must atone for all my recent sins of neglect by visiting my uncle today."

Farnam caught up to him on the stairs. "Er, see here, Lucas, are you sure that you have no objection if I step in to fill the void with Mathilde . . . so to speak?"

"None whatsoever. Nature abhors a vacuum," replied Lucas with some cynicism.

"Er . . ." Farnam cast him a puzzled look.

"Never mind. It's merely one of the many scientific observations my uncle is fond of pointing out." Lucas quickened his step, anxious to order his valise packed and his team of grays harnessed. "You are welcome to avail yourself of Mademoiselle M's company."

"That's awfully sporting of you." Farnam grinned and lowered his voice to a conspiratorial whisper. "Admit it— all this talk about your uncle is pishposh. I take it you are running back to an even more delectable morsel."

Lucas was loath to confess the truth. "What do you think?" he drawled.

His friend let out an admiring whistle. "You have the devil's own luck with women."

Or was it a curse? Sometimes he couldn't help but wonder if everything came just a little *too* easily for him. The truth was, the lack of a challenge had left him feeling bored of late.

Brushing off such unsettling thoughts, he flicked a mote of dust from his sleeve. "Care for a bit of advice?"

"Hell, yes!"

"The secret is in not giving a damn."

"Er, about what?"

"About anything at all."

# Chapter Two

$S$till upset by the ugly snippet of gossip, Ciara decided to vent her agitation by walking through the park rather than taking a hackney to her meeting. It was still unfashionably early, and the day was cool, with scudding clouds, so the chances of encountering anyone who might recognize her were slim.

*And what did it matter if someone made a snide comment?* One more nasty word could hardly do any further damage.

Turning down one of the side carriage paths, Ciara quickened her pace, edging onto the grassy verge to stay deep in the leafy shadows of the trees. Preoccupied with her thoughts, she wasn't aware of having company until a trilling laugh brought her up short.

"Come now, Annabelle, now that you've dragged us to this secluded spot, you simply *must* tell us all about that magnificent beast you've taken into your bed."

Ciara looked up with a start. Through the netting of her veil, she recognized Lady Annabelle Merton, a renowned beauty of the *ton,* strolling along the graveled path, arm in arm with Lady Caroline Guilford and Lady Mary Hurlbutt.

She froze, praying that her dark clothing would blend into the shade and allow her to go unseen.

*Dear God, don't let them look around.*

But the trio were too busy talking to notice they weren't alone.

"Yes, do give us all the delicious details." Another loud titter. "Is Hadley as good a lover as all the rumors say?"

*Hadley.* Ciara grimaced. The man seemed to be on everyone's tongue this morning.

Lady Merton fingered the curling plume of her stylish bonnet. "He's absolutely divine, Caro," she replied with a cat-in-the-creampot purr. "You've seen for yourself those broad shoulders and sculpted thighs. I assure you, every other part of his body is equally impressive."

"Is it true that he's hung like a stallion and has the stamina of a racehorse?" asked Lady Hurlbutt eagerly.

"Let us just say that the earl takes a lady on quite a wild ride."

As the trio dissolved into knowing laughter, Ciara was about to retreat and take another route. But they suddenly stopped and formed a more intimate circle, so she dared not move.

"His performance is perfectly splendid, even after several times around the track," went on Lady Merton. "I vow, the man can go on from dusk to dawn without a hitch in his stride." Her gloved hand gave a little flutter. "But, my dears, it is not just his own pleasure that Hadley cares about. The earl believes that both mount and rider should enjoy the gallop."

*Enjoy?* Ciara was sure she must have misunderstood. In

her experience, sex was naught but a hurried humping—
an awkward, painful process that a female was expected
to endure but certainly not enjoy.

And yet, Lady Guilford heaved a breathy sigh. "You
are the luckiest lady in London."

"I have heard that some rakes are very skilled with
their fingers," pressed Lady Hurlbutt.

"Mmm, Hadley has very clever hands," replied Lady
Merton. "But it's his sinfully sensuous mouth that does
such delicious things to a lady's most intimate places."

"You mean to say . . . the Grotto of Venus?" asked
Lady Hurlbutt.

Lady Guilford let out a gasp. "He doesn't. Not down
*there.*"

"Oh, but he does. Lush little licks, tiny teasing nibbles . . ."

Ciara had never in her life heard such shockingly
explicit talk. Her ears were burning, but in spite of
her loathing for gossip, she found herself straining to
hear more. It was merely out of scientific curiosity, she
reasoned.

However, the details were cut off by the sound of an
approaching carriage.

"Well, speak of the devil," murmured Lady Guilford.

"Good afternoon, ladies." The deep, masculine voice
sounded a little rough around the edges. Its raffish tone
was echoed by the gentleman's appearance. Beneath a
high-crown beaver hat, his long black hair fell in wind-
tangled disarray around the collar of his driving coat. A
dark stubbling shaded the strong line of his jaw, and his
eyes—

Ciara quickly took shelter between two oak trees.

Set off by his sun-bronzed skin, his eyes were a mesmerizing shade of sapphire blue. *The infamous earl in the flesh.* As he smiled, she felt her breath catch in her throat. He might be a scoundrel, but there was no denying that he was handsome as sin.

*A dark, dangerous devil.*

"La, Hadley," called Lady Merton. "What a surprise. I read in this morning's newspaper that you had left Town."

"I had," he answered. "But a pressing matter required my return."

"I hope you haven't taken a chill, sir," said Lady Merton with a saucy laugh. "Bathing outdoors in the damp night air can be very unhealthy."

"So I have been told." His lips curled up at the corners. "Luckily I've suffered no lasting ill effects. But in the future I shall be more discerning. Cold water leaves much to be desired." His lidded gaze slowly fixed on Lady Merton. "As I recall from a certain summer afternoon in Kent, submerging in a tub of sparkling champagne is a far more pleasant experience."

Her two friends giggled.

"Its effervescence arouses a delightful tickling sensation in"—the earl winked—"in places which I shouldn't mention in polite company."

"Naughty man!" Lady Merton laughed. "Now that you are back, I expect you to call on me soon."

"I shall try not to disappoint you, madam," replied the earl. "Do forgive me, ladies, but I must be off. I'm already a trifle late." With a jaunty salute, he flicked his whip.

As Hadley passed, his eyes seemed to linger for an instant on the shadowed spot between the trees. Ciara flinched as if touched by an open flame, even though she knew he could not possibly see her.

"You are never a disappointment, Hadley," murmured Lady Merton, watching him until he disappeared around the bend. Sighing, she looked back to her friends. "Shall we stop at Guenter's for lemon ices before returning to my townhouse?"

Ciara waited for them to move on and then slipped from her hiding place and hurried on her way.

Lady Charlotte Gracechurch Fenimore repressed an unladylike snort.

Having finished with their formal agenda, The 'Sinners' had circled their chairs around the tea table and were engaged in reading Ciara's latest additions to the Little Red Book.

"Perhaps we should consider shortening the title of our magnum opus," continued Charlotte. "Instead of 'The Immutable Laws of Male Logic—A Scientific Study Based on Empirical Observations,' we could call it 'Men—An Essential Compendium to Managing the Brutes.'"

"Ha, ha, ha." Lady Ariel Gracechurch, who at age sixty-five was the younger of the two Gracechurch sisters, peered over Charlotte's shoulder. Unlike her sibling, she had never been married. "Oh, I like your touch of using scarlet ink for the headings, Ciara. Was it meant to emphasize the self-indulgence of their behavior?"

"More like their sheer bloody-mindedness." Charlotte snapped the journal shut. Arthritic knees were beginning to slow her step, but her wit was as quick as ever. "I take it Sheffield's nephew paid you another visit this past week."

Ciara gave a tiny nod.

Kate Woodbridge grimaced. "Don't tell me he's trying to bleed more money out of you." Although she was, at age twenty-two, the youngest of the five 'Sinners,' Kate more than made up for her tender years in worldly experience. "The slimy little *gilipollas*."

"Language, my dear," reminded Ariel.

"Oh, I know a lot worse words than that," said Kate darkly. The daughter of an American sea captain—some high sticklers were more apt to call him a pirate—and an English mother, she had spent much of her youth in exotic ports around the globe, acquiring an expertise in botany. Not to speak of a multilingual fluency in cursing that would put a sailor to blush.

"Er, yes, I am sure you do. Just remember that saying them aloud in Polite Society will get you in hot water."

"Not you, too." Kate made a face. "His Grace has already lectured me on the subject of proper English manners."

Ciara sighed in sympathy. She was not the only one having trouble with a family member. A deathbed promise to her fever-stricken parents had forced Kate to seek reconciliation with her maternal grandfather. But things were not sailing along very smoothly.

"But let's not worry about my family travails," added Kate after a slight pause. "It's Ciara we are concerned about."

"Oh, Arthur is harmless enough," murmured Ciara. "He reminds me of a sulky child."

"Don't they all," muttered Charlotte. Mild-mannered about most things, she tended to turn a tad sardonic when financial matters were discussed. Her own late husband had hidden a ruinous weakness for gambling, which had nearly landed her on the street.

In spite of her worries, Ciara found herself smiling. She counted the decision to attend a lecture at the Royal Botanical Society two years ago as one of the most fortunate choices of her life. A chance encounter with the sisters had blossomed into a deep-rooted friendship. Their tart humor made her laugh, which had been a godsend during the bleak months after Sheffield's death. But they also possessed a more serious side, sharing their hard-won wisdom and experience with heartwarming generosity. In many ways, the sisters had become surrogate mothers to the three younger members of the circle, mused Ciara. Both Kate and Alessandra . . .

Charlotte cleared her throat.

Realizing that her friends were waiting for her to go on, Ciara replied, "Arthur's mother is a terrible harridan." She had never liked her late husband's sister. "No wonder he drinks to excess."

"That's the least of his faults," said Ariel. "Cousin Archibald says the young man has taken to playing vingt-un at one of the more disreputable gaming hells in Town. Apparently he has trouble counting past ten, for he's lost a considerable sum over the last quarter."

"That's hardly surprising." Ciara set down her cup. "Gambling for high stakes seems to be a weakness that runs in the Sheffield family." Along with a number of other nasty vices, though she kept that bit of information to herself. Her friends knew how unhappy her marriage had been. No reason to reveal all the sordid details.

"You aren't in any danger of losing the townhouse, are you?" Kate's brow creased in concern. "Or your money? It was, after all, yours to begin with."

Ciara shook her head. "My man of affairs assures me

the legalities are quite clear. The inheritance left to me by my grandfather cannot be touched, so Lady Battersham is not really a threat." She said it lightly, but she felt her cheeks pale on recalling the note her nephew had brought from his mother, along with his wheedling request for a loan. "Even though she is dropping new hints about seeking formal guardianship of Peregrine—which would of course include control of his inheritance."

"Don't underestimate the old Bat," counseled Charlotte. "Like a vampire, she's out for blood. Preferably yours."

"Seeing as Sheffield and the coroner did not succeed in sucking the life out of me, I daresay I shall survive any further attacks from his sister," replied Ciara.

Despite the announcement, Ariel looked troubled. "I applaud your courage. However, I'm worried over these new stories. It seems to me that the attacks by Sheffield's family are escalating."

Kate cleared her throat. "I wasn't going to say anything, but I saw a new satirical print by Gilray hanging in a shop window this morning. It . . . well, it wasn't pretty."

A sigh slipped from Ariel's lips. "I should like to set all our joking aside and speak to you frankly, Ciara."

It was one thing to dissect the inner workings of a *Cynara cardunculus* under a microscope, but to have her own feelings subject to scrutiny, even by her closest friends, was not something Ciara wished to encourage. Still, as she looked down at the dregs of her tea, she gave a reluctant nod.

"Unlike me, you are still young and possess both beauty and brains," said Ariel. "I would hate to think you have hardened your heart to the idea of ever meeting a man worthy of respect. There *are* some admirable members of the opposite sex."

"Ariel does have a point," murmured Charlotte. "From a purely practical point of view, marriage would offer a measure of protection—"

"So would a mastiff," muttered Ciara. "And I wouldn't have to let it sleep in my bed."

"Ciara!" Despite her diminutive size, Ariel could match the booming shout of an artillery officer.

Kate stifled a laugh.

"Oh, very well. I concede that the possibility exists." Ciara paused. "In theory."

"I am quite serious, my dear. Charlotte is right—we can't ignore the fact that Sheffield's family is growing more vocal of late. I fear they mean to stir up new trouble. And it's my opinion that this problem calls for a change in strategy," announced Ariel after a few moments of silence. "We will, of course, continue to attack scientific conundrums in our weekly meetings. But we are also going to have to marshal our forces for a different sort of engagement . . ."

*Engagement.* Ciara choked on a bite of biscuit.

"Why, what a brilliant idea, Ariel! You are quite right. A campaign to find Ciara a suitable husband is in order." Charlotte drummed a military tattoo on the tabletop. "We should be able to squeeze that in between writing a rebuttal to Asherton's *Treatise on Chemistry* and cataloguing the new shipment of botany specimens from Jamaica."

"Any idea of where to begin looking?" Ciara could not keep an edge of sarcasm from her voice. Her eyes fell on the newspaper beneath the tea tray, and she felt her cheeks begin to burn as she recalled her recent encounter. "Oh, well, I suppose we could always start with the gossip column. I see the infamous Lord H's name appears in boldface type . . . look there, just three lines below my own."

Charlotte bit at her lip, but Ariel was quick to regroup. "Well, he *is* devilishly handsome. With those flowing, black-as-sin locks and smoldering sapphire eyes, it's no wonder he has seduced half of Society. And the cut of his trousers reveals a pair of divinely muscled thighs." She paused. "He also has a wicked sense of humor, to go along with those sculpted legs. The limericks he recited at Lady Wilton's ball had me laughing so hard it brought tears to my eyes."

"The man may be a rogue and a rascal, but at least he's not boring," mused Charlotte.

Amusement won out over indignation. Ciara laughed. "I could not ask for more loyal or stalwart friends. But honestly, even if I were interested in remarrying—which I am not—Lord Hadley would be the last man on earth I would consider."

"Now, my dear," said Ariel quickly. "No one is seriously suggesting that the earl would make an ideal husband. However, it is the principle we need to consider. I am sure if we put our heads together, we can come up with a list of more acceptable candidates."

"After all, we solved Thackery's theorem of calculus in three days." Kate, who had been listening in silent mirth, finally schooled her face to some semblance of seriousness. "This is not nearly so complex an equation—one plus one equals two."

*Things did not always add up so simply,* thought Ciara.

However, she decided there was no harm in humoring her friends. Like the satirical compendium on male behavior they were drafting, this proposed list of gentlemen was merely an exercise in whimsy.

"Alessandra is invited to a number of Society entertainments on account of her mother's family," added Kate. "And though she doesn't choose to attend many, I'm sure she will have some interesting ideas."

"Speaking of Alessandra, will she and the children have returned to Town by our next meeting?" asked Ariel.

"Yes. If all goes well." As she gathered her notes from the meeting and rose, Ciara tried not to dwell on the irony of her words. Since when had life gone smoothly for her? But seeing Charlotte's eyes cloud with concern, she forced a smile. "By the by, whose turn is it to take 'The Immutable Laws of Male Logic' for the coming week?"

"Mine," piped up Ariel. "Though I fear I am not nearly as creative as the rest of you. I have only Cousin Archibald for inspiration, and that is not quite the same as a husband."

"Granted, you haven't experienced the full range of male behavior," Charlotte said with a grin. "But don't worry, I'm sure you get the gist of it."

"Yes, but . . . a scientist should always depend on empirical knowledge rather than hearsay." Ariel's cheeks turned a delicate shade of pink. "I cannot help but wonder what I am missing."

"Curiosity killed the cat." Ciara smoothed the sardonic quirk from her lips as she rose and gave her friend a quick hug. "We ought not ignore folk wisdom. Its truths are, after all, based on centuries of experience."

"I have another old adage—The apple does not fall

far from the tree." Charlotte polished off the last pastry. "Keep an eye peeled on Sheffield's sister. She is rotten to the core."

No clever quip came in response. Instead, Ciara felt her throat tighten.

"And murder is a very serious crime to be accused of—"

Kate's butter knife slipped from her fingers and fell to the floor with a clatter. Her face seemed a shade paler as she bent to retrieve it. "Let us not speak of murder. We all know Ciara is innocent of any wrongdoing."

"Of course we do. But truth is not always clear-cut in the eyes of justice," said Charlotte. "I am simply cautioning her to take care."

Ciara drew in a deep breath. She would *not* let fear poison her life. "Thank you for the warning. But I assure you, I am prepared for any trouble that might come my way."

Cursing the sudden rain shower, Lucas shrugged out of his caped driving coat and slapped his sodden gloves down on the side table.

"A foul day to be traveling, milord." With his usual show of quiet efficiency, his uncle's butler gathered up the discarded garments and blotted the drops of water from the mahogany veneer. "Shall I inform Sir Henry of your arrival?"

"No, thank you, Higgins. I'll announce myself." The earl's boots left a trail of tiny puddles as he crossed the checkered marble tiles and took the stairs two at a time to the library.

"Lucas!" His uncle looked up from his manuscript,

a fond smile wreathing his gaunt features. "Why, I had heard you left Town. I didn't expect to see you here for at least another week." Setting down his pen, the elderly scholar grasped the wheels of his Bath chair and rolled out from behind his desk. "You are looking a trifle damp," he remarked, a mischievous twinkle dancing in his eyes.

There was not a hint of reproach in his uncle's humor, yet the reference to his recent escapade in the fountain made Lucas feel a little juvenile. "Sorry," he began, angling his gaze to the orderly rows of leatherbound books.

Henry's smile faded. "I was not intending any criticism—"

"No, you wouldn't." Lucas traced a finger along the gilt spines. "You are far too tactful to tell me how dismayed you are that I have so little interest in intellectual pursuits. The fact that I chase far more tangible pleasures must be . . . a great disappointment."

"What is meat to some men is gristle to others." His uncle gave a wry grimace. "I am hardly in a position to pass judgment on how you live your life, Lucas. And besides, it doesn't matter what I think. The only person you have to please is yourself. You must do what makes you happy."

"I don't really give it much thought." Lucas took care to sound nonchalant.

"Ah." Henry fixed him with a pensive stare. "I daresay at some point you will. I have found that having a passion—a true passion and commitment—is a source of great satisfaction in life."

"I've plenty of passion in my life. And if I achieved any more satisfaction, I might expire from overexertion," drawled Lucas. "So you see, things are quite perfect for me as they are."

"Well, then, enough of curmudgeonly advice," murmured Henry. "I did not ask you to call on me in order to subject you to a prosy lecture."

Relieved to let the matter drop, Lucas was quick to reply, "I have been wondering as to the specific reason. Your request did seem to have a certain note of urgency."

"It's hardly a matter of life or death, but I was hoping that I might ask a small favor of you."

"Of course. Anything."

A chuckle sounded. "A few last words of wisdom, my dear boy—always look before you leap. It's ill-advised to commit yourself to action until you know what's expected."

"I'll take my chances." The earl grinned. "What do you have in mind—something illegal? Immoral?"

"Alas, nothing half so interesting." His uncle heaved a mock sigh. "You had better wheel me down to the library, so that I may show you."

As the Bath chair glided over the polished parquet, Lucas could not help noticing how his uncle seemed to weigh no more than the mohair shawl wrapped around his frail shoulders. There were other changes as well. They were subtle, like the whispered creaks of the wood and iron, but spoke all too clearly of the inexorable march of time.

". . . how much do you know of Bishop Raymond of Seville and his work in preserving the wisdom of the ancient Greeks?"

The earl thought for a moment. The name had a vaguely familiar ring to it, but other than that . . .

"The extent of my knowledge on the subject would likely fit on the head of a prick," he replied dryly.

As he had hoped, the waggish remark drew a bark of laughter.

"Yours or mine? The difference, I fear, would be considerable. My brain may not yet be shrinking, but unfortunately, the same cannot be said for the rest of me." Henry looked up and, without a trace of rancor, added, "It's damn depressing to grow old, Lucas. Would that there were some draught—other than hemlock—to make the process more palatable."

Lucas swallowed hard. Lud, he would miss the self-deprecating wit and pithy wisdom of his guardian when he was gone. "The Scots have a potent brew they call *uisge beatha*—water of life. I can vouch from experience that it's highly effective in killing any ill that ails you . . . at least temporarily."

"I was thinking more along the lines of encouraging rational thought, not oblivion," replied his uncle with a bittersweet sigh. "However, while my wits are still alive and kicking, I should like to exercise them." He motioned to one of the windowed alcoves overlooking the gardens. A thin sheaf of papers, bound with a red ribbon, lay centered on a small worktable.

"I discovered this manuscript hidden inside the binding of an old Bible I purchased from Lord Fannerton's estate." Excitement animated his voice. "My Arabic is rudimentary at best, but I think I make out the name of Hippocrates and the title of the essay. If I am right, it's a work that has been lost for centuries to Western scholars. Have you any idea what that means?"

Lucas shrugged. "I can't say that I stay up late at night to ponder the mysteries of the ancient world. I have other subjects on my mind."

Henry smiled, a deceptively mild expression that did

not blunt the sharpness of his gaze. But after a moment or two he turned his attention back to the dog-eared parchment. "Assuming my hunch is correct, its value is incalculable, and not just to serious scholars. I've made some notes, but the complexity of the data is beyond my knowledge of the subject. More than that, a good deal of the writing seems to be in code—which was used to hide radical scientific ideas from religious censors. All in all, I suspect it may be a momentous medical discovery."

"You don't say," murmured Lucas. It was hard for him to get excited over a bit of moldy parchment, but he was happy to see Henry's enthusiasm had brought a touch of color to his cheeks.

"Indeed. You see, from what I make out from the scribe's opening notations, he seems to imply that the manuscript contains some sort of miracle cure for wounds." Henry looked up. "Intriguing, isn't it?"

Lucas nodded. "Yes, I can see that."

"So did my friend Lord Lynsley, who as you know is Assistant Minister to the Secretary of State for War," continued Henry. "When I happened to mention it to him, he was quite interested and agreed that I should have it looked at by the leading expert in the field. After all, such a finding would have special significance for the military." He slipped the manuscript into a leather portfolio and tied its flap shut. "However, seeing as he would like me to be discreet about the discovery for now, I would rather not entrust transporting such a treasure to anyone but you."

"That's all?" Lucas wasn't sure whether he felt relieved or disappointed at being asked to do so little. "In truth, I was expecting a more daunting challenge than a quick jaunt to Oxford—"

"Oh, you needn't travel any farther than Pont Street. Judging from all I have read in my scientific journals, there isn't an Oxford don whose knowledge can compare to that of Lady Sheffield."

"The witch who poisoned her husband? Surely you are joking."

"Scurrilous rumors." Henry added an extra loop of cording around his precious package. "You, of all people, should know how the newspapers take liberties with facts. I have been assured by unimpeachable sources, including Lord Lynsley, that the widow is a brilliant scientist."

*So, not only was the lady a murderess, but she was a bluestocking, to boot?*

Lucas wasn't sure which was the lesser of two evils. Grimacing, he closed his eyes, envisioning skin the color of book paste, mouse-brown hair scraped back in a bun, bony shoulders stooped in a scholarly hunch, and thin lips pinched in perpetual disapproval. Spectacles would no doubt round out the picture. And definitely a squint. Maybe even a wart or two.

In his wildest nightmare, he couldn't have imagined a female he would less like to encounter.

"Indeed, Lynsley was the one who suggested that I ask her for help. He would have done so himself, except he has been called away from Town on an urgent government matter." Henry hesitated. "However, if you would rather not . . ."

"No, no." It was not as if he were being asked to confront a fire-breathing dragon or a snake-haired Medusa whose stare could turn men to stone. It was a simple errand, a small penance to pay for the sins of neglect.

He held out his hand for the manuscript.

# Chapter Three

*B*loody hell.

Of all his recent stunts, this was perhaps the most out-rageous. But the reclusive widow had left him no choice.

Cursing again as his boot slipped on the smooth lime-stone, Lucas caught at the vines just in time to prevent a nasty fall from the back wall of her townhouse. He paused for a moment and slanted another measured look at the window ledge. He had overcome far more difficult obstacles in the course of arranging an intimate rendezvous. Granted, the ladies in question had been aware of his intentions, but still, the logistics would present no problems.

It was not as if he had any alternative to stealth. Lady Sheffield's ancient butler had turned away every proper approach he had made to her residence on Pont Street. The last time around, the old curmudgeon had refused to even open the front door and accept his card. Lucas had slid it under the paneled oak anyway, after scribbling yet another note beneath the engraved script.

His mouth quirked up at the corners. *The widow wished to challenge him to a battle of wills?* Well, he had tossed down a gauntlet of his own, so to speak. And whether or not she read between the lines, the bit of stationery announced his intention of accepting the fight.

His inquiries up and down the street had finally turned up a neighboring bootboy willing to exchange information about "Lady Murder" for a handful of coins. She hardly ever went out—a fact he had ascertained on his own—but according to his source, the widow did have one regular appointment each week that she kept without fail.

*Ha!* He would simply make himself at home in her private quarters and wait for her return.

But as he slipped through the window and ran headlong into a swirl of vapor, Lucas was no longer feeling quite so smug. Perhaps this was not such a good idea, after all. Given the lady's reputation, he eyed the boiling cauldron with great wariness. However, as he crinkled his nose and gave an experimental sniff, he found that the moist air had a rather pleasant scent to it—a woodsy tang, softened with a floral sweetness. Hardly the sort of poisonous Underworld potion he would expect from the Goddess of Witches.

Indeed, despite all the odd-looking instruments, the room had a rather comfortable, cozy feel to it that reminded him of his uncle's study. He peeked inside one of the heavy tomes stacked on the worktable. Ah, yes—the same Latin nomenclature, the same complex equations.

Letting the cover fall shut, he moved on to her desk.

The usual assortment of pens and paperknives was arranged at the head of the blotter. The bottle of scarlet ink—at least he assumed it was ink and not the blood of her latest victim—was the only odd touch. Setting down his own packet of papers, he leaned in for a closer look.

"Damn."

Retrieving the little book he had knocked to the carpet, Lucas gave the marbled paper cover a dusting with his sleeve and then turned to put it back in its place. As he did, its ribbon bookmark slipped and the pages fluttered open.

*How interesting.* Perching a hip on the desktop, Lucas flipped through the rest of the chapter.

*Naughty girl.*

Not only did Lady Sheffield's proficiency in arcane languages appear to include a rather racy dialect of Italian, but the pictures showed a more intimate interest in anatomy than he would have expected in a prim bluestocking.

He turned the book upside down and stifled a laugh. On second thought, perhaps she was studying physics and the laws of gravity. Such a position would require a great deal of leg strength to maintain. Having tried something of a similar nature on the balcony of Lady Wilton's bedchamber, he could vouch for the fact that—

"What the devil!" A shout, shrill with shock, interrupted his study.

Lucas looked up and smiled. "Free feel to call me Lucifer. No need to stand on formalities, seeing as we are in a private—and some might say intimate—setting."

The lady was still wearing the same hideous headcovering as when she had left the house. Its voluminous clouds of black gauze made her look like a walking storm cloud.

"Get out!" Her thunderclap of fury did nothing to dispel the impression. "This instant."

Strange, but for a heartbeat he had a prickling feeling that they had encountered each other before. He shook it off and replied, "Not until you do me the courtesy of hearing me out."

"How dare you accuse me of bad manners! You are hardly entitled to lecture anyone on proper behavior."

Lucas tapped his forefinger to the erotic etching. "Neither are you."

Her shoulders stiffened, and her head came up a fraction. She was taller than he had imagined, and for some odd reason he had the impression that beneath the crow-black coverings, the arch of her neck was graceful as that of a swan's.

"Get out," she repeated. "I warn you, I don't mean to tolerate this invasion of my privacy."

Lucas crossed his legs and waggled a boot. "What do you intend to do—pull out a pistol and shoot me? I had heard that poison was your preferred weapon."

"If I gave you a choice, I should imagine you would choose a blade. Word has it you fancy yourself quite a swordsman."

He laughed. "Touché, Lady Sheffield." Pressing a hand to his chest, he exaggerated a grimace. "I appear to be hoisted on my own petard."

The gauzy veil did little to blunt her daggered look. He could feel a thousand little points of steel prick into his flesh.

"Your petard will not be hoisting itself—much less anything else—in this house," she retorted.

The widow had a rapier wit, he gave her that. Which she wielded with surprising dexterity. Lucas rose and smoothed the wrinkles from his trousers. Rather than aggravate him, the idea of matching thrusts and parries with a skilled opponent intrigued him. Demure young ladies bored him to perdition.

"It's rather warm in here," he drawled. "If we are to engage in a verbal duel, you might be more comfortable taking off your cloak and bonnet. As I said, I am not going anywhere until I have my say."

"You are not used to being told no, are you?"

"No."

There was a pause, and a flutter of black wool, as she moved to her worktable and spooned out a measure of white powder. Steam shot up as she emptied it into the cauldron.

"Come now," he murmured. "It's only sporting that I be allowed to see the face of my opponent." Deliberately toying with the top button of his coat, Lucas added, "It strips the combat down to the bare essentials, so to speak, when you look at each other, eye to eye."

She edged back. "I'm not interested in playing your game."

"Are you sure?"

Her hands betrayed a tiny tremor. "Q-quite sure."

"As a gentleman, I cannot force you to listen," he said softly. "But I'm getting rather desperate, and desperate men cannot be counted on to mind the rules."

He heard her breath catch in her throat. "I cannot imagine how your concerns could have anything to do with me." She stirred the bubbling liquid. "We do not move in the same circles."

"And yet our paths have crossed." He stepped around a stack of brass canisters. "Aren't you the least bit curious as to why?"

"I am curious about a great many things, Lord Hadley. You are not one of them."

Though Lucas admitted he deserved some measure of scorn, her tone pricked his pride. He was not about to let a reclusive widow have the last word. "Before you presume to pass judgment, why not hear me out?"

"And if I do?"

"Then you have my promise that I will not trespass on your hospitality a moment longer."

The widow hesitated, then abruptly unknotted the strings of her bonnet and set it atop the stack of books. "Very well," she said, turning to face him.

Surprise rendered him momentarily speechless.

His image of her had been completely wrong. Save for the thinned lips.

But that was only because at the moment they were compressed in a tight line. In their natural state they were full and finely shaped—he was enough of a connoisseur of feminine beauty to recognize their exquisite form, even when distorted by anger.

Lucas was transfixed by a sudden, thrumming awareness of every fine-boned, graceful detail of her face. His pulse quickened, and his heart thudded against his ribs.

*Lud, how was it he had not heard the lady was an absolute stunner?*

He stared for an instant longer before slowly releasing his pent-up breath and raising his eyes to meet hers.

Disapproval had dulled their seafoam green color to a stormy gray. Beneath the surface swirled a deeper emotion. *Distrust.* Darkened with a tinge of fear.

Lady Sheffield appeared wary of men. He wondered why.

But before he had time to give the matter further thought, she snapped, "Do go on, sir. I haven't got all day. You might not have anything better to do with your time, but I do."

Arched brows accentuated her displeasure. Like the curls that had come loose from her hairpins, they were a subtle shade of russet gold, sparked with glints of copper. The fiery highlights reflected her smoldering impatience. With a toss of her head, she shrugged off her cloak.

Forcing his gaze away from her willowy body, Lucas turned to retrieve his portfolio of papers. *Shake off this strange bewitchment,* he chided himself. He had seen far too many naked—and willing—women to feel such a visceral reaction to a widow dressed like a nun.

"It might be better if you had a look at these before I explain myself."

⟞⟝

Ciara took her time in untying the flap. "Is this some sort of joke, Lord Hadley? Some drunken bet scrawled in the betting books for all of White's to ogle over? Let me guess the gist of it—five hundred pounds says Hadley cannot penetrate the widowed witch's lair."

A last little yank snapped the strings. "You may enjoy all the lurid attention, and the notoriety of having your name become a byword for bad behavior. But I abhor being the subject of idle gossip, of sordid speculation."

His eyes narrowed slightly at her words. In the wink of scudding sunlight, Ciara could not be certain of what she saw. Surely it must have been anger, and not regret.

A wastrel like Hadley was not the sort of man to repent his sins.

Still, the urgency of his reply took her by surprise. "As you say, my exploits are well known. I don't have to engage in any such prank to prove myself."

"Then I ask again—what do you want of me? I have nothing a rake would desire." She knew that was true. Her late husband had made it clear that she was much too thin to stir a man's lust. And her hair wasn't the bright guinea gold coveted by most gentleman but was marred by Hibernian highlights. Sheffield had mocked the reddish tint, calling it the stain of her Irish mother.

She closed her eyes for an instant, hearing his drunken shouts cursing the king, the country, the Little Corsican—anyone but himself—for the empty coffers that forced him to marry for money. She had been no happier about the arrangement than he was. A lofty title was paltry recompense for the abuse she had suffered.

*God rot his cruel bones.* The man had been a bully and a lout. She was not at all sorry he was dead.

When she lifted her lashes, she saw that the earl had come closer. Close enough for her to breathe in the masculine scent of sandalwood and spiced tobacco. Close enough for her to feel the heat of his body caress her cheek.

"On the contrary, Lady Sheffield. You have *exactly* what I want."

His silky murmur sent a shiver skating down her spine. Reaching her belly, it did a slow, curling somersault as his sapphire gaze darkened to a deeper brilliance. What madness had come over her? It was utterly unreasonable to respond in such a physical way to a rogue.

*Don't.* Oh, don't stare at his sin-black hair, curling

around the chiseled line of his jaw. Don't wonder how the glossy strands would feel twined around her fingers.

Ciara smoothed her hands over her gown, unconsciously tightening the silk around her hips.

His eyes followed the gesture, and he smiled. "Not your fine bosom, or your long legs or your shapely derriere, but your learned mind."

She fell back a step, mortified to find herself stammering like a schoolgirl. "I . . . my . . . you . . . are speaking outrageous nonsense, sir. You know absolutely nothing about my person."

"No? I'm rather expert at assessing a lady's charms, even when they are buried in the depths of a dowdy gown. One can tell much from the curve of a neck, or the lithe grace—"

"That's enough," she interrupted, trying to quell the flutter in her belly.

"Aren't you curious to hear more?" he asked softly. "Most females like to hear a man appreciate their beauty."

*No—I'm not curious!* But for some perverse reason, the words remained stuck in her throat.

"As I was saying, you've a lovely, lithe grace to your movements. Your hips sway just enough to provoke . . . improper thoughts. As for your bosom . . ."

Her hand flew to her chest.

"Your breasts look to have the lush roundness of perfectly ripe peaches," he went on slowly, as if savoring the sweetness of each syllable. "Soft, yielding—"

"Please get to the point of this visit, Lord Hadley," said Ciara, finally regaining control of her voice. "My patience is wearing thin."

"A pity it is not taking that ill-fitting nun's collar along with it."

"Sir!"

The earl took another step closer. "Is it true what they say?"

To her dismay, she felt a rush of heat color her face.

"About your intellect," he added.

Ciara dragged her gaze away from his mouth, supremely sensuous in its curl of silent laughter. "Enough of your insolent arrogance, sir," she whispered, shoving the package back at his chest. "Whatever your game, it has gone too far."

The earl touched her hand. "Forgive my teasing. It's hard to resist the temptation when anger brings such a lovely glow to your features."

"And you are not a man much given to resisting temptation, are you?"

For an instant, the look of unholy amusement seemed to fade from his features.

"Well, I, too, am sorely tempted to give in to an urge," she added. "The one prompting me to consign you and your cursed papers to the flames of hell."

"You may wish a quick glance at that manuscript before tossing it in the fire." His nonchalance was back. "I'm told it is an ancient scientific treatise, as yet unknown in the West. For a serious scholar, its importance would be incalculable. But that is for you to judge."

Intrigued in spite of herself, Ciara took a peek at the first page. It did indeed appear to be very old, the ink faded to a spidery tracing. However, considering the source, it was probably a hoax. "Why bring it to me?" she demanded.

"Because my uncle does not wish to trust it to just anyone. He believes you are the most qualified to examine its contents and make an accurate translation. Some of it is written in a complex code, which he seems to think won't pose a problem to a lady of your intellect."

She snorted in disbelief. His explanation only confirmed her suspicions. "What fustian! I am quite certain I have never met any relative of yours in my life."

"No, but Sir Henry Phelps is very well acquainted with your writings and holds you in the highest esteem."

Now, *that* was an unexpected discovery. Ciara would never have guessed that the bookish baronet shared anything in common with the rakish earl. She had read some of the elder gentleman's essays and found them to be articulate and insightful.

The only ink Hadley created was page after page of prurient gossip in the scandal sheets.

"If what you say is true, why didn't he come himself?" she asked.

The earl took a moment to answer. "These days, he finds it difficult to manage the short journey from his bedchamber to his study. But it is pride as much as his infirmities that prevent him from leaving his townhouse. He does not like people to see he is confined to a Bath chair."

She was surprised by the hint of pain in his voice. Was it possible that a devil-may-care rake might give a damn about someone other than himself? "Do you share his interest in intellectual pursuits?"

"Not in the least. There are other, far more interesting things to pursue." He said it with a smirk, but once again, it seemed that the cynicism did not quite reach his eyes.

*Don't be a fool,* she chided herself. It was only a quirk of light that made him look rather sad.

"However, this means a great deal to him." There was no mistaking the note of affection in his voice. "And so,

I am willing to do whatever it takes—even if it means going through walls—to make him happy. It is the least I can do to repay all his kindness."

She felt her initial animosity softening ever so slightly. "You speak as if you are very fond of him."

He nodded. "I am. It cannot have been easy for a confirmed bachelor to find himself the guardian of a hellion adolescent. Yet he tolerated my youthful follies with extraordinary patience and good humor."

Ciara had assumed that Lord Hadley took nothing seriously, save his own pleasures. But as he looked to the windows, his profile a stark silhouette against the glass, she felt a small prick of conscience. Had she cast his character in too harsh a light? She, of all people, ought to know that the glare of public scrutiny often distorted the true picture.

"He sounds like a saint." To mask her confusion, she began a careful perusal of the manuscript.

"As opposed to the devil of a nephew?"

She turned a page. Had he read her face so easily?

He seemed amused by her refusal to answer. Much as she tried to concentrate on the arcane Arabic letters, Ciara caught a quick glimpse of his smile as he strolled to the workbench. After toying with a set of glass vials, he moved on to a tray of seedlings.

"You ought to know better than to touch anything in a laboratory," she muttered, annoyed that she was allowing herself to be distracted.

"It's one of the reasons I would make a poor scientist." He lifted a beaker to the light, nearly spilling its contents. "I am constantly forgetting the rules."

Her willingness to give him the benefit of the doubt quickly evaporated. "*Ignore* is more likely the precise word."

"Ah, yes, you are an expert in languages, too." The dratted man was far too fast with his hands. He once again had hold of the erotic book and began thumbing through the pages. "Tell me, do you enjoy the nuances of the Venetian dialect?"

"What makes you think it's written in Italian?"

"Contessa Francesca di Musto is a close friend. I've learned enough of the language from her to recognize—"

"I'm sorry I asked." Ciara cut him off with a brusque snap and forced her attention back to the ancient handwriting.

He waited several moments before asking, "Well, what do you think?"

"A-about what?" *The audacity of the man!* Did he actually mean to provoke a discussion on the highly improper verses and pictures he was ogling? There was a perfectly reasonable explanation for the book's presence in her workroom. She had been doing a bit of research for "The Immutable Laws of Male Logic" and had discovered that its text displayed a well-endowed sense of humor . . . to go along with its graphic illustrations.

The earl's brow arched. "The manuscript, of course. What else would I be referring to?"

Ciara found herself blushing again.

His cough sounded suspiciously like a chuckle, but when he spoke it was in all seriousness. "Will you take on the task of translating the text for Sir Henry?"

"I haven't yet decided." Reaching for her magnifying glass, she made a show of studying a small sketch in one of the margins.

To her chagrin, he resumed his wandering about her

work area. It was impossible to concentrate, hearing the scuff of his boots, the rustle of paper and rattle of glass. At the faint pop of a cork, she abandoned all pretext of examining the intricate brushstrokes and spun around.

The earl was dabbing a bit of jade-colored oil on his wrist. "Essence of juniper," he read from the label. "It's rather nice—not at all like a whiff of cheap gin."

"Put that down!" Grabbing up a rag, Ciara rushed to his side. "It's not meant to be used undiluted. It will burn right through your flesh. Here, let me have a look." She peeled back his cuff and set to wiping off every trace of green.

His hand had none of the softness expected of a fashionable fop but was strong and solid, the sinew and muscle well defined. A scar cut across his knuckles, and a dusting of dark hair ran along his forearm. Turning it over, she saw the palm was callused, as were the tips of his long fingers. Yet their touch was surprisingly gentle as they closed around her wrist.

Up close, he radiated a rampant masculinity, and against her will, she found herself thinking of all the naughty things she had overheard in the park.

"I haven't finished," she murmured, hoping he didn't hear the odd little catch in her voice.

"Neither have I."

Ciara had every intention of pushing him away, but some strange alchemy kept her frozen in place. He kissed her lightly, the brush of his lips feathering across her cheek. Suddenly she was no longer cold, but hot all over. Somewhere in her core a flame licked up. Her flesh began to burn as his palms slid up her arms.

*No. No. No.* This could not be happening.

Dazed, she opened her mouth to protest, only to find it captured in a far more intimate embrace. His tongue traced over her lips, and his teeth nipped her flesh. Then he was inside her, tasting of salt, of smoke, and of some earthy spice she could not put a name to.

Her attempt at speech came out as a wordless moan. It had been so long since she had been kissed. So long since she had been desired. So long since she had felt this alive.

The earl deepened his teasing tempo of slow, swirling thrusts. Mindless of all else, she opened herself to his sinuous rhythm, tentatively at first, then with increasing abandon.

*Wicked, wicked.*

The tantalizing touch and taste of him were suddenly withdrawn, and his mouth—still lush with heat—was tracing the line of her jaw.

Ciara closed her eyes and gasped for breath.

"Heaven help me." Was it a plea for strength? Or a signal of sinful surrender? She wasn't sure she knew herself.

In response, he framed her face with his palms, and that terrible, tempting mouth was once again suckling the swell of her lower lip. Gently, sweetly—as if such a thing were possible from a notorious libertine—his kisses fell like a soft summer rain. On her chin, her cheeks, her brow.

Clutching at the solid, sloping slant of his shoulders, Ciara found herself melting, molding against his body. *Dear God.* Had every sensible bone in her body turned to putty? She knew she should summon the resolve to force him away. Yet as her fingers curled, it was only to rake at his coat, digging for a deeper feel of every nuanced contour.

He stilled.

The awful truth was, she wanted him to keep kissing her. No matter that he was a practiced rake, a lustful libertine. She was suddenly tired of having to be strong and sensible when inside she was feeling alone and frightened. And unwanted.

She had buried her need so deeply, she had thought it beyond reach. But in a matter of moments, the earl's lithe hands had stripped away her defenses, exposing that need to light and heat. No amount of scientific study had prepared her for the chemical reaction. It was explosive.

"Dear God." She said it aloud, finding her voice had the ragged pitch of a total stranger.

He looked up and slowly smiled. "Whatever potions you brew here are potent as sin," he said rather thickly. The sandalwood scent of his cologne was now mixed with an elemental essence of his own exertion. The effect was intensely erotic.

Her mouth quivered. "I-I cannot explain this alchemy."

A sound—somewhere between a laugh and groan—tickled her earlobe. "Nor can I. But a man could die happily in its embrace."

Ciara blushed. "It makes no sense when you . . . analyze the ingredients. We are too different . . ."

"I seem to recall hearing that opposites attract."

That *must* be the answer. Otherwise, there was no way to explain the forces drawing them together. "Logical thought would—"

With a smooth, stroking touch, his finger stilled her lip. "Some things defy logic. Don't think, just feel."

She was acutely aware of the chiseled contours of his muscle. Oh, he felt wickedly good.

The earl's whisper tickled her ear. "Sheffield was an even bigger fool than I thought," he added. "To have sought his pleasure elsewhere."

The mention of her late husband saved her from surrendering completely to the madness of the moment.

As reason returned, she somehow summoned the strength to pull back. "Like most men, Sheffield lusted after what he did not already have."

His heavy-lidded eyes narrowed even more. "You think I planned to seduce you?"

Ciara didn't know what to think. Or feel.

"And if I did, is that so very bad? It seems to me that you have experienced very little pleasure in your life."

Confused, she sought release from the weight of his presence. "My personal life is none of your concern."

He did not object as she pressed her fists to his chest and gave a little shove. His grip slipped away and he stepped back, watching in silence as she smoothed her skirts.

The loss of his heat left a dull ache imprinted on her flesh.

"I—I must ask you to leave, Lord Hadley. And to take your papers with you." Like her fingers, her voice was now stiff with embarrassment. "I granted your wish—you have had the chance to state your desire." She drew in a breath. "It was, to be sure, an eloquent performance. But I have decided to say no to your request."

His gaze turned opaque, his expression hardened, betraying no emotion save for a sardonic curl at the corners of his mouth. "You have not yet heard the rest of the details about the manuscript."

"Whatever they are, I am not interested."

"Where is your sense of adventure, Lady Sheffield? I

thought all scientists were excited by the possibility of new discoveries."

Ciara looked away, appalled by her lapse in judgment. "It is not really my field of study," she lied. "Your uncle will have no trouble finding someone else."

"He wanted you."

Her hands fisted in the folds of her skirts. "Well, we all must learn to live with disappointment in our lives."

The earl acknowledged his dismissal with a slow, mocking gesture at the row of instruments aligned on the table. "A strange sentiment for someone who clearly has a passion for exploring the unknown."

She bit at her lip, unwilling to admit the truth of his words.

"You may want to add an observation to your laboratory journal." He retrieved his overcoat but made no move to pick up the manuscript as he turned for the door. "Even the most carefully controlled experiments can have unpredictable results. I will keep my word—for today. But be advised that you haven't seen the last of me."

# Chapter Four

*D*ismissed. Given his *congé*. Rather than dull the prick to his pride, Lucas found that the walk to White's only honed his temper to a more dangerous edge. Tossing his overcoat to a club porter, he stalked into the reading room and signaled for a bottle of brandy.

Lady Sheffield was right. He wasn't used to taking no for an answer, especially from a female. He had become accustomed to having the opposite sex beg for a favor, rather than the other way around.

*Bloody hell.*

Swearing under his breath, he slouched into one of the chairs by the hearth and stared at the dancing flames. The tiny, teasing tongues seemed a mocking reflection of the heat still lingering in his limbs. *Hiss. Crackle. Snap.* Was there smoke coming out of his ears?

Two quick drinks finally cooled his fury. By the third, Lucas was in a more reflective mood. The fire-gold flickers now seemed to sway in unison—wagging, scolding fingers of conscience. *Had he behaved badly with Lady Sheffield?* The urge to kiss her had been irresistible—and he wasn't very good at self-discipline or denying himself what he wanted.

But intriguingly enough, despite her protests, she hadn't been averse to his attentions. Indeed, her words had said one thing, but her body had said quite another.

Lucas pursed his lips and set his glass down. An experienced rake should have no trouble charming an unworldly widow into granting him a favor. However, to do so he would need another meeting. And by now Lady Sheffield had likely nailed every door and window shut.

She was smart . . . so he would have to be exceedingly clever.

But no matter how hard he thought on it, his mind remained blank.

*Damn.*

He looked around, desperately searching for some familiar face to distract him from his dark musings. But none of his rakehell friends were present—with his closest comrades-in-mayhem still rusticating in country, their ranks were a bit thin. The only other person in the room was a sober, serious-looking gentleman who was reading the newspaper as he smoked a cheroot.

Lucas cleared his throat. Even stuffy Lord Brewster was better company than his own thoughts. "Any fresh news from Russia?" he asked.

"General Kutusov may be old, fat, and blind in one eye, but it seems he has Boney in full retreat." Brewster turned the page with a low snort. "Now, if our navy can keep the French fleet bottled up, we may have a chance to end this interminable war."

"Indeed," murmured Lucas.

"Speaking of water . . ." The viscount cocked a bushy brow. "Thought you had sailed out of Town until the outrage over your latest escapade had a chance to blow over."

"A pressing family matter required my return," he replied tersely.

"Hmmph." Brewster pulled a face. "Well, at least you aren't expected to show your phiz at Lady Becton's soirée this evening. Don't know why my wife insists that I attend. The guest list always includes a gaggle of eccentric old ladies who share the dowager's interest in art and science." The newsprint crackled. "Perhaps if *I* got written up for cavorting with a naked whore, I could get banished to the country for the duration of the Season. Just think of it—hounds, horses, hunting." The viscount sighed and blew out a plume of smoke. "Heaven."

*Somehow, his recent prank no longer seemed so uproariously funny.* Lucas slouched a little lower in his chair. "Yes, but there might be hell to pay. I've been told that wives don't find that sort of behavior amusing. Which is one of the reasons why I don't have one."

"Smart man," growled Brewster. "I fear you are right. I have little choice but to suffer through a long evening of music and learned conversation. The only saving grace is that the lady serves a very decent claret." The baron rose and set the newspaper aside. "Enjoy your devil-may-care freedom while you can."

Lucas feigned a smile, but he wasn't feeling overly smart at the moment. In retrospect, he should not have allowed lust to overpower reason in dealing with Lady Sheffield. Clearly the widow was wary of the opposite sex—and he had only added more empirical evidence that the male species were louts. He should have reined in his baser urges. Instead, he had reacted like a randy stallion.

His uncle would be so deucedly disappointed.

Swearing under his breath, Lucas reached for the

brandy. However, with his hand a mere hairsbreadth from the bottle, he held back. Hell, he was Mad, Bad Had-ley. He would *not* give up so easily. Henry did not yet know of the rejection. There was still time for one last assault on the lady's Ivory Tower. But it would have to be done with brains rather than brawn.

Steepling his fingers, Lucas thought a bit longer. While trying to arrange the first audience with Lady Ciara Sheffield, he had done a little research on his quarry. He knew of her scientific society and her small circle of friends. Recalling Brewster's mention of Lady Becton's soirée, Lucas decided to do penance for his earlier sins by making an appearance. It was the sort of staid affair that he would usually avoid like the plague.

However, Brewster's grousing had sparked an idea. The elusive widow never made an appearance in Society, but as for her fellow 'Sinners' . . .

Ciara eyed the Arabic manuscript, half expecting a green-horned *djinn* or *affreet* to rise in a puff of smoke from the ancient vellum. However, the only demons were those inside her head. And unfortunately they were speaking the king's English, loud and clear.

*Fool! Fool! Fool!*

Stepping over the broken glass, she slumped into her desk chair and took her head in her hands. "Oh, you wicked, wanton woman," she whispered. "How could you be so *woefully* stupid?"

A handsome face, a teasing kiss—she ought to know better than to fall for a flirt's superficial charms. The first time she had been oh, so young and innocent in the ways of the world. Now there was no excuse for such an abominable lapse in judgment. All men were charming when they wanted something.

Well, she would *not* be manipulated or used. Lord Hadley and his wicked, wanton mouth could go kiss Lucifer's arse . . .

Out of the corner of her eye, she couldn't help but notice the intricate little painting in the margin of the manuscript page. The fine brushstrokes, skillfully rendered in muted shades of greens and grays, seemed to depict a caravan of camels passing through a grove of palm trees,

Intrigued, she picked up her magnifying glass and pulled the pages closer. "The traders returned from the East, bearing strange plants and spices previously unknown to our world," she translated slowly.

The tantalizing words raised gooseflesh on her arms. Sitting back, she reached for her pen and a fresh sheet of foolscap.

~⌒~

"Why, Lord Hadley, I fear you are going to ruin my reputation . . ." The dowager Countess of Becton paused to lay a gloved hand on Lucas's sleeve. "For throwing a boring party."

"I am always happy to oblige a lovely lady," he replied, lifting her frail fingers to his lips.

"So I have heard," said the countess dryly. "But unless you have an interest in archaeology, you ought not waste your charms on me. I'm old enough to be an artifact."

"A very well-preserved artifact," murmured Lucas. "I

would never guess that you and my mother were close friends at school."

"It was your *grand*mother, as well you know."

"Impossible."

"Naughty man." Lady Becton chuckled. "I see why you have no lack of willing partners for your head-over-heels escapades."

Lucas winced inwardly. Put that way, he sounded like one of the acrobats at Astley's Circus.

The dowager squinted through her quizzing glass. "Which begs the question of why you are here. A cello recital does not attract a very risqué crowd. Indeed, most of my guests are not a day under sixty, and bluestockings to boot."

"Maybe I'm interested in improving and expanding my mind," he answered.

Light glinted off the gold-rimmed lens. "That appears to be the only portion of your anatomy that needs any such attention."

Lucas choked down a laugh. Age had not dulled the dowager's sharp sense of humor. He seemed to recall mention that the lady had been quite a hellion in her day.

"But if you are looking for intellectual stimulation, you have come to the right place. Do let me introduce you to some of my close friends. It isn't every day that the old ladies get to ogle a flesh-and-blood rake." Lady Becton drew him toward the main drawing room. "Let us hope that none of them faints dead on the spot."

"Indeed. At the moment, I have enough sins laid at my feet."

She silenced him with a slap of her fan. "And enough ink blackening the front page of the newspaper." Her brow arched. "Tell me, are you planning to do anything shocking?"

He assumed an angelic smile. "I assure you, my intentions are above reproach." The last notes of a Boccherini concerto floated out from the music room. "However, like your virtuoso musicians, I sometimes feel the urge to improvise."

"Well, if you have the urge to submerge yourself in another scandal, the least you can do is let me watch."

Before Lucas could reply, he was led to a small group of ladies standing near the tea table at the far end of the room. It was hard to tell which they were enjoying more—the lemon tarts or the lively discussion on the cross-pollination of tropical fruit trees.

At his approach the voices rose a notch higher, and in a twittering of ostrich plumes, several of the ladies took cover behind the potted palms.

*Like hens fleeing from a fox.*

The others, however, stood their ground with admirable sangfroid as Lady Becton moved down the line, performing the introductions. The last in the group was a short, silver-haired female who had wandered off for a moment to study a framed set of botanical prints.

"Lady Ariel." The dowager tapped her friend's shoulder. "If you can tear yourself away from *Cannabis savita,* I should like to introduce you to Lord Hadley—you know, the champion swimmer."

Lucas heard a splash behind him as someone spilled her tea.

"I am acquainted with the gentleman." The lady slowly turned, her oversized steel-rimmed spectacles giving her the air of a startled owl. "We met briefly at Lady Wilton's ball. In addition to your sporting skills, sir, you have quite a gift for reciting entertaining poetry."

"I am flattered that you recall such details," replied Lucas as he lifted her hand to his lips. *Appalled* was a far more accurate word. The limericks she had overheard were bawdy enough to make a sailor blush.

"It's hard to forget such pithy verses as 'There once was a lady from Exeter, so pretty that men craned their necks at her. One was even so brave as to take out and wave the distinguishing mark of his sex at her.'" Lady Ariel paused. "Do you know any more?"

"Lots. But most are even more improper to repeat in front of a lady."

"Then come stand *beside* me, Lord Hadley. At my advanced age, I find there is little that shocks me. Besides, I am a scientist, and as such, I like to keep an open mind about things."

Perhaps all was not lost, thought Lucas.

"Alas," sighed Lady Becton, "I am going to have to take my leave, just when things are getting interesting. I see Lord Highstreet has cornered Mr. Battell, and if I don't intervene, they may come to blows over whether Beethoven's music ought to be banned in polite society."

Lucas smiled. "And here I thought intellectual gatherings were staid affairs."

"Oh, you wouldn't believe some of the things that go on," replied Ariel. "I know for a fact that when scholars roll out the guns, they can make the Battle of Trafalgar look like a yachting regatta."

He cleared his throat and decided to test the waters. "Lady Becton mentioned you have quite a keen interest in science."

"Very much so. In fact, I belong to a small circle of learned ladies who meet every week to discuss a wide range of fascinating topics."

*Including a certain Italian sex manual.* Lucas wondered whether they considered the subject of its contents biology. Or physics.

"Indeed," he murmured politely. "I believe our hostess said something of the sort, and that your sister is a member, along with Marchesa della Giamatti and the Duke of Clyne's granddaughter."

"And the Marchioness of Sheffield," added Ariel.

"Ah, yes. The chemistry expert." He signaled to a passing footman for two glasses of champagne. "Seeing as she is not here, I assume the wine is safe to drink."

The thick lenses magnified the flash of indignation in her eyes. "Really, sir, Ciara is a *very* serious-minded scholar, sir. Her work—and every other thing about her—is above reproach."

"I did not mean to make light of the matter. The truth is, my uncle, Sir Henry Phelps, shares your good opinion." Lucas hesitated and then made up his mind to take the plunge. There was nothing to lose in trying to win over the elderly lady. He had a feeling that she could be a powerful ally, despite her diminutive size.

"In fact, he was quite anxious to engage Lady Sheffield's expertise regarding an ancient medical manuscript he recently discovered. But alas . . ." He exaggerated a sigh. "She refused."

Ariel's brow furrowed. "Refused? That does not sound at all like Ciara. She is exceedingly generous in sharing her knowledge with other scientists. We have all read your uncle's essays and have a high regard for his scholarship."

"Apparently that opinion does not extend to me, the messenger. Lady Sheffield turned me down flat. Wouldn't even take a look at it." Lucas took a small swallow of his wine. "A pity. My uncle suspects it is a long-lost work by some Greek fellow with a funny name. Hippo . . . Hippo . . . potamus?"

Ariel sucked in a breath. *"Hippocrates?"*

"Yes, that sounds about right. Not that I can tell one from the other." Was he going a bit overboard on the theatrics? Doing things to excess was, he knew, a real weakness in his character.

"A lost manuscript by Hippocrates?" she mused. "Hmmm. Let me have a word with Ciara at our next meeting. I may be able to help."

"I would be extremely grateful," said Lucas. "And if there is any favor I might do for you in return, Lady Ariel, you have only to name it."

She flexed her frail fingers. "Would that you could thrash the stuffing out of that nasty writer for the *Morning Gazette*. You know, the one who pens the gossip columns."

"Don't tell me you've been a naughty girl." Lucas kept his tone light, but he couldn't help but wonder what had sparked her remark. He hadn't bothered to read the newspapers for the past few days. Could it be that Lady Sheffield had made some slip that could be used as a bargaining chip? He was determined enough to resort to any means, foul or fair.

"Not me. Unfortunately, I'm too old to get into any trouble." Ariel sighed. "It's Ciara I'm worried about. You, of all people, ought to know how the newspapers love to blow a story into lurid proportions."

"In my case, I'm afraid the *ondits* are not overly exaggerated," murmured Lucas.

"Well, in her case, they are greatly distorted," assured Ariel. "Sheffield's family is planting scurrilous rumors about her in the press. Having failed to have her indicted for murder at the inquest, they now hope to obtain custody of her young son—and his considerable inheritance."

Recalling her wary gaze, he felt a stab of sympathy for Lady Sheffield, one made all the sharper by his own devious strategy. It seemed he was not the only person who wanted something from the widow.

"Ciara hasn't a family or a gentleman to protect her from slander. Or prison. We—that is, our Circle—are very concerned for her. And so, we have embarked on a campaign to find her a protector—oh, dear . . ." Ariel's cheeks turned pink. "That did not come out exactly right. What I meant was a suitor. Someone smart enough to see beneath the shroud of lies and recognize what a warm and wonderful person Lady Ciara is."

He could vouch for the warm part.

"Someone with enough stature and connections in Society to counter their malicious machinations. Someone with . . ." Ariel stood on tiptoes and lowered her voice. "Someone with the bollocks to stand up to their bullying."

"That's a rather lengthy list of qualifications. It narrows the field considerably."

"I'm afraid so." Her chin came up. "It's a difficult challenge, but not an impossible one. It is amazing what levers can be moved if you put your brain in gear."

"You sound very much like my uncle." As he spoke, Lucas heard a little whisper echo inside his own head—it was the voice of Reason, warning him to walk away. But as usual, a more primal force kept him rooted in place.

"A very intelligent man, to judge by his writings," mused Ariel.

"Yes, he is."

Ariel regarded him thoughtfully before clearing her throat. "The way I see it, each of us has a complicated problem . . ." She took a moment to polish her spectacles on her sleeve. "But you know, sir, our little group of scholars prides itself on solving complex conundrums."

Lucas smiled. "I'm not a scholar, but it seems to me that there is a simple solution."

"Hardly simple, Lord Hadley," murmured Ariel. "However, it might just work." She sipped her champagne. "In any case, it is worth pursuing."

Recalling Ciara's sensuous body and lush mouth, Lucas offered her his arm. "Yes, definitely worth pursuing. Come, let us take a comfortable seat by the fire and put our heads together . . ."

# Chapter Five

*A*re you *mad?*" Ciara nearly choked on a bite of biscuit.

"Actually, I think Ariel's actions were eminently reasonable," said Charlotte. Encouraged by her sister's vigorous nod, she went on. "We all agreed that finding you a husband made a great deal of sense."

"We also agreed that Lord Hadley was the last man on earth I would consider for the opening," countered Ciara.

"From what I have heard, the gentleman would fill the void rather nicely," murmured Kate.

"*Katharine!*" chorused the elderly sisters in unison. However, their shock quickly dissolved into unladylike chortles.

"He is a very virile specimen, especially up close," observed Ariel. "And quite amusing."

"Then *you* marry him," muttered Ciara.

"Now, my dear, no one is suggesting that you actually go through with the ceremony," said Charlotte. "You heard Ariel—Hadley has agreed to announce an engagement, and go through the motions of squiring you through the rest of the Season. During that time, he will use his influence to pressure Sheffield's family into stopping their slanderous talk. And once you are introduced into Society, and forge friendships of your own, your late husband's relatives will find it nigh on impossible to renew their attacks." She paused a fraction. "It is also agreed that at the end of that interlude, you are perfectly free to cry off."

"A lady may do so with no harm to her own reputation," pointed out Ariel.

"But doesn't it reflect badly on a gentleman?" asked Kate, who was still struggling to understand all the complex rules of Polite Society.

"Oh, pish!" Ariel waved off the question. "Hadley doesn't give a fig about that. He says one scandal more won't do his name any harm. Indeed, he assured me that half the fun of this arrangement would be thinking of some truly outrageous exploit to give you a reason to break off the engagement. And he was quick to point out that such a strategy would only generate more sympathy for you among the *ton*." She paused for a dainty nibble of her strawberry tart. "You know, I am aware of his reputation as a mindless rake, but I am beginning to believe that he is far more clever than most people think."

"Speak for yourself," snapped Ciara, unwillingly recalling the sensuous slide of the earl's mouth over her flesh. She put down her teacup, hoping to hide the tremor of her hand. "Let me get this straight. One of London's most celebrated wastrels is willing to play the noble knight—at considerable sacrifice to his own pleasures. And all I have to do in return is translate his uncle's manuscript?"

Ariel nodded.

"I don't believe it," said Ciara darkly.

"Frankly, I don't really see the harm of Hadley's proposal, my dear," mused Charlotte. "After all, you will likely enjoy the task of studying the ancient text, especially if it is a long-lost work of medicine."

"There *must* be an ulterior motive. Lord Hadley did not strike me as altruistic by nature." Recalling her shameful response to his kisses, Ciara bit her lip. The earl, with his undeniable aura of animal magnetism, was . . . dangerous.

*But given the alternative, what choice did she really have?*

Yet another headline in the morning newspaper had stirred dire forebodings. It could only have been planted by her late husband's family. Even more alarming was the missive she had received from her man of affairs earlier in the day. Sheffield's relatives—led by his sister, Lady Battersham—seemed intent on stirring up new trouble with the estate. Ciara had no doubt that having failed to have her arrested, they were now redoubling their efforts to get custody of her son and his inheritance.

Her hands went suddenly cold. She couldn't bear the thought of losing Peregrine. She would do anything—*anything*—to keep him safe.

"Perhaps you are judging Lord Hadley too harshly," said Ariel softly. "His affection for his uncle seemed genuine."

"Despite his rakish reputation, he's titled and rich. And that, in the end, is what influences Society—rank and money," pointed out Charlotte. She was no longer smiling. "Hadley has both and will use them to your advantage."

"My dear," murmured Ariel after an uncomfortable

silence. "It is an unfortunate truth that the wheels of justice do not always roll in a straight path. A word here, a favor there—there are many little things that can alter its course."

Charlotte was quick to add her assent. "Believe me, I have seen enough of the world to know. Sheffield's family will use every rotten little trick they can to harm you. Much as you might wish not to stoop to their level, you, too, must fight dirty to defend yourself. As a lone female, you are already at a disadvantage."

Ciara knew in her heart that they were right. Still, she felt her cheeks flush. "I cannot believe you all are encouraging me to do this."

"As scientists, we must look at a problem objectively and apply logic to seeking the solution," said Ariel. "Even if the answer conflicts with our own personal feelings or assumptions."

"That's all very well in theory. But in practice . . ." Ciara let her voice trail off, knowing she was running out of arguments.

"So, what do you say?" demanded Kate.

*Dangerous.* Once again, the word leapt to mind.

But she would risk anything, even a date with the Devil, to keep her son safe from the clutches of her late husband's family.

"Very well, I'll do it," she muttered. "You've all been very persuasive. Let us hope this little experiment does not blow up in my face."

"It has all the ingredients for a very entertaining Season." Kate's grin suddenly faded. "Oh, hell. We are going to miss all the fun!"

Charlotte looked crestfallen, as well. "Good heavens,

I had forgotten all about our trip! What a pity that we agreed to attend the symposium in St. Andrews."

Ciara recalled with a start that Charlotte and Kate were scheduled to leave for Scotland the day after the morrow. "Traitors!" she exclaimed. "You convince me to take a leap of faith and then are leaving me in the lurch?"

Charlotte looked a little guilty. "You have Ariel for moral support. And Alessandra, who is far more comfortable in Society than we are."

"Right," chimed in Kate. "You'll do just fine without us."

She glowered at her friends. "I wish I was as certain about that as you are."

~⌐

Lucas paused for a moment in the doorway, watching as his uncle turned the page of his laboratory journal and continued transcribing his notes. Perhaps it was merely a quirk of light, but his guardian looked a little frail and faded against the mullioned windows.

The scratch of the pen covered his approach. It wasn't until he cleared his throat that Henry looked up.

"Lucas! How nice to see you, my boy." He gestured to the sideboard. "Pour yourself a brandy and have a seat by the fire. That is, if you are not pressed for time."

Lucas took up two glasses. "Will you join me?"

"Perhaps a spot of sherry. The doctors want me to swear off spirits altogether. But life is deucedly boring without an occasional indulgence."

"That I wouldn't know," said Lucas dryly.

The remark elicited a chuckle. "There is something to be said for moderation."

"Yes—to hell with it." As Lucas had hoped, his uncle laughed louder. He handed over the sherry and clinked glasses.

"Have we something to celebrate?"

He could tell that Henry was trying to keep the note of anticipation from his voice. Which only made Lucas feel more determined not to disappoint him.

"Not yet," he replied. "But I have reason to believe we may be coming close." Shifting a stack of botany books, he perched a hip on the corner of the desk. "Lady Sheffield is like one of your wild English roses—tough, twisting vines and prickly thorns discourage any contact."

"A lady who keeps you at arm's length?" Henry waggled a brow. "That probably hasn't happened since you were a skinny schoolboy with spots on your face."

Lucas shifted uncomfortably. Had he been such a skirt-chasing hellion even then? The answer was oddly depressing. Perhaps the specter of old age—his thirtieth birthday was not far off—was weighing more heavily on him than he realized.

"With all due modesty, I don't think it's just me she doesn't like. The widow seems to be wary of men in general."

"With good reason," mused his uncle. "From what I have heard, Sheffield was a drunkard and a violent brute."

His own inquiries had left Lucas with the same impression. The lady's parents, a wealthy baronet and his ambitious wife, had been willing to barter a handsome dowry for a lofty title. Leaving their daughter to pay the real price.

"Is she pretty?" asked Henry.

"Very," he replied slowly.

Henry's mouth curled in a wistful smile of longing. "Brains and beauty. A rare combination indeed."

Lucas was suddenly struck by an unsettling realization. In all the years that he had lived with his uncle, he had never asked him why he had never married.

Moving back to the sideboard, he refilled his glass. "Were you never tempted to take a wife?"

"Ah, work is a hard enough mistress." His uncle laughed, but the sound was strangely hollow.

Lucas looked away, the brandy burning the back of his throat. What a selfish sot he had been for never being curious about his guardian's life. Henry had always been there to listen, to share every little triumph and disaster. He had never thought to return the favor.

Youth was naturally self-centered, supposed Lucas. But platitudes didn't dull the edge of his regret. "No doubt science is satisfying—up to a point," he said softly. "But surely you looked up from your books once in a while."

Henry didn't answer for some moments. "There was a young lady once. A long time ago." He stared down at his sherry. "We met at a lecture . . . the professor from Oxford was a prosy bore, and as I sat squirming in my chair I caught her eye, and we both made a face. Afterward, I took her to Guenter's, where we discovered that we shared a taste for strawberry ices and botany."

"Did you not pursue the relationship?" asked Lucas softly.

"With a passion." Henry crooked a tiny smile. "Though you probably can't imagine me interested in aught but ink and vellum." He sighed. "Her name was Elizabeth. Elizabeth Sprague. Her father taught philosophy at Merton College."

"And?"

Henry took a long swallow of his sherry. "Unfortunately, she was as delicate as some of the ancient manuscripts we loved to study. Six months after we met, she died of consumption."

Lucas felt a lump form in his throat. "I am very sorry."

"Don't be. Life is too short for regrets."

"I should have . . . known," he added lamely.

"You were just a boy at the time." His uncle gave a nonchalant shrug. "As for now, it's ancient history—not a subject that ever appealed to your fancy."

He forced himself to grin at the joke.

"You need not look so queasy, my dear boy. I'm quite content with my life," finished Henry.

Rather than seize the chance to drop the subject, Lucas pressed on. "Did you never meet anyone else?"

"Never really cared to, I suppose," replied Henry. "I had my books. And you."

*And what had he given Henry in return, save for more heartache?*

For an instant, Lucas wished he had never returned from the country. He could be carousing with his friends and his fancy whores. Laughter and lust—not a care in the world. Instead, he felt a cold weight settling on his shoulders.

Responsibility? Good God . . . Repressing a shiver, he downed the rest of his brandy. "Somehow I doubt that I was more fun than a roll in the hay."

"You had your moments," replied Henry with a twinkle in his eye. "Besides, I get vicarious pleasure out of your exploits."

Lucas set aside his glass. "Well, as I said, I hope to

have more material gratification for you in the near future. I've a meeting scheduled with Lady Sheffield on the morrow."

"What makes you think you can change her mind now?"

"Because the lady is smart enough to realize that I may be the answer to her prayers."

Henry snorted in amusement. "Kisses will get you only so far. I fear that the widow will require a more convincing argument."

"We'll see about that."

# Chapter Six

Ciara drew in a deep breath, trying to slow the skittering beat of her heart. Lud, she hadn't felt this nervous since the night of her first ball.

Back then, she had been an innocent girl, fresh from the schoolroom and untutored in the ways of the world. Entering the Mayfair mansions had been like stepping into an enchanting fairy tale. The titled gentlemen, resplendent in their finery, had all appeared like Prince Charmings.

Her education regarding the true nature of men had come swiftly, though not swiftly enough. Sheffield had been no prince. He had been a . . .

*Prick* was the word Kate had used. When its meaning had been explained, Ciara had filed it away in her private vocabulary. Yes, Sheffield had been a prick. Never again would she be so naive as to be fooled by a gentleman's superficial charm.

*So why was she experiencing butterflies in her stomach?*

Fisting her hands, she sought to get a grip on her fears. A part of her could not believe she was voluntarily re-entering that glittering world of glamour and gaiety. Of silken whispers. Of satin lies. And in the company of a devil-may-care rakehell, a gentleman whose only interest was the pursuit of pleasure.

In both sense and sensibility they were complete opposites.

*Opposites attract.*

Ciara bit her lip on recalling one of the basic laws of physics. Just because she had, in a moment of weakness, allowed herself to enjoy the intimacy of a physical touch, the sweetness of a kiss, didn't mean that she was attracted to Lord Hadley. Not in any meaningful way. It could have been anyone—

A knock on the door interrupted her thoughts. "Lord Hadley is here, milady."

Ciara stiffened her spine. "Please show him in, McCabe."

The lady looked so rigid and pale that she might have been carved out of marble. *Was she nervous?* Strangely enough, Lucas found that he was, too.

He entered the parlor and made a polite bow, hoping to dispel the awkwardness of the moment. Perhaps this time around, he could get things off on a more civilized footing.

That hope, however, was quickly dispelled.

Clenching her arms across her chest, the widow moved brusquely toward the mullioned windows. "Let me begin the meeting with a reminder that this is just a business arrangement, nothing more."

Shadows wreathed her face as she turned to stare out at

the garden. Her expression was unreadable, but contempt was written plainly in her tone.

"It seems that my friends have it all worked out," she went on. "You get the manuscript translated for your uncle, I get a titled fiancé and some semblance of respectability in Society."

"Tit for tat," he replied with matching coolness. "In other words, we both get what we want."

"Speak for yourself," snapped Ciara. "I'm not at all convinced that your name will offer me much protection from the malicious lies being spread by my late husband's family. However, my friends insist that I have no choice but to agree to this absurd proposition."

*Hell.* It wasn't as if the arrangement suited him perfectly, either. Squiring her through the Season would require a number of sacrifices on his part. Stung by her scorn, Lucas responded with deliberate sarcasm. "One always has a choice, Lady Sheffield. We are all responsible for our own actions."

"That is true," she said softly. "But some of us are responsible for more than our own selfish wants or needs. I have a young son, sir. And to keep him safe from the clutches of his father's beastly family, I would do anything."

It was evil to tease her, but Lucas couldn't resist the temptation. "Even kiss me again?"

A flush rose to her cheeks. "I pray it won't come to that."

She looked even more lovely with her color up and her eyes sparking with fire.

"No need to appeal to the heavens for protection, Lady Sheffield. I am not in the habit of forcing my attentions on an unwilling partner," he drawled.

Her face flamed to a deeper shade of scarlet.

Suddenly sorry for upsetting her, Lucas stopped smiling. "But speaking of force, do you really think that Sheffield's family is seriously seeking to take custody of your son? I understand that they said some nasty things during the inquest, but—"

"It was more than mere words, Lord Hadley. Someone tried to bribe the chemist from whom I purchase my supplies to say that I had bought some highly toxic poisons right before my husband's death. Thank God, he was a man of integrity and informed my solicitor, so the trick could not be tried at another shop."

Ciara took a moment to steady her breathing. "And before you ask why, I will tell you that the answer is simple—money. Arthur Battersham has gambled himself into debt, and his mother, my late husband's sister, knows that if I am declared an unfit mother, the current legal guardianship can be changed. Whoever is appointed to take charge of my son will control the purse strings of his considerable fortune." Another pause. "So be assured that I am not imagining the threat."

"It would not seem so," replied Lucas as he watched her wet her lips . . .

*Forget about her lips,* he warned himself. Forget about the tiny tremor of her mouth when she spoke about her son. Forget about the shade of fear that darkened her eyes when Society was mentioned.

*And most of all, forget about the inexplicable desire that came over him when she was near—the desire not only to kiss her witless, but to pick up a sword and slay her dragons.*

"Have you other questions, sir?"

"Not at the moment." Reminding himself that he was a rakehell libertine, not a high-minded hero, he shoved aside such strange thoughts. "Shall we move on to the business at hand?"

She nodded curtly.

"For this to work, we are going to have to be a convincing couple. That means we shall have to begin appearing in Society."

"When?" she whispered.

"As soon as possible." He took a piece of paper from his pocket. "I've made a list of the influential hostesses and the parties where I think we should make an appearance. I suggest we make our debut at the Countess of Saybrook's soirée. She's one of the leading arbiters of style in London, and word will spread like wildfire. After a week or so of us being seen together, the betrothal announcement can be sent to the newspapers."

Ciara grimaced. "I can't imagine how anyone will really believe we have a *tendre* for each other."

Lucas smiled. "In my experience, when it comes to telling a bouncer, one should always stick as close to the truth as possible. We shall say that we met through my uncle, whose scholarly interests are well known. I was smitten by your charms . . ."

She made a strange sound in her throat. "Or we could announce that I bewitched you by slipping a potent love potion in your drink, a powerful drug that addled your judgment."

"My judgment has never been considered very steady to begin with," he replied. "No one will blame you for its demise."

"Ah, well, one less crime I am guilty of." For an instant

her eyes flared with an odd light, somewhere between anger and longing. And then her mask of composure was back in place, her gaze unflinching as it met his. It could not be easy facing the smug censure and prurient gossip, yet she had retained a dignity and grace that did her proud.

Lucas was aware of how sublimely stupid his antics must appear to her. *Another indolent aristocrat, wasting away his days with drinking, gambling, and womanizing.*

He smoothed a wrinkle from his sleeve. To hell with what Lady Sheffield thought of him. He didn't give a damn for Society's opinion, so why should hers matter? There was, he reminded himself, nothing personal about this arrangement. It was simply an exchange of services.

"Lady Sheffield, it's obvious you think I am a wastrel and a fool. But much as it might shock you, my brain has grasped the fact that you are not at all pleased with the proposed arrangement," he said. "I understand that you are sacrificing your scruples. Well, so am I. The ballrooms of Mayfair bore me to perdition, yet I'm willing to dance in circles—not for any personal pleasure but for the sake of my uncle."

Ciara looked down at her hands.

"So unless you have changed your mind about protecting your son—"

"Never!" she exclaimed.

"Then it seems we are fated to be in each other's company quite frequently over the next several months. And to be frank, I'd rather not be subjected to your constant scorn and sarcasm. Why don't we try to make the best of it? Who knows, you might even enjoy the experience."

"And pigs might fly," muttered Ciara.

"My understanding of biology may not be as advanced as yours, but that seems anatomically improbable. The legs are too stubby, and the ratio of weight to length is a decided drawback. Not to speak of a curly tail, which offers little directional stability."

Her lips twitched.

"I thought that perhaps Lady Ariel was exaggerating . . ." Lucas paused. "But thank God, you *do* have a sense of humor."

"I am going to need more than a sense of humor to survive the Season," she murmured.

"Right. You are going to need *me*." Lucas moved to the hearth and leaned an elbow on the mantel. "So, do we have a deal?"

Her answer was almost lost in a sigh. "Yes."

He smiled.

"But . . ."

"But what?"

Ciara looked away for a moment, unwilling to allow the sensual spread of his lips to distract her. "Now that we have agreed in principle to the arrangement, let's get down to details, Lord Hadley," she said through clenched teeth. "As I said, I am willing to go through with this charade, but only if you agree to certain conditions."

"Which are?" he asked.

"No overt whoring, no drunken debaucheries, no outrageous stunts for the duration of the Season."

He cocked an eyebrow. "Ah. So I must be boring?"

Ciara averted her eyes. Damn the man for being so devastatingly handsome when he made that face. "No doubt it will seem so to you."

The earl took a lazy turn in front of the hearth and then leaned back against the marble mantel. "What shall I do with my time, then, if I am not allowed to cavort and carouse?" he asked. "Try to improve my mind?"

"Why not?" she replied impulsively. "If I must subject myself to frivolous balls and parties, you, in turn, should have to expose yourself to my world. Not that it is likely a rakehell rogue will *ever* comprehend the first thing about logic and discipline."

"Is that a *challenge,* madam?" he said softly.

"Yes," snapped Ciara, her patience dangerously frayed. "Put it in the blasted betting book at White's." She paused to think. "The Wicked Witch wagers Lord H that he cannot complete a basic course in . . . chemistry." She paused for breath. "No, that's too unfair—make it ornithology, a far simpler subject for a layman to grasp."

Lucas didn't respond for a moment. "Done," he said softly. "I accept your wager, but we shall, for the sake of propriety, not record it at any club. It will be a more private accounting."

Ciara felt a flare of heat prickle along her arms. Oh, Lord, had she just made a dreadful mistake? If there was one thing a man couldn't tolerate, it was a jab at his pride. But she couldn't very well back out now. She, too, had her own unyielding pride.

"The thing is," he continued, "a wager needs a prize. And a penalty. Tell me, Lady Sheffield, what are you willing to forfeit if you lose?"

"I have no intention of losing," she replied.

"Am I misinformed, or is a scientist expected not to have preconceived ideas about the outcome of an experiment?"

She thinned her lips. "Very well, Lord Hadley. Name the stakes."

"If I win, you must grant me one wish."

"Too vague," she objected. "I'd be a fool to agree."

"What's the worry? I thought you didn't intend to lose."

*Damn the rogue.* For a man who claimed to have no interest in intellectual pursuits, he was awfully clever with his tongue . . .

Ciara felt herself flush as she recalled Lady Annabelle's risqué comments about Hadley's sinful mouth and the taste of its naughty pleasures. Looking up, she saw he was smiling. The crescent curve of his lips showed a peek of pearly white teeth.

"So, you wish for me to be specific? Very well." He paused. "If I win, you must submit to a kiss."

"I suppose that I can agree to that—" she began.

"Wait. I haven't finished." Smoothing a crease on his trousers, he added, "To be bestowed on a place of my choosing."

"Th-that's . . . outrageous," she whispered.

"Is it?" His gaze drifted ever so slowly over her body, as if peeling the layers of silk and cotton from her flesh. "There are, you know, so many exquisitely sensitive parts of the female body—it's devilishly difficult to decide on just one."

She gave an involuntary gasp.

"I could suckle one rosy red nipple," he said in a smoky murmur. "Then again, I could feather my lips over the dimpled little button of your belly." His voice dropped a notch. "Or I could delve even lower."

Sure that her face was on fire, Ciara looked away, hoping to hide her reaction. His words were titillating, but she didn't wish to admit it. "The decision is yours, sir. It makes no difference to me."

His husky laugh teased against her flesh. "Ah, but it should. You, too, have much to learn."

Seeking to deflect his attention, she demanded, "What do *I* win?"

"What do you want?"

"Nothing you can give me," replied Ciara, ruing the tightness that took hold of her throat.

"Don't be so sure," said Lucas.

A tiny trickle of sweat tickled along the crevasse between her breasts.

"Think hard—is there really nothing you want from me?"

She didn't trust herself to speak.

"No need to reply right now." With a lazy flick of his finger, he straightened the folds of his cravat. "I am willing to let you defer your choice of spoils for victory until a later time."

"That's taking a chance, sir."

"As you know, I am not afraid of taking chances." He stepped closer, and she was acutely aware of his heat, his scent—sandalwood, tobacco, and a mysterious musk that was dark and dangerously male.

Quelling the odd little quiver of her insides, Ciara managed to regain her composure. "Some would call that arrogance, Lord Hadley."

"I prefer to think of it as confidence. I have a good deal of experience in beating the odds."

"I am glad to hear it. We are going to need a good deal of luck to get through the next few weeks."

"There is an old English adage, Lady Sheffield. Luck is the residue of desire."

# Chapter Seven

$S$anta cielo, I go away for a fortnight, and look what happens! All hell breaks loose." Alessandra della Giamatti cut a small slice from the pear on her plate. "And here I thought I was doing you a favor, taking the little devils with me."

Ciara tore her gaze away from the two children, who were chasing butterflies in the garden. "I swear, I did not go looking for trouble. Trouble came looking for me."

"At least Trouble is handsome as sin," quipped her friend.

"That is entirely beside the point," she exclaimed, dismayed that her voice sounded so brittle. "I have absolutely no interest in the rogue, other than to make use of his connections in Society."

Alessandra arched her elegant brows. "A more intimate connection might make the interlude more enjoyable, no?"

"No!"

Her friend nibbled at the fruit. "Have you something against the man that I don't know about? It's hard to find fault with his physical appearance."

"He's far too . . ." Ciara faltered.

"Too what?" asked Alessandra.

"Too different." *Too dangerous.*

"You know, there is a scientific theorem . . ." began her friend.

"Please—not you, too!" muttered Ciara. "I had hoped that you, of all people, would understand."

The marchesa was the most worldly of all her friends. A poised, polished Renaissance beauty—her ethereal face had inspired several ardent admirers to compare her to Botticelli's painting *Mars and Venus*—Alessandra had arrived in England a year ago, seeking reconciliation with her mother's estranged family. Their acknowledgment, however lukewarm, had elevated her into the highest circles of London Society. She attended the balls and soirées on occasion, but for the most part she had settled into a quiet life, dividing her time between scholarly studies and her daughter.

Ciara slanted a sidelong look at Isabella and Peregrine at play. A fortuitous meeting at a Royal Scientific Society chemistry lecture had revealed that they both were mothers to energetic eight-year-olds. But the bond between them had quickly grown deeper than shared advice on skinned knees and sore throats. Along with her intellect, Alessandra possessed an incisive eye for judging character and a sardonic sense of humor.

A sigh escaped from her lips.

"I do understand, *bella,* more than you know," replied Alessandra with a graceful wave of her hand. Glimmers of gold and green sparkled as her ornate emerald ring caught the sunlight. "I was merely trying to tease the lines of worry from your face."

Her smile was equally brilliant, but Ciara knew there was also a dark side to her friend. Alessandra was very private about her personal past and spoke very little about her life in Italy. As for the reasons why she had chosen to leave the country, aside from a dark hint or two, they remained shrouded in mystery. *Sins and secrets.* Yet another bond between them.

"Would that I could laugh them off." Ciara forced a self-mocking grimace. "But to be honest, I'm beginning to think I have made a grave mistake. Tomorrow—tomorrow!—I must swathe myself in silk and appear in Society as if I hadn't a care in the world." She had not yet mentioned the wager to her friend. "I . . . I am not sure I can carry it off."

"Of course you can. And you won't be alone. I am so sorry I cannot be there for you, but Hadley will offer moral support and an arm to lean on."

"Ha," muttered Ciara. "More likely he'll be off in some dark corner, trying to put his hand up some lady's skirts."

"I grant you, his reputation doesn't inspire much confidence. And yet, I have heard . . ." Alessandra hesitated and then shrugged. "But you must judge for yourself."

She wasn't sure whether to feel disappointed or relieved that her friend did not finish her words. Unwilling to appear in any way curious about the earl, she didn't pursue the subject. Now, if only the rogue and his wicked wager would stop plaguing her thoughts.

*Risk and reward.* Such challenges excited a gambler's nature. However, for her they held no allure. Ciara knew herself too well—she was, by temperament, steady and serious. Disciplined and decisive.

So why was she feeling so uncertain about . . . everything?

"A penny for your thoughts?" murmured Alessandra.

"You would be making a bad bargain," she replied with a rueful grimace.

Alessandra sat in silence, slowly curling a lock of her raven hair around her finger.

"Besides, I'm not quite sure I could express them in any coherent order," she added.

"Sometimes it helps to simply talk, *cara*."

Ciara refrained from pointing out that was rather like the pot calling the kettle black. Instead she asked, "If you had been at our meeting, what would you have advised me to do?"

The hesitation was barely perceptible. "To follow your heart," said Alessandra.

"Good Lord!" The answer took her completely by surprise. "You are the most pragmatic, practical person I know! Never in a thousand years would I have guessed that you are a secret romantic!"

The reflections from the mullioned glass formed flickering patterns of sun and shadow across her friend's face. "Romance has nothing to do with it. What I meant was, sometimes one has to rely on instinct rather than intellect. This is true even in science, *si?*"

"I—I suppose I see your point." But instead of casting any light on her quandaries, Alessandra's words of wisdom only muddled her mood. "Kate said much the same thing to me as we were leaving our weekly meeting."

"I am not surprised. I suspect that the three of us share more than an interest in science." Alessandra did not elaborate but returned to her earlier comment. "Mind you, I am only suggesting—"

A cry from the garden cut short the exchange.

Both mothers shot up out of their chairs as Peregrine dropped to the ground with a thump. Ciara was first through the French doors, with Alessandra a scant half step behind.

"Girls!" Peregrine blinked back tears as she smoothed the tangle of curls from his forehead. A lump the size of a goose egg was already forming smack between his eyes. "Why can't they ever learn to throw a ball straight?"

"It slipped." Alessandra's daughter, Isabella, leaned in for a closer look. "Ewwww, it's turning a really horrid shade of purple, Perry. Why didn't you duck?"

"Because you were supposed to be aiming at the wicket. Which was near my feet, not my head, nitwit."

Isabella's lips quivered. "Cricket is a stupid game."

"So is playing with your silly dolls. But *I* don't cosh you over the head with them."

*Sniff.* The little girl's eyes started to water. "I didn't do it on purpose."

"Of course you didn't," soothed her mother.

"No harm done," said Ciara, hugging her son close. "A cold compress and some jam tarts will soon make everything right."

"I think I should take Isabella home." Alessandra made a wry face over the top of her daughter's head. "Before bruised feelings turn truly ugly."

The children were usually perfect playmates, but the journey home from Bath had been a long one, due to the rains, and even the best of friends could grow tired of each other's company.

"Perhaps that's a wise idea," agreed Ciara. It seemed her blue-deviled mood was rubbing off on everyone around her.

"*Ciao, tesoro.*" Alessandra kissed Peregrine, then Ciara. "I look forward to hearing all about tomorrow's ball at our next meeting."

Her current sentiments on the subject were best left unsaid.

Gathering her son in her arms, Ciara accompanied her friend to the front door and then sought the soothing sanctuary of the kitchen. The sweet smells of melting sugar and cinnamon immediately enveloped them in a buttery warmth. So, too, did Cook, who dusted the flour from her yeasty hands and quickly set a pan of milk to heat on the hob.

Ciara bit her lip as she watched the elderly woman fuss over Peregrine's bruised forehead. It suddenly struck her that her son was surrounded by females. The only men of the household were the butler McCabe and Jeremiah the footman—and neither was a day under seventy. It couldn't be good for a boy to grow up without a strong male influence in his life. She didn't want him to be cosseted and petted until he became a spoiled brat. Suffering a few scrapes was all part of life. He must learn to take his lumps and laugh them off.

Not that Sheffield would have made an ideal role model. Ciara repressed a shudder. A drunken wastrel with a hair-trigger temper was hardly an example to emulate. She knew that her late husband wasn't all that different from many aristocratic fathers. But she wished for something more for Peregrine.

Warmth. Laughter. *Love*.

She had no illusions that he would get any of those things from Sheffield's family. The only reason they were trying to gain guardianship of the boy was on account of his money and his lands.

Fear froze her throat, and for a moment she couldn't swallow. As Peregrine smiled and bit into one of the freshly baked pastries, she turned away, hoping to hide her worries. Lud, she was really in no mood for making a reentry into Society. Amid the gaiety and glitter of the evening, she would be like . . . a fish out of water. Especially if Hadley chose to plunge headlong into some new scandal.

However, Ciara reminded herself that she had survived far worse than a London ball. Be damned what the *ton* whispered behind her back. *Sticks and stones could break her bones, but words could never hurt her . . .*

Now, if only there were a grain of truth to the old adage.

~~~~~

"You look bored."

Lucas glanced up from his half-empty glass.

"I had heard you were rusticating in the country for a bit." Lord James Jacquehart Pierson—known to his friends as "Black Jack" on account of his shoulder-length raven hair and olive complexion—flopped into one of the leather armchairs and signaled to the club porter for another bottle of brandy. "What happened—did the fountains all dry up in Kent?"

He gave a gruff grunt. Would those particular jokes never evaporate?

"Or have you plans to make another splash in Town?" Jack propped his boots on the brass fender and lit a cheroot. "Whatever you have in mind, count me in. It's been dull as dishwater around here."

"Stubble the witticisms, Jack. Lest you wish to be fishing your teeth out from the bottom of the Serpentine."

"In a foul humor, are we?" Jack blithely ignored the warning. "What's dampened your enthusiasm for fun—other than a pair of black and blue cods?"

His answering oath would have made a sailor blush.

"Oh, very well. We'll paddle along to another subject." Blowing out a plume of smoke, Jack offered a refill of brandy. "Or perhaps you would prefer whisky. Did you know the word derives from Scotch Gaelic?" His friend paused ever so slightly. "*Uisge beatha* means water of life."

"My, my, aren't you a font of knowledge." Lucas set aside his drink and flexed a fist. "A pity your brain will soon be taking a bath in the club's punch bowl."

Jack chuckled. "Cry peace, Hadley. I promise to put a cork in it for the moment."

He slouched back in his seat. "You damn well better."

"Don't be a prig. Things have been sadly flat around Town, especially with Sandhurst away in Scotland on his honeymoon." Jack stared morosely into his brandy. "He returned yesterday, but he's so besotted with his bride, he has no interest in making the rounds of the gaming hells in St. Giles." His mouth pursed in a wry grimace. "Not that I blame him. Lady Olivia would tempt any man to settle down."

"Settle down?" growled Lucas. "Good God, what a depressing thought."

His friend's expression brightened considerably. "That's the spirit. I knew I could count on you to be hell-bent for some fun. Tomorrow evening, there's going to be a special high-stakes game of vingt-un at the Wolf's Lair.

And from there we'll move on to a charming little bordello that I have discovered in Southwark. The girls—"

"Sorry," interrupted Lucas. "I have a previous engagement."

Jack flicked a bit of ash into the hearth. "The more, the merrier. Bring your current lady along. In my experience, they often find a naughty adventure exhilarating."

"This one won't." Realizing that he was sounding awfully sardonic for a man about to announce his betrothal, Lucas added, "She's not . . . that sort of lady."

Frowning, Jack drew in a mouthful of smoke and spirits before letting out a rumbled laugh. "Damnation, you had me fooled for a moment." The sound grew louder. "You with a respectable female? What a bouncer!"

Lucas didn't crack a smile. "Actually, it's true. I am engaged to escort Lady Ciara Sheffield to the Countess of Saybrook's ball."

The ensuing paroxysm of coughing woke up the elderly gentleman napping in a nearby chair.

"Harrumph. You young men should switch to a mild Virginian tobacco if you can't stomach Indian cheroots."

Jack sputtered an apology before turning back to Lucas. "Your wits must have been left permanently waterlogged by your latest stunt."

"Jack . . ." warned Lucas.

"Nothing else could explain this sudden delusion."

"Delusion?" repeated Lucas.

"That you somehow fell into a baptismal font and emerged a saint."

"You think I am not capable of change?" Lucas was beginning to enjoy seeing his friend's agitation. Simply to annoy him he added, "Perhaps I am ready to shed my old skin."

"Pollywogs turn into frogs, not princes," muttered Jack.

Lucas lifted his glass and swirled the brandy. Firelight winked through the cut crystal, turning the amber spirits into a shimmering vortex of liquid gold. It stirred a sudden recollection of Lady Sheffield's glorious hair, alive with highlights of copper and sunshine . . .

"Damn it, Lucas." His friend shook his head. "Are you demented? Deranged?"

"I'm perfectly sane," he replied.

"Then listen to reason! Steer clear of any involvement with the Wicked Widow. Need I remind you that her first husband ended up dead?"

The sneering remark brought to mind Ciara's vulnerable face, her gaze shaded with fear . . .

His grip tightened on the glass. She was all alone, and yet she had the courage to stand up to the vicious gossip and nasty rumors. Damnation—she deserved more than scorn. She deserved someone to come to her defense.

"From what I have heard, it's a wonder she didn't kill him sooner."

"Ye gods." Jack refilled his glass. "Why *her* when you have your choice of any number of willing wenches?"

"Maybe I'm attracted to her mind," drawled Lucas. "My uncle has nothing but the highest praises for her intellect."

His friend snorted in disgust. "Since when have you favored a female's brain over her body?"

"Have you met Lady Sheffield?" he asked, unwilling to admit that he *did* find her intelligence intriguing.

His friend shook his head. "Like the Grim Reaper, she seems to live in the shadows."

A smug smile crept to his lips. "Well, I assure you, beneath her black shroud is more than skin and bones."

"Because she feeds on the blood of her victims." Jack exaggerated a ghoulish grimace. "I still don't understand—why go out of your way to seduce a suspected murderess . . ." He thought for a moment, and then his expression brightened. "A wager—tell me it's on account of a wager."

"You know very well that a gentleman does not discuss his relations with a lady in public," replied Lucas. "Code of honor."

"Mad, Bad Had-ley lecturing me on morality? Someone must have spiked my cigar with opium."

His friend's unrelenting sarcasm was beginning to rub him a little raw. "Are you implying that I'm not a gentleman?"

A bark of laughter jabbed deeper. "No, I'm not implying it—I'm saying it straight to your face."

"Damn it, Jack, that's unfair," said Lucas defensively. "I've never cheated at cards or reneged on my vowels. And you know that my word is good as gold."

His friend shrugged. "Of course I'm not questioning your honor among your peers. But as for your antics in Polite Society . . . Hell, Lucas, your name has become a byword for bad behavior. Admit it—you are a rake who takes great glee in thumbing his nose at the rules." Jack flicked the butt of his cheroot into the fire. "Not that there's anything terribly wrong with that. All your friends consider you a capital fellow. But in a pinch, you would hardly be the first man I'd want to depend on."

*Bloody hell*. Lucas took a long swallow of brandy. And then another. What a sobering sketch of his character.

Jack reached for the bottle and refilled their drinks. "You are looking a little green around the gills. Dare I hope you are having second thoughts about taking the plunge with the Wicked Widow?"

Lucas didn't answer.

His friend arched a questioning brow. "Don't tell me you've taken offense at my words. If I've been blunt, it's only for your own good."

He forced a sardonic grin. "Don't worry. It's not as if I haven't heard the lectures before."

"Then cry friends and come along with me to Southwark tonight. I know where we can find some very pretty whores who will make you forget all about Lady Sheffield."

"You go on," he said softly, unsettled by the conflicting urges to be both noble and naughty. "Perhaps I'll join up with you later."

"You *are* ill." Jack gave him a fishy stare. "Go home and get a good night's sleep. I shall save you a seat at the gaming table tomorrow night. Play will be for high stakes—it promises to be an interesting interlude."

"As I said, I've already given my word to escort Lady Sheffield to the ball tomorrow night," replied Lucas. "And much as it might surprise you, I intend to honor it."

Jack expelled a long-suffering sigh. "Well, it's your funeral." Rising, he drained the dregs from his glass. "I'm off to Cupid's Cave." He hesitated a fraction before flashing a parting grin. "I shall leave you to sink or swim on your own."

Lucas swore a silent oath at his friend's retreating rump.

Save for the cracking coals and an occasional snore, the reading room was quiet as a crypt. Lucas shifted uncomfortably in his seat, his mood growing more on edge as he mulled over the conversation. It seemed that his recent soggy slip had turned his whole world upside down. Forced to look at himself from a new perspective, he wasn't sure he liked what he saw.

*Damn.* He closed his eyes and touched his fingertips to his throbbing temples. His head ached, and the brandy had left a stale taste in his mouth. Maybe he *was* sick.

Or perhaps the widow's kiss had possessed a potent poison after all. That would account for the strange shivers of fire and ice that took hold of him whenever he thought of her. And for the temporary insanity of agreeing to all her terms.

Starting tomorrow . . .

No, he wouldn't think about the consequences of his actions. He had always lived for the present, so why change now?

Raising his glass, he mouthed a silent toast to his real self. Mad, Bad Had-ley. A man who knew how to have a good time.

It was all very well to feel a twinge of sympathy for Lady Sheffield, but he owed no real allegiance to her. Some faraway time in the future he might be caught in the Parson's Mousetrap, but for now, it was all a sham. He was still free to do exactly as he pleased.

Pushing back from his chair, Lucas hurried for the door, hell-bent to catch up with Jack and have some fun.

# Chapter Eight

$T$he townhouse torchières were ablaze, the golden flames casting a pattern of dancing shadows across the pale Portland stone. Turning up the collar of her cloak to ward off the evening breeze, Ciara stepped down from the earl's carriage, glad that the dark velvet hid her face from the other guests for a few moments longer.

All too soon she would be bared for all to ogle. *The Wicked Widow in the flesh.* No doubt her presence would stir a swirl of lurid speculation. She shivered, wishing she could turn and slink off into the darkness.

As if sensing her thoughts, Lucas tightened his hold on her arm. "Nervous?" he asked.

"A little," she admitted.

"Don't be," came his whispered reply. "All eyes will be drawn to you—"

"That's what I'm afraid of," she muttered.

"On account of your beauty, grace, and regal bearing," continued Lucas smoothly. "You are looking exceeding lovely tonight, Lady Sheffield. You should always wear that shade of indigo blue. It sets off your golden hair and ivory skin to perfection."

The earl was, of course, a practiced flirt, but his flatteries helped her relax as they passed through the portico and into the entrance hall.

"Though of course," he added in an exaggerated whisper, "I would prefer to see you wearing nothing at all."

"Shhhh." Ciara slanted a swift look around as a footman approached to take her wrap. Oh, Lud, she had forgotten how very grand and glittering these gatherings were. The sparkle of the ornate cut-crystal chandelier seemed to magnify the splendor of guests making their way across the checkered marble tiles. For an instant, it all ran together in a blur of sumptuous color—the costly jewels and colorful silks of the ladies, punctuated by the elegant black-and-white formality of the gentlemen. Pomp and polish, privilege and pedigree.

*Propriety.*

What a fool she had been to think this charade might work. She felt like a drab sparrow amid all the brightly feathered finery. And beneath the peacock plumage, they were hawks at heart.

*Ready to eat her alive.*

Lucas leaned close, shielding her for a moment from the sidelong stares. "Smile, my dear," he murmured. "In my experience, nothing stops the *ton*'s scrutiny better than to act as if you haven't a care in the world."

Though her lips felt as if they were carved out of ice, Ciara forced them to curl upward.

"That's the spirit." He placed her arm on his, a gesture that was strangely protective. "Another trick is to stare back and imagine them all naked." He flashed a roguish wink. "You will find that quickly strips away their aura of smug superiority."

Despite her nervousness, Ciara had to choke back a laugh. Heavens, he was right. The short and stout dowager Duchess of Stamford did not appear nearly so intimidating without the armor of her gaudy gown and brilliant baubles.

"Shall we go up and greet our hostess?" asked Lucas.

Seeing that the curved staircase was already crowded with a long line of guests, Ciara was tempted to hang back. But on recalling the earl's exhortation, she nodded. "Yes, go ahead and lead the lamb to slaughter," she said under her breath.

His light laugh tickled her cheek. "Trust me, you will find that most of these people are sheep in wolves' clothing. Don't let them frighten you."

Ciara let out her breath, surprised to find how much his banter helped relieve the tension. There was something to be said for humor . . .

Lucas escorted her into the line and immediately began an amusing anecdote about the mansion's history. That is, Ciara assumed it was entertaining. She caught only bits and snatches as she lowered her lashes and ventured another glance around at her surroundings.

The architectural details were magnificent—the carved balusters, the ornate moldings, the decorative wall niches filled with exotic flowers. Equally impressive was the procession of ancestral portraits on the cream-colored walls. Peering down from their gilded frames, the Saybrook family looked to be a rather stiff-rumped lot, she observed. But then again, the starched ruffs and pinched corsets of Elizabethan times did not encourage any show of a smile. She could only hope that the current flesh-and-blood countess, a hostess noted for her style and wit, would be more welcoming.

As for the other guests . . .

Ciara was aware of the surreptitious scrutiny from all sides. She could feel the heat of the hurried looks against her bare arms, and could hear the whispers of silk and speculation. Wondering, no doubt, what had drawn the Wicked Widow from her lair.

"Ah, Lord Hadley!"

A throaty laugh from their hostess drew Ciara from her own inner musings.

"How delightful to see you have returned to Town." With a flourish, Lady Saybrook extended a gloved hand to Lucas. "Things have been sadly flat around here without you making a few waves," she added.

"My dear Alison, I shall try not to stir the waters tonight."

The countess winked. "It looks like you have already caused a tempest in a teapot—or rather the punch bowl." Turning to Ciara, she flashed a warm smile. "How delightful to finally meet you, Lady Sheffield. I have heard so much about your scientific accomplishments."

"Y-you are too kind, Lady Saybrook," stammered Ciara.

"I fear you will find me a complete scatterbrain when it comes to scholarship, but I do love gardening." The countess had raised her voice so that those nearby could hear every word. "So I do hope you will tell me about your latest work with medicinal herbs."

"Gladly," she replied.

"Excellent. Come sit with me at supper, if you please." Lady Saybrook waved Lucas toward the dance floor with a flick of her fan. "Don't keep her all to yourself, you naughty rogue."

"I—I cannot believe the countess's kindness to a total stranger—a stranger with a sordid reputation," mused Ciara as they made their way through the crowd. In her experience, the ladies of the *ton* could be even more ruthless than the gentlemen. Too often their satin smiles and velvet voices cloaked a killer instinct worthy of Attila the Hun. "Perhaps she has me confused with someone else?"

"Alison owes me a small favor or two, the details of which I won't go into," said Lucas. "And besides, she's led a rather interesting life herself and thinks that rigid respectability is vastly overrated."

*So far, so good.* She breathed a sigh of relief at having made it through the receiving line without suffering a direct cut. However, the respite didn't last more than a step.

"The musicians are striking up a waltz." Turning smoothly, Lucas took up a position on the polished parquet.

"Lord Hadley, must we—" she began.

"Yes. We must." His gloved hand pressed lightly against the small of her back. "This will be an exercise in futility if we don't appear to be enjoying ourselves."

"But—"

"Don't look so apprehensive. I won't tread on your toes."

Ciara pressed her eyes shut for an instant. "It's not *my* toes I am worried about, sir," she said in a low voice. "You forget that I have been out of Society for some time. I don't know the steps of this new dance."

Lucas drew her a touch closer. "Just follow my lead."

To her surprise, it proved rather simple to do. The earl had an easy, elegant grace, and after the first few spins Ciara relaxed into his rhythm, matching his moves without conscious thought.

"You see, it's not so hard to unlace your corset," he murmured.

Ciara was acutely aware of his overpowering closeness—his hand holding hers, his palm pressed to the small of her back, radiating heat through the layers of soft glove leather and silk. Already her skin felt a little singed.

"When you allow yourself a little freedom, your movements have a lovely, liquid flow to them," he went on.

The heat flooded to her face. "Why is it that you always make sexual innuendos, sir?"

"Why is it that references to your beautiful body always bother you?" he countered.

"I—I'm not beautiful," she stammered.

"Then why is every man in the room staring at you?" said Lucas with a spinning twirl that set her skirts to flaring.

Ciara slanted a peek around. Oh, Lud—people *were* watching them. She drew in a gulp of air.

"You see? Their eyes are drawn to you, like moths to a flame," said Lucas.

"Fire is dangerous," she whispered.

"Ah, but danger adds to the allure." His eyes glittered in the brilliant light of the chandeliers. "As I well know."

Another glance showed that men were not the only ones watching them dance. For an instant she felt a little giddy. Why, the belles of Town were envious of *her*. Here she was, the Wicked Widow of Pont Street, dancing with the most desirable rake in London.

"Your cheeks are a very luscious shade of pink," murmured Lucas. "It's the same shade as . . . another hot spot of the feminine form." He looked at her through his dark lashes. "Can you guess which one?"

Resisting the urge to fan her face, she asked, "Do you flirt so outrageously with every lady of your acquaintance?"

The corners of his mouth curled up. "But of course. The point of a party is to have a little fun."

Ciara sighed. "Life seems to be one unending party for you."

Before he could answer, one of the ladies whirled close with a lilting laugh. "La, Hadley, I hear there is a new ballet opening—it is called *The Fountain of Youth,* and I'm sure you won't want to miss it."

Her partner guffawed.

"Does it never bother you to be the butt of gossip?" she asked, once the figures of the dance drew them away from the others.

"Why should it?" replied Lucas after a slight hesitation.

Though the question was likely rhetorical, Ciara considered it seriously for several measures of the music before finally replying, "I don't know . . . it's just that if I were you, I would begin to wonder whether people were laughing *at* me, rather than with me."

"We all must be comfortable in our own skin," he replied lightly. "My hide is obviously a good deal thicker than yours, for you see, I don't really give a damn about what people say or think." Lucas stepped through an intricate twirl without missing a beat. "Why do you?"

"I don't have the luxury of thumbing my nose at Society. This may come as something of a shock to you, Lord Hadley, but there are two sets of rules in the Polite World. Ladies are held to a far more rigid standard. One misstep can mean ruin."

Looking around, she suddenly realized that she was a part of the spinning whirl of sights and sounds—blazing colors, winking lights, trilling laughter, clinking crystal. *All the things she had run from in the past.*

Tonight there was no escape—and strangely enough, that didn't seem as terrible as she had feared. Not with the earl's hard, muscled body providing a comforting measure of support. Swept along in the circle of his arms, she didn't feel quite so vulnerable or alone.

As the last notes of the violins died away, Lucas led her to a secluded spot by the potted palm trees. "Would you care for some champagne punch?"

"Yes, thank you." Ciara had forgotten that dancing could work up quite a thirst.

"I won't be long." Before she could protest being left by herself, Lucas hurried off.

Repressing a shiver, Ciara forced her gaze up from the parquet floor. No matter how awkward she felt inside, she must not appear intimidated by her surroundings. Predators pounced on any show of weakness.

Through the crowd, she saw Lucas pause to exchange a few words with a tall, broad-shouldered gentleman whose chiseled profile and military bearing made him a rather formidable figure. The stranger turned and eyed her for a moment before nodding gravely to Lucas.

To her surprise, he suddenly excused himself from his companions and started in her direction. His expression was austere, aloof—some might even consider it arrogant. As his piercing green gaze honed in on her little oasis amid the palm fronds, she willed herself not to flinch.

As he came closer, Ciara realized who he was.

*The Marquess of Haddan.*

A highly decorated war hero, the marquess was also a Fellow of the Royal Scientific Society. He was held in awe by most of Society, and according to the newspapers, he did not suffer fools gladly—

Her musings were interrupted by his baritone voice. "I beg your pardon, Lady Sheffield. Might I ask if you are free for this set?"

Seeing as her dance card was conspicuously empty, save for Hadley's name by the two waltzes, Ciara wondered for a moment whether he was mocking her. The leafy shadows made his expression hard to read, but in her experience, titled gentlemen sometimes took perverse delight in playing cruel games.

"I shall endeavor to beat off my many admirers with a stick to make room, sir," she replied softly.

His rumbled chuckle was surprisingly pleasant. "I have saved you the trouble. It seems my approach has scared them away. Rather like a magnet whose force has been reversed."

Ciara gave a tentative smile.

"Your expertise in science is quite impressive, Lady Sheffield," he went on. "I've read several of your essays and would enjoy discussing them, if you would care to dance."

"I . . . I would be honored, sir."

Once again, she found herself spinning across the polished parquet in the arms of a handsome gentleman. The conversation was so interesting that she forgot to be nervous, and somehow her steps stayed in harmony with the trilling violins. To her surprise, Ciara was almost sorry when the music came to an end.

"Thank you," she began.

But rather than return her to the shadows of the potted palms, Haddan angled his steps for one of the brightly lit refreshment tables. "I shall hand you off to my friend Woodbridge, if you don't mind."

Ciara nearly tripped over her own feet. Known for his charm and wit, Devlin Woodbridge was the darling of London Society. She couldn't think of why he would risk exposing himself to censure by standing up with her.

"Oh, please, Lord Woodbridge need not trouble himself." She drew a deep breath, wondering where Lucas had run off to. *Wretched man—how dare he abandon her to the mercy of strangers.*

"No trouble at all." Haddan stepped back with a small bow. "Ah, here he comes now. Enjoy the rest of your evening, Lady Sheffield."

*Clever.*

Smiling, Lucas congratulated himself on enlisting the help of his old friends in reintroducing Ciara to Polite Society. They could always be counted on to come through in a pinch. Haddan was respected, and even a little feared, while Woodbridge's sunny charm assured that he was well liked by most everyone who mattered. A show of favor from such powerful personages would go a long way in influencing the *ton*.

Yes, let Haddan and Woodbridge do his work, thought Lucas with an inward grin. Leaving him free to saunter off for a stroll in the garden with the buxom Baroness Blenheim. The lady had indicated an interest in a dalliance . . .

And yet, as he slanted a sidelong look at the spinning couples, Lucas felt his smugness slip a notch. Ciara and Haddan were moving through the last figures of the dance with an élan that stopped him short. His friend's natural reserve must have melted a good deal since his recent marriage—the marquess had never been one to engage in superficial flirtation, yet he seemed to be enjoying Ciara's company.

*Bloody hell.* There was no need for Nicholas to smile *quite* so frequently.

Gritting his teeth, Lucas snatched a glass of champagne from a passing footman and began to stalk around the perimeter of the dance floor. The ladies greeted him with smiles and sly winks. By the time he was halfway down the room, he had collected several whispered invitations for a late-night assignation. And from the gentlemen came good-natured gibes and guffaws. *Three cheers for Mad, Bad Had-ley, who kept them all so deucedly amused.*

Lady Sheffield was all wrong. He was a great favorite, not a great fool.

And yet the sparkling wine suddenly tasted a bit flat on his tongue. He switched to claret, and then to brandy.

All to no effect. Perhaps the close proximity of the scholarly scientist was having a strange chemical effect on him.

*Was her presence more potent than drink?*

He would have to test out that theory during their first private lesson.

For now, though, Lucas let his gaze drift back to Ciara. As she glided through a series of intricate steps, he couldn't help but admire her lithe grace, her cool composure. He had been close enough to sense she was quaking inside, yet she had the fortitude to face her fears with an outward show of dignity and determination.

*Brave girl*, he applauded.

He saw he wasn't the only one watching her. All around, speculative gazes gleamed, bright as the blazing chandeliers. Fortune hunters were drawn to a rich widow, no matter how notorious, like moths to a candle flame. His brows pinched together, and he felt a flicker of fire inside his chest. Let any grasping bastard come too close and the fellow would find his fingers roasted over the coals.

"The minx may be a murderess, but I'd die happy swiving such a shapely strumpet." Lord Dunning, a casual acquaintance, sidled up to his shoulder. "She has a fine arse, eh?"

Lucas swallowed a savage oath, along with a mouthful of his wine.

"You must fancy a poke, yourself," Dunning chortled. "Can't be after her fortune. Your coffers are bloody well full."

Repressing the urge to shove the other man's teeth down his gullet, Lucas set down his drink and flexed a fist. "My interest in Lady Sheffield is not a subject I intend to discuss with you. Code of honor and all that."

"Er, right." Dunning stepped away, looking both puzzled and peeved. "No need to get your hackles up, Hadley. Just making a little joke."

"Do so out of my hearing," he said softly.

The other man shot him a sour look and moved on.

It was all part of their plan, Lucas told himself. Word would spread like wildfire that Mad, Bad Had-ley had fallen under the spell of the Wicked Witch of Pont Street. The drawing rooms would soon be abuzz with speculation on what his next outrageous action would be.

Well, they were all in for a big surprise.

# Chapter Nine

Ciara was still feeling a little off balance as Lord Woodbridge exchanged places with Lord Haddan.

"I confess, sir, I am a bit overwhelmed by your kind attentions." She was well aware that dancing with two such exalted gentlemen would go a long way to smoothing her acceptance in Polite Society. "I cannot . . . that is, I am quite grateful—"

Woodbridge silenced her stammering with a brilliant smile. "The pleasure is all mine. It is not often that Lucas needs help with a lady. So I am happy to oblige. And you may be assured that I shall tease him unmercifully about it for some time to come."

"That makes me feel marginally better," said Ciara. "Have you and Lord Haddan known Hadley for a long time?"

"Lud, yes. Since we were pups at Eton, cutting our teeth on boyish escapades. From there, the three of us went on to Oxford together. In fact, it was Hadley's idea for a prank that got us all the boot."

Ciara was curious. "Which was?"

"Don't ask about the details. Suffice it to say it involved a cat, a courtesan, and the rector of Merton College."

Her lips twitched. "Oh, dear."

"It was more like 'Oh, hell.'" Woodbridge's eyes twinkled with unholy amusement. "Haddan and I joined the army, where, I am ashamed to admit, we continued to act like devils. Our unit was called the Rakehell Regiment, though we are thoroughly reformed now, thanks to our new brides."

That sounded like an interesting story, but her first concern was her errant escort. "Hadley did not join the army, too?" It seemed odd that he would not choose to follow his friends.

"No, Lucas was extremely sorry to cry off, but he did not want to go abroad and leave his guardian alone," explained Woodbridge. "Sir Henry was already beginning to suffer some serious physical ailments."

Ciara bit her lip. That the earl—an unrepentantly reckless young rascal—had been unselfish enough to think of his uncle at that age came as yet another surprise. The more she learned of Lucas, the more she found herself confused. He was a contradiction.

*A conundrum.*

She was usually very good at working out puzzles, but so far, the earl was a real enigma. On the surface, he seemed a man of shallow pleasures. But perhaps he had more substance.

"That seems rather out of character for Hadley," she mused.

"Ah, beneath the devil-may-care antics, Lucas is not quite such a fribble as he appears," replied Woodbridge. "He's a good and generous friend, loyal to a fault, though he takes care to hide it. I think he's just never had anything to challenge the better side of his nature."

"I see." The steps of the dance separated them for a moment. "Actually, I don't. I . . ." She let her words trail off.

He flashed an encouraging smile. "Yes?"

Something about his sunny manner made her abandon her usual reticence. "In my experience, gentlemen of title are vain, selfish, and manipulative," she blurted out. "Yet you and Lord Haddan have gone out of your way to be kind."

"Perhaps you have been moving in the wrong circles, Lady Sheffield," said Woodbridge softly.

Ciara was grateful that the music ended, for she was suddenly feeling a little light-headed. The evening was certainly taking an entirely different turn than she had expected.

"Thank you for a most delightful dance." Woodbridge bowed gracefully over her hand. "Here comes Lucas, so I shall hand you back to your escort. With great pleasure, I might add. It's about time that he gets serious about leaving the follies of his youth behind him."

"You are mistaken, sir, if you think that there is anything serious between us. As his closest friend, you must have been informed that our arrangement is purely business," said Ciara softly. "A bartering of services, if you will. Hadley has no intention of swearing off his old way of life."

"Yes, he did make mention of the circumstances," murmured Woodbridge. "However, if I may offer a parting word of advice, a rake is usually the last one to admit when he is ready to reform."

The profusion of flowers was drooping in sleepy splendor, and the candles were burning low, their flames dancing slowly to the last notes of a quadrille. From the card room came the faint chime of the clock.

"Lud, it's late." Ciara stifled a yawn. "I can't remember the last time I was up at such an ungodly hour." Some of the guests were beginning to take their leave, while others lingered by the French doors, watching the play of moonlight over the terraced garden.

"On the contrary, the night is young." Lucas couldn't resist a little teasing. "It's only a little past one, and the darkness before dawn hides a multitude of sins. Would you care for a stroll outside to admire the heavenly stars?" He waggled a brow. "And other celestial bodies."

Her mouth thinned and then slowly curled up at the corners. "It's a pity our wager concerns a course in ornithology. If we were studying astronomy, you would have a head start."

Was it the champagne that had the lady letting down her guard enough to banter with him? Spying a half-empty bottle amid the arrangement of peonies, he quickly refilled her glass. "In some subjects, I'm a very quick study."

"Save your efforts for the laboratory," said Ciara, trying to draw back her hand. "I will expect you to master the basics before conceding you a victory."

"Don't worry, I have the stamina of a stallion." The wine bubbled up, light winking off the explosion of effervescence.

"I was referring to *mental* efforts, Lord Hadley," she said dryly.

Lucas slouched a shoulder against one of the carved colonnades. "Come now, I deserve some credit. I was smart enough to ask Haddan and Woodbridge to pay court to you," he answered smugly. "By virtue of their marriages, they are now respected members of Society. God knows why they chose to sacrifice their freedom, but it certainly served our purpose tonight. As you noticed, after their attentions, several other gentlemen dared ask you for a dance."

"Yes, it was extremely kind of them to risk censure for someone they had never met before."

He shrugged. "They are my friends. I knew I could count on them."

A flutter of gold-tipped lashes blurred her expression. "You are fortunate to have such stalwart support. I confess, before tonight I had doubted whether there were any titled gentlemen worthy of admiration."

"Oh?" He straightened slightly.

"But I enjoyed conversing with your friends more than I ever imagined possible." Ciara took a tiny sip of champagne. "They are intelligent and articulate, not to speak of charming. Please thank them for going out of their way to put me at ease."

So, it was Haddan and Woodbridge who got all the credit for her mellow spirits?

Irritated, Lucas responded with a low laugh. "Trust me, they are not saints. Together we used to raise holy hell."

"They indicated that they have outgrown their youthful indiscretions," she replied.

His jaw tightened. It was true. His own life had continued to career out of control, a blur of gaming hells, brothels, and boudoirs. But as Haddan and Woodbridge had abandoned the old haunts, the three of them had drifted apart. He hadn't realized until now how much he missed their company.

"That's what marriage does to a man. Sucks all the fun out of him."

"They seem quite happy with their wives," she said softly. "However, I agree that such unions are rarer than hen's teeth. On the whole, you are absolutely right. Marriage is a fate worse than death."

"I couldn't agree more. Being leg-shackled to one bed would be a ghastly way to go. I imagine that one would finally expire from sheer boredom."

"You are incorrigible," she murmured. "Do you really think of nothing but satisfying your baser urges?"

"No. I'm a dissolute, debauched sybarite, and really quite proud of it."

She stared at him for a moment before asking, "Why?"

Lucas shifted his stance. "Does there have to be a reason for everything, Lady Sheffield?"

"I have always thought so," she answered.

"Perhaps you think too much, and should learn to just *feel*." Flicking out a finger, he brushed a curl from her cheek. "Have you ever unpinned your hair and enjoyed the silky slide of it over the arch of your neck?"

She gave a little gasp.

He flashed a sardonic smile. "As for me, I love the sweet burn of costly brandy on my tongue. I love the lush scent of exotic perfumes tickling my nostrils. And I love the feel of sensual textures against my skin—the finest fabrics, a whisper-soft breeze, a woman's velvety flesh."

A flush of red rose to the ridge of her cheeks. "I think it's time to take our leave, sir."

A voice in his head warned him to stop, but he

blithely ignored it. Doing things to excess was, after all, what he was known for. "You might find that you actually enjoy unlacing your corset from time to time," he whispered.

Ciara pulled back, as if singed by a flame.

"Easy, sweetheart." He widened his grin. "And don't scowl. People might get the wrong idea."

Her eyes flared, but she forced her face to relax. "Then please stop trying to spark a quarrel with your lewd remarks, Lord Hadley."

"There is a difference between lewdness and light teasing, Lady Sheffield. Shall I explain?"

She shook her head.

Lucas offered his arm. Why had he deliberately ruined the mood, he wondered. The night had been going smoothly. But then her simple question had cut deeper than he cared to admit.

Until lately, he hadn't thought to question his way of life. Carousing with like-minded scamps like Farnam, Greeley, and Ingalls was great fun, with each one of them striving to outdo the others in excess.

*Every man for himself.*

And what was wrong with that?

"Hadley."

Lucas forced himself to focus on the cluster of guests at the foot of the stairs.

"We are having a soirée next Wednesday evening to celebrate Ashton's birthday. Do say you will come." The Viscountess of Ashton was known for the elegant opulence of her parties. Invitations were highly coveted. After a slight hesitation, she added, "And you, Lady Sheffield."

Surprised, Ciara started to stammer.

"We would be delighted to attend," he responded smoothly.

"Wonderful. I shall count on it." The viscountess eyed them with undisguised interest before turning back to her friends.

"Lud, since when have *you* become such a respectable fellow," murmured one of the gentlemen standing by the coatroom as Lucas brushed by. "Next thing we know, you'll be attending church on Sundays."

"Good God, imagine Hadley walking down the aisle of St. George's in Hanover Square," quipped another of the group, mentioning the most fashionable venue for Society weddings.

Ignoring the low peal of laughter, Lucas signaled the porter for Ciara's wrap and hurried her to the line of waiting carriages.

She expelled a pent-up breath but said nothing as they walked to the corner of the street.

He, too, stayed silent. Be damned if she was angry, he thought with an inward oath. *How dare she question or criticize his way of life?* The lady had no right to complain about the evening. It was *he* who had exerted considerable effort. The least she could do was to thank him, rather than ceding all the credit to his friends.

Wrenching the carriage door open, Lucas helped her inside. Her unspoken disapproval chafed even more in the tight space. The lacquered walls seemed to be closing in on him with every turn of the wheels.

Lud, how he hated the feeling of being constricted, confined.

"If you have something to say, sir, I would prefer that you speak your mind, rather than mutter under your breath," said Ciara over the clatter of hooves on the cobblestones.

Unwilling to admit to any weakness, Lucas decided to cover his inner conflict by taking the offensive. After all, he reminded himself, with his reputation as a rake and a lecher, self-indulgence was all anyone expected of him.

And he was happy to comply.

"Would you?" he answered with a sardonic smile. "I rather doubt it."

Ciara made a face. Which only goaded him on.

"But then again, perhaps you should decide for yourself." He angled his legs so that their thighs were touching. "However, I warn you that my mind has a naughty habit of thinking . . . improper thoughts. Shall I go on?"

"Wicked man."

"Oh, trust me, Lady Sheffield, I have not yet begun to be wicked."

Her eyes widened.

"And wait until you see me get truly evil."

Ciara tried to slide away, but his fingers were fisted in the folds of her skirts.

"Unhand me, sir," she whispered.

He chuckled. "That sounds like a line from one of Mrs. Radcliffe's novels. You know, the ones where the helpless heroine is trapped in a gloomy castle by a lecherous villain." Lucas tightened his grip. "Who is intent on stealing her virtue."

"This isn't a novel, it's a nightmare," she said through gritted teeth.

"But you are no virginal schoolgirl, who needs a white knight to ride to her rescue."

"Lord Hadley," she warned.

Lucas eased back a fraction, only to slide his hand up over her belly and cup the weight of her curve in his palm.

Another wordless sound slipped from her lips.

"I think it's time to explore some of those other prime kissing spots on the feminine form," he murmured against her mouth. Holding the kiss, he slowly teased his long, lithe fingers over the peaked flesh. Then all at once, it was not his hand but his tongue tracing a circle over her bodice. His teeth closed gently, drawing a cry from her as the wet silk tickled her sensitive flesh.

Threading her hands through his long, tousled hair, Ciara lost herself in the sensuous texture of its sin-dark satin. Twisting, twining, she reveled in its softness, the strands wrapping around her roving touch like spun sugar.

It felt like Heaven—or was it Hell?

One of the carriage wheels hit a loose cobblestone, setting the oil lamp to flickering wildly as a plume of smoke swirled around the glass globe. Dazed, Ciara tried to blink the haze of passion from her eyes.

Lifting his head, Lucas hooked his thumb in the top of her gown and slowly inched the fabric down. Another fraction and her rosy areola would be fully exposed . . .

It was the draft of chill air against the wine-kissed spot of wetness that snapped the spell.

Uncurling his hand, Ciara slowed released herself from his hold. He made no attempt to stop her.

"I—I'm sorry. I—I can't . . ." She bit her swollen lip. "I don't know what came over me."

Lucas straightened. Shadows splayed across his face, making it impossible to read his expression. "I suppose it is I who should apologize. I meant to tease you, but I should have showed more restraint. It's a failing of mine, I'm afraid."

"*I* should know better." Ciara closed her eyes. "Oh please, let us simply forget this happened?"

"Forget?" he echoed.

"Yes. You were drunk. And I was . . ."

*Delirious.*

"And I was clearly affected by the champagne. It's been ages since I've had a taste," she finished lamely.

"It's true that I often can't remember what I do when my wits are soused with drink," replied Lucas slowly.

"Perhaps a breath of fresh air will clear your head—and mine." She quickly cracked the window. "Or maybe you need a splash of cold water."

He choked back a laugh. "Touché."

Ciara sighed, doing her best to banish the last few minutes from her mind. "Would that we did not always have to be at daggers drawn, sir."

"Sorry," he murmured. "I can't help myself. However, I shall make a more concerted effort to . . . keep my sword sheathed when we are together."

"Please do." She tried to appear angry, but given her own transgressions, it was hard to muster much show of maidenly outrage. The effect was further spoiled as she was forced to stifle a yawn. "Lord knows, I'm too tired to fight any more battles tonight."

"You've no need to worry about the party. You emerged victorious on every front," he murmured. "Your dignity and grace won over a number of influential people to your side. In a word, you were magnificent, madam."

Surprised by his compliment, she felt a blush steal to her cheeks. It was kind of him to say, seeing as she was feeling neither dignified nor graceful. "Th-thank you, sir."

Lucas watched her fumble with the strings of her reticule, but to her relief, he pretended not to notice. "No need for thanks, Lady Sheffield. I'm simply keeping up my end of the bargain." He, too, seemed to have decided it was safer to move away from any more personal interactions. "Now, about my uncle's manuscript . . ."

# Chapter Ten

*B*rilliant, brilliant! Lady Sheffield's expertise is even more impressive than I dared to hope for."

Henry set aside the first batch of Ciara's notes, which had arrived that morning. "There are a number of questions I should like to ask . . ." His voice trailed off on a wistful note. "But I am sure she will explain the nuances of her research as she goes along."

Lucas turned from the window. "If you like, you might jot down a few specific queries and I could pass them along to her."

"Oh, it's just several simple things, like how she thought to research the routes of the early Arabic spice caravans from the East, and what—"

"You had better put it all down on paper," he interrupted. "Seeing as the subject hasn't anything to do with wine or women, I will likely get it garbled."

Henry's smile was fleeting, and as he looked up, he fixed Lucas with a searching stare. "I doubt that," he said softly. "You have a very sharp mind when you choose to use it."

Lucas exaggerated a yawn. "Perhaps. But intellectual

endeavors require a great deal of effort, with little recompense. I'd rather expend my energies in pursuits that offer immediate gratification." He paused for comic effect. "Fucking is far more fun than thinking."

The quip didn't elicit the expected chuckle. For a moment, the only sound was the faint crackle of paper as his uncle smoothed the sheaf of notes. Then came a soft sigh. "My dear boy, you might be surprised."

"I can't imagine how." Lucas answered with a bit more edge than he had intended. "And I have a *very* vivid imagination."

Henry tactfully changed the subject. "By the by, on your way out, will you ask Higgins to send one of the footmen to Hatchards," added Henry. "My order of books from Boston has arrived."

"I'll pick them up myself," said Lucas.

"No need to trouble yourself."

"It's no trouble at all," he insisted. "The fact is, I have a package waiting there, as well."

"If it's a book of erotic etchings, I do hope you'll allow me to have a peek," joked his uncle. "Seeing as vicarious pleasures are all that I have left these days."

Lucas was undecided on whether to admit that the volume in question was a detailed history of British ornithology. Henry was aware of his bartered arrangement with Ciara. But he had not yet told him about the side wager. He wasn't quite sure why.

*In case it blew up in his face?*

Ciara had passed her first test with flying colors. This afternoon, it was his turn to be under the microscope. And thinking about it only seemed to magnify his current way of life. *Drinking, gambling, womanizing . . .* the litany of his vices would likely cover more paper than the widow's scholarly research notes.

His gaze strayed to the gilded spines of Henry's scientific essays. If his own accomplishments were written down in stark black and white, there wouldn't be much to be proud of.

"Lucas?" Henry's gentle voice stirred him from his mordant musings. "You are looking a bit green around the gills. Perhaps you ought to sit for a bit and pour yourself a brandy."

"Thank you, but no. I've an appointment and I ought not be late."

Henry chuckled. "The lady would likely forgive you."

"Not this one," muttered Lucas under his breath. In a louder voice he added, "I'll be by later with your books. If you write out your questions for Lady Sheffield, I will pass them along. We are scheduled to make an appearance at Lady Hillhouse's soirée."

"How is your experiment with her progressing?"

"I'm still alive," he quipped.

The slanting sunlight accentuated the hollows of Henry's cheeks. "*Carpe diem*. Do try to make the most of that gift, my dear Lucas."

Steam rose from the boiling water, misting the rack of glass vials. The blurred labels and muddled colors forced Ciara to hesitate for an instant before making her choice.

It was not like her to lose focus in the laboratory. Here was the one place on earth where she counted on seeing things with a sharp-eyed clarity. But this afternoon, her head seemed to be in a fog.

Slapping down the spoon, Ciara scribbled a note in her logbook. Worrying would not keep Lord Hadley from his appointed lesson. Perhaps she could concoct a magic potion that would turn him into a frog. That would solve two problems at once—she would not be tempted to indulge in improper thoughts, and Peregrine would have a male playmate.

*Peregrine.*

Ciara sighed. Her son was a far more serious concern than a rakehell rogue. The boy had been a bit moody since his return from the country, but her gentle probing had so far uncovered no specific reason. Had he somehow overheard some nasty gossip during the trip? A whispered reference to the Wicked Widow?

Her grip tightened on the pen. Perhaps she ought to consider a retreat to the country, despite the fact that her legal advisers strongly advised against such a move. Or perhaps she should seek shelter in some foreign land. Peregrine would lose the trappings of title and privilege but gain the freedom to live his life untainted by her sordid scandal.

The sound of steps in the corridor warned that she would have to set aside such complex conundrums for the next hour. Lord Hadley was here, and though the effort would likely be a waste of time, instructing the earl in the rudiments of scientific inquiry might at least provide comic relief.

Assuming he didn't set the laboratory on fire.

Ciara was aware of a slow burn spreading across her cheeks. *Damn.* The powders and potions were not the only things at risk to the earl's incendiary touch. She would have to keep a tight lid on her own reactions to the man. But it was growing harder and harder. Try as she might to ignore his smoldering sensuality, his looks—*his kisses*—sparked a volatile reaction deep inside her.

It was best not to analyze why. The answer was too . . . dangerous.

"Lord Hadley is here for his appointment, milady." McCabe's reedy voice announced the visitor.

Drawing a deep breath, Ciara opened the door. "I see that you are punctual," she observed, slanting a look at the mantel clock. "That is a step in the right direction, sir. In all disciplines of science, one must be precise in measuring minutes and seconds, else the results can be disastrous."

"I make it a point never to be late for an assignation," replied Lucas with a languid flutter of his sable lashes. "You are right—the repercussions can indeed be disastrous."

*No man should possess such sinfully beautiful eyes.* She forced herself to slow her skittering heartbeat. "Lord Hadley, you are only wasting precious lesson time by trying to provoke me with more of your innuendos."

"I can think of worse ways to spend an hour than in trying to bring a blush to your lovely cheeks," he murmured.

Ignoring him, she went on, "Let us get something straight. While you are here in my laboratory, I expect you to behave and follow my instructions to the letter."

"More rules?" Lucas heaved a martyred sigh. "You know, it's not really allowed for one party to add restrictions once a wager is agreed to. But seeing as you are new to this, I will grant you a little leeway."

"I . . ." Ciara opened one of the cabinets, unwilling to be put on the defensive. "I have here the basic textbook on ornithology that we will be using for the course of our lessons." She held up a weighty volume for his inspection. "The author is a noted expert, and his writing offers a clear, concise introduction to the subject."

As she turned back, Lucas placed the package he had under his arm on the worktable and removed the wrapping paper. The gilt title sparked in the sunlight—*Birds of Britain—A Detailed Compendium of Observations and Methodology by Fitzwilliam Bergemot.*

"I took the liberty of acquiring my own copy," he said. "The clerks at Hatchards were very helpful in helping me choose. I am happy to see that we guessed right."

"Lesson number one, Lord Hadley," she said sternly. "Do not presume anything in science. And don't make guesses."

"Even educated ones?" he replied.

"Sir—"

Lucas held up a hand. "Yes, yes, I know. I am to be serious at all times." He schooled his face to a sober expression. "I shall strive to be an attentive student."

She thinned her lips against the temptation to smile at his teasing. The man had a quick wit, she granted him that. And a quick tongue—

*No.* It was best not to think of his tongue, or the soft, sensuous slide of his mouth on hers. This was not an anatomy class. Ornithology was, she hoped, a far less dangerous subject.

But with the earl, it was hard to tell.

"Let us start out with a quick survey of the instruments and their proper usage," she began. "Although we won't be using them until later on in our studies, I think it best to give you an overview. The mechanisms are extremely delicate and must be handled with great care."

Lucas looked on the verge of speech but then merely nodded.

"Follow me."

Ciara led the way to the work counter by the window. "This microscope is the latest model from Heidelberg, with a magnifying lens ground to a precise specification of . . ."

She moved down its length, explaining the different areas and the orderly array of implements. Lucas listened to the detailed discourse without comment. Though whether he was taking it all in or was merely bored to perdition was impossible to gauge.

Finishing up a warning to him about the chemical compounds stored above the small gas burner, she indicated the bookshelves. "There are a number of reference books that you will need during the coming weeks—" She stopped short, seeing him pause to pick up a round object from her desk.

"Lesson number two, sir—never touch an item in my laboratory without permission."

The object in question flew into the air for an instant and then landed back in his palm with a soft slap. "Are you a secret sporting enthusiast, Lady Sheffield? Or am I deluded in thinking that this is a cricket ball?"

Ciara flushed. "It belongs to my son," she replied tersely. She didn't add that she was practicing throwing it against the pillow propped in the far corner, so she might prove a more proficient partner than young Isabella.

"Ah." He seemed intent on examining the stitching of the

leather. "You ought to buy them at Silliman's Emporium. These ones made by Brompton are of inferior quality."

"Thank you for the advice," she said a bit curtly. "But can it really matter?"

"Very much so. You see, the seams can greatly affect the flight of a ball. Observe how uneven they are here."

Ciara leaned in a little warily, wondering if he was playing games with her. But closer inspection showed he was right. The raised cording was indeed irregular, with noticeable lumps in the waxed thread.

"They should be uniformly smooth and even, otherwise it's hard to be accurate with a throw." He tossed the ball from hand to hand. "Physics, you know."

"I hadn't realized that sport was such a science," she said dryly.

"You might be surprised how seriously we frivolous fellows take our pursuits of sports. As for flight patterns, ask any bird about—"

The earl's reply was cut short by a tentative knock on the door. "Mama?" called Peregrine. "May I come in?"

Masking her surprise, Ciara turned quickly and clicked open the latch. Her son knew better than to interrupt her work, save for something important.

"Shouldn't you be at your lessons, young man?"

"Mr. Welch let me go early as reward for getting a perfect score on my mathematical test," replied Peregrine. "I wanted to practice my pitching against the garden wall, but I can't find my ball anywhere. I thought perhaps you might have seen it?"

The brisk slap of leather echoed against the earl's palm. "It was serving as a physics specimen, but I'm sure it could be put to better use outdoors."

Ciara saw her son's eyes widen at seeing an unfamiliar face inside their townhouse. "Perry, this is Lord Hadley, who has come to consult me on a scientific question." She slanted a sidelong look at the earl, praying he would not make some mocking remark. The boy was shy around strangers. "Lord Hadley, my son, Peregrine."

"You like cricket, lad?" Lucas dropped to a casual crouch, so that he was at eye level with her son.

"Yes, sir," answered Peregrine.

"So do I. Do you play often?"

"N-not really." Her son made a face, accentuating the bull's-eye bruise on his forehead. "The trouble is, my only playmate is a girl, and her aim isn't very good."

"A problem," agreed Lucas gravely. "Have you tried teaching her a corker pitch? The spin helps add control."

Peregrine looked downcast. "I—I don't know how."

"It's actually quite easy." Lucas cocked a brow. "If your mother would allow a short recess from our lessons on ornithology, I'd be happy to accompany you to the garden and give you a few pointers."

Ciara nodded in answer to her son's pleading look.

"Come then, let us fetch your bat, lad." Lucas gave the boy a conspiratorial wink. "Before your mother changes her mind about letting me scamper on my lessons."

She took a moment to put her workbench in order, then trailed along behind them, amazed at how quickly her son's reticence receded in response to the earl's easy banter. A tentative query turned into a peppering of questions on the sport, and all of a sudden, Peregrine was chattering like a magpie. Laughter—male laughter— echoed off the wainscoting in a counterpoint of baritone and alto notes.

The sound tugged at her heartstrings. A boy ought to have a man in his life. And yet . . .

Lucas laughed again, and despite the bright afternoon light dappling the glass-paned doors, the sound was like the rumble of distant thunder, presaging a coming storm.

Shaking off such dark musings, Ciara forced a sunny smile as Peregrine looked back at her with a grin and then pelted into the garden. Trouble might be hovering on the horizon, but the skies were clear.

For the moment.

⌁

"Just a tic, lad." Lucas stripped off his coat and draped it over the garden bench. "I can't afford to split a seam," he joked as he waggled his limbs. "Throwing requires vigorous movement, and my valet tells me that Weston's tailoring costs me an arm and a leg."

The boy giggled.

"Now, first of all, show me your grip." He handed over the ball.

Laying his small fingers in line with the seams, Peregrine took a tentative hold and looked up.

"No wonder you've got no one to play with but girls." Lucas rolled his eyes in mock despair. "I can see we've got a lot of work to do here." He moved the boy's hand, showing him how to position his thumb and forefinger. "Use a bit of pressure here. And here. It will give you better control. Go stand by the statue and I'll show you what I mean."

The boy scampered across the graveled path.

"Make a target with your hands," called Lucas. Taking

aim, he lobbed a soft toss that hit square on the mark. He crouched down and held his palms in front of his chest. "Now you try."

The ball sailed high over his head.

Peregrine's face pinched in embarrassment.

"Relax your arm, lad. Make the muscles like macaroni." He demonstrated with a deliberately silly shake. "You can't throw well if your elbow is stiff."

The boy's next try was a bit better. "Good, good," encouraged Lucas. "You're getting the hang of it."

Out of the corner of his eye, Lucas saw that Ciara had taken a seat on the terrace steps and was watching in solemn silence. Did she disapprove of frivolous fun? It was impossible to tell from her expression.

*"Mens sana in corpore sano,"* he murmured to her as he passed close to retrieve an errant throw. "A healthy mind in a healthy body—the ancient philosophers believed that vigorous physical exercise was important to intellectual well-being."

"I'm not sure the ancients were referring to some of your favorite activities," she replied with a cryptic smile. "But I agree that the principle makes a great deal of sense."

"You need not worry that I am going to lead your son down the path to perdition. Lads his age need to expend a great deal of energy. A game of cricket will do him no harm."

A shadow flitted across her face, accentuating the hollows of her cheeks. She looked troubled, though he wasn't sure why. "I am aware of that, Lord Hadley. And I . . . I am grateful to you for taking the time to teach him some of the basic skills."

"My motive is purely selfish. I've escaped a stuffy

classroom. Dare I hope that I get good marks for sportsmanship?"

"You've a passing grade so far," murmured Ciara.

"Just passing? I guess I will have to try harder—I take pride in earning high honors in hijinks." Turning, he tossed the ball back to Peregrine. "Remember, keep your thumb firm on the seam, lad."

"Yes, sir!"

The boy reminded him of an awkward young puppy, so willing and eager to please. Lucas felt an odd constriction in his chest, remembering how lonely it could be for a child living with a single adult. The widow's notoriety no doubt limited her son's contact with the outside world even more. No wonder the boy was trying so desperately hard.

"Well done, lad. Well done!" he called, twisting to field the throw before it hit the grass. "A bit more practice and you'll be a corking good bowler."

The simple praise drew a grin from Peregrine. Ducking his head, he darted a sidelong look at his mother, who answered with an encouraging smile. "I have not Lord Hadley's experience in sports, but your skills certainly seem greatly improved to me, lambkin."

"Mama!" Peregrine rolled his eyes in embarrassment. "I'm no longer in leading strings."

Ciara's smothered cough sounded suspiciously close to a laugh. "My abject apologies, Perry."

Lucas masked his mirth, as well. "Sporting champions must become accustomed to adoring female spectators," he said gravely.

Her gaze narrowed ever so slightly in warning not to tread on dangerous ground with any risqué innuendos.

Much as he enjoyed seeing her cheeks flare with crimson

fire, Lucas decided to back off. He was having too m⁻ ⁻n
fun. Lud, it had been an age since he had played cricket.

Grabbing up the bat, Lucas took a few cuts through the
air. "How are your hitting skills?" he asked.

"Awful," admitted Peregrine with a rueful grimace.

"It's all a matter of timing and proper vision. The stance
is very important. Here, let me show you . . ."

For the next quarter hour, he worked with Peregrine on
the rudiments of play. The boy was a quick study, and the
*thwack* of wood against leather was soon echoing through
the garden, along with whoops of exuberant laughter.

Lucas rubbed the ball between his palms. "Oh ho,
showing me up in front of your mother, eh? What a blow
to my manly pride." He winked at Ciara. "Let's see if you
can hit this one."

Cocking his wrists, just as he had been shown, Peregrine took a mighty swing at the pitch. The bat connected with a resounding crack, but the angle was a little
off and the ball flew off in an errant arc. Ricocheting off
the brick wall, it shattered a terra-cotta flower urn, which
in turn knocked a pot of garden fertilizer—a mixture of
watered manure and fishmeal—onto Lucas's expensive
coat. Drenched in slimy muck, the garment slithered from
the bench and fell into a small reflecting pool.

The boy dropped the bat and ran to retrieve it.

Lucas joined him at the water's edge and reached out,
only to see Peregrine flinch and cover his head.

"I'm s-so s-sorry, sir," stammered the boy. "I swear I
didn't mean to ruin your coat. I was clumsy—it won't
ever happen again. I promise."

Ruffling the boy's hair, Lucas gave a hearty chuckle.
"Think nothing of it, lad."

Ciara had shot up, but she sat down without a word.

He nodded in silent approval and went on, "You're not a real player until you have destroyed at least a dozen innocent bystanders. I shattered six of my uncle's windows in one afternoon."

"D-did he birch you?" asked Peregrine.

"No, he hired the star player from Lord's to teach me to hit it straight. Said it was far cheaper than to be constantly repairing the glass panes." Suddenly aware that the boy was still rigid with apprehension, Lucas scooped him up and tossed him in the air. "Actually, I owe you a debt of thanks. I have always disliked that particular shade of green but have been too cowed by my valet to get rid of it."

Peregrine relaxed enough to giggle as Lucas set him down.

"Now fetch your missile and let's continue to play," he added.

However, a moment later the cook appeared in the doorway and summoned the boy for his tea.

Peregrine looked loath to end the session, but a gentle chiding from his mother reminded him of his manners. "Thank you for the pointers, sir. It was awfully sporting of you to take the time to work with me."

Lucas dusted his hands on the seat of his trousers. "Next time we'll practice some basic batting drills to improve your timing."

The boy's eyes widened. "You mean we can do it again sometime?"

"If your mother agrees." He lowered his voice a notch. "So you had best obey her, so she doesn't decide I'm a bad influence on you."

As her son marched dutifully toward the door, Ciara turned.

"Th-thank you," she said in a halting voice. "Our bargain did not include playing games with an eight-year-old."

"He's a nice lad," said Lucas.

"I'm surprised . . ." Her voice trailed off as she tugged at her shawl.

"Surprised that he is nice?" he said dryly.

Her mouth quirked. "Surprised that you are so good with children, sir."

Lucas shrugged. "It's hard not to enjoy their exuberance."

"No, it's more than that," she insisted. "Some people have a natural rapport with adolescents. Peregrine's father got very angry when he made a youthful mistake."

"Did Sheffield strike him?"

There was a perceptible pause. "Only when I couldn't move fast enough to intervene."

"So that he could beat you?" said Lucas, somehow managing to keep his voice calm, though a surge of hot bile rose in his throat. Only a craven cad would mistreat his own wife and child. He found himself wishing that the lout were still alive—so he could thrash him to a pulp.

Ciara looked aghast at her slip of the tongue. She tried to cover up by quickly adding, "No, of course not! As for Peregrine, his father did on occasion use a firm hand for discipline, but I am told that all boys feel a birch on their backsides from time to time."

"True." Forcing his jaw to unclench, Lucas leaned down to scoop up the soggy remains of his coat. "Shall we call it a day?"

"Yes," she agreed with obvious relief. "It makes sense to wait until the next lesson to start on our program of study—" Her gaze suddenly seemed to focus on his shirtsleeves. "Oh dear, how on earth are you going to walk through Mayfair like that! Shall I call my carriage for you?"

He waved off the suggestion. "No need. If anyone asks, I'll simply say I was taking my daily swim."

"But you will catch your death of cold."

"Lady Sheffield, I hate to distress you, but I have gallivanted through the streets of London clad in far less than this."

"You are sure you don't want a carriage?"

"Quite." Lucas retied his cravat and ran a hand through his disheveled hair. "Speaking of studies, I nearly forgot." Fishing a piece of paper from his waistcoat pocket, he handed it to her.

She smoothed at the wrinkles, looking a little uncertain of whether to unfold it.

"Don't worry, it's not some passionate billet-doux or erotic poem. My uncle jotted down some questions he had regarding your research," he explained. "Sorry if the writing looks a little rushed. Henry is quite excited about this project." He paused. "The truth is, it's brought a gleam to his eye that's been missing for ages."

"Please assure Sir Henry that I will study his queries and send him a prompt reply."

"I fear you have been stuck with the harder part of the bargain. So, if anyone should be giving thanks, it is I."

"Let us call it even," said Ciara softly.

"Sportsmen don't really like a draw. It's considered something akin to kissing your sister—there is no pain, but no pleasure, either."

She fixed him with a thoughtful stare. "Must there always be a winner and loser?"

"That is usually how the game is played."

Interestingly enough, she did not inquire as to which game he was referring. Holding his coat by its dripping collar, Lucas took his leave with a polite bow. But rather than flag down a hackney, he decided to walk for a bit, despite the stares.

The outdoor interlude had left him in a pensive mood. He had seen Ciara's pinched expression as she watched her son at play. She was obviously a doting mother, and did her best to put on a cheerful face. Yet beneath the surface smiles, she looked worn and worried.

*Damn.* The thought of what they must have suffered stirred a new wave of anger at her late husband. A lady of her youthful years ought not have so many responsibilities weighing on her shoulders. Her eyes should be lit with laughter, not clouded with fears for her future.

Slowing his steps, Lucas turned abruptly and entered a store on the corner of Albemarle Street. It took only a few minutes to have his purchases wrapped and sent on to his townhouse—along with his still damp coat. Then it was on to Hatchards. A glance at his pocket watch showed there was plenty of time to stop off at Henry's with the promised books before returning home to dress for the evening.

# Chapter Eleven

*D*espite being the last full gathering for several months, the meeting of the Circle seemed to move a little faster than usual.

"So," said Charlotte, rapping her teaspoon for silence. "Now to the most important matter of business. We expect a full report on how things are proceeding with Hadley."

"So far, the earl has refrained from acting like Lucifer Incarnate," admitted Ciara. "No smoke, no brimstone has filled the laboratory with sulphurous smells." The only hellfire was from her own heated reactions to the man's devilish charm.

Dreading any discussion of her feelings, Ciara quickly changed the subject to her work with Henry's manuscript.

"I would rather talk about the manuscript. I have reason to believe that the parchment is all about some sort of plant with miraculous healing powers," she began. "As you all know, the ancient Greeks were engaged in the spice trade with India and the Far East long before the Europeans."

"True," murmured Kate. "I've seen an early *periplus,* or navigator's guide, which describes in great detail the trade routes through the Eastern oceans. The journeys were timed to the monsoon winds. In fact, it was a Greek by the name of Hippalus who first recorded the phenomenon—"

"Such nautical history is fascinating," said Charlotte dryly. "But let's not stray from the main topic."

Ciara tried to keep the topic on the current course. "Kate is right. The merchant ships made great use of the strong prevailing winds. A major port of call was Malabar, where the Greeks exchanged tin, glass and Mediterranean coral for ivory, silks, pearls, and exotic spices and plants unknown to the West—"

"Charlotte is right," interrupted Ariel. "Tell us more about Hadley."

"There really isn't much to tell," she replied evasively. "So I don't know what to say."

"You could start with how you feel about him," suggested Alessandra dryly. "Now that you've spent a little time with him."

"He is handsome as sin, and there is no denying he has a certain devilish charm . . ." Her voice trailed off.

*"And,"* pressed Kate.

Ciara felt herself color under the scrutiny of pairs of eyes. "And . . . and the truth is, I'm not sure how to feel. One moment I'm hot, the next moment I'm cold." She made a face. "As if that makes any sense."

Alessandra gave a sympathetic murmur.

"Has he tried to kiss you?" asked Kate.

Her cheeks were now on fire. "Please, if you don't mind, I really don't care to talk about Hadley. We are supposed to be discussing *science,* not sex."

"Sex is science," quipped Kate. "It's a core element of biology."

"Oh, very well, we'll stop teasing you." Charlotte pursed her lips. "Getting back to the manuscript, if the plant in question has remarkable healing powers, why was it kept such a secret?"

Grateful for the respite, Ciara hurriedly explained, "During medieval times, the Christian Church tended to view science as heresy. So many scribes recorded their texts in secret codes, in hope that they would survive."

"Secrets," muttered Kate darkly. "Hell, society is always so ready to savage anyone who dares to challenge convention."

*Secrets.* Ciara gave an inward sigh. She was certain that she was not the only 'Sinner' plagued by private demons . . .

"We, of all people, are aware of that," observed Alessandra dryly. "But do go on, Ciara. This is sounding interesting."

She shook off her musings and returned to the subject of science. "Yes, well, I've read through only the first few pages; however, I have a feeling that it is going to be something truly special."

All shared her excitement, but Ariel seemed especially intrigued. Botany was her special field of interest.

Ciara went on to mention Henry's list of questions.

Kate broke off a bit of biscuit. "You know, I recently read one of Sir Henry's essays for reference, and I must say, I like his style. It's clever, lucid, and witty. He seems to have a sense of humor—"

"He must, to have raised such a hellion as Hadley without murdering either himself or his ward," said Ciara under her breath.

Kate ignored the interruption. "Only one thing puzzles

me. Why have we never encountered the gentleman at any of the Scientific Society lectures?"

Ciara bit her lip, unsure if Lucas had meant for the information about his uncle's infirmity to be kept in confidence.

"Perhaps he dislikes a crowd," pointed out Alessandra.

"A good point. Many deep thinkers dislike disturbing their routine." Ariel tapped her chin. "I know—we could consider calling on him."

"That's an excellent suggestion," said Charlotte. "A meeting with the baronet might help solve the mystery of the manuscript sooner."

Ciara decided to agree. If Sir Henry did not want visitors, his servants would know how to turn them away.

Ariel thumbed through an ink-smudged notebook. "Excellent, excellent," she murmured, echoing Kate's sentiment. "The fact is, I should very much like to ask Sir Henry his opinion on Kingston's essay on Indian orchids." She pushed her spectacles back up to the bridge of her nose. "Shall we go tomorrow afternoon?"

Ciara saw no reason to defer the trip. "Oh, very well."

"My, my, aren't you the clever fellow."

Lucas looked up from the pages of the sporting journal. The florid face was vaguely familiar, but he couldn't connect a name to it. Cocking a quizzical brow, he replied, "I beg your pardon?"

The reek of spirits grew more pronounced as the man leaned down over the leather armchair. "I'm no fool, Hadley. I know what you have in mind, but I'm telling you that we won't tolerate any meddling in my family's affairs."

"Apparently your wits are more slurred than you think. I've no idea what you're talking about." He returned to reading about the upcoming races at Newcastle. "Toddle off and annoy someone else."

Rather than retreat, the man grew more belligerent. "It's you who had better back off."

A hush fell over the club's reading room.

"We've heard word that you have interest in making my aunt a respectable offer—though God knows why you, of all people, would have any need for her fortune. You're rich as Croesus."

*So, the obnoxious oaf was Arthur Battersham, Lady Sheffield's nephew.* It took a concerted effort for Lucas to keep his temper in check.

"You are welcome to toss up the she-bitch's skirts any time you like," continued Battersham. Although it was early in the evening, it was clear that he had been drinking heavily, and the brandy had made him bold—and unsteady on his feet. His beefy bulk was now perched on the arm of the chair. "However, be advised that we won't let anyone steal her fortune from our family. It rightfully belongs to us, and we mean to see that the witch pays for the perfidy of poisoning my uncle."

Lucas slowly set aside the journal. "Thank you for the warning. Have you anything else to add?"

Battersham smirked and shook his head. "No, I think I've made my points perfectly clear."

"Indeed you have. Now allow me to return the favor." His hand shot up and caught the man's cravat in a stranglehold. "First of all, if you ever utter a disrespectful word about Lady

Sheffield in public again, I shall thrash you to a bloody pulp."
He tightened his hold. "Secondly, if you ever imply that she
is guilty of any crime, save to misjudge the character of your
slimy uncle, I shall kick your arse from here to Hades."

Battersham's face was now turning a mottled shade of
purple.

"Thirdly, if you ever presume to threaten me again, I
shall meet you at dawn—and it won't be me who eats
grass for breakfast, you miserable spawn of a slug—"

"Enough, Lucas, enough." Black Jack Pierson shot up
from his chair by the hearth and hastened to intervene.
"Come, let him go," he added in a low voice.

Lucas gave Ciara's nephew a last shake before loosening his grip. "Have I made myself perfectly clear?"

A squeak slipped from Battersham's lips.

"Good. Now get out of my sight."

As Battersham slunk off, Lucas flexed his fist and
sought to get a hold of his raging emotions. He had come
damn near to murdering the man on the spot.

"Here, have some wine to cool your temper." Jack
signaled to the porter for a bottle of claret. "Bloody hell,
what's got into you of late? I'm beginning to have serious
worries about your state of mind."

"No need for concern." Lucas saw his hand was still
shaking as he reached for his glass. "I simply dislike
cowardly, craven, contemptible cheats. Lady Sheffield is
being threatened by her late husband's family."

"It's not your responsibility to defend her," said Jack.
"She has kin, doesn't she?"

"Her own family won't lift a finger to help her."

Jack took a long swallow of his wine. "So the task falls
to you?"

Lucas found that he couldn't compose a coherent answer. "Damn it, Jack," he grumbled. "It's hard to explain."

"And even harder to comprehend." His friend sighed and shook his head. "I hope you know what you are getting into. The Battershams are a despicable bunch of characters, but we both know that doesn't matter. Their blood connection to the Sheffield title gives them prestige and power, along with a certain degree of influence within the highest circles of Society. So if I were you, I would not go out of my way to make enemies of them."

"So you, too, feel compelled to offer me a warning?" said Lucas rather acidly. "Thank you, but despite what you and that worm seem to think, I'm perfectly capable of making up my own mind concerning Lady Sheffield and her situation."

Jack frowned. "Well, I would think twice about getting too involved, if I were you." He looked around and lowered his voice. "Before you came in, I happened to overhear Battersham talking with his cousin. The family is putting pressure on certain people to have the inquest reopened. I got the impression they won't rest until they have seen her arrested and formally charged with murder."

"Look, I've asked around about the proceedings myself. The first inquest uncovered no tangible evidence of a crime," replied Lucas. "The case is closed."

"That does not mean some new bit of proof won't come to light," said his friend slowly.

Lucas felt his jaw tighten. "Let them try. They will not find it so easy to slander Lady Sheffield this time around.

Now that she is reentering Society, she is making her own set of friends."

"Lucas—"

He held up a hand. "Thank you for the warning, Jack. But as I said, I'll make up my own mind on this."

"In that case, I shall refrain from further comment." Jack lit up a cheroot, inhaled deeply, and then puffed out a perfect ring of smoke. "Save for one last suggestion."

"Which is?"

"If you mean to continue your pursuit of the Wicked Widow, take a shovel with you." Another exhale sent a plume of ghostly gray floating up toward the ceiling. "Just in case you have to dig your own grave."

The butler cleared his throat and squinted in the afternoon sun. "I fear you have mistaken the gateway, madam. Lady Jervis lives next door—"

"We are not looking for Lady Jervis," replied Ciara. She and Ariel were standing on the steps of an elegant townhouse on the north edge of Grosvenor Square. Handing the man her calling card, she added, "We've come to see Sir Henry. Is he in?"

The question seemed to throw him into a state of confusion. "Er, um, I—shall have to inquire."

"Might we wait in the entrance hall while you do so, rather than out here on the steps?" she asked politely, seeing he was about to shut the door in her face.

Now thoroughly flustered, the butler yanked his arm back and bowed them inside. "The baronet is not in the habit of receiving visitors."

"So it seems," murmured Ariel.

The man crabbed toward the staircase. "Please excuse me."

As they waited, Ciara took the opportunity to have a look around. For some reason, she was curious to see where Hadley had grown up. Stepping around the massive bearskin rug, she started a slow circle of the room. The entrance hall had an eccentric charm—a sculpted marble head of Julius Caesar sported an Oriental turban, while Caligula wore a lacy Spanish mantilla. The paintings were an eclectic mix of style and periods. She guessed they had been chosen more for personal enjoyment rather than for show.

"Oh, look." Ariel ventured a peek into the side parlor. "Isn't this delightful?" A tall Chinese tea chest, lacquered in a brilliant vermilion hue, was topped by an ornate brass dragon with a jade ring through its nose. "Sir Henry seems to possess a whimsical side to his character," she added.

"That, or his nephew has a schoolboy sense of humor," observed Ciara.

"Arrhumph." The butler cleared his throat with a brusque cough. "Ladies, if you will be so kind as to follow me."

The Oriental runner muffled their steps on the stairs, but at the top of the landing, the floor was bare wood.

"This way," said the butler, beckoning them down a corridor. At its end was a set of polished oak doors. "Sir Phelps is waiting inside." He knocked and then stepped aside.

"Come in, come in." The voice was faint, like the flutter of old parchment.

Ciara exchanged a look with Ariel before taking hold of the handles and passing through the portals.

"What an honor, Lady Sheffield."

It took Ciara a moment to make out the baronet. His Bath chair was sitting directly in front of the mullioned windows, and in the slanting sunlight, his wraithlike figure was nearly indistinguishable from the shadows.

"Please forgive me if I don't get up and greet you," he added.

"I never stand on ceremony, sir," she replied quickly. "As you see by our barging in unannounced on your privacy."

Her words drew a hearty chuckle. "To be visited by two lovely ladies is hardly call for complaint. In fact, maybe I ought to check my pulse—for all I know, I may have died and gone to Heaven."

"We are not angels, sir, only scholars," piped up Ariel. "I trust that does not mean you wish us to Hades."

His chuckle turned into a laugh. "Even better."

"Allow me to introduce my friend and colleague, Lady Ariel Gracechurch," murmured Ciara.

"The author of 'Variations in the Poppies of Punjab'?" asked Henry.

Ariel blushed like a schoolgirl. "Why, yes. But in comparison to your work, it's hardly worth mentioning."

"Not at all, not at all. I was fascinated to read about your comparisons to the tropical species of India . . ." He stopped short and made a rueful face. "Lud, here I am forgetting any semblance of civilized manners. Please sit down and let me ring for tea before we plunge into scholarly talk."

Ciara liked the baronet immediately. And so, by all appearances, did Ariel. The quieter of the two Gracechurch sisters—which of course was not saying much—she usually allowed others to carry the conversation. However, as the scientific talk resumed, her manner seemed different. And oddly enough, so did her appearance. Her cheeks were pink as rose petals.

The touch of color was quite becoming, decided Ciara.

"Ah, that must be our refreshments," said Henry in answer to the knock. "Come in, Jenkins," he called. "I do hope you have brought some of Cook's excellent walnut tarts."

Still engrossed in reading over a passage of the scientific journal he had just purchased, Lucas entered the room without looking up. "Sorry, no tarts. But I could order a few delectable trollops from Madame D's bordello if you like." Turning the page in midstride, he went on without a pause. "Henry, don't laugh, but I have a question on—"

"Slow down, my boy," cautioned his uncle. "Our guests already have reason to question my manners. I would rather they didn't think I have raised a household of heathens."

*Guests?*

Lucas stopped short, surprised at how the sight of Ciara sent a frisson of heat through his limbs.

"Forgive me." Masking his reaction with a droll twitch of his brows, he quickly added, "Had I known you were entertaining a ménage à trois, I should never have been so indiscreet as to interrupt."

Henry grinned. "We are having a *very* stimulating discussion on poppies."

"Poppies," repeated Lucas. "Well, I shall leave you and the ladies to your pleasure." He bowed a polite greeting to

Ciara and Ariel, taking care to obscure the printed pages of the journal in a tight roll. "I just stopped to see if you needed anything picked up at the apothecary."

"There is no need to act as an errand boy, Lucas," replied his uncle softly.

"I pass right by the door on my way home from Manton's." He gave Henry's shoulder a squeeze and then reached down to smooth the lap robe.

"No need to act as nursemaid, either," said Henry wryly.

"Ah, no doubt you would prefer the ladies to take liberties with your person," replied Lucas. "I can't say I blame you."

"Won't you join us for tea, Lord Hadley?" asked Ariel. "We promise not to bore you with talk of leaf structure and cross-pollination."

"Yes, do, my boy," said Henry.

Lucas noted that Ciara said nothing.

"Speaking of which, you've yet to ask your question," added his uncle.

"Never mind. It's not important." He perched a hip on a corner of the desk. "I'm afraid I can't stay. I am meeting friends at Jackson's boxing saloon and then going on to test a new pistol at Manton's shooting range." Flicking a speck from his cuff, he drawled, "As you see, the life of an indolent idler keeps me busy."

"What is that you are reading, Lord Hadley?" asked Ciara abruptly.

*Damn.* Lucas casually tucked the rolled journal into his coat pocket. Hopefully she had not spotted the cover. He didn't wish for her to know he was reading the *Ornithology Review*.

"Why, the latest racing forms for Newcastle," he drawled. "Would you care to place a wager on the horses?"

"Not really," she replied coolly. "I am not a great fan of trusting my fortune to luck or chance."

"How very wise," he replied.

"Perhaps you ought to take a page out of Lady Sheffield's book," said Henry with a smile.

"Perhaps." Lucas rose. "However, at present I must be off to trade punches with a sweaty, half-naked pugilist."

Ciara continued to regard him with an inscrutable stare.

As he turned, he couldn't help looking at Henry with a touch of concern. "I asked Cook to send up an egg custard along with the tarts. You are looking a little too thin these days."

Henry gave a low snort. "Don't waste your time gazing at *my* body. I daresay you have far prettier sights to feast your eyes on."

Ignoring his uncle's warning glance, Lucas came around to brush a kiss to the top of his silvery head. "Behave yourself. I shall stop by this evening with your medicines."

"Bah." Henry made a face. "For some reason, the boy seems to think I'm an invalid."

"Don't worry, Lord Hadley," said Ariel. "We shall see that Sir Henry finishes every bite of his custard."

"If he balks, you could consider tying him to his chair and using a whip. Some people find that very stimulating to the appetite." Dodging the book that Henry tossed at his head, Lucas flashed a parting grin and took his leave.

"I hope my nephew did not shock you," apologized the baron. "He has a rather wicked sense of humor, but he means well."

"Oh, that is quite clear," assured Ariel.

"Given Lord Hadley's other exploits, I imagine we got off quite lightly," murmured Ciara. In all honesty, she had been more intrigued than shocked by the earl's behavior. His superficial teasing could not disguise the depth of his feelings for his uncle. *Love?* She would not have thought him capable of such emotional attachment. But the truth was impossible to deny.

Though he took great pains to hide it, Hadley had a serious side to his character. She wondered why he was so loath to let it show. The more she thought about it, the more she realized that the earl was far more complex than she had first thought. He wasn't just a selfish simpleton but . . . a conundrum. One that was proving as difficult as the ancient code to decipher.

However, the arrival of the tea tray forced her to set aside such musings for another time.

The baronet seemed to have come more alive since their arrival. A sparkle lit his eyes, and his frail form seemed to gain a little strength as he broached the subject of the manuscript.

"Yes, your nephew passed on your questions," she replied. "You raise a number of very interesting points, so rather than write reams of pages in reply, I thought it best to come discuss them in person . . ."

The next half hour passed in a detailed discussion of her research so far. "I confess, the complexities of the code are slowing down my progress," she finished. "The next section seems to be written in a new system, which is proving difficult to decipher. I plan to show a sample to my friend Lady Giamatti, who is more conversant with cryptology than I am."

"I've little experience in that sort of thing," mused Henry. "However, I do have a number of rare books on the subject here in my library, if you think that might help."

"It couldn't hurt to take a look," said Ciara. "In the meantime, let me write down the names of the other reference books I mentioned." She set aside her teacup. "Several of them must be ordered from Edinburgh."

While she wrote, Henry and Ariel resumed their discussion on the medicinal properties of opium poppies.

Indeed, the baronet was growing more and more animated. "I have a very interesting folio edition from India on the subject. If Lady Sheffield would be so kind as to look on the shelf above the bust of Pliny the Elder . . ."

"Perhaps we ought to leave that for a later visit." Ciara rose. Despite his enthusiasm, the baronet looked to be tiring. Hadley would not thank them for overtaxing his uncle's strength. "It is getting late, and we really should not overstay our welcome."

Henry looked a trifle crestfallen. "On the contrary, I haven't enjoyed myself so much in a long while. Please do not feel obliged to follow social conventions and run off so soon."

"Unfortunately, I must return home and dress for an evening engagement." She paused. "With your nephew."

"Lucky fellow." He pursed his lips. "I trust the rascal is behaving himself."

"No scandals so far." Try as she might, Ciara could not quite keep the sardonic edge from her voice. "Though the tattlemongers are likely placing wagers on which one of us will be the first to stir up trouble. Indeed, I'm not sure who has the worse reputation in Society—Lord Hadley or me."

"Hmmph." Henry blew out an expressive snort. "The tat-tlemongers are all jackanapes! No person who has read your thoughtful essays could ever think you capable of murder."

"I daresay we are all capable of extreme acts if pushed hard enough." Seeing the look of concern on Ariel's face, Ciara quickly added, "At least, in theory, that is. But of course, most of us will never be put to such a test."

Ariel cleared her throat. "I look forward to viewing the engravings some other day, Sir Henry."

"Anytime," replied Henry. He gave a self-deprecating chuckle as he rolled his Bath chair back from the work-table. "You know where to find me."

Ciara felt a little awkward about how to take her leave. "Please don't let us take you from your studies, Sir Henry. We shall see ourselves out."

"I should like to enjoy the company of two learned— and lovely—ladies for as long as possible, so I will escort you to the head of the stairs." Henry's eyes twinkled, but then lost a little of their sparkle. "Unfortunately, to descend beyond that point, I must suffer the indignity of being carried, a spectacle that I do not wish for others to see."

As the small front wheel of the chair snagged on the carpet, she hesitated, and then quickly moved a step closer. "May I assist you, sir?"

"Oh, I'm not quite the invalid I appear," he replied firmly. "Does me good to do a little exercise. Lucas won't let me lift a finger when he is here. And he insists on mol-lycoddling me—the dear boy wraps me in so many lap robes, I sometimes feel as though I were an Egyptian mummy, or some priceless artifact being shipped off to a museum."

Ciara smiled. "I have the distinct impression that he wishes to keep you around a little longer."

"Indeed," murmured Ariel.

"I should like to oblige my nephew." The creak of the spokes echoed off the bookcases. "I have a great deal of work I would like to finish yet. And I should also like to see him settled in life before I shuffle off this mortal coil."

"Lord Hadley a reformed man?" she said dryly. "I hope your work includes concocting an elixir for eternal life."

A chuckle. "Hope springs eternal."

"Thank you for your time, Sir Henry," murmured Ariel. "It has been a most enjoyable afternoon."

"That it has," he said with a wistful sigh. "I hope you will come again."

Ciara offered her hand. "I think you may safely wager on it, sir."

# Chapter Twelve

*I* have been thinking . . ." Lucas slid smoothly through the first few figures of the waltz. Lady Ashton's ball was in full swing, and the room was packed with a host of prominent people. "It seems to me that now is as good a time as any for our betrothal announcement. Do you agree?"

Ciara nearly tripped over his foot. "Don't you think it's a little fast?"

"I thought you were anxious to get it over with. You said earlier that you were tired of the speculative stares."

"Yes, so I did. B-but . . ."

He spun her apart from the other dancing couples. "Did you see the morning paper?" Yet another nasty headline about the Wicked Widow had been featured on the front page of the gossip section.

Her hand clenched against his. Beneath the soft kidskin, he could feel her palm was cold as ice. "Yes."

Lucas waited for her to go on.

"By all means then, do it," she said after a twirling spin. "You are quite right. What difference does it make?"

"Some men might take offense at that," he said lightly.

"But not you, Lord Hadley. You are far too sure of your appeal to the opposite sex to need any compliments from me."

"Lud, you make me sound like a pompous peacock."

"Your plumage is far too subdued for a peacock." She hesitated a fraction. "I would have expected a notorious rake to favor bright colors like cerulean or chartreuse, rather than such staid shades of navy and charcoal."

Lucas exaggerated a leer. "We raptors have no need of gaudy feathers. We simply sharpen our talons and grasp what we want."

"I am glad to see you have started your study of ornithology," she replied. "Raptors are indeed hunters, well known for their soaring grace and lethal speed. Pretty to look at, but dangerous."

"Yes, if you are their prey. But hawks can also be helpful. They have been used for centuries to rid the land of harmful rats and vermin."

She didn't answer for a long moment, and when she did, it was to obliquely change the subject. "Speaking of feathers, I trust your coat was not ruined beyond repair."

"Weston assures my valet that the stained sleeve can be replaced," he replied. "As for its plunge into the pool, I can personally attest to the fact that water leaves no lasting damage."

Ciara's mouth quirked. But as the music faded, so did her smile. "Oh Lud, what do you wish me to do now?"

Lucas gave her hand a reassuring squeeze. "Relax, sweetheart, and just follow my lead."

Moving through the milling crowd, Lucas congratulated himself on having had the foresight to discuss his plan with their hostess ahead of time. Lady Ashton was shrewd enough to realize that a surprise betrothal at her party would only add to her celebrated reputation as a hostess. And so, she was only waiting for his signal to quiet the crowd for an announcement.

Catching her eye, he gave a quick nod.

She gave him a last dubious look, as if questioning his sanity, then shrugged and made her way onto the raised stage, where the musicians sat tuning their instruments for the next dance.

A whispered word to the flute player resulted in a sudden trilling adagio.

Conversation ceased as an air of anticipation descended over the ballroom.

The guests gathered around the stage amid the soft rustle of silks and the clinking of crystal.

"As you all know, we've gathered tonight in celebration of Ashton's birthday," began the viscountess.

Someone proposed a toast, but she silenced him with a quelling stare. "We shall all raise our glasses in a moment, but I've made the delightful discovery that we have yet another special milestone to mark."

An expectant murmur rose.

Clearly enjoying the drama, Lady Ashton was in no hurry to relinquish her role. "I am sure you will all be as surprised as I was. I daresay you will *never* guess the news."

Lucas felt Ciara stiffen. "Must we make such a sordid spectacle of this?" she said softly. "I would rather be put on display in the Tower menagerie than endure this."

"Actually, we are trying to avoid cages with iron bars," he reminded her. It was cruel, perhaps, but necessary. For this to work, she must play her part.

Ciara paled but refrained from further complaint.

"I will try to make it as quick as possible," he added. "Try not to look as though you were facing the executioner. You are supposed to be a lady in love, remember?"

"And how is that supposed to feel?" she asked in a small voice.

"I wouldn't know, my dear. So we will both simply have to fake it." On impulse, he lifted her hand and slowly kissed the tip of each finger.

"*Hadley!*" she whispered. "People are starting to stare."

"That's rather the point, sweetheart." He winked. "I could have chosen a more intimate spot to embrace, but I wouldn't want you to fall into a swoon."

With that, Lucas broke away and leapt lightly onto the stage. "Come, Lady Ashton, let us not keep your guests in suspense."

"What is Mad, Bad Had-ley up to now?" asked someone in the first row.

"Something outrageous—you can count on it!" came the answer.

"Actually, I have come to announce quite the opposite," said Lucas with a jaunty bow. "From now on, I am a reformed man."

A rude sound rose from the back.

"No, no, I am quite serious. I mean to give up my former way of life and embrace the pleasures of matrimony."

"Ha! I'll lay two-to-one odds at White's that any engagement doesn't last a week," called one of his fellow club members.

Lucas ignored the jibe. "Indeed, I consider myself the most fortunate man in the world that Lady Sheffield has consented to be my bride."

There was a moment of dead silence, then a burst of excited voices. Several ladies shrieked. Lucas wasn't positive, but one of them appeared to faint on the spot.

"I'm sure I speak for everyone when I offer you and your intended all the best wishes for future happiness." Lady Ashton handed him a glass. "Have a drink, Hadley," she murmured. "It may be the last one you enjoy without wondering what has been added to it."

"To my future bride." Lucas quaffed the champagne in one long swallow.

There was a smattering of polite applause.

Knowing that Ciara would rather die than be displayed on the stage, he quickly thought of a compromise. "And now, let the musicians strike up another waltz. My elation is such that I find I can't stand still."

As the violins struck up the first chords of a lilting Viennese tune, Lucas hurried to claim Ciara's hand. "Just smile," he murmured, leading her out to the middle of the dance floor. "And look at me with adoring eyes."

"Thank you," she whispered. "You handled that extremely well, sir."

"Not that I've had much practice in announcing an engagement," he said wryly.

She quickened her steps to match his. "I'm sure next time around, you will be even smoother."

Lucas kept a smile on his face. "Lud, I hope there won't be a next time."

Her gaze remained intent. "You will have to set up your nursery at some point and beget an heir."

"I'm not about to cock up my toes anytime soon," he replied. He spun her in a circle. "Am I?"

"That is *not* funny, Hadley." However, her lips did

quirk. "How can you joke at a time like this?" she added under her breath.

"These are precisely the sort of moments when humor is called for." Lucas acknowledged a call of congratulations with a broad grin. "Life is full of little absurdities. You cannot take them so seriously, Lady Sheffield, or they will crush you."

She was silent for several steps. "You think me too serious, and I think you too serendipitous . . . I wonder if there is any middle ground?"

Lucas pivoted on the polished parquet. "I wouldn't know. My path in life seems to veer from highs to lows, with nothing in between."

Ciara's expression took on a strange pinch.

"Come, sweetheart, you are not allowed to look pensive, remember? Trust me, this will all work in your favor. Society loves nothing so much as a roguish rake reformed by love."

She forced a smile.

"That's better. Let us enjoy the moment. This is an evening for merriment and celebration." But as he turned to escort Ciara from the dance floor, he saw several members of the Sheffield family, circled like grim vultures near the colonnaded archway.

*If looks could kill* . . .

Angling his shoulders to shield her from their stares, Lucas countered their scowls with a cool nod.

They said nothing as he passed by, but he felt a prickling at the back of his neck, like daggers dancing against his flesh. He sensed that he hadn't heard the last of them.

At breakfast the next morning, Ciara decided not to look at the newspaper. Alessandra was coming for luncheon, and no doubt her friend would give her a detailed report of the news in the gossip columns—discreetly editing out the nastier comments.

To his credit, Lord Hadley had been surprisingly sensitive in arranging the events of the previous evening. She watched a tendril of steam float up from her teacup, recalling every nuanced sensation of his body as they danced—the warmth of his hand on the small of her back, the strong, solid feel of his thighs brushing her skirts, the sure-footed grace of his rhythm. *The sensuous sound of his laughter, the silky stretch of his smile.* She swallowed a tiny sigh. Indeed, he had taken it upon himself to bear the brunt of the *ton*'s reactions, deflecting both the well-meaning wishes and inquisitive comments with a mixture of humor and charm.

It was rather nice to let someone else step in and solve a problem—she certainly had enough of them to share. But such musings were unrealistic, she chided herself. She could not depend on it happening again. Despite his well-muscled shoulders, Lord Hadley could not be expected to bear her burdens for much longer.

Forcing her thoughts away from the earl, Ciara put aside her cup. With that in mind, she had better get back to work on Henry's manuscript. The code was proving perversely difficult to decipher, but she had a few new ideas to try.

The hours passed quickly, and before she knew it, McCabe knocked to announce that her guests had arrived. Hurrying down to the entrance hall, she found Peregrine already there and proudly displaying his newfound knowledge of cricket.

"See, Isa—you hold the ball like so!" he exclaimed, showing the grip that Lord Hadley had taught him.

"Perry, why don't you take Isabella to the garden for a more detailed demonstration," suggested Ciara.

"So, the deed is done?" asked Alessandra, once the children had raced off.

"Yes."

Her friend untied the strings of her bonnet and set it on the side table. *"And?"*

"You have probably read all the grisly details," said Ciara.

"Actually, it sounded rather romantic."

Her breath caught in her throat for an instant as she once again recalled the glittering candlelight, the lilting music, the feel of the earl's body moving in perfect rhythm with hers.

"How can you say such a thing!" she exclaimed, trying to quell the flutter of longing in her chest.

"Lord Hadley is a sinfully attractive man, *cara*," replied her friend. "You would have to have ice water in your veins not to have enjoyed the moment just a little."

"'Sinful' is the key word." Ciara busied herself rearranging the objects on the side table, unwilling to meet her friend's gaze. "At midnight, the man was waltzing with me. An hour later, he was likely dancing beneath the sheets with one of his fancy ladybirds."

"You aren't sleeping with him, then?"

*"Alessandra!"*

"Just asking, *cara*." Her friend took her arm. "Come, I shall stop my teasing, as it seems to be upsetting you."

"I'm not upset. I'm merely . . ."

*Confused? Conflicted?* Ciara left the sentence unfinished.

Alessandra waited for a moment and then carefully changed the subject. "Tell me, how is your work coming on the baronet's manuscript?"

"I am glad you asked," she replied. "I'm having a devilishly difficult time with a section of the code and could use your advice."

"My skills in ancient cryptography patterns are a little rusty, but I shall be happy to take a look."

"I will fetch my notes and meet you in the morning room." With the French doors open to the garden, they would be able to keep an eye on the children at play. "Today, the sporting session should pass without any serious bodily injury."

"Yes, Peregrine seems to have acquired an expertise in cricket since the last game," remarked Alessandra. "Don't tell me you managed to decipher that manual on pitching techniques." She waved her bejeweled hands. "Good heavens, to me it was more puzzling than ancient Egyptian hieroglyphics!"

"No," admitted Ciara. "It was Lord Hadley who gave him a few pointers."

"Hadley? With Perry? How did that come about?"

"It's not important." For some reason, she had not told the 'Sinners' about her side wager with Lord Hadley. Not even Alessandra. Feeling a little foolish, she added, "Please, let us forget about the earl, if you don't mind."

That, however, proved easier said than done.

They had no sooner spread out the notes on the table and settled into their chairs when a knock at the door drew a muttered oath from Ciara.

"Blast, I wonder what that could be?" Sighing, she

added an apology to her friend. "McCabe usually knows better than to disturb us when we are working."

The butler cracked the door in answer to the call to come in. "Forgive me, madam, but you have a caller."

"Inform whoever it is that I am not receiving visitors," she muttered.

"I did so, madam," replied McCabe with a sniff. "But he—"

"He refused to take no for an answer." Lucas shouldered his way around her baleful butler, his arms laden with several odd-shaped parcels.

"S-sir," stammered Ciara, rising so quickly that a sheaf of notes slid from her lap.

"Forgive the intrusion, Lady Sheffield. I did not realize you were already entertaining," he said, smoothly shifting the packages to retrieve the fallen papers. Eyeing Alessandra through the spill of his sable hair, the earl turned the gesture into an artful bow. "Might I have the honor of being introduced to your lovely friend?"

*Lud, nothing seemed to throw the earl off balance.* He probably contrived to look graceful even when falling naked into a fountain.

Aware of her own skittering pulse, she tried to control the quaver of her voice. "But it's far too early for morning calls."

"Ah, but a fiancé should be allowed a few small liberties, should he not?" replied Lucas with a charming smile.

"No—" began Ciara.

"Why, yes," countered Alessandra. "Of course." Her friend rose gracefully and extended a hand. "You need no introduction, Lord Hadley."

"Alas, it seems that my reputation precedes me," he murmured, his lips brushing her rings.

"Allow me to introduce Marchesa della Giamatti," said Ciara, feeling a little flustered. "She is privy to our business arrangement, sir," she added softly. "So there is no need for false flatteries."

Arching a brow, Alessandra waggled a subtle reproach.

However, the unexpected sight of Hadley's smiling face was having an unnerving effect on her. "As you can see, sir, we are rather busy with a session of serious scholarship. So if you don't mind . . ."

"I did not intend to interrupt your work, Lady Sheffield. I just stopped to leave off these packages."

"What are they?" she asked suspiciously.

Lucas slowly peeled the wrapping paper from the top item. "First of all, these are for you."

A rush of air slipped from her lips on regarding the bouquet of flowers. Instead of the usual formal arrangement of roses or tulips, the individual blooms were a mixture of sizes and shapes, their subtle palette of pale blues and delicate lavenders set off by curling green fronds of lacy ferns. The effect was striking—the natural forms seemed so gloriously alive.

*"Bellissimo,"* murmured Alessandra.

"Y-yes, they are quite beautiful," intoned Ciara, feeling her heart give a lurch as he passed them over.

"The other parcel is for Peregrine." Lucas glanced at the two children tossing the ball back and forth. "I take it the young lady is the errant marksman who hit him square between the eyes."

"My daughter, Isabella," explained Alessandra. "As for

her aim, it is improving." After a fraction of a pause, she added, "That is to say, there have been no near-fatalities this morning."

"Miss Isabella looks to have excellent form. I daresay with a few more pointers—and the correct equipment—both she and Peregrine will pose no imminent peril to each other." Untying the twine, Lucas parted the paper to reveal several varnished cricket bats and a half-dozen new balls. "Silliman's finest," he said. "I took the liberty of selecting the proper models for children. With your permission, Lady Sheffield . . ." His brow winged up in question.

Ciara gave a tiny nod.

"Excellent." Lucas moved to the door. "I shall leave you ladies to your work, while I indulge in a little play." He had the audacity to wink. "As you can imagine, we dissolute rakes are not up to any intellectual efforts this early in the day."

A whoop of delight from Peregrine greeted the earl as he sauntered outside. The new sporting gear elicited even more excitement, and after a brief interlude of eager inspection, both children were pleading for him to join in the game.

"Hmmm. This is becoming more interesting by the moment." Her friend watched Hadley remove his coat and roll up his shirtsleeves. "I have a feeling there is more to this affair than meets the eye."

"Let us focus on the manuscript," said Ciara quickly. "Its secrets are far more important than my private life."

Alessandra took the bouquet and inhaled deeply. "*Cara,* far be it for me to lecture, but I have learned from experience that life's mysteries cannot always be solved with reason. Sometimes they unravel themselves in the most unpredictable ways."

"Your advice is always welcome, Alessa." She crooked a wry grimace. "Even when you are speaking in riddles."

Her friend rang for a vase and then returned to the table. "Now, where were we?"

Ciara settled down to work, but despite her own words, she found it impossible to concentrate. The peals of light-hearted laughter were distracting. As were the occasional glimpses of Hadley romping with the children. Peregrine looked so carefree, swinging his new bat under the earl's tutelage, and Isabella was not left out of the play. The sight of the broad-shouldered rake showing the little girl how to hold the ball forced her to swallow a smile.

The summons for luncheon was a welcome interruption. Ciara called the children in from their game. Hadley followed, looking boyishly disheveled with his cravat loosened and his hair ruffled by the breeze.

"Will you join us for some refreshment, Lord Hadley?" asked Alessandra.

"Thank you, Lady Giamatti. But I fear that I have already trespassed on Lady Sheffield's hospitality too long."

"On the contrary, sir," said Ciara, managing a show of outward composure. "We would of course welcome your company."

"Would you?" murmured Lucas, so that only she could hear. Dusting his trousers, which had several large grass stains on the knees, he added in a louder voice, "Unfortunately, I've a previous engagement to meet some friends at Manton's shooting gallery."

"Well, then let us not keep you," she answered quickly.

"Relax, sweetheart." Lucas untied the ribbon and eased off the smooth satin.

"But—"

He began massaging her toes. "We could, of course, stop at the Berkeley Square fountain, but I assure you that the water is quite frigid against bare skin." Teasing his thumb across her arch, he said, "Perhaps this will serve as an acceptable alternative."

Ciara tried to wiggle free. "It's *not* acceptable," she mumbled. "It's . . . inappropriate."

"Ah, but who will know except us?" Keeping a firm hold, he deepened the pressure of his strokes. "How does this feel?"

"Divine," she said after a moment of hesitation. "Though I shouldn't admit it."

In the swirl of light and shadow, her expression looked achingly vulnerable. "Why not? There's no sin in allowing yourself to indulge in a little naughtiness once in a while."

"That's hardly a surprising sentiment, coming from you." She tried to sound firm, but a tiny smile played at the corners of her mouth. "You are, after all, an expert in sin."

Lucas fingered the delicate texture of her stocking. "A connoisseur," he agreed with a soft laugh.

Her hips twitched against the soft leather as she tried to jerk free.

"Stay still, Ciara," he said. "Why not just"—he tickled the ball of her foot—"let yourself lie back and enjoy a little pleasure."

"That would be wanton," she whispered.

"And wicked," he replied. "But haven't you ever wanted to be a little wicked?"

No. *Yes!* No.

Ciara couldn't find her voice to reply.

"I, on the other hand, have no compunction about indulging in wickedness."

*Rip.*

The sound of tearing silk jolted her upright. *"Hadley!"* she gasped as he peeled her now-ruined stocking down to her ankle. The touch of night air against her now-bare skin was shockingly intimate.

But not half so intimate as the flick of his tongue against her toes.

"Oh, that is . . . depraved," she protested. But her wiggling proved too weak to break free his hold.

"Mmmm, yes." He nibbled at her flesh. "But I am a rakehell scoundrel, remember?"

*How could she possibly forget?*

"And a rakehell scoundrel is wont to kiss a lady in all sorts of shocking places."

*Oh, Lud—was he really suckling her big toe?* The wet warmth of his mouth sent a surge of heat through every nook and crevasse of her body. The sensation somehow dissolved every last bit of rational thought, for she heard herself blurt out, "Like the Grotto of Venus?"

As Lucas lifted his head, the fire-gold lantern flame danced along his smile. "Why, Lady Sheffield, have you been reading more erotic books?"

"N-no," she exclaimed with a guilty start.

"No?" He arched a brow. "I doubt you discovered that term in one of your scholarly textbooks."

"If you must know, I—I overheard some ladies discussing your sexual prowess in the park," she confessed.

"Did they sound satisfied?" asked Lucas slowly.

"Very." She hesitated a fraction before adding, "Though I cannot imagine what they . . . implied."

"A kiss to a lady's quim?"

"Quim?" she repeated.

"It's one of the terms that I prefer for that feminine spot. *Grotto of Venus* sounds a bit gothic, don't you think? While *quim* reminds me of a sweet, ripe piece of fruit."

Ciara squirmed, embarrassed and yet intrigued. "There are . . . other names?"

*"Cunny, muff, notch, nick-nack, honeypot, pipkin,"* he recited slowly.

The wicked little words seemed to slide over her skin like melted butter.

"And simply, *paradise*. There are lots more, of course, but that should give you the idea."

"Yes," she replied, trying to repress the tingle running up her legs. "How very illuminating."

"You see, there is much to learn outside the quiet confines of a library or laboratory," murmured Lucas. "As for naughty kisses . . ." A slow, sensuous lick traced the length of her sole. "Perhaps you simply need a little help in stimulating your imagination."

As his hands caressed her ankle and then stole up her calf, she didn't dare think about such erotic fantasies. Never in her wildest dreams did she picture a man . . . and a woman . . .

*Oh, surely that was wicked beyond words.*

And yet. And yet, Ciara was suddenly aware that her foot was not the only part of her body growing moist.

She squeezed her thighs together to stop his roving touch. "Th-that's far enough," she said thickly.

His hands stilled on her knee. The lamp swayed, casting his face in darkness. After a moment, his voice drifted out from the shadows.

"Very well." Leaning back, Lucas smoothed her stocking down and slipped her shoe into its rightful place.

The satin felt oddly cold after his warmth.

Ciara sat up, just as the carriage came to a halt. Grateful that the low light hid her flaming face, she gathered her skirts. "It appears that our evening has come to an end. I bid you good night, Lord Hadley."

"Good night, Lady Sheffield." As the coachman came around to the door, he added, "I hope that the lovely, virginal hymns we heard will inspire sweet dreams."

Lucas rose earlier than usual the next morning and rang for his shaving water.

"I beg your pardon, sir?" said his valet as he set down the basin and razor on the washstand. "Is there something else you need?"

"Hmmm?" It took a moment to realize he was humming a passage from Handel's *Messiah*. "No, no, that will be all, Humphrey. Please tell Cook I shall be down shortly for breakfast," replied Lucas. "I shall dress myself today."

A long-suffering silence greeted the remark.

Lucas turned from the mirror, his jaw half covered in soap. "Is something amiss, Humphrey?"

"Aside from the shocking state of your wardrobe, sir?"

The valet folded his hands across his chest. "Perhaps you would prefer for me to hand in my resignation. It appears that you are unhappy with my services."

"Are you crying over a stained sleeve?"

"Your best coat will never be quite the same, sir. And the dove gray trousers . . ." Humphrey shuddered. "They are utterly ruined."

"So order another pair." Lucas patted his face dry. "Hell, order a half dozen if it will wipe that scowl off your phiz."

"Fashion is nothing to laugh about, milord. Allow me to point out that no one has ever dared criticize your clothing."

"No, only my lack of it," he quipped.

Humphrey sniffed.

Moving to the dressing room, Lucas picked out a navy jacket, buff breeches, and a pair of his most comfortable boots.

"Those are in need of a good buffing, sir," said Humphrey, eyeing the scuffed leather with horror.

"Don't bother. I'll be walking through the muck at Tattersall's," said Lucas. He paused, brushing a hand to the boots. "Tell me, did I have a pony when I was a small boy?"

"Yes, milord. Sir Henry gave you one for your seventh birthday."

"I thought so." He took a moment to knot his cravat. "Every boy ought to have a pony."

"So long as he doesn't try to ride it up the marble staircase of his great aunt's mansion in Grosvenor Square," said his valet.

"Aunt Prudence had no sense of humor, if I recall."

Humphrey coughed. "Apparently not. You and the animal were banned from the premises for life."

"I doubt Ajax went to his grave lamenting the loss. And nor shall I." With that, Lucas slipped his pocket watch into his waistcoat and went down for breakfast.

He was just digging into a plateful of shirred eggs and gammon when the door gave way to a shove.

"What are you doing, keeping country hours?" called Farnam.

"We expected to find you abed," added Ingalls, his voice suspiciously slurred. By the look of their wrinkled clothing and bleary faces, neither of the two men had slept the night before.

"Coffee?" asked Lucas, holding up the steaming pot. "Or kippered herring?"

"Oh, God, I think I shall puke if you mention food." Ingalls sprawled into one of the dining chairs and took his head between his hands. "I had better have another brandy."

Farnam brought over the bottle. "I'll drink to that."

*Lud, was he always such a sorry sight after a night of carousing?* Lucas slowly chewed a bite of his toast, finding the mingled reek of smoke, sex, and stale perfume was leaving a rather sour taste in his mouth.

"When did you arrive back in Town?" he inquired. "I thought you planned to spend the month in Kent."

"Yesterday," said Farnam. He frowned. "Or was it the day before?"

"'S'hard to remember," agreed Ingalls with a grimace. "Hell, it's hard to tell time when you never see a wink of daylight."

Lucas watched his friend slosh another helping of spirits into his glass, spilling half of it onto the carpet. "Er, why *did* we come?" muttered Farnam. "I know there was a bloody good reason . . ."

"The mill!" Ingalls straightened somewhat.

"Oh, right, the mill!" Farnam slapped a hand to his head. "We just got word—Booker, the Negro champion from Jamaica, is set to meet McTavish, the Hulk of the Highlands, in the village of Cookham this afternoon."

"For a purse that is rumored to be over a thousand pounds," added Ingalls. "The betting is already astronomical."

"Aye, it promises to be the fight of the decade! And if we don't get moving, we'll never get near ringside." Farnam struggled to his feet. "Where the devil is Greeley with the carriage? He should have been here by now."

"Going the last few rounds with Mathilde—you know, Lucas, the ladybird you left behind." Ingalls lewdly rocked his hips and guffawed. "A few stiff jabs and his opponent will cry surrender."

Funny, but such schoolboy chortlings did not seem half so witty when one was sober, observed Lucas.

"Mad, Bad Had-ley ain't interested in Mathilde anymore. He no doubt has a luscious new set of feathers to pluck." Farnam leered. "Who is she?"

Lucas poured himself another cup of coffee.

"You can squeeze his whirligigs for the answer once we are in the carriage, Freddy," said Ingalls. "Bolt down your eggs, Lucas. We have to be off."

He made no move to rise. "Sorry, gentlemen. You will have to go on without me."

"*What!*" Both of their jaws dropped in unison.

"I have a previous engagement for the afternoon."

"Bloody hell! Break it! What could be more important than watching two goliaths try to batter each other into submission?" added Ingalls.

*Champion pugilists, raucous crowds, oceans of ale* . . . For an instant, Lucas was sorely tempted. "Sorry, I can't."

His friends blinked in disbelief.

"But why—"

Farnam's sputtering was cut short by Greeley, who sailed through the door with his shirttails still flapping around his thighs. "By God, I'll tell you why. I just ran into Jervis on the street, and he filled me in on the latest news." Making a mock bow of obeisance, Greeley went on to explain. "Our Mad, Bad Had-ley has upstaged the prize fight. Indeed, he has knocked all of London on its ear. He's announced his engagement." He burst out laughing. "To the Wicked Widow."

His other two friends doubled over in mirth.

"Do be a sport, Lucas, and let your friends buy into the bet, whatever it is," said Greeley, once he had caught his breath.

"Aye, we want to share in the fun," urged Farnam after another chortle. "What buffle-headed idiot was willing to wager that you wouldn't dare do it?"

"The fellow doesn't know you like we do," said Greeley.

"What I want to know is what stunt you have planned to get out of it." Ingalls fixed him with an expectant grin. "It's got to be a real corker."

Lucas calmly consulted his pocket watch. "You are going to be late if you don't leave now. And so am I."

"Leave off your joking, Lucas. Our carriage is waiting."

*Comrades. Cavorting. Not a care in the world.* He drew in a deep breath, the devils in the back of his head all urging him to say yes.

"Sorry, but no."

"Satan's arse," growled Ingalls. "What in the devil has got into you?"

*Perhaps a modicum of good sense.* Lucas couldn't explain it, even to himself. Shrugging, he rose. "Nothing. I simply have something else to do."

"If you are sneaking off to swive the widow, just say so." Farnam winked at the others. "We can keep a secret."

His hand shot out for his friend's throat, but he caught himself in the nick of time. Tapping a light pat to Greeley's shoulder, he smiled. "Let's leave the lady out of this, shall we?"

Dumbfounded, Greeley could only stare in mute surprise.

"Now, if you all will excuse me, I must be on my way."

~⁓

"Are we really going for a walk in the park?" asked Peregrine.

"Yes," replied Ciara, trying to decide which bonnet to wear. All of a sudden, they all looked so dowdy.

"With Lord Hadley?" persisted her son.

"Yes." She sighed. "Unless he changes his mind. Gentlemen like His Lordship lead very busy lives in Town, so it's possible he may have to cancel at the last moment."

It was also possible that Hadley would forget. Or decide that such a public display of courtship was unnecessary, after all. Last night, she had tried to dissuade him from the idea of attending the *ton*'s daily ritual. The only purpose of the fashionable afternoon promenade was to see and be seen. But Lucas had been strangely stubborn about it, raising his voice enough to attract sidelong glances from the other guests. His argument that Peregrine would enjoy seeing all the fancy had silenced her misgivings.

Now she wasn't so sure. Ciara smoothed a tangle from the ribbons. She was a little nervous. A Mayfair ballroom had been bad enough, but all of Society strolled along Rotten Row, eager to keep up with the latest *ondits* and scandals.

No doubt she and Hadley were the talk of the town.

"I like Lord Hadley, Mama," said Peregrine after a lengthy pause. "Do you?"

"He has been very kind in showing you the fine points of cricket," she said evasively.

"Marianne says . . . she says that you are going to marry him."

*Damn.* She would have to speak to the maid about repeating gossip in front of her son.

"Perry . . ." Turning from the cheval glass, Ciara took a seat on her bed beside the boy. "Lord Hadley and I have agreed to help . . . a friend. And to do so we must . . ." She hesitated, unsure of how to explain things to Peregrine.

He looked up at her, his blue eyes very solemn and serious. "You must tell a little white lie?"

*Oh dear, this was going to be even more difficult than she imagined.*

"To tell a lie is very wrong, Perry. The earl and I have announced that we are engaged to be married, which is the truth. But whether we actually become man and wife is another thing altogether. We are allowed to change our minds."

"Oh." He dropped his gaze. "I think I understand."

Her heart gave a lurch, but any further attempts to

explain the situation were ended by the maid's announcement that Lord Hadley was waiting downstairs.

Peregrine was very quiet as they left the townhouse
and headed for the park, but the earl quickly coaxed
him into lively discussion on upcoming cricket matches
at Lord's. Ciara listened in silence, wondering if she
had made a mistake in allowing Lucas to get close to
her son.

*Right and wrong.* If only there were a scientific formula
that spelled out the difference in no uncertain terms.

As they walked through the Cumberland Gate, Lucas
headed toward the wide carriageway straight ahead.

"That's the famous Rotten Row," he said to Peregrine.

The boy giggled. "What a silly name."

"It's said to derive from the French *Route de Roi*, or
King's Road," replied Lucas. "King William III built
the avenue in 1690, in order to have a safe way to travel
between St. James's Palace and his new court at Kensing-
ton Palace. At night, it was lit by over three hundred oil
lamps."

Her son appeared suitably impressed.

"Today, it is a popular spot for a promenade," continued Lucas. "The Tulips of the *ton* like to come and
show off their horses and carriages. See, there goes
Lord Huntfield in his new high perch phaeton. And
over there is Sir Sidney, mounted on a chestnut hunter
from Ireland . . ."

Hadley kept up a running commentary as they joined
the strolling crowd. Ciara was aware of the sidelong stares
and whispers, but the earl merely smiled and returned the
greetings with a nonchalant wave.

"Don't look so apprehensive, Lady Sheffield," he murmured. "If you will notice, you are garnering your share of pleasantries."

To her amazement, Ciara saw that he was right. The looks were not all hostile, and a number of people met her gaze with a polite nod.

"Do you ride, lad?" asked Lucas in response to one of Peregrine's eager questions.

"A little, sir." The boy looked longingly at the parade of horses. "Mama says perhaps when I am a little older she will hire a riding master for me."

"No reason to wait. I happened to be at Tattersall's this morning and saw a splendid pony for sale." Catching her eye, he flashed an apologetic grin. "I took the liberty of purchasing the animal, so if your mama has no objection, I could give you some basic lessons."

Peregrine's mute appeal was impossible to deny. "That is very kind, Lord Hadley. An occasional ride will be fine, but, Perry, you must not pester him too much."

"I promise, Mama!"

On seeing her son's beaming face, Ciara didn't have the heart to be cross with Lucas for making such a move without her permission. Still, it *was* a little unsettling. Her life seemed to be slipping out of her control.

"Sorry," he murmured, inching a touch closer as they walked. "I hope you don't disapprove."

"It was very thoughtful of you. But next time, please consult me in advance before making decisions about my son," she replied. "I don't like surprises."

He answered with a wink. "Ah, but surprises are what add a little spice to life."

Ciara could not help but smile. "Perhaps. But please do not pepper Peregrine with too many new things. Our life may seem bland and boring to you, sir. However, I prefer that it stay predictable."

They walked on for a way in silence, and then halfway down the drive, Lucas turned down one of the graveled footpaths. "Enough of horses, lad. Let's have a look at the Serpentine. At this hour of day, there are sometimes some boating enthusiasts sailing their pond yachts in the shallow waters."

She couldn't help but admire his sangfroid. "You are certainly taking this sudden upheaval of your life in stride, sir."

"My life was not exactly stable to begin with." He smiled as Peregrine raced ahead, following the antics of a small dog playing with a stick. "Besides, it doesn't take much exertion on my part to indulge in a pleasant walk with such charming company."

Ciara expelled a sigh. The thought of how soon the charade was likely to end made her reply a little sharply. "You need not wax poetic when we are in private."

"What makes you think I am exaggerating my sentiments, Lady Sheffield?"

"The fact that you are a shameless flirt and notorious womanizer," she said, unwilling to meet his gaze.

"You left out 'lewd libertine,'" he murmured.

"The litany of your sins probably stretches from here to Hades," said Ciara, repressing a smile. "But I saw no need to go on past the first few."

"Thank you for sparing my delicate sensibilities."

*Oh Lud, there was no denying that he had a devilishly sly sense of humor.* She would miss their banter.

"Be serious for a moment, sir." Seeing his gaze drift to a wooded area bordering the path ahead, she let her words trail off. Perry had veered off to chase the dog across a wide expanse of grass—

Suddenly, from out of the trees burst a horse and rider at full gallop. Hooves slashing like scimitars, the big black stallion thundered over the turf, kicking up clods of earth.

Ciara opened her mouth to scream, but Lucas was already making a mad dash for her son.

With a last, desperate leap, he managed to knock Peregrine down and keep him from being trampled beneath the pounding stride.

*"Hadley!"*

In twisting to shield her son, Lucas had caught a flailing kick to his chest. He now lay on the ground, still and silent.

Gathering her skirts, Ciara raced to his side. After a quick hug of her son assured her that Peregrine was unharmed, she fell to her knees. "Hadley!" Her breath was barely more than a whisper as she struggled to loosen his cravat.

"Is he hurt, Mama?" Peregrine, his face pale as a ghost, stared down at the earl.

"I pray not, lambkin," she replied, feeling for a pulse.

To her relief, the earl's eyes fluttered open. "P—erry?" he croaked.

"Is unharmed," she answered. "Thanks to your heroics."

Lucas tried to sit up but fell back with a wince. "Oh, hell. Another coat ruined," he said, feeling at the large tear at his shoulder. "My valet will never let me hear the end of it."

"Hush, and don't try to move." Ciara bit her lip to keep

it from quivering. "I've not yet had a chance to check for any broken bones."

"I'd rather that you move your hand lower, sweetheart—" His words cut off in a grunt of pain.

She smoothed the tangle of hair from his brow and undid the top fastening of his collar. People were starting to gather and someone cried out, "Send for a surgeon!"

Lucas swore a ragged oath. "I don't need a bloody surgeon. I've just had the wind knocked out of me. Help me up."

"Lie still, sir." Ciara kept her hand on his chest. Despite his protest, he looked to be hurting.

"Hadley!"

She looked up to see a tall, dark-haired gentleman elbowing his way through the onlookers. "What happened?" he demanded, dropping to his knees beside her. "How serious are his injuries?"

"It's hard to say until I get a closer look at him," she replied.

"Remind me to get trampled by a horse every day." Lucas lifted an eyelid. "Jack, I must say, you are a sight for sore eyes. Clear a path through this cursed crowd and help me home."

"Run over by a horse," repeated Jack. "Hell, didn't I warn you that consorting with the Wicked—"

"Jack," interrupted Lucas. "Allow me to introduce Lady Sheffield and her son."

Ciara saw the stranger grind his jaw in embarrassment.

"Lady Sheffield, this is Lord James Jacquehart Pierson."

"A pleasure, madam," said Jack gruffly.

"I doubt it," she said softly.

The retort drew a grudging twitch of the gentleman's

mouth. "Forgive my rudeness. Concern for my friend caused me to speak without thinking."

"I am concerned, as well." She turned up Lucas's lapel to ward off the breeze. "We need to move him. The earth is damp, and I don't want to risk the chance of his catching a chill."

"My curricle is close by. Perhaps I can lift him—"

"Damn it, Jack, I'm not deaf. Or dead," muttered Lucas. "Give me a hand and I can stand."

He did, but only barely.

"Slowly," she cautioned, slipping her arm around his waist. Between the two of them, they managed to get Lucas settled in the curricle.

"Where to?" asked Jack, taking up the reins.

"Home," answered Lucas.

"Absolutely not," said Ciara, overriding the earl's order. "Drive on to Pont Street, Lord James, so I may ascertain that Lord Hadley has not suffered any internal injury."

Jack hesitated and then flicked his whip. "Pont Street it is."

# Chapter Fourteen

As he lowered himself from the curricle, Lucas felt as if he had been pummeled by a half-dozen pugilists. If this was the reward for doing a good deed, no wonder he had chosen to be an imp of Satan.

"Bloody hell," he muttered, leaning on Jack more than was manly.

"Please have Lord Hadley lie down on the sofa, while I take my son up to his room and see him settled." Ciara showed them into the side parlor. "I'll not be long."

Gritting his teeth, Lucas nodded. His ribs ached abominably, but he tried to temper his limp.

"Lord James, there is brandy on the sideboard. Perhaps you would be so good as to pour the earl and yourself a glass." After a pause, she added, "I assure you, it's straight from Wendell & Briggs, so is untainted by any additives."

Jack did as he was asked and then drained his drink in one gulp.

"Stop fidgeting," muttered Lucas. "She's not coming back with a wizard's wand or dragon's tooth to cast some evil spell over you." He eased his shoulders back against the pillows. "As you see, she is a perfectly normal lady."

Clasping his hands behind his back, Jack went to look at the art above the mantel. "An interesting choice," he mused after admiring the watercolor of the sea at sunset for some moments.

Lucas knew that his friend was extremely knowledgeable about art, though he kept it a secret from all but his closest comrades.

"Mr. Turner has a bold eye and daring imagination when it comes to light and color," continued Jack. "He breaks a host of traditional rules, so not many people appreciate his genius."

"Lady Sheffield is not bound by convention," replied Lucas. "She's not afraid to make up her own mind about things."

"Hmmph." Jack turned slowly. "I'm worried about you, Lucas—"

"Hell, I've suffered far worse knocks falling from my horse in a drunken stupor," he interrupted. "I'll live."

"This time, perhaps," said his friend darkly. "But I fear—"

He stopped abruptly as Ciara reentered the room with a tray of medical supplies.

"Kindly hold this while I cut away the remains of Lord Hadley's coat." She handed Jack a basin of steaming water. "Pass on my apologies to your valet, sir," she murmured over the snip of the scissors. "And direct him to have Weston send me the bill for refurbishing your wardrobe. Acquaintance with my son seems to be hazardous to the health of your clothing."

"A small price to pay for the chance to resharpen my cricket skills." Lucas winced. "Er, speaking of sharp . . ."

"I'm so sorry." Looking flustered, she hurriedly cut

through the last threads of the coat sleeve. "But this outer garment must come off, so I may have a closer look at your ribs." Her hand pressed gently just below his heart. "Take a deep breath," she said.

He slowly filled his lungs. Despite his discomfort, he bit back a smile. It was rather nice having her fuss over his injuries. No lady had ever shown such concern over a few bumps and bruises.

"It does not appear that any bones are broken." She took the basin from Jack. "Tilt your head back."

"Why—"

The sponge feathered across his cheek. "Once this mud is cleaned away, I've a special arnica salve that will help ease the swelling. And this draught of willowbark will dull the pain. I will make up several measures for you to take home. Drink it every four hours for the next few days and it will keep you comfortable."

"You appear quite an expert in medicine, Lady Sheffield," said Jack as he watched her mix a powder into a glass of water.

"My interest in science has led me to study the basics . . ." She paused ever so slightly. "Of the healing arts, Lord James. Despite what you have heard, this potion will not turn your friend into a frog."

"I apologize if I have given you the wrong impression," began his friend. "I did not mean to imply any insult."

"No need to apologize, sir." She turned in profile, and Lucas was struck by how very young and vulnerable she looked in the slanting sunlight.

*And how very beautiful.* Her hair glinted like spun gold, the wind-curled strands accentuating the finely chiseled shape of her features.

"I am aware of the rumors swirling around my name," she went on. "You can hardly be blamed for assuming the worst."

"Jack is smart enough not to form judgments based on hearsay," said Lucas. "Isn't that right, Jack?"

"I'm friends with you, aren't I?" retorted Jack. "That should speak volumes about my loyalty, though not my sanity."

Ciara ducked her head to hide a smile. "I've not yet thanked you for your help, sir. I'm not sure how I would have coped with getting two muddied males home on my own."

"I am sure you would have managed quite well, madam," said Jack, his tone considerably thawed.

Lucas shifted slightly. "How is Peregrine, now that the first shock has passed? You are sure he was not clipped by a flying hoof?"

"He's just a little shaken, that is all." She dabbed a bit of ointment on his scraped jaw. "However, he is quite concerned about you. The only way I could prevent him from plaguing you with his presence was to promise a full report as soon as I am finished ministering to your injuries."

"I shall look in on the lad myself and assure him my pitching arm survived unscathed." An involuntary shiver shot down to his fingertips on recalling the sight of the huge stallion charging down on the small boy. "You are sure he is unhurt?"

"Boys his age are very resilient," said Ciara. "I'm more worried about you. Now please sit still."

Lucas rolled his eyes, only to find Jack was looking at him rather oddly.

"Seeing as you look to be in good hands, Lucas, would

you have any objection to my leaving you here?" asked his friend. "I'm already late for an appointment to be fitted with a new hunting gun by Mr. Purdey. And the old curmudgeon has a deucedly short fuse when it comes to promptness."

Lucas waved him on. "Don't worry about me, Jack. I am perfectly fit enough to get home on my own."

"Godspeed, then." Jack bowed politely to Ciara. "It was a pleasure to make your acquaintance, Lady Sheffield." As he headed for the door, he turned to add one last comment. "Do try to keep clear of any more mischief, Lucas. After all the years I've spent keeping your carcass in one piece, I should hate to see all my efforts go for naught."

⁓

As the door clicked shut, Ciara finished tending to the scrapes on Lucas's face. "The two of you seem to have known each other for some time." Setting aside her reserve, she went to work undoing the rest of the shirt's fastenings.

"Yes," he answered with a crooked grin. "Jack was part of our pack of little devils at Eton. So we have been raising hell together for ages."

"I see." She was trying very hard not to stare at the triangle of tanned skin and dusting of dark curls now exposed to view. *Science,* she reminded herself. This was simply a dispassionate exercise in . . . skeletal zoology. "Lift your arm, sir."

He winced.

"Sorry," she muttered.

"By the by, Jack approves of your choice in art," said

Lucas. "Not many people know it, but he is quite knowledgeable on the subject."

"I daresay that's the only thing he approves of about me," she replied, trying to work her hand under his sleeve. "Not that I blame your friend for his concern."

"Jack is no cabbagehead. He will change his mind when he gets to know you better."

Ciara didn't reply. Lord Hadley was not thinking straight—of course his friend would not get to know her better. The sham engagement would end soon, severing all contact with the earl and his comrades. What man in his right mind would risk the censure of Society to consort with the Wicked Widow?

It didn't matter, she told herself. She was quite capable of surviving on her own.

Shifting awkwardly, Ciara tried to work the salve down to the spot that had borne the brunt of the blow. "Blast," she finally muttered. "You will have to remove your shirt, sir."

His mouth twitched in silent amusement. "Is that an invitation, Lady Sheffield?"

"No, it's an order."

He tugged the linen over his head and let it float to the floor. "Do with me as you will."

She began to massage the healing ointment over his ribs, trying to keep her eyes off the sculpted planes of his chest. As her gaze dropped, she saw that his right side was already a mottled mass of purple bruises. *An ugly reminder that she had dragged an unwitting stranger into her troubles.*

A sound slipped from her throat. "Oh, Hadley, I fear you must hurt like the devil," she whispered.

He grinned, making light of her worries. "You ladies

take such things far too seriously. Trust me, I have suffered much worse at Gentleman Jackson's boxing saloon. The former champion may be aging, but he still has fists of iron."

*"Men,"* she muttered, shaking her head. "Why you make it sound as if such a thing were fun is beyond me."

"There is no rational explanation," he agreed. "It must be some deep, dark, primitive urge that courses through our blood."

Ciara was suddenly aware of a primal pulsing through her own veins. As her hands slid over his ribs, tracing every chiseled contour of muscle and bone, every fiber of her being was intimately aware of *HIM*. A rampant masculinity, from the earthy scent of sweat and coarse curls of hair to the sun-roughened texture of his skin and the bulging—

"Sorry," she mumbled, feeling her nails dig into his flesh. Jerking back, she reached for the jar of ointment.

"Don't you think that's enough?" he joked. "I'm slippery as a greased pig."

"It helps hold the bruising at bay—" she began, staring at the darkening welts spreading across his flesh. The brutal truth was, she didn't want to stop touching him. She wanted to slide her hands up to his shoulders and hold on for dear life. She wished to share her fears and seek solace in his strength. Most of all, she yearned for him to kiss her into sweet oblivion.

Oh, the gossips were right—she was truly the Wicked Widow.

"The bruising is nothing to worry about, sweetheart. I'll be a bit sore tomorrow, that's all."

"How can you say that! You . . ." Now that the first

shock was over it suddenly hit her with a force that nearly took her breath away—the earl had risked his life for her son. "You could have been killed!"

"But I wasn't," he replied lightly. "Though come to think of it, my demise would have saved you the trouble of crying off from this engagement."

A sob slipped from her lips. And another, giving voice to all her wordless longings.

Lucas gathered her in his arms. "Don't cry, darling," he soothed.

Ciara answered with a fresh torrent of tears.

He held her close, rocking her gently and stroking her hair. Through her trembling, she could feel the strong, steady beat of his heart.

"I won't let anyone hurt you or Peregrine. On that you have my word."

"Oh, Hadley, don't make vows you cannot keep. I cannot bear any more broken promises from men." She pushed away from his embrace, blinking the droplets from her lashes. "Besides, we are not your responsibility."

"No, but you are . . . my friend, Lady Sheffield. And I don't leave my friends to fend for themselves."

"Men may have that sort of bond between themselves, but I am under no illusion that they ever form *that* kind of friendship with the opposite sex," she said, striving to sound unemotional. "There is only one thing that you want from females, and it is not conversation or camaraderie." A watery sniff then ruined the whole effect.

"We are, for the most part, despicable creatures," he murmured. "But on rare occasions we are capable of rising above selfish desires."

A tremulous smile tugged at her lips. "I grant you that,

Hadley. Indeed, I—I have not thanked you enough for your kindness to Peregrine."

"You give me too much credit," replied Lucas. "Perry is a nice lad and I enjoy his company—and the chance to play a bit of cricket. So you see, my motives are not entirely altruistic."

"Yet you are patient and encouraging." Ciara drew a ragged breath. "His father treated him as if he were naught but a disgusting nuisance. Small children are a bother. They piss, they cry, they cast up their accounts. Sheffield used to say that he had done his duty in begetting a brat. After that, his only interest in his son was to stay as far away as possible."

To Ciara's dismay, tears once again spilled down her cheeks. What an idiot she was to turn into a watering pot in front of Hadley. No doubt he was used to weepy women, but she prided herself on controlling her emotions. Only in her most private moments did she ever allow pain or weakness to show.

He would think her wheedling or . . .

His arms were suddenly around her again, his hand gently stroking her hair. "Easy, sweetheart." His voice was soft, soothing, as he hugged her close and pressed her cheek to his shoulder. Strangely enough, despite his half-naked state, there was none of the sexual tension of their last few encounters. The intimacy radiated simple, solid warmth.

Even the brush of his lips to her brow, and then to her mouth seemed innocent.

All too soon, Lucas drew back from the gentle kiss and remained silent as she shuffled away.

"Sorry." Ciara finally gathered her wits and raised her head. "Dear God, I don't know what has come over me."

"No apologies are necessary," he chided. "You have been strong as granite for your son. But even granite must chip here and there in the face of the elements."

"G-good heavens, Hadley. H-have you been studying philosophy along with ornithology?" she said lightly.

"Me?" Lucas exaggerated a grimace. "Perish the thought. Even your alchemy could not brew up a potion that could turn a rakehell into a respectable scholar."

A strange feeling bubbled up inside her breast. *Longing, regret?* The earl had a very sharp mind, but he had chosen to hone a different side of his character. That he took his greatest pleasures in drinking and carousing was something that set them fundamentally apart. No matter that some inexplicable force seemed to draw them together.

*Rather like a magnet and steel shavings.*

Well, the last thing she needed in her life were slivers of sharp metal cutting too close for comfort.

Ciara felt a sudden chill, as if a knifepoint were teasing down her spine. She must set aside her attraction to this man—if not for her own sake, for that of her son. Despite his moments of kindness, Hadley was unstable, unsound. Lud, on one hand he played cricket with children, and on the other hand he cavorted bare-arsed with a courtesan in the middle of Berkeley Square! She could not subject Peregrine to the vagaries of another wastrel.

"Hadley," she began.

"Lucas," he corrected. "Seeing we are engaged, it's only proper that we start calling each other by our Christian names, Ciara." His breath stirred a strand of her hair. And a longing she dared not define. "What a lovely name—the sound is like a soft wind blowing through pine boughs."

"Hadley," she repeated. "I—"

"I should like to hear my name on your lips."

She hesitated. *No, no, no. That was too dangerous.* Yet the word seemed to slip out of its own accord. "L-Lucas . . ."

His mouth quirked in an odd little smile. "Hell, it sounds uncomfortably close to Lucifer, doesn't it? But then, I suppose that's only fitting. A pity that it's not nearly as poetic as yours."

"I wonder that you always feel compelled to paint such a black picture of yourself." In spite of her own misgivings, she couldn't help adding, "You are far from evil."

"I'm far from good, sweetheart." His features suddenly hardened. "Don't be a fool and forget that."

Heeding the warning, Ciara finally drew back from the comfort of his arms. He made no attempt to keep her close. "Thank you for the reminder, Lord Hadley. You need not worry—I'm not about to join the legion of ladies chasing at your coattails."

"It's not my coattails they are after," he murmured.

*Ah, back to being the lewd libertine.*

It was just as well, she told herself. Lucas had so much practice sliding in and out of the role. It now fitted him to perfection, like the soft York Tan leather of his fancy gloves.

Fisting her hands in the folds of her skirts, Ciara matched his cynical tone. "You need not explain the graphic details. I am well aware of the thrust of your comments. As well as your feelings on sentimental attachments." She feigned a careless shrug. "But Peregrine is not."

Lucas ceased smiling. "Whatever my faults—and God knows they are legion—I would never hurt a child."

"No, perhaps not deliberately," she replied. "Yet I fear he is forming an emotional attachment to you. One that will only lead to pain and heartache when it is broken." She drew in a gulp of air, trying to steady her voice. "Perry is too young to understand our arrangement, and he's already experienced enough rejection." *Oh no, not tears again.* It was absurd to be acting like a horrid novel heroine. "He's so vulnerable. I beg you, do not encourage his—"

"Ciara."

She fell silent.

"You think I mean to toss aside Peregrine, like a defective cricket ball?" asked Lucas.

Her gaze remained riveted on the tips of his boots.

"Whatever comes of our situation, I should be happy to continue my friendship with your son," continued Lucas slowly. "He's an engaging imp, and, well, I rather like showing him some of the basics of being a boy." After a moment, his expression turned a touch more serious. "You need not fear that I will introduce him to any of my vices."

Somehow, Ciara sensed that she could trust his word on that. "I don't. But . . ." She heaved a harried sigh. "I don't know, it just all seems so complicated."

He touched her cheek. "You have been teaching me that a scientist must step back and break down a complex problem into a progression of simple steps. Let us not jump ahead of ourselves. Somehow, if we exercise care and caution, things will work out."

Ciara felt her mouth quiver. "Oh, how very humbling it is to be reminded of my lectures. Do I really sound so pompous?"

"Wisdom is always worth repeating," he murmured.

Fighting the flutter of her heart, Ciara wagged a finger.

"Now you are doing it too brown, Hadley. Flattery will only get you so far."

"And from there?" His tone was light, and yet the fringe of his lashes did not quite obscure the odd glint in his eyes.

She regarded her hands, which were still knotted in the folds of merino wool. "I—I suppose we will just have to cross that bridge when we come to it."

# Chapter Fifteen

*W*icked, wicked, wicked.

Lucas propped his slippered feet on the fender and stared at the fire licking up from the burning logs. *Oh, he was an evil man.* Only the worst sort of depraved devil would be thinking such impure thoughts.

The flames flared, nearly singeing his soles.

Lady Sheffield—the sinfully sensuous Ciara—had turned to him for comfort, and he had been all too happy to oblige. He had held her, stroked her, offered her a shoulder to lean on.

And said it was all in the name of friendship.

*Liar.*

*Lecherous, lascivious liar.* Loosening the sash of his dressing gown, Lucas shifted uncomfortably against the soft leather cushions of his chair. Damnation, an honorable man would not have taken shameless advantage of her momentary weakness.

Then again, he had never pretended to be a paragon of virtue.

Making a face, he poured himself a drink.

Lud, her body had felt so damnably good against his

bare flesh. The pliant curves molding perfectly, as if made to fit him. A part of him—admittedly a *very* small part of him—wanted only to offer stalwart support. The rest of his body wanted to slide up her skirts and make mad, furious love to her.

The voice of reason in a shouting match with the howl of carnal desire?

It didn't take a genius to figure out which one would overpower the other.

The coals hissed and crackled, setting up a plume of smoke. *Wicked man,* he repeated. Most likely his cods would roast in the deepest pit of hell for all eternity.

But the warning did not cool the heat of lustful, lecherous longings swirling deep inside him. He had never been a good man. He lived for sybaritic pleasures. There was no reason to think he could change now.

He was, after all, Mad, Bad Had-ley. *Wasn't he?*

Reaching for the brandy, Lucas saw that the bottle was empty. *Like his own craven soul?* With a sardonic snarl, he tossed it over his shoulder. Yes, it had been rather nice having a lady look up to him as a hero for once. A knight, not a knave.

But it was too damn hard to be noble. Playing the ruthless rake was far easier than girding his loins to joust at fire-breathing dragons.

Ciara didn't really expect anything more, having been disappointed by all the men in her life. Lucas felt a twinge in his gut. She deserved better, of course. And yet he wasn't altruistic enough to walk away. Life was full of bitter disappointments. If he couldn't give her peace of mind, he could at least offer her physical pleasure, if just for a fleeting moment.

*What was wrong with that?*

Prying the cork from a bottle of claret, he wet his lips with the wine. It was not as if she was a sheltered miss, innocent in the ways of the world. She had experienced the slings and arrows of scorn. Right now what she needed was someone to make her feel wanted. To make her feel alive again. He had sensed her softening.

Seduction, he reasoned, would be doing her a good turn. She might even thank him in the end.

*Evil, evil,* chorused the tongues of flame.

He didn't need their wagging whispers to know that the rationalization was a self-serving twisting of the truth. But closing his eyes, Lucas chose to listen to the dark side of his nature. Their bargain was for an equal exchange of services.

She meant to teach him all about intellect?

Well, he would give her some lessons in lust.

So far their exchanges had only been foreplay . . .

~⌒⌐

Uncorking a vial of juniper essence, Ciara set about brewing a batch of medicinal bath oil for one of Ariel's invalid friends. The pungent evergreen was a powerful balm for calming both body and spirit.

Perhaps she had better make up an extra tub of the stuff. Both her mind and her muscles felt as if they were tied in knots.

*Relax,* she scolded herself. All things considered, they had escaped the accident relatively unscathed. Peregrine seemed to be suffering no lingering effects of shock. As for Hadley, by the time he had taken his leave last night, his limp was hardly noticeable. This morning he would probably be a good deal stiffer . . .

*Oil.* It was time to add oil to the mixture.

She hurried through the last few ingredients, and then left the pot to simmer over a low flame. In the meantime, she could spend the next hour with the baron's manuscript.

"Milady?"

Repressing a sigh, Ciara paused in the doorway of the library. "Yes, McCabe?"

"There is a gentleman downstairs to see you."

"Please tell Lord Hadley that I am too busy for visitors this morning."

The butler cleared his throat. "It is not Lord Hadley, milady."

Her blood froze. The only other male who dared to call at Pont Street was her nephew. "Sir Arthur?"

"Yes, madam."

"Tell him I will be down in a moment."

As the servant headed for the stairs, Ciara caught a glimpse of her reflection in one of the glass-framed botanical prints. *Hardly a pretty picture.* Steam had reddened her cheeks and curled her hair into unruly ringlets. Tucking an errant lock behind her ear, she smoothed at the folds of her work dress. Not that it mattered what she looked like.

The Sheffields were blinded by their own selfish greed.

"Good morning, Aunt." With an insolent shrug, Arthur placed the small Roman bronze of Mercury back in the curio case. "What an odd collection. You seem to have a fondness for pagan deities."

"I collect classical antiquities," she replied coolly. "As do a great many educated members of Polite Society."

He flushed slightly at the subtle barb. "You also appear to collect misfortunes, Lady Ciara. I just heard about the accident in the park and came to inquire about my young cousin."

"Peregrine is perfectly fine, thanks to Lord Hadley's quickness."

Arthur's eyes narrowed to a razored squint. "Perhaps if you had been keeping a careful watch on your son rather than making mooncalf eyes at your lover, the boy would not have been in any danger to begin with."

Ciara drew in a harsh breath.

"Perhaps he would be better off with more attentive guardians, Aunt. You seem more concerned with brewing up black magic than in looking after your child."

She couldn't contain her indignation. "How dare you accuse me of neglect."

"Oh, I assure you, it's not just me." A casual flick of his finger knocked over the statue of Juno. "The drawing rooms are all abuzz with talk about the Wicked Widow." He paused. "And have you seen the morning headlines?"

Though a frisson of fear ran down her spine, Ciara lifted her chin. "You may not find it quite so easy to turn all of Society against me. I am not without . . . friends."

Arthur's face darkened for an instant, and then his lips parted to reveal a flash of teeth. "You dance through a few balls and so think that you are a match for us? Trust me, my family knows the *ton* far better than you do. They know who wields the power here in Town— and who does not."

She didn't trust her voice to answer.

"So you see, it really would be best for everyone involved if you would agree to our earlier suggestions and cede legal guardianship of the boy to us, his father's family," continued Arthur. "That way, Master Peregrine would get the attention he deserves, and you, dear Aunt, would be free to pursue your unnatural interests."

"Over my dead body," she muttered through clenched teeth.

"Oh, that can be arranged. Perhaps sooner rather than later." He gave a nasty laugh. "You do know, don't you, that the magistrate is considering our petition to reopen the inquest into my uncle's untimely demise. If we were to withdraw it, the case would remain closed . . ." The unspoken words hung heavy in the air.

Ciara took a moment to master her outrage. "Are you threatening me, Sir Arthur?"

"Think it over, Aunt." His sneer became more pronounced. "You really think Hadley will protect you? Ha—what a farce! God knows what secret wager has him playing the besotted swain. But he'll tire of the game soon enough."

"Get out, sir," she whispered.

Arthur shrugged and sauntered for the door. "Suit yourself," he called. "But then be prepared to call Newgate prison your new home."

Ciara waited until the click of his boot heels died away before allowing herself to sink into one of the parlor chairs. Only then did she realize her hands were trembling so badly that the fringe of her shawl was tied in knots. As were her insides.

Arthur was a despicable dullard, but his words were not idle boasts. The Sheffield family did indeed have power and influence. Was it enough to poison Society against her and make good on their threats to convene a second inquest?

She stared down at tiny loops of silk and felt her throat constrict. *As if she needed any reminder that murder was a hanging offense.*

The soft rap on the door caused her head to jerk up. Looking around in a blind panic, she sought for some means of escape. If only she could slip away to somewhere safe—Italy . . . India . . . a remote South Sea island far, far from the lies of London.

"Your pardon, milady, but you have another caller. The gentleman says he will take up only a moment of your time."

Standing in the shadow was Lord James Jacquehart Pierson.

*Coming to voice his own disapproval?* Try as she might, Ciara couldn't muster the strength to stand.

"Forgive me for calling at such an early hour, but I found this in my curricle"—he held out a small gold earbob—"and thought you might be worried about it."

"Thank you," she said numbly, making no move to take the piece of jewelry. "I assumed I had lost it in the park."

"Er. Well." Jack shifted his feet. After waiting a moment longer, he took a few steps and placed it atop the curio cabinet. "I'll just leave it here." However, his hand remained hovering over the burled walnut. "By Jove," he murmured. "That is a remarkably fine example of Octavian bronzework. It is by Flavius, is it not?"

"Yes," she replied without looking up.

He looked up abruptly. "Are you all right, Lady Sheffield?"

"Yes," she whispered, stifling the urge to break out in hysterical laughter.

"You look a little faint," he insisted. "Please allow me to pour you a glass of sherry."

"Tippling from the bottle is not one of my bad habits, sir," replied Ciara a trifle sharply. "We witches and warlocks usually wait until midnight to drink our black-magic libations."

To his credit, Jack accepted the sarcasm with a show of good grace. "I suppose I deserved that. Would it help matters any if I apologized once again for putting my foot in my mouth? I am not usually so clumsy, or so rude." He hesitated. "I am sincere in saying that I was mistaken in jumping to conclusions based on hearsay and innuendo."

"It is I who ought to be making an apology, sir," she assured him. "I—I am a bit overset at the moment, but that does not excuse my taking it out on you."

He nodded. "I saw Battersham leaving just now. I assume he has something to do with your current state of mind."

"You could say that," she said softly.

"Hadley says the fellow is threatening you." It was half statement, half question.

"You did not come here to listen to a litany of my woes, Lord James." She rose, unwilling to unburden herself any further. "I imagine every family has its skeletons in the closet."

"True." Jack moved away from the curio cabinet, though his gaze seemed to linger for a moment on the display of Roman art. "Don't let him rattle you. He's a toad, and all of the *ton* knows it."

"I agree that Sir Arthur is a reptile, but I see him as

more of a serpent. And unfortunately, the Sheffield species have poisonous fangs."

"Hadley seems intent on pulling out their teeth," he replied after a hint of hesitation.

"I cannot blame you for sounding unhappy about the fact that your friend is putting himself at risk, sir. I am aware that Hadley's association with me is . . . dangerous."

"As you may have noticed, Lucas isn't afraid of taking a risk," murmured Jack. Averting his eyes, he quickly changed the subject. "Speaking of risk, I was admiring your Turner watercolor yesterday. The artist is not afraid of defying convention by using a bold palette, is he?"

"Or a bold imagination." She studied his profile as he approached the painting and subjected it to a closer scrutiny. Strange, but at first blush, Jack had not struck her as a man who would care for art. Like Lucas, he was quite handsome, but his features were a little harder, his gaze a little darker. His olive complexion and long black hair only added to the aura of brooding introspection.

*Intimidating.* Ciara stared a moment longer. An occasional *ondit* in the newspaper hinted that he was almost as rakish as his friend, but the particulars were never mentioned. Whatever his escapades, "Black Jack" Pierson kept them very private.

"Have you seen the current exhibit at the Society of Painters in Water-Colours?" he asked abruptly.

She shook her head. "I don't go out much in public."

"You ought not miss it. I shall tell Lucas to take you. You should also see the latest works that Mr. Turner has on display at his gallery in Harley Street."

"I doubt Hadley would know a Turner from a turnip."

Ciara made a face. "I've inflicted enough punishment on the poor man, I'll not ask him to spend hours in an art gallery."

"He might surprise you," replied Jack. "Have you ever had a look at his sketchbooks?"

"Hadley draws?" she asked.

"Quite well, actually." He paused a fraction. "Perhaps because he had such a devil of a time learning his letters. We used to laugh ourselves sick over the pages of his copybook."

"What do you mean?"

"He wrote the letters in reverse—E's and F's facing left instead of right. It seemed funny to us; however, the teachers were not so amused. They used to birch him until he was black and blue. The trouble was, he didn't do it on purpose."

"Yes, I have heard of such a thing," said Ciara.

"I believe he eventually outgrew it."

"Still, it must have been very hard on him," she mused.

"Who enjoys being the butt of ridicule, Lady Sheffield?" replied Jack slowly. "Lucas was not stupid. Quite the contrary. So he quickly figured out how to deflect the jeers and catcalls of 'imbecile.'" He paused for a fraction. "A devil-may-care recklessness tends to draw whistles of admiration."

"I see." Her eyes had certainly been opened to a whole new facet of Hadley.

"Well, I had best be on my way." Jack inclined a polite bow. "Good day, Lady Sheffield."

"Where are you going?"

"For a ride," replied Lucas.

Jack leaned against the adjoining stall. Hearing a shrill whinny, he peered inside. "What is *that?*"

"*That* is a pony."

"Let me rephrase the question. What is *that* pony doing in *your* stable?"

"Eating hay." He cocked an ear. "And making a pile of shite."

"You're an arse. You know that, don't you?" grumbled his friend.

"What has you in such a sour mood?" Gathering the reins of his stallion in one hand, Lucas tightened the saddle's girth.

Jack didn't miss the wince. Ignoring the question, he countered with one of his own. "Should you be riding today?"

"Probably not. But when have you ever known me to do the sensible thing?"

"At least you are not trying to prance through the park on half a horse," retorted Jack. "What prank are you planning for the poor beast?"

"If you must know, the pony is for Peregrine."

"Lucas—" began his friend.

"Hell, the lad is lonely, Jack. What's the harm in taking him out to the park for a few basic lessons in horsemanship?"

"Harm?" echoed Jack. "I would say that the risk is very great indeed. I have been making a few inquiries, and it sounds to me as if the incident yesterday was no accident."

Lucas checked his stirrups. "I'm not so bacon-brained

as to think that it was merely coincidence that a strange stallion burst from out of the blue and tried to trample Lady Sheffield's son." His hand tightened on the leather. "I've done a little asking around myself. Were you aware that Arthur Battersham is heir to the Sheffield title and lands if anything should happen to the boy?"

Jack swore under his breath. "Did you get a look at the rider's face?"

"No, he had a broad-brimmed hat and a muffler wrapped around his face. But my questions also uncovered information on where one may hire that sort of ruffian." Repressing a grunt, Lucas swung himself into the saddle. "Make my apologies to Gentleman Jackson. I won't be joining you for the weekly sparring session this afternoon."

"Wait." Jack signaled for the stable boy to bring out the chestnut hunter. "I'm coming with you."

"It's not your concern," replied Lucas gruffly. "You warned me about Sheffield's family, so consider your duty done."

"Bloody hell, as if I'd stroll off and leave a friend in the lurch."

"Damn it, I can fend for myself."

"Nonetheless, I am not letting you go on alone."

Lucas muttered several rude words but held his mount in check as the stableboy saddled another horse.

"Where are we headed?" asked Jack.

Lucas patted his pocket, checking that the scribbled directions were there. "Several livery stables in Southwark. My informant has heard some whispers in the stews about a band of thugs for hire."

"By the by, Battersham paid a call on your betrothed this morning. Judging from the look on her face as he left,

I assume it was not to offer his felicitations for a long and happy marriage."

A jerk on the reins drew a whinnied protest from his stallion. Hooves thudded against the cobbles, kicking up a cloud of dust. "How the devil do you know that?" demanded Lucas.

"Because I stopped by myself"—Jack held up his hand to cut off the curses—"to return an earbob that Lady Sheffield dropped in my curricle."

Somewhat mollified, Lucas muttered a few soothing words to his horse before replying. "You could have given it to me."

"I thought you would be laid up for the day—with one of your usual cyprians to minister to your physical comfort."

"You are one to talk," retorted Lucas.

"I am not the one engaged to be married," pointed out his friend. "So my habits are irrelevant. And besides, I was curious." He fingered his watch fobs. "You did not mention that Lady Sheffield is interested in classical art."

"She is interested in a great many subjects. Her intellectual abilities are most impressive."

"Well, she can't be all that smart," drawled Jack.

Lucas scowled. "Now see here, Jack—"

"She agreed to an engagement with you."

He waited for his friend to mount, then urged his stallion into the narrow alleyway leading to the street.

"It's a little complex," muttered Lucas as they turned the corner.

"Well, keep it simple," countered Jack. "You are, after all, Mad, Bad Had-ley. A fellow not given to thinking too deeply about things."

Lucas swore under his breath.

"I'm just trying to make you think twice before you get involved in something you'll regret."

The observation touched a sore spot. "Damn it, Jack," replied Lucas. "People *do* change."

The low snort did not come from one of the horses. "True, for right now I hardly recognize my fellow rakehell reveler. Indeed, if I wished to be snide, I might imply that the widow slipped some potent potion into your medicine."

Lucas felt his jaw harden.

"But I won't," continued Jack quickly. "I shall merely ask if the transformation is a permanent one?"

Lucas wasn't quite sure how to answer. "Look, it's a long story."

Jack slanted him a sidelong look. "It's a long ride."

Ciara dabbed a drop of lavender oil to her temples and breathed in deeply. Mingled with the piney tang of the steam wafting up from the simmering cauldron, the floral fragrance helped her knotted nerves to unwind.

*"Ciao, cara!"* The lilt of Italian floated in from the corridor.

Ciara pushed a damp curl behind her ear. Was her head in such a fog that she had forgotten an appointment with Alessandra? Her friend did not make a habit of dropping in without warning.

"I have something very interesting to show you," announced Alessandra as she sailed through the door without knocking. "But first, you must tell me—has Lord Lucifer a rival for your affections? I just saw the Prince of Darkness leaving your door."

"Oh, you must mean Hadley's friend, Lord James Pierson." Ciara went back to measuring the bath oil into a set of glass bottles. "Though from what I understand, his friends do call him Black Jack."

"Whatever his name, Hadley's *amico* is a handsome devil. But he looked as if someone had stuck a red-hot pitchfork up his arse. I swear, there was smoke coming out of his ears." Alessandra sniffed at the cloud of steam. *"Bella, bella,"* she murmured, rubbing at her neck. "I should like to soak for hours in a tub perfumed with—" She stopped short. "Good God, you look pale as a ghost!"

"I may soon be one," she said with an attempt at humor. "If my late husband's family has any say in the matter."

Alessandra clasped her hand. "Is that man—Black Jack—part of their cabal?" she demanded. "Did he come here to torment you on their behalf?"

Ciara shook her head. "Lord James's only quarrel with me is that he doesn't approve of Hadley's involvement in my affairs. He's afraid that his friend may suffer from getting too close to me. I can't say I blame him." Sighing, she went on to recount what had happened in the park.

*"Santa cielo,"* muttered Alessandra. "This is bad."

"And likely to get worse." Ciara tugged off her apron. "Alessa, although you speak little about your life in Italy, I have a feeling that you are acquainted with certain circles of . . . radicals. Do you know anyone who could help me . . . disappear?"

Her friend looked away, hiding her expression in the scrim of steam. "Oh, *tesora,* I counsel you to think very long and hard before taking such an extreme step. To be a fugitive, always looking over your shoulder, is not a life that I would wish on anyone."

"I know, I know. But I am desperate."

"To run now will give truth to the rumors that you committed murder." The mist had formed droplets of water on the tips of her lashes. Alessandra blinked and one fell away, etching a path down her ashen cheek. "Before you take that fatal step, I would advise you to be very sure that you have no other alternative."

Ciara reached out and touched her friend's hand. Their fingers curled together. "Oh, Alessa," she began.

Alessandra pulled free, her rings flashing with fire as she gestured for silence. "So let us put our heads together and decide on the best course of action."

Sensing that her friend would not talk about her own travails, Ciara gave a tiny nod.

"Has anything else happened to alarm you?"

"Sir Arthur was here this morning. The threats from Sheffield's family are growing worse. And I have been thinking . . ." Ciara's voice caught in her throat for an instant. "Is—is it possible that Perry's mishap was no accident?" she said, forcing out the terrible words. "When you look at it dispassionately, it is only logical that they seek to get rid of him. Why go through all the trouble of raising Perry, when his demise means that the family lands and title go to Battersham, whose loyalties are not a question?"

Alessandra's eyes flooded with compassion.

"Besides, they would kill two birds with one stone," went on Ciara. "If anything happened to Perry, it would cast more suspicions on me. The hue and cry for my neck would have me on the gibbet at Newgate in no time."

"Let us not panic," counseled Alessandra. She thought for a moment. "Have you mentioned your fears to Hadley?"

"Lord, no!" Ciara hoped the quivering of her lips was

not too obvious. "The man was nearly killed yesterday on account of us. Risking life and limb was not part of our bargain. I can't in good conscience drag him any deeper into my travails. It is *my* responsibility to figure out a solution to this problem."

"And we will, *cara,*" assured Alessandra. "The Circle may be somewhat smaller right now, but the three of us are clever enough to outwit the Sheffields."

Ciara felt her insides unclench. "Oh, what would I do without such stalwart friends?" she murmured, wiping a sleeve across her eyes.

"No tears." Her friend wagged a bejeweled finger. "Men like that bullying oaf Battersham think that women are capable of naught but hysterics. It will be a great pleasure to prove him wrong, *si?*"

"*Si.*" She smiled through a sniff. "You are right, of course. We shall beat them at their own game."

"That's the spirit." Alessandra gave her a quick hug. "For the moment, you must put on a brave face and go on in society as if you haven't a care in the world. Perception is part of the battle—let the *ton* see you smile and make merry and they will assume you have nothing to hide."

"Hmmm." She blinked. "Hadley said something similar the night of our first appearance in public."

"Ah, so he has both beauty *and* brains," quipped her friend.

Ciara wasn't quite sure how to reply. Hadley played the careless rakehell well, but she, too, was starting to believe that there was a great deal more to him than a sinful smile.

"*Bene.*" Linking arms, Alessandra led her to the door. "Now, let's go to the library. As I said, I have something very intriguing to show you."

# Chapter Sixteen

*L*ucas uttered a grim oath as he slipped out of the dank stable. "Let's be gone. This place stinks of shite," he muttered.

"Filth begets filth," agreed Jack, untying his reins from the rusting railing. "It's a nasty business the fellow runs, but the sad truth is, the government gives many of our ex-soldiers little choice but to turn to a life of crime to survive. At least we've a lead to follow."

He grunted. "I've no doubt it will take us to Battersham's doorstep. I swear, I will beat the bastard to a bloody pulp."

"You won't be able to protect your lady if you are swinging from a gibbet," warned his friend. "We'll need to gather proof of Battersham's perfidy."

Lucas swore again.

"Look, why not leave this to me? I'll enlist Haddan and Woodbridge to help. Between the three of us, we have enough connections with former military men to call in a few favors."

Lucas urged his horse to a quicker pace through the twisting alley. "Well, if you are serious about helping . . ."

"Of course I will help," interrupted Jack. "And so will

Nicholas and Devlin. We are friends, Lucas. No more need be said."

*Friendship.* Jack made it sound so simple.

"It looks like you will have your hands full looking after the lady," added Jack dryly. "Why is it I hadn't heard what a stunner she is?"

"She's been careful to keep her charms under wraps," he replied. "Her experiences with men haven't been overly good."

Jack slanted a sidelong look. Lucas felt it linger a little longer than he would have liked.

"Don't say it," he muttered, feeling a stab of guilt for his thoughts of the previous night. "My reputation may not be lily white, but I've no intention of being a blackguard with Lady Sheffield."

That would, of course, depend on what shade of meaning was given to the word.

His friend seemed to be reading his mind. "I trust you will act honorably. The lady has enough trouble."

"I thought you didn't approve of her," said Lucas a little snidely. "Why the sudden concern?"

"I didn't approve of you involving yourself in her affairs," corrected Jack. "And I still don't, despite your explanation." Lucas had told his friend about Henry's manuscript and the bargain of mutual aid with Lady Sheffield. "As to the lady herself, I admit that my preconceived notions about her were wrong. However, there are too many things that can . . ."

"Blow up in my face?" suggested Lucas.

"Both of you are playing with fire." Jack frowned. "This sham courtship could reflect badly on Lady Sheffield and leave your reputation in complete tatters."

"It was awfully frayed to begin with," quipped Lucas.

"That's my point—you are hanging on to your position in respectable Society by only a thread. It would be a pity to cut all connections with the Polite World."

"Respectability and manners are a crashing bore," snapped Lucas. Even to his own ears, the retort had a hollow ring.

"You sound like a schoolboy, Lucas."

"Since when have you turned so staid?" he retorted.

Jack didn't deign to answer the gibe. "All I am saying is, be careful." He guided his horse around a lumbering dray cart. "Any chance you are actually going to marry the widow?"

Lucas jerked on the reins. "Why do you ask?"

"Just curious."

"What do you think?" he snapped.

"Given your erratic behavior of late, it's impossible to guess what you'll do next."

⁓

Ciara studied the sequence of letters one more time. "Why, I believe you are right," she mused. "Whatever inspired you to make such a guess?"

"Something you said earlier got me to thinking." Opening an old leatherbound book, Alessandra pointed out several passages. "See here, the chronicler speaks of a colony of Egyptian traders based in India. So it seemed logical to look to the dialect of ancient Cairo for a clue to the code."

Ciara read over the text. "I would never have thought of that," she said admiringly.

"Only because cryptography is not your usual field of study."

"You are being far too modest." She carefully refolded the sheets of papers with her friend's transcription. "That leaves just one last section of the manuscript to figure out."

"The most important section," pointed out her friend. "I will keep working on it."

"Yes, we still have work to do, but deciphering this mention of *Penicillium notatum* is a critical discovery." Excitement edged into her voice. "I am sure it is key to the manuscript's secret."

"Isn't *Penicillium notatum* a form of . . . mold?" asked Alessandra.

"Yes."

Her friend made a face. "It's hard to imagine how mold can be of medicinal benefit."

"Which makes the last section of code even more intriguing," replied Ciara. "May I take your notes to show Sir Henry? He will be very excited to see what progress we have made."

"Of course." Alessandra slanted a look at the clock on the mantel. "Forgive me for rushing off, but I promised Isabella to take her to the Tower menagerie. She wishes to make some sketches of the lion."

Ciara smiled. "She is showing quite an aptitude for art. The pictures she did of the monkey were quite wonderful."

"She enjoys it, so I am doing all I can to encourage her interest," replied her friend. "I've just hired a Swiss drawing master, who comes very highly recommended. The only trouble is, he is said to be a trifle temperamental. How he will do with a child remains to be seen. The first lesson is tomorrow."

"Isabella is not easily intimidated," assured Ciara.

"That is true." Alessandra rose and pecked a kiss to her cheek. "Chin up, *cara,* and don't lose heart. We shall fight fire with fire."

She nodded, trying to dispel the lingering fear of Sheffield's family.

After seeing her friend to the door, Ciara returned to the library, intent on spending the next few hours studying the manuscript. But her mind kept wandering between the past and the present. The ancient code was not the only thing proving perversely difficult to decipher . . .

Giving up on trying to puzzle out her emotions, she gathered her papers and rang for her carriage. Given her current mental state, perhaps two heads would prove better than one in reviewing Alessandra's discovery.

Sir Henry's butler greeted her arrival with a solemn nod. "Please follow me, madam," he intoned. "The baronet has informed me that he is always at home when his fellow scholars pay a call."

From behind the library doors came a lilt of laughter.

Ciara stopped short. "Oh, I do not wish to interrupt if Sir Henry has other guests—"

The butler, however, had already knocked.

"Come in, come in," came Henry's voice.

She entered the room and was about to voice an apology when two silvery heads looked up in unison from the display table.

"Lady Sheffield! What a delightful surprise," exclaimed Henry.

*Surprise was an apt choice of words*. Ciara was momentarily speechless.

"We were just studying the stamens and pistils of these

poppies," said Ariel, her blush matching the exact shade of pink tinting the colored engraving. "Sir Henry has such a fascinating portfolio of prints. And he has been kind enough to share his expertise on the subject with me."

"It has been my pleasure," said the baron.

Ciara shifted her case. "Don't let me interrupt. I shall stop by another time—"

"No, no, I was just leaving." Ariel rose hastily and shook out her skirts. "I must be getting home."

"You must promise to return soon," said Henry. "We've not yet looked at the collection of species from Afghanistan."

"Thank you, I—I shall."

Ciara bit back a smile as her friend fumbled with her reticule. Ariel appeared embarrassed, which was rather endearing. Was something blooming in the room besides exotic species of *Papaver somniferum?*

Henry cleared his throat. "Er, have you made any headway on the code, Lady Sheffield?"

"As a matter of fact, yes," she replied. "Lady Giamatti had made a breakthrough in decoding the middle part. All that is left to figure out is the last section."

His face lit up. "Ah, what wonderful news! I knew I could count on you to solve the mystery."

"We still have a long way to go, sir."

Henry dismissed her words with a wave. "I have every confidence in your ability to come up with the answer."

Ariel voiced her agreement. "As well you should, Sir Henry. Ciara has one of the sharpest minds I've ever encountered."

*Then why couldn't she cut through her doubts and fears?*

"Actually, I'm feeling a little dull-witted at the moment," admitted Ciara. "I thought perhaps a fresh pair of eyes might see whatever it is that I am missing."

Henry maneuvered his chair to make room at the table. "Are you sure you won't stay, Lady Ariel?"

"I am sorry, but I promised Mrs. Taft I would drop off a tisane for her sore throat before the supper hour."

*Interesting.* So the two of them were spending time together. However, Ciara forced herself to remain focused on the main conundrum.

She handed Henry the notes from Alessandra. "Perhaps you would care to read through this while I lay out the manuscript's last section. I have brought along a special magnifying glass in case you care to examine the nuances of the pen strokes." She made a wry face. "I confess, I have studied the writing from every possible angle and can see nothing that sparks a flash of inspiration."

Henry pursed his lips. "Let me see what I learn here before I have a look. But I am not sure I shall be of much help."

As he pored over the papers, Ciara walked Ariel to the door. "Thank goodness our next meeting of the Circle is tomorrow, for the three of us need to have a . . . council of war."

"Have the Sheffields been rattling their sabers?" whispered her friend.

"They have fired the first shot, so to speak," answered Ciara. "I think they are gathering their forces for a new attack. But I will tell you all the details later."

"Hmmph." Ariel's eyes narrowed. "Don't worry, my dear. They will soon discover that they have underestimated their enemy."

〜⁀〜

"I'm not surprised that your eyesight is fading, Ciara." Lucas saw her frown at the use of her given name as he entered the library and approached the worktable. "Do you never take a break from your studies?" he added.

She set down the large magnifying lens. "I rarely idle away the hours, Lord Hadley. I am happiest when I am expanding my mind."

"And I," he added softly, "am happiest when I am expanding a very different section of my anatomy."

"Lucas," chided his uncle. "Remember your manners."

"I'm not sure I ever knew them to begin with." He wasn't quite certain why he was going out of his way to be provoking. The morning had left him in a brooding mood. Ciara and her son were so vulnerable to attack. It was impossible to anticipate how their enemies might strike next.

"Is the swelling around your ribs any better today?" she asked softly, ignoring his risqué innuendo.

"The area is still a bit black and blue, despite your tender ministrations."

"You ought to be in bed," she murmured

"I could be convinced, if you would come tuck me in."

"Lucas . . ." Henry's voice turned sharper.

"It is quite all right, Sir Henry. I have grown used to your nephew's rakish teasing." Ciara jotted down something in her notebook before applying the glass to another section of yellowed parchment.

Curious in spite of himself, Lucas edged closer to the table. "What are you doing?"

"Looking for clues," she said without glancing up.

"To what?" he persisted, leaning down. The scent of her perfume—a beguiling blend of exotic spices—tickled at his nostrils. Cinnamon, cloves . . . he could barely refrain from licking his lips.

"Patterns," she replied tersely.

Lucas stared at the squiggles.

"The manuscript is written in a series of codes," explained his uncle. "Each section is increasingly complex. Lady Sheffield has solved all but this last one, which spells out the exact secret hidden by the ancient scholar." He turned to her. "By the by, I think we should send a progress report to Lord Lynsley. If what we suspect is true, and this really does reveal the secret of a new medicine for healing wounds, then the discovery will be of great interest to the government and the military."

"Yes, by all means, if you think he would wish to hear of it." Ciara nodded absently as she moved her magnifying glass across the page.

Lucas studied her for a moment longer before asking, "Are you looking for the frequency of certain forms?"

"How did you know?" She sounded surprised.

"I am a gambler, remember? And any gambler worth his salt learns to count cards. That way, one has a better chance of predicting the odds of what will turn up next."

Henry looked thoughtful.

"I imagine you are trying to determine how often a symbol appears," Lucas went on. "Then, based on the most common usage of vowels and consonants, you make an educated guess as to which letter is which."

"It takes patience and a devilishly clever mind," said Henry. "And even then, it's a process of trial and error."

"Hmm." Intrigued, he held out his hand for the magnifying glass. "May I?"

Ciara passed it over without comment.

"Part of the trouble is that we don't know what language it's based on," explained Henry. "Lud, there are so many arcane dialects from the Arab world at that time."

Lucas continued his study. "Have you tried classical Greek? The fellow was, after all, copying a treatise by that fellow Hippo . . . Hippo . . ."

"Hippocrates," murmured Ciara.

Henry tapped his pen to his chin. "Sometimes the correct solution is the simplest one."

Ciara slowly traced a finger along the lines of writing. "You are not merely guessing. You *do* see a pattern, don't you? It makes sense, given your artistic eye, and the fact that you had to study your letterforms far more closely than the other boys."

Lucas stiffened. "What do you mean?"

"Lord James mentioned your difficulty in the schoolroom," she replied softly.

"Jack is an arse," snapped Lucas. "He has taken a minor childhood incident and blown it all out of proportion."

"There is nothing to be ashamed of, Lord Hadley. I have heard that a good many children suffer through the same problem."

"What problem?" asked Henry, his face wreathed in concern.

"Your nephew had trouble reading and writing on account of seeing the alphabet reversed."

"Is that why you never wrote to me?" asked Henry softly.

"Damnation, no," he growled. "I didn't write because I

was too busy raising hell." Dropping the magnifying glass, as if it were a burning coal, he turned on his heel and stalked to the door. "Speaking of which, you will have to excuse me. I'm late for a game of vingt-un at White's."

Lucas was still seething as he entered the club. Jack was about to have his beak bloodied. *How dare he reveal such private, painful secrets to the lady?*

"Why, look! It's the besotted bridegroom!" Peering over the back of his armchair, Ingalls raised a bottle of brandy in mock toast and started to hum a wedding march.

Greeley joined in, whistling the melody slightly off-key.

"You two are idiots," muttered Lucas.

"You know why he's dressed in such somber shades of black and charcoal?" sniggered Farnam. "He's in mourning for his sex life."

"Speaking of black, what happened to your phiz?" asked Ingalls. He squinted at the bruise on Lucas's cheekbone. "Looks like you went a few rounds in the boxing ring."

"I got hit," replied Lucas. "By a horse."

"Damned clumsy of you, man," remarked Greeley. "Were you drunk?"

"I'll bet he was bewitched by his intended," said Farnam in a dramatic whisper. "A potent love potion that had him stumbling like a mooncalf through the streets."

The other two chortled.

In no mood for teasing, Lucas summoned a scowl. "Freddie, another insulting word about the widow and you will find your cods roasting over the fire."

"Cool down, Lucas. What's happened to your sense of humor?" groused Ingalls.

"It seems to have evaporated after his latest splash in the newspapers," muttered Farnam.

"I haven't changed," he said defensively. "It's just that . . ." Damn, it was unfair that Ciara was the butt of nasty jokes. She deserved respect rather than cruel innuendos on account of her intellect. Perching a hip on the back of the long leather sofa facing the hearth, he motioned for his friends to draw in a bit closer.

"I do have a secret, but you must promise not to tell anyone."

His friends solemnly crossed their hearts.

"Lady Sheffield is engaged in a very important scientific project . . ." Lucas recalled that Henry had said Lord Lynsley was following Ciara's work on the manuscript with great interest. After all, the discovery might be of great medical value to the military.

"For the Marquess of Lynsley," he continued. "Who is heading up a special military research committee for Whitehall."

"Whitehall?" echoed Farnam.

"Yes, the lady's intellect is held in the highest regard by the government." Lucas dropped his voice a notch, forcing his friends to edge closer. "It's all very hush-hush, but she's working on deciphering the secrets of an ancient medical manuscript—and she's *this* close to completing the task." He held his fingers a hairsbreadth apart.

Ingalls pulled a face. "You mean to say she's about to make a momentous discovery?"

Lucas nodded. "If her hunch is correct, it may be a miracle drug that will save countless lives among our soldiers. Just think—such a medicine would give our military a powerful new weapon." He saw no reason not to embellish the story. *In for a penny, in for a pound.* Above all else, men were impressed by money. "And the truth is, the government is willing to pay her a bloody fortune for the patent."

Farnam let out a low whistle. "Now I understand your interest in the wid—er, that is, the lady."

"Not that you need to marry money," added Ingalls.

"No," agreed Lucas. "I don't."

Greeley fixed him with a strange stare. The bottle rose again, this time in a more serious salute. "Er, well, good luck to the lady. Especially as she is working for God and country."

Lucas allowed a grim smile. The Sheffield family would soon discover that two could play the game of rumor and innuendo. Oh, his friends would keep their word, but there would be plenty of winks and hints that the Wicked Widow was not so evil after all. Word would spread through the drawing rooms of Mayfair, countering the latest sordid lies being spread about Ciara.

"Have any of you seen Jack?" he asked, recalling his original mission.

"In the card room," answered Ingalls. "Getting foxed."

"Good." Lucas straightened and flexed a fist. "Then he won't feel much pain when I punch out his deadlights."

"Oh, this should be entertaining," sniggered Greeley. "Maybe Mad, Bad Had-ley is not beyond redemption, after all."

Farnam signaled the others to follow along.

As the four men strolled from the room, not one of them noticed Arthur Battersham sit up on the sofa and slink away through the side portal.

# Chapter Seventeen

*Chin up.* Ciara reminded herself to smile and appear carefree as Lucas guided her through the figures of the gavotte. By Alessandra's decree, she had ordered a few new gowns, all of which were a shade bolder in cut and color than her usual style. The one she was wearing tonight was her friend's favorite—a smoky sapphire blue with a neckline that revealed a goodly amount of cleavage.

Ciara wasn't so sure of the changes . . .

But the strategy seemed to be working. Her dance card had only a few blank slots, and she had just received an invitation to an afternoon poetry reading from the Duchess of Devinhill.

"You have changed your *modiste*," remarked Lucas from out of the blue.

"You don't approve?" she asked hesitantly, a little embarrassed that she cared what he thought.

"On the contrary." His eyes lingered on her bosom. "Jewel tones accentuate every facet of your fair coloring."

"A very pretty speech," she said dryly.

"A very pretty partner."

*A very pretty dilemma.* She should not be finding his company so pleasurable. And yet . . .

Despite knowing that his flirtations meant nothing, Ciara felt a small thrill steal through her. *Don't be blinded by folly,* she chided herself. The glitter in his gaze was fool's gold, a mere wink of light from the gilded candelabras.

Still, it was nice to be admired, even if the sentiment was not serious.

As the dance came to an end, Lucas suggested that they walk out to the terrace. Several other couples were admiring the grouping of Greek marbles in the sculpture garden, while a quartet of men were gathered by the stairs, smoking and discussing the latest war news from Russia.

"Let's get away from the crowd for a moment, shall we?" After taking up two glasses of champagne, he slowly led the way to the far end of the railing.

The night breeze ruffled the garden greenery, and the shadowed whisper of the leaves was redolent with roses and the lush perfumes wafting out from the ballroom. From the darkened walkways came the sound of muted laughter and the crunch of gravel underfoot. Torches swayed in time to the music, smoke and flame flickering in the moonlight.

Ciara inhaled deeply, savoring the coolness on her cheeks.

"Enjoying yourself?" he asked.

*Was it that obvious?*

"Yes," she admitted. "Though I should not be taking pleasure in such frivolous entertainment."

Lucas cocked his head. "Why not?"

"How can you ask that?" She couldn't hold back a

sigh. "There are so many daunting problems to confront, so many serious matters that I must resolve."

"All the more reason to relax and allow yourself an occasional respite from worry, Ciara."

The sound of her name, soft as the stroking of a feather, stirred a pebbling of gooseflesh on her bare arms. "Really, sir," she reminded him. "You must not be so personal in public."

"Because it implies an intimacy between us?"

"Y-yes." The tiny bubbles prickled her tongue as she took a sip of wine.

"But you can't deny that a certain closeness has formed between us, sweetheart."

Ciara felt a jolt of heat as his thigh brushed against hers. "The connection is . . . purely a practical one, Lord Hadley."

"Speak for yourself, Ciara," he replied. "And my name is Lucas, in case you have forgotten."

She swallowed in confusion.

"No one can hear us here, so feel free to use it."

"Th-that wouldn't be proper."

"Mmmm." His fingertips touched the nape of her neck. "Then I imagine you don't think I ought to be doing this." He started to toy with a tendril of hair.

She tried to edge away, but the wall of Portland stone was against her back.

His laugh was low and lush. "Caught between a rake and rock, my dear?"

Ciara sucked in her breath, only to find the musky scent of his maleness sent a shiver down her spine.

"No one can see us, sweetheart. It's dark, and the flower urn is blocking the view."

"You must stop this, sir," she whispered, trying not to allow his smile to curl her toes. *Toes.* Oh, Lud, she must not think about his intimate kisses in the carriage.

Lucas ignored her warning. "You know, instead of returning to the ballroom for our waltz, I would much rather dance you into my bed." His breath tickled her ear. "The first thing I would do is unfasten those pretty little pearl buttons on your bodice . . ." He brushed a fingertip lightly over her breasts. "Then I would ease the silk down to the swell of your hips . . ."

Her flesh began to prickle.

"And let it fall to the floor, leaving you clad in only your corset and shift." A glint of moonlight sparked in his eyes. "But not for long."

Ciara was shocked, yet fascinated. Suddenly it was not merely her toes that were responding to his murmurs. She felt her body clench and react in the strangest way. "Wh—what are you doing, sir?" she demanded.

"Giving you a lesson in lovemaking," he replied in a silky-soft voice. "It's called foreplay, my dear. Suggestion can be very stimulating."

"Lord Hadley—"

He kept talking. "Have you any idea how very desirable you look tonight? I would love to see you naked, your glorious body bathed in shimmering starlight. I would place my palms on the inside of your thighs and gently—ever so gently—coax your legs apart. Imagine your skin sliding over a petal-soft bedsheet, and my caress growing . . . intimate."

She squirmed. No wonder the man had seduced half the ladies in London. That silvery tongue . . .

"Remember our little discussion on the Grotto of

Venus?" His smile stretched wider. "Have you thought about what it would feel like to be kissed there?"

Mesmerized by his mouth, Ciara found it impossible to utter a further protest. Its shape was supremely sensual. *Sinuous. Sinful.*

Oh, Lord, she wanted his lips on her, doing all the delicious things he was describing.

*Was that wicked?*

He turned abruptly. "But you are right, we had better go back in."

Strangely enough, disappointment coursed through her. She felt overwhelmed by a fierce longing, though, of course, even so much as a fleeting kiss was out of the question. *Too risky.* Their behavior in public must be above reproach.

But would he renew his lascivious advances in the privacy of the carriage ride home? Ciara wasn't sure whether to be eager or afraid.

Lucas escorted her back to the ballroom, exchanging polite small talk with acquaintances along the way. His manners were perfectly proper, and for one moment she wondered whether she had merely imagined his naughty whispers.

*No, never in her wildest dreams could she have made up such words, such longings.*

After handing her off to the next name on her dance card, Lucas seemed to ignore her. Without so much as a backward look, he moved along the perimeter of the dance floor, flirting shamelessly with every lady he encountered.

Ciara maintained an outward show of indifference, but she couldn't help watching him out of the corner of her eye. She found herself feeling strangely sorry that she knew so little about wielding her womanly wiles. How was it that some women seemed to have an intuitive understanding of the art of attracting a man—the subtle play of a laugh, a look, a gesture?

*Was she jealous?* The thought took her aback.

How absurd. She was *not* jealous of Hadley. Indeed, she ought to be annoyed that he had been playing such wanton games with her. He was incorrigible.

*Incapable of acting responsibly.*

The last little interlude had been a graphic illustration of his faults.

"Er, the set seems to be forming, Lady Sheffield. Shall we dance?" Ciara's current partner, a colonel serving with General Burrand's staff, offered his arm with a formal bow.

*Chin up.* Alessandra's exhortation echoed once again in her ears. Determined to appear unmoved by the earl's desertion, Ciara made a concerted effort to engage the colonel in an animated conversation.

"What an impressive array of medals, sir. You must explain to me what they all mean," she said archly, repeating a line she had overheard a lady use earlier in the evening.

Obviously flattered by her interest, the colonel flashed a smile that was nearly as bright as the bits of gleaming brass.

As he launched into a detailed explanation, Ciara realized with a start that this was easier than she had ever thought possible. It was not hard to figure out that people liked to talk about themselves.

Growing more confident with every step, she relaxed and began to enjoy the dance. Why, a little flirting was actually fun. The colonel, an acquaintance of Lord Haddan, turned out to be a pleasant fellow who possessed a dry wit and engaging manner. And a gaze that was frankly admiring. She was almost sorry when the music ended.

"Thank you for a delightful dance, Lady Sheffield." He brushed a kiss to her glove. "I look forward to the pleasure of partnering you again."

"I would welcome it, sir," she replied truthfully.

"Then allow me to pencil my name in for later." He angled a peek at her dance card. "I had better move fast, for it appears you have only a few spots left for the rest of the evening."

The statement took her by surprise. She hadn't been paying much attention to the scribbles, but it seemed that the colonel was right. If Lucas didn't hurry . . .

She stole a surreptitious glance around the room.

And quickly discovered she need not have bothered. He was still busy flirting with a trio of lovely ladies.

Lifting her head with what she hoped was regal indifference, Ciara moved on to her next partner.

*Wretch,* she muttered to herself as she spun by him.

The rest of the ball passed by in a blur, and by the end of the evening she had caught only one other glance of him—waltzing with a young Yorkshire heiress who seemed to be hanging on his every word.

"What a pleasant time," remarked Lucas as he helped her on with her wrap. "Did you enjoy yourself?"

"Quite," she replied a little coolly.

He didn't appear to notice.

The carriage ride home was equally annoying. Lucas was polite but distant, both in body and spirit. The space between them seemed to be a yawning chasm, growing deeper with every turn of the wheel.

*Rake's rules.* Whatever his game, she was in the dark as to how it was played. She knew she ought to ignore him, but try as she might, Ciara found that her limbs were taut and her mood unaccountably irritated as the horses came to a halt in Pont Street.

*Why?* She couldn't explain it, save to say that the earl had somehow gotten under her skin with his hot and cold teasings. In spite of herself, a shiver coursed through her limbs as she thought over his suggestive words on the terrace.

"You had better hurry inside, before you catch a chill." Lucas made no move to help her descend from the carriage. Nor did he offer his arm for the short walk up the front steps of her townhouse. "Sleep well," he murmured with a bow. "I shall see you tomorrow for our scheduled lesson."

"Be prepared for a quiz on the first chapter of the textbook," she warned. "Despite all the recent distractions, I don't mean to let you off lightly from our wager."

"I confess, I am curious to see how I shall perform on the test."

"So am I, Lord Hadley." Ciara restrained the urge to bang the door shut in his face. "So am I."

~⁓~

The scratch of the pen seemed unnaturally loud in the scholarly silence of the laboratory. Lucas finished writing out his last answer and glanced up. Ciara was standing across the room, her back to him as she carefully measured out portions of powder from the array of jars above her gas burner.

To his surprise, the test had been easy. The answers had flowed smoothly, like a nightingale's song, from his head. Strange how much interesting information could be stored in his brainbox when it wasn't overflowing with brandy.

And the truth was, he found the subject quite fascinating. As a boy, he had spent countless hours in solitary rambles along the seaside cliffs near Henry's country estate. Observing all the different birds had been a source of constant wonder. But now, as he was beginning to understand some of the scientific reasons for the different appearances and behaviors—things like feather patterns, wing shape, migratory habits—he felt an even greater appreciation for their beauty.

Perhaps Henry had not been exaggerating in saying that knowledge enriched the experiences of life. It definitely had a certain allure, reflected Lucas. Over the last week, he had spent several nights at home reading about gulls and fish hawks rather than joining his friends in carousing with ladybirds. Lud, his comrades-in-revelry would laugh themselves sick if they knew.

Lucas was feeling rather virtuous for studying so hard . . . but all thoughts of virtue flew out the window as Ciara turned slightly and bent over the table.

*Hell.* Fire lit in his loins on seeing the figured muslin stretch across her shapely derriere. *Think of ornithology, not zoology,* chided the voice of Reason.

*Too late.*

It was not his intellect being put to the test, it was his sanity. She looked so achingly lovely, so damnably desirable.

And he was Mad, Bad Had-ley—a man not used to resisting his baser urges.

Before he could get hold of himself, Lucas had moved out of his chair and past the bookshelves. The oilcloth floor covering muffled his approach. Intent on her task, Ciara was unaware of his presence until he tickled the goose quill pen against her neck.

"Hadley!"

He caught the glass vial in midair. "Sorry. Did I surprise you?"

"By now, nothing you do should come as a shock." However, she appeared a little flustered.

Lucas set the container down on the counter. "Not even the fact that I've finished my written examination ahead of schedule?"

"I wouldn't crow quite yet, sir." Ciara carefully wiped her fingers on her apron. "I have yet to read over your answers."

He traced the feathered tip along the shell of her ear. "Oh, I think you'll find yourself quite satisfied with my efforts."

Her cheeks flushed, and the pulse at her throat seemed to grow a little erratic. "Well then, if you are done, you are dismissed from the classroom early. I have some tests for my upcoming meeting of the Circle that I need to get finished."

"Actually, I have another suggestion for how we could use the time."

Ciara tried to evade his tickling touch. "Which is?"

"I thought we might switch roles," he replied. "You be the student, and I'll be the teacher for a change."

"Please, Hadley. I have serious work to do." She

flicked the feather from his fingers. "And you are distracting me."

"Afraid of learning something new?"

Her hands shook slightly as she added a teaspoon of vermilion powder to her cauldron. "What lesson do you have in mind?"

"An elemental experiment in chemistry."

"A subject about which you know absolutely nothing," she pointed out.

"On the contrary, I know a great deal about certain aspects," he said, moving in close enough that his coat brushed her shoulder blades. "Like what effect heat and friction have on a volatile substance."

The scent of perfume rose up from her blush-warmed flesh, enveloping him in a cloud of longing. All semblance of self-control dissolved into a need too strong to keep bottled up. Lucas reached out his hands.

She went very still.

"Yes, that's it," he whispered in her ear. "Don't move. Don't speak. Just feel." He pressed his palms to her hips and drew them back slowly. "You've a lovely arse, Ciara. So smooth, so shapely."

He heard her breath quicken as he caressed her curves. *So far, so good.*

A hitch of his hands raised her skirts to her knees.

Ciara made a sound somewhere deep in her throat.

"Pay attention to the teacher." He touched his lips to the nape of her neck, tasting the salty sweetness of her skin. "Be still, darling."

The whisper of lace ruffled softly as he skimmed his palms up the front of her thighs.

"Hadley—"

"Lucas," he corrected.

"L-Luc—" She sucked in her breath. "Lud!"

Lucas rubbed his rigid shaft against her derriere and began a slow, rhythmic massaging of her lithe legs, coaxing her body into a sensual, swaying slide of arousal.

Her hands were braced on the countertop, her knuckles white against the dark-grained wood.

"Steady, steady," he crooned, watching the whirl of wonderment spasm across her profile. Tendrils of steam wafted up from the cauldron. Her face was turning rosy, the rising heat of her flesh intensifying her scent. The sweetness of verbena mixed with the earthy essence of her womanly passion.

Inhaling deeply, he nearly came undone.

*Hell's teeth.* He pulled her a little roughly against him as pure primal lust threatened to overwhelm all rational thought. But much as he wanted to rip open his trousers and sheath himself in her heat, he held himself in check. As she turned her head in profile, a flutter of her gold-tipped lashes reminded him that this was not about his own selfish satisfaction.

Perhaps it was a paltry gift, but he wanted to give her pleasure.

She moaned, her body softening as she arched herself into him.

"Yes, sweetheart, spread your legs a little wider."

Her slippers slid over the painted floorcloth.

"Let me touch you here." A scrim of delicate lace tickled against his fingertips. "And now here."

The sound that slipped from her lips was neither a yes nor a no. It was something far more elemental. Lucas sensed the need quivering through every fiber of her being, though she feared to let herself give voice to it.

Ciara was too strong, too unselfish to ask for anything for herself. He suddenly longed to free her from fear, to sweep her into sweet oblivion. A special place where for a few precious moments she could feel herself at the very center of the universe.

*What else could a rakehell rogue give her?*

Skimming his hands up over her legs, Lucas found the fastenings of her garters. The knots yielded to a tug, and the silky stockings slipped down from his probing touch.

She flinched ever so slightly as he found the slit in her drawers.

Skirts frothing against his legs, Lucas turned her to face him. "I won't hurt you," he promised, never meaning anything as much in his life.

Slowly, hesitantly, Ciara lifted her hips in answer.

Easing through the finespun cotton, he found her folds of feminine flesh flooded with a pulsing, honeyed heat. The sensation was sweet beyond his wildest words. With a low groan, he stroked through the dampened curls, feeling his fingers grow slick with her essence.

She sucked in her breath.

Willing himself to go slowly, he centered a circling swirl on her pearl.

Ciara gasped, the rush of air hot against his cheek.

*Oh, yes, oh, yes.*

Lucas kissed her, teasing his tongue in and out of her mouth to match the quickening tempo of his touch. Her lips parted—hungrily, it seemed to him—allowing his thrusts to go deeper and deeper. Moving his free hand to her breast, he felt her nipple harden against his palm. The sensation of her intimate flesh peaking with pleasure was intensely erotic.

A growl—or was it a groan?—rumbled in his throat. Lucas had thought himself an expert in every nuance of sexual play, but this feeling spiraling through his belly was something utterly new. Something utterly different. *Just who was teaching whom?*

A little dizzy at the thought, he paused for an instant to catch his breath and steady his stance. Making sense of his reaction could wait. Suddenly the only thing that mattered was to make the moment one that she would never forget. A memory etched indelibly on her mind and her body.

"Oh, please." Her eyes widened and winked with a luminous light. "Don't stop."

"Lucifer and a legion of his dark angels could not drag me away, sweetheart." Lucas parted her petals and probed at the entrance to her passage. "Do you like this?" he asked, his voice oddly urgent.

Ciara clenched around him. "Y-yes."

He withdrew and then thrust his finger inside her again, a little bit deeper.

Burying her face in the folds of his cravat, she sank her teeth into the knotted linen. He heard her whimper and gulp for air.

His own breath was a little ragged. "Have you any idea how beautiful you are, Ciara?" he whispered against her hair.

Her body tightened. "N-not me—"

"Yes, you, sweetheart."

She twisted against him, squirming, sliding, seeking release from the coiling tautness that had taken possession of her body.

*So close, so close.*

She arched back, knocking a glass to the floor.

Though he felt the urge to shatter into a thousand tiny shards, Lucas kept a grip on his self-control. Uttering her name, he delved into her depth with another stroking caress.

She came undone with a shuddering cry.

Lucas covered her mouth with his, sucking in the lush, liquid sound of her climax.

She clutched weakly at his shoulders. Only the weight of his body holding her hard to the edge of the counter kept her from slipping to the floor. With her hair loosened, her lips lush with his kisses, she looked wildly, wantonly, womanly . . .

*Wonderful.*

He held her close, allowing her heartbeat to come back to normal before attempting to speak. Perhaps in a moment he would think of a clever quip, but for now he was bereft of words. Strangely enough, he wasn't quite sure what he wanted to say.

"Mama?" The silence was suddenly broken by a knock on the door. "May I come in? Is Lord Hadley here?"

In an instant, the dreamy glow was gone from Ciara's eyes, replaced by a flare of fear. "Oh, dear God." Slumping against the counter, she looked around in a blind panic.

"Aye, lad. Give me just a moment—I'm finishing up the last part of my lesson." Lucas quickly helped her shake out her skirts into place and then tugged his coat in place to hide his arousal. After running a hand through his hair, he hurried to the door. It took several tries for his fumbling fingers to work the latch open.

"What a fine afternoon, lad," he said with a forced heartiness. "I've been cooped up here long enough. What say you to getting some fresh air? Shall we practice our hitting skills?"

To his relief, the boy was too delighted with the suggestion to notice that anything was amiss. "Hooray! I'll fetch the bat and ball, sir!"

"Excellent, excellent! I'll meet you in the garden." He glanced back at Ciara, who had already begun sweeping up the powdered pigments that had spilled to the floor.

She didn't look up.

Lucas hesitated for a fraction, then turned and quietly closed the door.

# Chapter Eighteen

Too restless to sleep, Ciara threw off the tangled sheets and rose from her bed. The scudding clouds hid all but a tiny sliver of the moon. Its light flickered for a moment across the carpet, then was quickly obscured by the storm-black shadows. A drizzling rain pattered against the leaded windows, and as she pressed her cheek to the glass, the chill seeping through felt good against her skin.

*Hot and cold. Black and white.*

Life was rarely defined in such simple terms.

Her sigh fogged the glass. Ciara was shocked and appalled at her wanton behavior. As well as curious and elated. She knew that she should feel ashamed of herself, but somehow guilt could not get a grip on her heart.

Was it wrong to seize a moment of pleasure?

Ciara wasn't sure she knew the answer. Far more learned minds than hers had wrestled with the philosophical question.

She wandered out into the corridor, hesitated, and then headed for the library. A book—preferably one on a soporific subject like crop rotation—might help to take the edge off her nerves. Then again, the topic of sowing seeds might not have the intended calming effect.

*What the devil did Hadley do to release his pent-up . . . frustrations?*

The man would not suffer in solitude, she told herself. He had plenty of women willing to satisfy his needs. Or he could visit a fancy brothel.

Neither option offered her much peace of mind. Not that it was any of her business how the earl spent his hours, or his money. He was, of course, free to do as he pleased—

A tiny *snick,* the scrape of metal on metal, suddenly caught her attention.

Ciara stilled her steps and waited.

It came again.

*Had she left a window latch loose in her laboratory?* She wasn't usually so careless.

She was about to move when she heard a scuff of leather. *Footsteps.* Picking up a heavy brass candlestick from the side table, she tiptoed to the door and pressed her ear to the oak.

A shuffling, and then a low snarl as a set of measuring spoons jangled against the counter. "Son of a poxy bitch."

The thought of an intruder pawing over her precious equipment roused her to action.

"Stop, thief!" she cried, throwing open the door and brandishing her weapon.

A chair overturned, its thump punctuated by the sound of breaking glass.

*Damn!*

"Stop!" Rage made her reckless. Without thinking, Ciara charged across the threshold.

From out of the shadows, she saw a shape lunge for the open window. For a brief instant, a burly figure was silhouetted in the mizzled moonlight, then disappeared.

"Milady!" Still in his nightshirt, McCabe stumbled down the stairs, a cudgel in his hand.

"Are you all right?"

"Yes." It was only now that Ciara realized how badly her hands were shaking. She set down the candlestick and drew a deep breath.

"I shall send Jeremiah for the magistrate immediately," said the butler. His brow furrowed as he watched her strike a flint to the oil lamp inside the doorway. "Er, perhaps you ought to wait until help arrives."

"Whoever was here, he is gone now." She stepped over the broken beaker, anxious to check on her microscope. *Thank God, no damage done.* Breathing a sigh of relief, she moved down the counter, carefully checking that all was in order. It was odd that someone would target this house, this room. There was nothing of real value for a common thief to pawn at a flash house.

It wasn't until she turned the corner that she spied the papers strewn on the floor. The neat stack of books on her blotter lay in disarray, and by the look of the open drawers, her desk had been searched.

Staring down at the muddy footprints, Ciara expelled a harried sigh. In the swirl of the storm, the intruder must have mistaken her townhouse for one of her wealthy neighbors. *Bad luck—but it could have been worse.* She set about straightening her work. At least she had scared him off before he could do any real damage.

*"What!"* Lucas let the library door bang shut behind him. Seeing Henry with a lady at this hour of the morning was a bit of a shock. But it was his uncle's announcement rather than his breakfast companion that froze him in his tracks.

"Lady Ariel just arrived a few minutes ago to tell me the news," replied Henry. "Apparently someone broke into Lady Sheffield's townhouse last night, but she managed to scare him off."

"No harm done," added Ariel. "I rushed over to check on her as soon as I received her note, but Ciara is fine and nothing was taken. She was awake at the time and heard a noise in her laboratory, so she went to investigate."

A wave of cold fury washed over him, and then his face was sheened in sweat. The idea of Ciara alone and at the mercy of an intruder made him feel nauseous.

"Her presence must have scared off the thief," finished Ariel.

Lucas tried to calm himself with a deep breath. "That was bloody stupid of her. He might have had a weapon."

Ariel tactfully ignored the oath. "Yes, I wish she would not take such risks. But I suppose in the heat of the moment, she wasn't thinking too clearly. Her scientific instruments and papers are very dear to her."

"Her life ought to be even more precious," he growled. "Damn it, she could have been hurt."

"Pour yourself some brandy, Lucas," said Henry softly.

"I don't need a drink, I need a . . . plan." He smacked a fist to his palm. "One that will keep Lady Sheffield safe from further threats until I can prove who all is behind these dastardly deeds and see that they are brought to justice."

"Why, that is an excellent idea, Lord Hadley," said Ariel. "Er, have you any suggestions?"

Pursing his lips, he began to pace the room. *Damn.* Surely he could come up with something. However, try as he might to concentrate on logistics and legalities, he kept thinking of Ciara.

Her face, her fears. Her eminent intellect, her unrestrained passion. She was so utterly unlike any woman he had ever met before. So utterly worthy of respect.

While he, on the other hand, had so little to be proud of. He found himself regretting his idle, rakehell existence. There wasn't an accomplishment he could think of that might attract her admiration.

"My dear boy, much as I wish that we could look to Buddha for guidance, I fear that the statue can offer no words of wisdom," murmured Henry. "Especially when you have its neck in a stranglehold."

Lucas placed the jade carving back on the bookshelf. "Right. Much as I'd like to crack a few skulls, we must use brains rather than brawn to protect Ciara." He took another turn by the hearth. "The attacks are getting more brazen. Whether real harm is intended, or Sheffield's family is simply trying to intimidate her into acceding to their demands, we cannot take any more chances."

His uncle nodded.

"So, first things first. We must remove her from London."

"Yes, that makes a great deal of sense," mused Henry.

Thus encouraged, he went on. "And we must ensure that she is not alone."

Ariel clutched at her teaspoon. "Most definitely not alone."

"The spot must be safe, secure." Lucas pursed his lips. "I think I've come up with an idea . . ."

~~~~~

"It's been decided—you can't stay in London any longer." Lucas marched into Ciara's study and closed the door. "The risks have grown too great."

Drawing in a sharp breath, she rose from her desk. Her nerves were already frayed, and his tone of command rubbed raw against her lingering fears. She needed someone at whom to lash out.

"You have no right to bark orders at me. Let me remind you that you are not yet my lord and master," she snapped.

"And let me remind you that you are not yet free of suspicion for your late husband's murder." He scowled. "Damnation, don't be a fool. Given the past rumors and current nasty innuendos, the authorities will be loath to take these threats against you seriously. And on your own, you cannot force Sheffield's family to back down."

She refused to meet his gaze.

"I tell you again, the only sensible thing to do is to take refuge in the country. It will be far harder for anyone to make trouble for you at my estate in Derbyshire."

Ciara knew that she was being irrational. Still, she set her jaw. "No."

He muttered something under his breath. She thought she overheard "stubborn" and "arse" mixed in with an oath.

Mention of the word *arse* brought a rush of heat to her cheeks. "Blast it all, Hadley, aren't we taking this charade a little too far? You have no real hold on me, you know."

Seeing a sardonic curl of his lips, she hastened to add, "And don't you *dare* bring up what happened between us yesterday."

For a moment, he looked blank. "Oh. That."

*Yes. That.*

"I agree," he continued in a brusque voice. "It has no bearing on the present situation."

How was it that men could dismiss sex with a casual shrug? Seeing how little it mattered to him did nothing to improve her mood.

"Well, at least we are in accord on *something*."

He looked at her a little strangely before resuming his gimlet glare. "You may be willing to risk your own neck, but what of Peregrine? Or have you forgotten that he may also be a target of attack?"

"That is a low blow, Hadley," she whispered.

"I'll stoop to any measure to get you to see reason." His tone softened. "Damn it, Ciara, I am not trying to hurt you. I am trying to help you."

"I know, I know." She swallowed a sigh, unable to articulate why she was acting like a peagoose. He was right, of course. She couldn't just stand by meekly while someone tried to harm her son. "Let me talk it over with my friends and get their advice," she muttered.

"Lady Ariel already agrees with me," he replied.

Her prickliness was back in a flash. "You went behind my back to conspire with her?"

He bristled at the accusation. "She was visiting Henry. Have you made up yet another new rule, one that says I cannot visit my uncle?"

She colored. "Forgive me. I—I am still a trifle overset."

"With good reason," he conceded, though his tone was a little stiff.

For a few moments, an uncomfortable silence hung between them, broken only by the ticking of the mantel clock.

"The Circle is scheduled to meet in an hour," she said after a sidelong glance at the gilded hands. "I will let you know my final decision later this afternoon."

He took up his hat and gloves from the side table. "Do."

*⌒⌒⌒*

"So." Alessandra added a splash of cream to her tea. "Lord Hadley wants you to seek refuge with him in the country?"

"Yes," answered Ciara, rather hoping that her friend would voice an objection. "I know—it's a bad idea."

"On the contrary," said Alessandra. "I think it an excellent plan."

Ciara felt her face fall. "You do?"

"And I agree wholeheartedly." Ariel pushed her spectacles up to the bridge of her nose. "Indeed, Sir Henry and I think there are a number of points in favor of Lord Hadley's plan."

"I didn't realize that you and the baronet have become such bosom friends as to meet first thing in the morning."

Her friend blushed. "Sir Henry and I have a mutual interest in *Papervira*. We talk about flowers."

"And perhaps the birds and the bees?" quipped Alessandra.

Ariel's face turned a vivid shade of scarlet. "Good

heavens, I am far too old to succumb to girlish fantasies," she stammered.

"Love knows no age," teased Alessandra.

Seeing that the conversation was making Ariel acutely uncomfortable, Ciara quickly changed the subject back to her own dilemma. "Much as I hate to nip this conversation in the bud, I promised to give Hadley my answer later this afternoon. So I must make a decision about what I should do."

"The country," advised Alessandra. "Without delay."

"But talk about gossip!" argued Ciara. "I can't just fly off with the earl to his country manor."

"Actually, Henry thinks it makes more sense to go to his own estate near Eastbourne. It's far closer than Hadley's lands, and the secluded location by the sea makes it a perfect retreat," said Ariel. "As to propriety, we have already agreed that no tongues can wag if he and I go along as chaperones." She thought for a moment. "What about you, Alessandra? I am sure that Ciara would welcome your company, too."

"Me?" Alessandra's usual mask of cool composure slipped ever so slightly. "I—I have a tentative engagement . . . however, I suppose I could change my plans."

"Isabella would be a welcome playmate for Perry," pointed out Ciara.

"Very well." Her friend thought for a moment. "I suppose I can come for a week. After that, I really must return to London and prepare for my trip to Bath. I promised the Antiquities Society that I would spend several weeks there to help oversee the excavation of a newly discovered site of Roman ruins."

"I don't expect to stay sequestered for longer than a

week," muttered Ciara. "I refuse to remain a prisoner to fear indefinitely."

"Until we have a better idea of what is going on, it is better to be safe than sorry," said Ariel.

Somehow, the idea of living under the same roof as Hadley seemed . . . dangerous. But Ciara kept such sentiments to herself.

Alessandra put down her cup. "Hadley is taking charge of discovering who is responsible for the attacks?"

"Yes, and he's enlisted some of his friends to help him. Lord Haddan and Lord Woodbridge are both former military men." Ariel tapped her chin. "Come to think of it, so is Lord James."

"The Prince of Darkness?" Alessandra rolled her eyes.

Ciara was puzzled. "I wasn't aware that you had ever conversed with the gentleman."

"We exchanged a few words when he was leaving your townhouse." Alessandra slowly peeled a grape. "Had I known he spoke Italian, I might have phrased my sentiments a little differently."

"Oh, dear," murmured Ariel. "I hope you were not too rude."

The shrug was eloquent in itself. "What was I to assume, seeing him storm out of Ciara's door at that hour of the day? I do not believe in standing by meek as a mouse if someone is harassing my friend." Alessandra popped the fruit into her mouth. "Perhaps it was not very ladylike of me to call him a goat's penis, but there is something about the man that simply rubs me the wrong way." After a tiny pause she added, "By the by, he knows a number of very naughty words in Roman slang."

"I appreciate your loyalty, Alessa," said Ciara. "But

Lord James is on our side—or at least he is a neutral observer. I have enough enemies as it is."

Ariel reached over to pat her hand. "Don't worry, my dear. Hadley and his friends will take care of everything."

"Would that I felt the same confidence," she murmured. However, as her own private doubts were far too hard to unravel at the moment, she chose not to elaborate. Seeing that Alessandra was about to speak, she quickly collected her notebooks and rose. "Well, seeing as we are settled on a course of action, I had best return home and start packing."

# Chapter Nineteen

$\mathcal{A}$ house party." Jack looked skeptical as he followed Lucas out of White's and into St. James's Street. "You really think that wise?"

"It is not exactly meant to be all fun and games," said Lucas defensively. "Lady Sheffield can't stay alone in her townhouse, not after what happened last night. Her late husband's family is getting more brazen."

"Or more desperate," said Jack.

Lucas quickened his pace and turned down one of the side streets. "The same thought has occurred to me, of course. But it doesn't quite make sense. In many ways, time seems to favor Sheffield's family. They can simply sit back and wait for their lethal lies to poison Ciara."

"Perhaps they fear that once she is remarried, and becomes reacquainted with the *ton*, it will not be so easy to slander her character."

"But . . ." began Lucas.

"They don't know the engagement is a sham," Jack pointed out. They walked on in silence for a few strides before his friend asked, "Is there any reason they would break into her workroom?"

"Not really," he answered. "She is working on deciphering an ancient manuscript, which may have some value for the government. But there is no way Sheffield's family could know about that. Lady Ciara hasn't told a soul, save for her scientific friends, who are very discreet."

"And you?"

"Hell, no." He hesitated. "Well, I might have hinted something of the sort to Ingalls, Greeley, and Farnam, but they promised to keep mum on the subject."

Jack greeted the statement with a snort. "Are you daft? That trio of loose-lipped tattlemongers stay silent? By now, the news has been trumpeted all over Town with God knows how many embellishments."

"It may have been a tactical error," conceded Lucas. "But that's yet another reason I need to get her away from London." He consulted his list of items needed for the trip. "Why don't you come join us for a few days? You've been spending too much time in the gaming hells lately. A breath of fresh air might do you good."

"Spare me the lecture on virtuous living." His friend made a face. "Who else is going?"

"My uncle and Lady Ariel Gracechurch have volunteered to serve as chaperones," replied Lucas. "Oh, and the Marchesa della Giamatti."

"The lady with the mouth," muttered Jack.

Lucas grinned. "Aye, it is quite a lovely one."

"What comes out of it could blister the paint off of a forty-gun frigate."

"Lady Giamatti?" Lucas shook his head in disbelief. "You are exaggerating."

His friend gave a baleful grimace. "Trust me, I am not."

"Oh, come now, she's the very picture of Renaissance refinement."

"Don't forget that the Renaissance included the likes of Machiavelli and the Borgias," shot back Jack.

As they passed Silliman's Sporting Emporium, Lucas was distracted from further comment by the shop window. "Wait here while I run inside. I'll just be a moment."

His friend grumbled, but gave a curt wave. "Try to hurry. I've a date to meet De Quincy at the Wolf's Lair."

The purchases were concluded quickly, but when he came out, Jack was nowhere to be seen. "Damn," swore Lucas under his breath. He, too, was pressed for time. Looking around, he finally spotted his friend in the adjoining arcade, perusing the wares of a print shop. He was about to call out when a lady emerged from the establishment next door.

*Alessandra della Giamatti.* Following right on her heels was a gentleman. They looked to be having a heated exchange of words.

Frowning, Lucas ducked through the archway, but before he could come to the lady's defense, Jack intervened.

"You heard the marchesa, Ghiradelli," said Jack in a tight voice. "She asked you to leave her alone. Whatever the manners are in Milano, here in London a gentleman is expected to honor such a request."

"Mind your own business, *stronzo*," snapped the other man.

Lucas hung back, hidden in the shadows, loath to interrupt. He vaguely recognized the fellow as a flashy young nobleman from the north of Italy, lately arrived in Town. Giovanni Marco Musto della Ghiradelli already had earned quite a reputation for his rakish ways with the ladies. However, Alessandra did not appear to be charmed by his attentions.

After darting the conte a dark look, she turned to Jack, her eyes sparking with ill-concealed ire. "Really, sir. You may save your heroics for some silly English chit who is in need of rescuing. I can handle this on my own."

"*Si, si,* the lady is convinced that she can take care of herself," drawled Ghiradelli. "If I were you, I wouldn't get too close. She has a dangerous temper."

Alessandra's aristocratic face turned red, and then white.

Jack didn't budge. "Sorry, code of honor compels me to see that this macaroni stops harassing you in public."

"*Men.*" She clenched her teeth in exasperation. "You and your silly rules. Both of you may go to the devil."

"The marchesa does not like rules," snapped Ghiradelli.

"But I do," countered Jack. "And Polite Society has strict ones about embarrassing a lady. So take your leave, before my boot quickens your step."

"Careful, *amico,*" said Ghiradelli. "Another word and I will shove those pearly teeth of yours down to the bottom of your bowels."

"I would like to see you try," retorted Jack.

"No," said the conte softly. "You would not."

Lucas had heard enough. He stepped out of the shadows before things could turn ugly.

"Ah, there you are, Jack." He tipped his hat politely to Alessandra. "Good afternoon, Lady Giamatti. A lovely day for a stroll, is it not?" He inclined a nod to the conte. "Lord Ghiradelli? I believe we met at Lady Wilder's soirée."

*"Si."* Ghiradelli narrowed his eyes in annoyance, but he backed off with an exaggerated bow. *"Ciao, signora.* I will leave you to your English admirers. But reminiscing about our homeland brings back such sentimental memories—I look forward to continuing our conversation very soon."

Alessandra's smile remained frozen in place, but Lucas saw a flush of color creep to her cheekbones. She remained silent until the conte disappeared around the corner and then let out her breath in a huff.

"Really, sir," she said in a low voice, fixing Jack with a glare. "Next time you wish to play the knight in shining armor, rattle your sword for someone else."

"You might say *grazie,*" muttered Jack.

She snapped something in Italian.

Lucas guessed it was not a word of thanks.

"Now, if you will excuse me, I have errands to finish," added the marchesa. "As you see, my maid is waiting for me next door, so I have no need of an escort."

"What was that all about?" he murmured as Alessandra stalked off.

"Don't ask me," growled Jack. "Talk about a haughty, hellfire female. I swear, she is worse than a bear with a thorn in his—or her—arse."

"A lovely arse, though," observed Lucas.

"God help any man who tries to pursue it." His friend's expression darkened as he watched the silky sway of her hips. "It's not worth the aggravation."

"Speaking of aggravation, Jack." Lucas was once again serious. "I'm leaving at first light to take Lady Sheffield and the others to the country. So I need your help tracking down another clue on the ruffian who rode roughshod over me in the park . . ."

Ciara listened to the faint echo of the ocean washing up against the rocky cliffs. There was a certain comforting rhythm to the sound of the sea. *Ebb and flow.* An elemental reminder that life was constantly in motion.

Her hands gripped the window latch. If only her own life were not caught in such dangerous crosscurrents.

Here, at least, there seemed to be an air of tranquility. Cracking the casement, she lifted her cheeks to the soft caress of the salty breeze. From what she had seen so far, Sir Henry's estate was indeed a sanctuary of splendid solitude. *A safe harbor from the threatening storm.* Dusk deepened the ridge behind the manor house to a haze of purpled shadows. Crickets chirped, and off in the distance a lone owl hooted.

All things considered, the trip from London had gone quite smoothly. Sir Henry had a special traveling coach, designed to accommodate his infirmity, and with the earl's constant cosseting at every stop along the way, Ciara did not doubt that the elderly baron had passed the hours in comfort. As for her own party, between Peregrine's lively chatter and Ariel's calming company, the journey had been a pleasant one.

Once they had turned off the main road near the coast, it quickly became clear that there were few inhabitants in the area. Indeed, over the last few miles of the journey, she hadn't seen another dwelling, and the entrance to the manor's winding drive was guarded by a large stone gatehouse.

Henry had made a point of informing her that it was inhabited by a gamekeeper and his family of four sturdy sons.

It was hard to imagine that Sheffield's family would dare to try and make trouble for her here. They would watch and wait.

But Ciara was tired of cowering, of waiting for their next move. It was time to confront their slanderous lies. *The question was how.*

Despite the rigors of the road, Ciara was too restless for sleep. A simple supper had been served on their arrival, though Henry and Ariel had chosen to take refreshment in their own rooms and retire for the night. The meal had passed pleasantly enough, despite having only Hadley and her son for company. There was still a frisson of tension between her and the earl, but Peregrine's peppering of questions about country life had kept the mood light. Alessandra and Isabella were due to arrive the day after the morrow, which would provide a welcome distraction from his company.

The more, the merrier, she thought wryly.

A shout from the lawns below drew her gaze. Streaks of pink and gold light still lingered in the sky, casting a mellow glow over her cavorting son. A large, hairy hound was chasing after a stick, much to Peregrine's delight. Hadley was laughing, too, his dark hair curling in boyish disarray around his collar as he wiped his hands on his trousers.

No doubt his valet would have a fit of apoplexy, seeing the sticky streak of mud and dog saliva now marring the superfine wool.

Looking up at that moment, he waved to her.

Ciara turned away quickly from the mullioned glass, pretending she hadn't seen the gesture. But much as she wished to be angry with him, she found it hard to remain resentful over the manner in which he had taken charge of her affairs.

*Manhandled.* A part of her chafed at his tactics, for she had been bullied enough in her life. And yet, a part of her was weak enough to welcome his assuming control. Ciara watched as the reflection of the setting sun cast quicksilver patterns of light and dark across her bed. Her own emotions were equally ill-defined. The edges blurred, the shapes shifted in the blink of an eye.

"Mama!"

Sighing, Ciara returned to the window.

"Isn't Mephisto magnificent?" Peregrine wrestled free of the dog's slobbering tongue. "Hadley says he has sired a litter of puppies and that I may have one—that is, if you agree."

"We shall see," she called. "But for now, you must come up and finish your bathing in your bedchamber."

"But Mama! I'm not tired."

"Your mama is right." Lucas took hold of the animal's collar. "It's nearly dark, and we've all had a long day."

"But—"

"Perry."

The single word of warning from Lucas silenced any further protest. "Yes, sir."

A cuff to his backside sent her son scampering for the terrace doors.

"Sorry." Lucas looked up with an apologetic shrug. "I did not actually make any promises, I merely said perhaps."

"Boys that age do not always grasp the nuances of language," she replied carefully.

"Ah." He flung the stick into the murky twilight and watched as the dog bounded off in pursuit. "Nor, would it seem, do grown men. Somehow, despite my best intentions, I have offended you." His tone was equally reserved. "Allow me to apologize again."

"I don't wish for you to think me ungrateful, sir." Yet even to her own ears, she sounded distant. Detached. "However, my life is very . . . complicated at the moment," she continued. "Please don't make it any more difficult."

"Oh, I am a very simple fellow," he answered with a shade of cynicism. "I tend to concentrate on the basics, madam. It makes things easier all around." Whistling for the dog, he strolled off into the lengthening shadows.

She sighed. *Was he being deliberately obtuse?*

However, the arrival of her son left her little time for stewing. Masking her misgivings, Ciara listened with a smile to his chattering about the stables and the kennels. Whatever her own feelings, she must not cast a cloud over Peregrine's enjoyment of their stay in the country.

It had taken some persuading for her to agree that Peregrine could occupy the earl's old childhood rooms, high in the manor's central tower. She and Ariel were quartered in the east wing, while the baronet and his nephew shared the west wing. But Hadley had assured her that Perry was perfectly safe. The main staircase was the only way up and down, and the entrance hall would be guarded by a footman throughout the night. As an added precaution, he had assigned a maid to sleep in the adjoining schoolroom.

Seeing as her son was taking the country sojourn as a grand adventure, Ciara hadn't had the heart to say no.

"Hadley says when his groom arrives with his horses, he will teach me and Isa how to do a somersault in the saddle," said Peregrine with a sleepy smile. "Just like the acrobats at Astley's."

"How nice." She helped him on with his nightshirt. "Do you wish for me to stay and read you a story for a bit?"

He rolled his eyes. "Have you seen the troop of lead soldiers atop the bookcases? Hadley says I may play with them whenever I wish to. There's a regiment of mounted Hussars and a battery of brass artillery."

"Well, I see that a book can't hold a candle to such excitement." Ciara pressed a kiss to his forehead. "You may have half an hour to command your army, and then Alice has orders to extinguish your lights."

Peregrine scrunched his face.

"Good night, lambkin. Sweet dreams."

"Good night, Mama."

Ciara shut the door before expelling a sigh. In addition to polishing their skills at cricket, Hadley had volunteered to teach her son and Isabella how to ride? The man really was marvelous with children. He ought to set up a nursery of his own . . .

The thought of dark-haired little imps with his devilish smile sent a stab of longing through her core.

*No, don't think of Hadley's babies.* Her insides clenched. *Or what it would take to make them.*

Past regrets had no place in the present or the future. She had long ago accepted the fact that Peregrine would be her only child.

Ciara hurried down the last few steps and turned to latch the door. Her only thought now was to keep him safe, whatever the cost.

The dog gave a *whoof* and then a whine.

"Sorry." Lucas stepped over the stick at his feet. "I know it's fun to cavort all night long, but it's time to return to the kennel."

The golden eyes fixed him with a baleful stare.

"Don't look at me that way. I am probably feeling far more frustrated than you are."

Mephisto pricked up his ears and wagged his tail, clearly hoping the words were a signal that the game was not over.

"Come along." Crossing the front lawn, Lucas headed for the stables. "You, at least, can gnaw on a bone for distraction."

After locking the pen and checking that the barn doors were bolted shut, he made a last inspection of the estate drive before doubling back for the manor house. The familiar scent of pine, fresh-cut grass, and sea salt wafted through the breeze, stirring up memories of his childhood. Despite the isolation, he had enjoyed his visits here. There was much for a small boy to explore. He must remember to show Peregrine the badger's burrow, and the smuggler's cave beneath the sea cliffs.

He realized with a jolt just how fond he had become of the lad. As for the lady herself . . .

Lucas stopped and looked up at the sky. The twilight clouds had blown over, allowing a clear view of the myriad stars and a full moon. No wonder he felt like howling at its shimmering, silvery circle of light. There was, he knew, a scientific explanation for its powerful effect on the natural world. Spin, rotation, gravity—perhaps that was what had his emotions ebbing and flowing like the ocean tides.

He hadn't meant to take Ciara seriously. For Mad, Bad Had-ley, life was best lived for naught but rakish pleasures. Yet somehow he had been caught in a strange current, a vortex that pulled him far from familiar waters. He had come to care deeply about her and her son.

*Was he a fool to imagine there could be any future between a scholar and a scoundrel?* She had suffered enough selfish men in her life. He didn't want to cause her pain. Already she was angry with him for ordering her out of London. His concern had been interpreted as bullying. *So much for speaking the same language.* He might as well have been mumbling in Mandarin when he tried to explain himself.

There were unspoken tensions, as well. Lucas was well aware that women did not consider sexual dalliances quite as dispassionately as men. She had implied that he had meant to use their afternoon interlude as a means of manipulating her. His jaw hardened. Hell, nothing could be further from the truth, but she had refused to listen.

A part of him said he should steer clear of any emotional involvement with Ciara.

And a part of him wanted to buck the tide of conventional wisdom and risk venturing into uncharted waters.

*Throw caution to the wind.* That certainly sounded like Mad, Bad Had-ley speaking.

Turning his gaze seaward, Lucas listened for a moment to the distant rumble of the surf washing up against the cliffs.

Or dare he hope that the better half of his nature was finally finding its voice?

He stood there a little longer, undecided on whether to seek his bed or make one more round of the grounds. Walking finally won out over tossing and turning between the sheets. Either way, he wasn't likely to get much sleep.

# Chapter Twenty

Ciara sat up suddenly in bed, roused from a fitful sleep by . . .

*By God knows what,* she admitted. Perhaps Sir Henry's country home was plagued by a ghost. Some specter seemed intent on haunting her dreams.

Looking around, she saw a twinkling of light dance across the ancient oak dresser. It was coming in through the leaded windows, and as she watched, a gust rattled the glass and the draperies twitched.

She threw off the covers, feeling a curl of apprehension inside her chest. It was just her nerves stretched taut, she chided herself. As Hadley had said, she must learn to relax. Cracking the casement, Ciara inhaled deeply, letting the calming scent of cedar and salt fill her lungs. It was silly to imagine that trouble was stalking close by. A peek outside showed only the leafy silhouettes of the garden plantings and the copse of oaks at the far end of the lawns . . .

Was there a movement stirring the shadows?

Ignoring her wrapper, Ciara unlatched the side door and stepped out to the terrace.

The rough slate tiles were cold against her bare feet. Another survey of the surroundings showed no cause for alarm. Feeling a little foolish, she was about to turn around when Lucas emerged from behind the hedge.

She held her breath as he crossed the stones. "Is something amiss?" she asked softly.

He shook his head, the dark fringe of his lashes shadowing his eyes. "Just making the rounds to check that all is in order. I've taken the precaution of having several men with dogs patrol the property. Have no fear, Lady Sheffield, I may be a bumbling bully, but I won't allow any harm to come to you or your son."

Her name sounded so formal.

She shivered, suddenly aware there was nothing between her and the night air but a thin scrim of silk.

"You are cold." Lucas moved to shield her from the night breeze. "Go back inside."

She meant to move, but the play of moonlight on his hair was like quicksilver, dancing and darting over the dark, curling strands.

"Ciara."

*Oh, no—God help her if he touched her body.*

The devil must have sensed her weakness. Her wanting.

His arms came around her. "You look breathtakingly beautiful with your golden hair spilling over your shoulders." A breeze spun the night mists in a soft, shimmering circle around their bodies. "Like some mystical, magical sea sprite in a fairy tale."

"This is no storybook fantasy," she replied, feeling the thud of his heart through his coat. "This is real life—"

"Aye, all too real. We are flesh-and-blood people,

Ciara gasped as he nipped at her flesh.

"Mmmm, just wait until I get to your toes, sweetheart. But that may take a while."

"Oh, Lucas . . ." A laugh quivered on her lips.

"Yes, that's it. Stop thinking." He feathered delicate kisses over the hollow of her throat. Teasing, tingling, tantalizing sensations that left her a little light-headed. "You have a magnificent brain to go along with your glorious body, but it sometimes gets in the way of the other parts."

His deft humor loosened the last of her inhibitions. Oh, how she wanted to give herself completely to him. With a hitch of her hips she arched against his thighs. "I will make every effort to leave intellect aside."

A feral growl rumbled in answer. *Dark. Rough. Masculine.* The sound reverberated somewhere deep in her core.

"You are doing a damn good job of it," he said.

She splayed her hands on his chest, savoring every nuanced contour of his shape. Men were for the most part a mystery. In wonder, she traced the trail of dark hair down to the top of his breeches.

Lucas held his breath for an instant and then let it out in a husky laugh. "We'll get there in a moment, sweetheart. But first, let me see you in all your splendor." He parted her bodice, revealing one breast, then the other.

She went very still.

"Oh, Ciara. You would tempt a saint to renounce his vows. And God knows I am no saint." He lowered his head and the warm wetness of his mouth covered her nipple.

Ciara gasped.

And then he drew it into him with a slow suckling

sound. His teeth nipped at its bud, the pressure sending a sharp and yet sweet jolt of heat through her. A moan caught in her throat as his tongue—his oh-so-clever tongue—lapped and laved the peaked flesh to a point of unquenchable flame.

She swayed, feeling her knees melt. No wonder rakes were considered so devilishly dangerous. One smoldering look, one hellfire kiss, and all heed of civilized rules went up in smoke.

"Lift your arms, sweetheart," coaxed Lucas, "I want to take off your night rail."

"Yes," she said thickly. "Yes."

The fabric skimmed up over her head and floated to the floor. She felt wickedly wanton standing there. Never had the full length of her body been exposed to a man's eye.

"Sweet Jesus." He stepped back, his gaze slowly sliding from her face to the triangle of red-gold curls between her legs. Through the scrim of his lashes, she saw a spark of molten blue.

Heat spread through her as Lucas tugged off his boots with a feral growl. His erection was pressing against the front of his breeches. Mesmerized, she watched his fingers wrench the fastenings free.

Half turning, he shucked off the buckskins, and then his drawers. Limned in the light of the moon, his phallus thrust forward from a tangle of midnight curls and the heavy sac of his sex.

A primitive sound stirred in her throat. Instinctively, Ciara reached out to touch him.

His response was immediate. She felt him throb and swell against her palm. Emboldened, she circled her fingers and ran a light caress down his length. Lucas groaned aloud as her thumb touched the ridge of his crest. What a fascinating new discovery—the sheathing of a man's steel was soft as fire-kissed velvet.

"Dear God," he groaned through gritted teeth.

Roused from her rapture, Ciara stilled. "Am I doing it wrong?"

"No. Exquisitely right."

She dropped her gaze, eager for a closer study of his maleness. Her marital encounters had all been quick, jerky fumblings under the cover. *Push and shove.* The experience had been more painful than pleasurable. She couldn't remember ever seeing Sheffield's shaft. Not that she had ever desired to view him naked.

But Lucas . . . Lucas was a sight to behold.

Ciara loosened her hold, letting the weight of his cock slip free. The head twitched up, erect and proud. In the flickering candlelight, the ruddy flesh appeared aflame. She grasped him again, ever so gently, and let her fingers slide down to the thatch of dark curls at the base of his belly. They sprang back at her tentative touch. Twining deeper, she marveled at the contrast in male textures—smooth flesh, taut muscle, coarse hair.

She could have spent hours exploring him, but Lucas shifted and angled her chin up.

"Look at me, Ciara. I want to see your eyes, sweetheart."

Her lashes lifted.

"Lud, you are a passionate creature."

"I'm not," she protested. On the contrary, she had always been ruled by reason. *So how to explain this?*

"Oh, yes. You are." His eyes simmered with a sensuous gleam. "I see it in your work, your dedication, your delight in discovery. You must trust in my greater knowledge of this subject." Lucas stroked her spine. "Do you, Ciara? Do you trust me?" he crooned.

Against all reason, she *did* trust him. With all her heart.

"Yes," she whispered. *Yes.*

Suddenly she was floating on air, her hair falling in shimmering waves over his back. A twisting spin, and she dropped onto the bed, her bare bum sinking into the tangle of silky sheets.

Lucas was laughing softly, and so was she. In her wildest dreams, she had never imagined that sex could be . . . fun.

*Wickedly so.*

He was on his knees, positioning himself at her feet. His hand took hold of her ankles and urged them apart. "I'm aching to taste you, to tantalize you, Ciara. Will you let me do that?"

In answer, she hitched her legs wider. Oh, how she wanted to experience such intimate pleasures with him.

He lowered his head, and all at once his open mouth was sliding along the inside of her thigh. The sensation was indescribably delicious—the heat of his lips on her skin, the coolness of the night air on the trail of wetness. She flinched a little shyly as he reached the notch of her curls. But her hesitation quickly yielded to the gentle probing of his tongue.

*The Grotto of Venus.* No wonder its mention had sparked a chorus of feminine sighs on that fateful afternoon in the park.

Parting her folds, Lucas opened her more fully to his lush kisses. Ciara whimpered, feeling her body respond with a clench. He licked again, and again. Some force—some fire—was burning inside her. Surely it must soon find release, else singe her to a crisp. Sensing her growing need, Lucas drew her pearl between his teeth.

A tiny nip ignited a heated cry, and an instant later, she convulsed in a shower of white-hot sparks.

As she lay limp, waiting for the waves of pleasure to subside, she managed a soft whisper. "I . . . I am . . . bereft of words."

His lips feathered across her belly. "Your body is exquisite in its eloquence, sweetheart." Then moving with the lithe grace of a panther, he was atop her, his legs straddling her thighs.

Oh, she knew—*she knew*—that Lucas had done this countless times with countless women, but somehow he made her feel special. As if the only thing that mattered at this very moment were the two of them joining as one.

It was just a length of engorged flesh, she told herself. Nothing more, nothing less. Friction, heat—the results of the experiment were really no mystery.

He parted her knees, opening her wide to his gaze. She closed her eyes, feeling oh-so-wicked, oh-so-wanton.

"Beautiful." Lucas sounded a little breathless as he leaned low and spread his hands across her middle. They inched up in a leisurely glide, caressing her ribs and then cupping her breasts. "So beautiful in every way." The warm length of his cock tickled against her belly.

*Beautiful.* He made her feel it was so.

"Spread your legs wider," he said in a husky whisper. His mouth replaced one of his hands, and he licked a slow, sensual circle around her peak.

Twisting, trembling against the weight of his legs, Ciara arched up into his embrace.

And then his fingers found her feminine slit and stroked through her slickened folds. "Your quim is ripe again," he said with rough satisfaction. "And ready for me."

*Now. Now.* Her breathing had become so feverish that she couldn't tell whether she had actually spoken aloud.

A laugh, low and lush, feathered against her flesh. "We mustn't rush, sweetheart." He delved deeper, finding her hidden pearl. "A scientist should never hurry the steps of an experiment, is that not right?"

She cried out in answer, no longer capable of coherent speech. The friction of his callused thumb was driving her a little wild with want. Her arms went around him, needing the feel of him hard against her. *Inside her.* The urgency was mounting. *Closer, closer.* Ciara pulled him down, dimly aware that her nails were scoring a trail across his shoulders.

Lucas rocked back with a grunt. His face glistened with exertion, and the dark tangle of hair shadowed his eyes. The long, curling strands gleamed like polished ebony in the winking light. Ciara felt a whisper of air as he parted her flesh. The momentary coolness was replaced by throbbing heat as he positioned himself at her opening.

She nearly surrendered her sanity.

His cock nudged in a fraction. Then withdrew.

Ciara squirmed within the rock-hard muscles of his thighs, moaning a wordless complaint. *So wrong. So right.* It went against all reason, she knew, but oh, she wanted him. Madly. Badly.

Lucas entered her again, this time a little deeper, before sliding out of her passage. The head of his cock rested against her slickness, pulsing with pent-up heat.

The sensation was unbearably wonderful.

Grasping his buttocks so he couldn't retreat, she arched up her hips to force him deeper.

For an instant, Ciara saw something akin to her own wonder reflected in his gaze. She must be mistaken, of course. A quirk of the stars and shadows. Coupling was such a commonplace experience for him. But perhaps that flash of baring his soul was what made him such a sought-after bedmate. He made a woman feel that she was the light of his life.

Such skillful lovemaking must take a good deal of practice . . . No, she would *not* think of that. Or anything, save the magic of the moment.

❧

*Oh, God.* Lucas gritted his teeth, praying for self-control. He must keep himself in check and go slowly. This was the first time for Ciara, and he meant for it to be special. Oh, to be sure, she had had a man inside her before. A quick ploughing of her flesh. A mere filling of her womb with seed. But he suspected she had never been roused to feel any joy in it.

For far too long, Ciara had been forced to keep her true self—her womanly passion, her scholarly brilliance—bottled up. She had been told to feel ashamed of her glorious body, her glorious mind.

*The Wicked Witch of Pont Street.*

Most men were afraid of a woman with brains. While he found her intellect and accomplishments inspiring. Exciting. Enchanting. Amazing. She made him wish to be a better man.

But not just now. Weak, selfish sybarite that he was, he could not pull back. His body was afire with crude, carnal lust. He thrust into her, feeling her liquid heat close around him. "You bedazzle me. Beguile me." *Bewitch me.*

She arched up to meet him, her eyes reflecting the luminous light of the stars. Their bodies rose and fell in a sinuous rhythm. Faster and faster, until her heartbeat was a wild drumming in his ears. *Or was it his own?*

Impossible to tell.

The pulsing beat drove him on. A last thrust and he felt her hips lift and a surging shudder dissolve into a liquid cry.

His own shout of savage satisfaction echoed her climax. She was *his* now—all his.

As she convulsed around him, Lucas pulled out just in the nick of time, his essence spattering over her cream-white belly.

"Sweetheart." Bracing himself on hands and knees, he covered her throat with kisses until her gasps subsided.

*Damn.* That had been a close call. Neither of them had given any heed to protection, and begetting a child on her would only add to her troubles. However, an odd pang of longing twisted inside him as he leaned back and gently wiped his seed from her skin with a corner of the sheet.

She now lay perfectly still, her lashes lowered, her hair fanned out on the pillows like a shimmering halo of gold. Strangely enough, he felt a little awkward about breaking the silence. Words somehow seemed inadequate for anything he might wish to say. Instead, he simply lowered himself down beside her, content just to savor the little details about her—the scent of her sex, the softness of her spent body, the gentle rhythm of her breathing.

After a moment, Lucas cuddled closer and curled a hand possessively over her hip, aware of an utterly unfamiliar sensation spreading through his limbs. It wasn't the purely physical thrum of sated pleasure. This was more . . . cerebral. *Contentment?* No, something far more profound. Perhaps *peace* was a better description. The aimless urge that drove him to seek ever-more desperate thrills seemed to have stilled within him.

Ciara stirred and opened her eyes halfway. "Mmmm." Her voice was slightly slurred, a sleepy, smoky, sexy sound. She blinked, trying to sharpen her gaze. "Luuu-cas." He loved the way she said it, drawing it out as if it were a length of melting toffee. "This was special—"

Smiling, he hushed her with a finger to the lips. "Yes, it was."

Ciara looked sweetly flustered, so unlike her usual self. "Th-that was not precisely what I meant." She shifted with a lazy wriggle, propping herself up on one elbow.

As Lucas watched the sheet slide over the curve of her breast, he felt his cock twitch. *Damn.* He did not want to overwhelm her with his carnal lust, but another fraction of an inch and he would be hard-pressed to keep from rolling her back and having her again.

"I meant, the circumstances were special." She bit her lip. "We can't . . . that is, we mustn't—"

"Shush." He brushed his lips to hers and tucked the sheet around her. "Sleep now, sweetheart. We'll try to make some sense of it all later."

# Chapter Twenty-one

*T*he Day After.

Ciara made a wry face. Oh, dear, that sounded so gothic. She wasn't some peagoose heroine in a novel. She was a rational scientist, trained to be disciplined and detached.

*So why were her thoughts swirling like puffs of pollen in the breeze?*

The mists had blown off, leaving the morning cool and cloudless as she approached the climb to the cliffs. Hiking her skirts, Ciara rounded the tangle of brambles and scrambled over the outcropping of granite. She had risen early and decided to take a long walk, rather than appear in the breakfast room. At some point she would have to face Lucas in the light of day, but she would rather not do it over kippers and toast—or the scientific patter of Ariel and Sir Henry.

The thought of a discussion on reproductive details, even if they were about flowers, made her stomach slightly queasy.

Winding through a last steep stretch of rock, the footpath finally brought her to the crest of the cliff. In the slanting sunlight, the blue of the ocean was nearly blinding in its brilliance, the aquamarine hue dotted with flecks of foamy whitecaps for as far as the eye could see. High overhead, gulls wheeled on the gusting winds, the echo of their raucous cries nearly drowned by the pounding of the surf below.

For an instant, she envied their freedom to fly away, to wherever their wings and their whimsy might take them. How exhilarating it would be to sail through the heavens without a care in the world.

*Don't be a bird-witted fool,* she scolded herself. Life was not so simple, even for a *Larus argentatus.* Every species on earth had predators lurking, ready to pounce at the tiniest slip in vigilance.

She, at least, had a brain to counter any threats.

Though it could be argued that hers was not in full working order at the present time.

*How else to explain the fact that she had made mad, passionate love to Mad, Bad Had-ley?*

Taking a seat on a sun-warmed slab of stone, Ciara shaded her eyes and stared out to sea. Had she cast off all common sense, leaving herself adrift in shoaling waters? The earl could not be counted on as an anchor—only look at how he had floated through life, content to bob along in whatever current caught his fancy.

She bit her lip and winced, the flesh still tender from the torrid force of his kisses. But at the moment, it was not Lucas who had to answer for his actions. She could have—should have—said no.

"No!" she cried, startling a plover from his roost on the rocks.

*No.* She would *not* let guilt drag her down to the depths of self-loathing. There was an old English adage . . . *if you make your bed, you must be prepared to sleep in it.*

That the sinfully sexy Earl of Hadley happened to be in it with her last night added an awkward twist to the sheets. One thing was certain, she couldn't make a habit of it. For any number of compelling reasons.

But no matter all the rationales against the relationship, she could not bring herself to regret the night. Lucas was not perfect—what man or woman was? But neither was he so wicked or wanton as he claimed to be. He had played the role of devil-may-care rake for so long that by now it was like a second skin. And yet beneath the careless carousing and shocking stunts was a compassionate, caring man. He was kind, he was funny, he was loyal, he was . . . lovable despite all his faults.

*Love?*

Oh, surely not. Her brain, however impaired, knew better than to let her fall in love with Mad, Bad Had-ley.

The only trouble was that the rest of her body was refusing to listen to the warnings.

Salt stung her mouth as Ciara sighed and rose. The mysteries of the heart defied all human logic. Better to concentrate her efforts on the ancient manuscript, whose arcane code was based on reason. Perhaps with the help of her friends, she could finally coax the secret from the last section of coding. Already, she had an idea about the final result. If she was right . . .

Lost in scientific thought, she began making her way back to the manor house. From what she had pieced together so far, she had a feeling that there was an important connection between the *Penicillium notatum* mold and—

"*Ciao, bella!*"

As Ciara crossed through the orchard, Alessandra's call roused her from her scholarly musings.

"I finished my business in Bournemouth a day early, so decided to come on ahead of schedule," continued her friend. "Ariel said you had gone for a walk in the hills, so I thought I would come meet you."

"Oh, Lord, I am *so* glad you are here."

Alessandra took her arm and fixed her with a searching look. "Has something else happened?"

"N-no. Yes." She caught her breath. "No."

Alessandra stared a fraction longer before shaking her head. "*Santa cielo,* I hope you know what you are doing."

Ciara colored under her friend's scrutiny. "Is it so very obvious?"

"Only because I recognize the subtle little changes," came the cryptic reply. "There are certain things a woman cannot hide." Her friend flicked out a finger. "And some that you can. Pull your collar a touch higher, *bella.* You've a love bite on your neck."

Blushing, Ciara fumbled with the soft merino wool.

"Not that I blame you in the least," added Alessandra. "He's a *very* attractive man."

"Still, it wasn't very smart of me," said Ciara softly.

"*Tesoro,* the heart is a perverse little organ with a mind of its own. Unlike the brain, it refuses to be ruled by logic or reason."

"So I have discovered." Ciara made a wry face. "Lud, as if I don't have enough trouble in my life right now without *this*."

"Or *that*," quipped her friend. "Tell me—"

"I will not," muttered Ciara.

"Tell me, does Ariel know?"

"No! And please don't tell her."

"Don't worry, *bella*." Alessandra regarded her rings for a long moment. "I can keep a secret."

Ciara heaved a ragged sigh. "Thank you."

They turned onto a path through the gardens, and for some moments, the only sounds between them were the soft crunch of gravel.

"I shall not say another word on the subject," murmured Alessandra as they rounded a trellis of climbing roses. "But if you feel in need of any advice, you have only to ask."

"Actually, I do have some pressing questions." Her mouth quirked. "But they concern Sir Henry's manuscript. I think I am coming close to the answer, but I would like your opinion, and that of Ariel, about my idea. It may sound crazy, but . . ."

⁓

Lucas watched the two ladies cross the lawn, heads bent together in deep conversation. He couldn't help but wonder what had them so engrossed. Some arcane archaeological discovery? The marchesa was, after all, a noted expert in the field.

Alessandra's sudden laugh rose above the twittering of the songbirds, then died away just as quickly.

*Hell.* He hoped they were discussing an ancient artifact and not some other subject. *Did ladies have the same code of honor as gentlemen about discussing the details of—*

"*HADLEY!*" Two juvenile voices chorused as one.

He started, a fraction too late. The cricket ball smacked

him square in the chest, knocking the wind out of him. With an echoing thud, his rump hit the ground.

Both Peregrine and Isabella came running.

"Are you all right, sir?" asked the boy, skidding to a stop.

"We called out," said Isabella. "Several times."

"My fault entirely," wheezed Lucas. "I must have been woolgathering."

"At least she didn't break your skull," pointed out Peregrine with a snigger.

Isabella scrunched her mouth in indignation. "I'll have you know that's *exactly* where I was aiming!" She looked at Hadley, her expression brightening quite a bit. "It worked, sir! I am learning to put a really wicked spin on the ball, just like you showed me. And now my throws are right on target."

"A splendid pitch, Isa," he assured her. "I'll wager that no wicket can stand up to your prowess."

The little girl beamed.

Peregrine waggled his bat. "She'll have to get the ball by me first."

"Ha!" She gave a toss of her ebony curls. "You still have a funny hitch to your swing."

"Let's have a look," said Lucas before any further words could be exchanged.

He rose rather gingerly and picked up the ball. *So much for intimate adult musings.* He made a wry face. It was probably all for the best that he kept himself occupied with other activities. Thinking of Ciara, stretched out in delightful dishabille among the rumpled sheets, was obviously dangerous . . .

"Hadley?" Peregrine gave him a fishy stare.

"Er, right." Lucas made a show of inspecting the seams of the ball. "Just checking that Isa didn't scorch the leather with her throw."

The little girl giggled.

"Now, Perry, take your place and let's see your form. Remember—elbows in, wrists cocked."

Their shouts and laughs were soon punctuated by a deliriously happy bark as Mephisto bolted from the kennels to join in play. The dog was delighted to fetch the batted balls, and though it took some wrestling to retrieve the chewed leather, his antics kept Peregrine and Isabella much amused. By the time they all traipsed into the kitchen for lemonade and jam tarts, the two children had finally been run ragged and agreed that the game was done for the day.

Lucas flexed his shoulders. Lud, he must be getting old—he had forgotten just how much stamina it took to keep up with two active eight-year-olds.

"Master Lucas." The elderly cook waggled a wooden spoon, just as she had when he was a boy. "How many times have I told you not to track your dirt into my kitchens."

"I'm afraid I've lost count," answered Lucas, cramming a bite of warm shortbread into his mouth. "I never was any good at mathematics."

The children chortled. Mephisto gave a low *whoof*.

"Incorrigible, as always," she scolded, though her mouth tweaked up at the corners. "Sir Henry wishes to see you in his study." The spoon stirred again. "And mind that you wipe your boots and tuck in your shirt."

"Yes, ma'am." He winked at the children before dusting his hands and heading for the corridor.

"Ah, there you are, my boy." Henry looked up with a smile from a sheaf of notes.

There must be some special tonic in the sea breeze, thought Lucas, for his uncle was suddenly looking years younger.

"Did you sleep well?"

*Damn.* Lucas shuffled his feet, hoping he wasn't blushing. "Quite. And you?"

"Extremely well. What a splendid idea it was to come here. I know that the country is probably boring for you, but your sacrifice of pleasure is much appreciated. I think it will prove an excellent respite for the others, too." The papers crackled. "Look! Already Lady Ciara has solved the final mystery!"

Lucas felt a surge of excitement for her, mixed with a touch of pride in her accomplishment.

However, he masked his feelings by clasping his hands behind his back with a careless shrug. "Is it as important as you all believed it to be?"

"Indeed it is." Henry adjusted his spectacles. "Let me explain." He cleared his throat. "The ancient Greeks established regular trade routes to India, bringing back exotic spices to the West. The merchant ships also carried fresh foodstuffs from the ports of call for the long voyage home. Well, by some fortuitous chance, a passenger interested in medicine noticed that a sailor with an infected wound made a miraculous recovery after eating a moldy Malabar melon."

"Mold." Lucas made a wry face.

"Science is all about the unexpected," said Henry with a smile. "The great Greek man of medicine, Hippocrates, did a number of empirical studies, which verified the result. Now that Lady Ciara has deciphered the original text, she plans to do some experiments of her own. We've sent one of the servants to town for cassava melons.

Apparently she needs to cultivate a certain mold known as *Penicillium notatum.* She will, of course, have to do some experimenting with how to distill its essence. But I've no doubt that she will come up with a formula that works. Just imagine—a miracle drug!"

"Amazing."

"Quite," replied Henry. "It is all so very exciting to be a part of such a momentous discovery. She is running some tests on moldy mushrooms right now, just to refine her procedures for handling the organisms."

Lucas looked up from the intricate patterns of the Oriental carpet. "She and her friends figured all this out on their own?" He crooked a rueful smile. "Clearly the Circle of Sin can run rings around the male intellect—save for yours, of course."

"Oh, no. My brain does not turn nearly as quickly." Henry chuckled. "Perhaps the current government ministers should cede their places to the ladies. The war would likely be over in a fortnight."

"I think they could solve any problem they put their minds to."

"Speaking of complex conundrums, my boy . . ." The whisper of papers fluttered against the leather desk blotter. "Might I ask if you have given serious thought to your situation with Lady Ciara?"

Lucas carefully avoided his uncle's eye. "I take it you mean the sham engagement?"

"Yes."

He chose his words carefully. "We haven't discussed it of late."

"Ah." There was a long silence, and Lucas assumed that Henry, with his usual tact, had decided to drop the subject.

However, before he could excuse himself, a desk drawer opened, then shut with a soft *snick*. "Have I ever shown you this?"

Lucas moved in closer to the desk as Henry opened a tiny leather case. "I bought this a long, long time ago." The ring, a strikingly simple design of flawless diamonds and sapphires set in burnished gold—seemed to sparkle with its own inner life. "And then I locked it away and forgot about it, leaving it to gather dust for all of these years."

Lucas shifted his gaze.

"Am I a senile old fool to think of asking Ariel for her hand?" Henry forced a rueful laugh. "It's a little late in life for romance, is it not?"

Through the mullioned glass, Lucas watched the play of sunlight on the freshly mown lawn. "You are asking my opinion on matters of the heart?"

"Yes, my boy. I value your judgment."

"I would think that it is never too late for love."

Henry's smile was a little tentative. "You wouldn't mind? Or feel abandoned?"

Lucas chuckled. "Good God, you have spent too much of your life worrying about me, Henry. I'm a grown man, though I might not act like it very often." Leaning over his uncle's chair, he pressed a quick kiss to his brow. "I wish you happiness," he murmured.

Henry turned red. "She hasn't said yes."

"Well, she hasn't said no," he replied. "The only way to know for sure is to ask. And I suggest you do it soon. *Carpe diem,* remember?"

"Right. I'm not getting any younger," quipped his uncle. "I shall try to screw up my courage. Tomorrow, maybe."

"Excellent. I'll help create a distraction, so that the two of you have the afternoon alone." He thought for a moment. "I'll take Lady Ciara bird-watching, and suggest that the marchesa ride over to see Pevensey Castle, which has the ruins of an old Roman fort on its grounds. One of the maids can take the children to play with the puppies."

"Lud, you should have followed your friends into the military." Henry grinned. "Wellesley could have used your tactical skills in the Peninsular War."

"Let's concentrate on making a different sort of conquest, shall we?" said Lucas dryly.

"By all means." Gripping the wheels of his Bath chair, Henry turned for the door. "Speaking of which, the ladies are still working on their experiment. Shall we go see how things are progressing?"

As Lucas entered the laboratory, Ciara looked up a little shyly, or so it seemed to him. They had yet to speak to each other since their parting just before dawn.

Their eyes met for an instant, and then, in a flicker of gold, she quickly lowered her lashes.

Strange, he felt a flutter inside, too. Other trysts had never affected him this way.

He didn't dare try to analyze why.

"How is it coming?" asked Henry, wheeling a little closer to the work counter.

"We have just one more test to run through." Alessandra added a touch of liquid to the measuring cup from her dropper. "Once we have established a proper procedure, the final results should prove Ciara is right—I am sure of it."

"Again, my congratulations, Ciara," murmured Henry. "I am truly in awe of your brilliance."

our friends mean to have a private discussion with the late marquess's relatives."

"Actually, they may leave that task to me. I mean to return with you to London first thing in the morning." After relatching the cellar door, Lucas took a moment to grab a corkscrew and glasses from his uncle's study. "By the by, if you mean to smoke those vile cheroots, Henry insists that it be done out on the terrace."

Jack lit the tobacco from a branch of candles. "No need to gallop off in a rush. I wouldn't have bothered to ride hell for leather just to inform you of something we could have handled on our own." The coal glowed a bright orange as he inhaled a puff. "The thing is, Battersham has disappeared from Town, along with his mother. Nobody seems to know where they have gone."

"The slimy little worm. He's probably crawled off to hide in some hole." Lucas tossed back his drink. "Am I supposed to be alarmed by the news?"

"We just thought you should know." His friend held his glass up to the fading light. "As a former soldier, allow me to offer a word of advice. Never underestimate the enemy. Battersham may be a craven coward, but that doesn't mean he isn't dangerous."

"Hmmph." Setting down his glass, Lucas surveyed the darkening woods. "I have taken precautions, Jack. There are men patrolling the grounds from dusk until dawn. And while I may not have your military experience, I assure you that if Battersham dares show himself, I'll beat him to a bloody pulp."

"I doubt he would be fool enough to risk a frontal attack." Jack blew out a ring of smoke. "He's already hired one band of thugs to do his dirty work. There's no telling whether he'll try again."

"I'm not about to let down my guard."

"Then enough said. Pour me another glass of wine. My throat is dry as dust from the road."

"Help yourself." Lucas handed his friend the bottle. "I had better go tell the housekeeper and cook that you will be staying the night."

"Bring some port with you when you return. By the look of the casks, that's a very fine vintage that your uncle has stashed underground."

Lucas snapped off a half-mocking salute.

"I don't suppose he has any London lightskirts tucked away in a discreet corner?" added Jack as he flicked a bit of ash from his cheroot.

"Don't you ever think of anything but drinking and wenching?" growled Lucas.

"That's rather the pot calling the kettle black," came the scathing retort. "What would you suggest?"

He thought for a moment. "Try enjoying the colors of the sunset and the sounds of the nightingales."

"On second thought, you had better bring some brandy, too," said Jack. "I need something stronger than wine to drown my fears for your sanity."

Lucas left his friend looking out over the gardens with a brooding stare.

⁓

Exhaling a sigh, Jack took a seat at the far end of the stone railing. He emptied the rest of the bottle into his glass and leaned back against the wall. Hazed with a violet hue, the shadows flitted over the pale limestone, reflecting the darkening palette of the twilight sky.

He was just about to light another cheroot when the sound of staccato footsteps rang out on the granite steps.

"How dare you follow me here!" In the play of pink and mauve light, Alessandra's face was rigid with fury as she looked back over her shoulder. "You have no right to intrude on my life here in England."

Moving with a slow, sauntering stride, a figure joined her on the terrace.

*Marco.* The Milanese macaroni.

"On the contrary, *bella.*" Ghiradelli leaned in closer, and lowered his voice, just enough so that the rustling of the ivy vines covered his words.

Whatever he said made Alessandra jerk away. Her hair had loosened, and a fall of ebony hid her face.

"Don't be angry with me, Alessa."

As Ghiradelli reached for her shoulder, Jack once again caught a snatch of the conversation.

"I am only trying to help do what is best for you and the child," said the conte.

"I know, I know . . ." The cool, composed marchesa sounded on the verge of tears. "Oh, Marco, I beg you, please do not press me for an answer at this moment."

"*Bene*—very well. But you can't put it off for long."

"No. I—I suppose I've always known that my past sins would come back to haunt me."

"*Ciao.* I will be in touch soon." Ghiradelli shifted his stance, and though Jack tried to avert his gaze, he couldn't help seeing the man's lips angle for the lady's upturned face.

For some reason he found his foul mood turning even fouler. "Alas, parting is such sweet sorrow," he sneered loudly, abruptly standing and stepping out from the shadows. "But if you don't mind, perhaps Romeo and Juliet could go enact their tragic love scene somewhere else. Here in England we try not to inflict our passionate embraces on innocent bystanders."

Alessandra whirled around. "So instead you take pleasure in spying on people? What were you doing, skulking in the shadows?"

"Enjoying a glass of wine and the lovely sunset," replied Jack. "At least I was until you two lovers interrupted the pastoral scene."

"You could have announced your presence," said Ghiradelli. "And avoided embarrassing the lady."

"I doubt that my voice would have been noticed. She seemed quite mesmerized by another pair of lips."

Alessandra answered with a huff of indignation. "*Not* that it's any of your business, sir. But Marco was kissing me on the *cheek*. As for being lovers, there is nothing amorous about our relationship."

Jack curled a contemptuous smile. "Funny, it didn't look like that to me," he said, striking a flint to his cheroot.

Her eyes sparked. "For your information, he is my *cousin*."

Jack nearly choked on the mouthful of smoke. "Cousin."

"*Si,* cousin," she snapped. "And unlike the English, Italians do not form intimate attachments with their cousins."

"Then it appears I owe you an apology, Lady Giamatti," he muttered.

"Yes. It does."

"Talk about theatrics, Lord James." Ghiradelli seemed to be enjoying the drama. "But much as I would like to remain until the end of the scene, I must return to Southampton without delay. Lord Lynsley wishes to be informed of Lady Sheffield's situation."

Alessandra looked away. "You may tell him that he will receive a full report on her discovery shortly. The final tests have yet to be done, but if all goes as expected . . ." She slanted a look at Jack. "The marquess will find the results of great interest."

"He will be pleased to hear it," replied Ghiradelli. "But I was referring to the lady's safety. Lynsley is quite concerned about her personal well-being. If you need guards—"

"Thank you, but Hadley seems to have everything in hand."

"Mad, Bad Had-ley?" Ghiradelli cocked a brow. "You are sure you wish to put your trust in him?"

She hesitated, but only for a fraction. "Yes, actually I am. He will see that no harm comes to Ciara."

"Very well." Ghiradelli squeezed her hand and then inclined a bow to Jack. "*Per favore,* Giacomo. Keep an eye on the marchesa for me, eh? She tends to get herself into trouble."

Alessandra muttered a rude word.

Jack gave him a baleful look. "If the marchesa won't listen to you, then she's certainly not going to listen to me."

"Stranger things have happened, *amico*." With that cryptic statement, he gave a flourishing wave. "I must be going, but before I leave, I think I shall stop and spend a few minutes with Lady Sheffield." His gaze flicked back to Alessandra. "I had better show her a few of the nasty little tricks I taught you for self-defense, *bella*—just in case."

"The cursed fellow knows how to make a grand exit from the stage," said Jack under his breath as Marco walked off.

She didn't reply.

To his relief, Lucas reappeared, several bottles of vintage spirits in hand. "Lady Alessandra. Er, I see that you, too, are enjoying the evening air." Clearing his throat, he added, "Would you care to join us in a toast . . . to the peace and quiet of the country?"

She shook her head. "Actually, I find it a little too chilly for my taste out here. I think I'll return to my rooms."

"Damn it, Jack," murmured Lucas as the door fell shut. "Why is it that you always manage to offend the marchesa?"

"Why is it that the sun always manages to come up each day?"

Lucas shrugged off the question. "Haven't a clue."

Jack reached for the brandy. Pulling the cork out with his teeth, he quaffed a long swallow straight from the bottle. "I'll drink to that."

# Chapter Twenty-two

*B*ird-watching?" Alessandra's raven brows winged up in skepticism. "Ah. More likely Hadley has a little love nest tucked away in the trees."

"No, really. He actually has an interest in the subject," said Ciara. She still had not explained why. Some secrets were not meant for sharing, even within her closest circle of friends.

"If you say so, *bella*." Alessandra checked through her satchel of books and sketchpads, and then signaled for her carriage to be brought up from the stables. "Don't do anything too naughty."

Ciara ignored the last comment. "Enjoy your afternoon at the ruins. I hadn't realized you had a particular interest in medieval stonework."

"I don't. But there are traces of an old Roman fort on the grounds, and Hadley seemed so insistent on getting all of us out of the manor house." Her friend smiled. "I think he wants Ariel and his uncle to have some time alone."

"Yes, I got the same impression," said Ciara. "He's even made sure that the children will not cause an unexpected interruption. They are going to the kennels to play with the puppies."

"Has he also offered to bathe them once they come home?" Alessandra crinkled her nose. "I shudder to imagine what substances will be sticking to their sweet little hands and faces."

"Let's not worry about that now." Ciara handed a picnic basket to the coachman, who then climbed to his perch on the box. "I feel a little guilty that you are spending the day on your own." She hesitated a fraction. "You are sure you won't come with us?"

Her friend waved off the suggestion. "I'm sure you two could use some privacy."

Ciara expelled a sigh. "I suppose Hadley and I had better have a talk. We need to come to an understanding about . . ."

"Sleeping with each other?"

"That," she said softly. "Among other things." Anxious to avoid further discussion of her relationship—emotional and otherwise—with Lucas, she quickly changed the subject. "It's a pity that Hadley's friend left at dawn. He could have accompanied you on the drive."

Alessandra grimaced. "The Prince of Darkness? Thank God I do not have to endure those fire-and-brimstone eyes, burning with disapproval."

"Hadley says he is very knowledgeable about art and antiquities."

"That may be so," replied her friend. "But I doubt that Lord Black Jack Pierson would deign to discuss them with me. He strikes me as a man who does not care for females who dare to voice an opinion, much less an expertise, on any intelligent subject."

"Perhaps you are being a little harsh in your judgment," said Ciara.

"And perhaps you are feeling overly romantic," countered her friend. She softened her sarcasm with a quick smile. "Don't worry about me, *bella*. I am quite content with my own company. As you say, the afternoon promises to be lovely, the children are occupied, and so we should enjoy a few carefree hours while we can."

A call to her coachman sprung the horses. *"Ciao, bella."*

*"Ciao,"* murmured Ciara, wondering why Alessandra seemed to have taken such a dislike to Lord James. Granted, the man did have an intimidating air about him, but once he relaxed his reserve, he was rather . . . interesting.

However, as Lucas crossed the graveled drive, she decided not to let worries about the others intrude on her thoughts. There was too much unspoken between her and the earl. *And unresolved,* she admitted. They had not had the chance to discuss in private the change in their relationship. Indeed, it almost seemed that he had gone out of his way to be distant. *Detached.*

Was he regretting their intimacy? Lucas was a man who made no secret of his aversion to complications in his life. He certainly hadn't bargained for getting involved in the dangers of her own sordid situation.

"Sweetheart, the day is far too fine for concern to cloud your face." Looking carefree as a boy, Lucas shifted the rucksack on his shoulder. "Come, let us enjoy the outing. It is, after all, the perfect opportunity to test what progress I am making in my studies." His eyes twinkled, green as the surrounding gorse. "I have yet to hear how my efforts have been graded."

"Hadley," she began.

"Lucas," he corrected.

She had to lengthen her stride to keep pace with him. "Lucas, let us not beat around the bush. We must talk—"

"Yes, yes, so we must. But there will be plenty of time later. Let us enjoy a lighthearted hour or two before turning serious."

She was just as happy to delay the discussion. "Very well."

The haze soon burned off, and as she and Lucas started up the steep path for the cliffs, the breeze turned balmy. Ciara lifted her face, breathing in the tangy scent of sea salt, wild thyme, and sunbleached cedar. The smooth stone mirrored the bright reflections of light and the shimmering blue of the seas.

"Look, a kestrel." Up ahead, Lucas stopped and snapped open his spyglass. "It's an immature male," he announced. "See the white feathers on the underside of its wings?"

"Yes." She shaded her eyes. "Is that a plover swooping down by the strand?"

"An oystercatcher," he corrected. "You can tell by the shape of the wings in flight."

He continued a running commentary on his observations, surprising her with the depth of his knowledge. Memorizing a few rudimentary basics was one thing, but his enthusiasm was unfeigned as he chatted about habitats, migration, and feather patterns.

Ciara dropped her gaze from the sky. "As a matter of fact, I did have a chance to read over your answers to the classroom test."

"Indeed?" For just an instant, his smile looked a trifle tentative. "And?"

"Actually, you earned a perfect grade." She tucked a windblown curl behind her ear. "I confess, I did not have very high expectations of you as a disciplined student. However, you've excelled at your studies, even though I didn't make it easy for you. You should be very proud of yourself."

"Learning a few facts about birds is hardly something to crow about," replied Lucas with an offhand shrug. However, as he turned away to watch a flock of seagulls take flight, she saw that her praise had brought a flush of color to his cheekbones.

Her heart gave a sudden, unexpected flutter at seeing him look so happy. "Go ahead and bask in the brilliance of your accomplishments for the present," she said. "Things are bound to get tougher as we go along."

"Very well. I shall listen to my teacher's advice and simply enjoy the moment." Eyes glinting with laughter, he grinned. "Now follow me."

On reaching the top of the promontory, Lucas led the way through the rocky outcroppings to a secluded spot overlooking one of the many coves that dotted the coast. The ledge was flat, and a tumble of wind-carved granite afforded shelter from the wind.

"You seem to know your way around these cliffs," remarked Ciara as he set down his rucksack and shook out the picnic blanket tied to its straps.

"I spent a lot of time here when I was a lad. Henry was often busy in his laboratory, and instead of studying my lessons, I would sneak off to explore." Lucas made a wry face. "Likely his hair would have gone gray a lot sooner had he seen me larking around the sheer drops and tidal currents." He threaded a hand through his own curling locks. "Lud, I was a horrid little devil. It's a wonder he didn't hire a stork to deliver me to some poor, unsuspecting family."

Ciara smiled. "Despite your many faults, he seems to have no regrets with having you in his life."

"I feel I've had far the better of the bargain," mused Lucas. He watched two ivory gulls circling overhead. "How do you and your friend feel about this *tendre* between Lady Ariel and Henry?"

"Nothing but joy that they have both found such happiness," she said softly. "I think it is a perfect match. And you?"

He chuckled. "I couldn't be more delighted. The two of them make a very endearing pair of lovebirds."

"Indeed." She sat down on the sun-warmed stone and drew her knees to her chest. "I know your opinion of matrimony is that it sucks the life out of a person. And yet I believe they will both find a second youth with each other."

A grunt was his only answer. Unbuckling the flap of his bag, Lucas began to unpack its contents—Stilton cheese, fresh bread, ripe pears, and a bottle of Mosel wine appeared from the wrappings of oilskin.

Ciara spotted a small sketchbook buried at the bottom. As he turned to lay out the food on the blanket, she edged a touch closer and took it up.

"Wait—"

*Too late.* She was already perusing the pages. The first drawings were a series of lovely pencil sketches depicting a robin atop her nest, a barn swallow with its beak full of straw, a hawk hovering in graceful flight.

"Why are you loath to show your talents?" she began.

But as the next page turned, she fell silent.

It was her own profile that stared back at her, a trio of variations done as quick doodles. The lines were spare and simple, yet so alive. Ciara caught her breath and turned again.

"Bloody hell," swore Lucas.

Ciara looked down at the drawing of her naked, amid a tangle of sheets.

He grabbed for the book, but she jerked it away. "Please, let me look."

"Damn it, they weren't meant for any eyes but mine," he growled.

*Did he really see her as such?*

There was a beauty, a passion to the strokes of graphite that nearly singed her fingertips. She touched the textured paper, letting her hand linger for a long moment before slowly shutting the covers. "Lucas, you have a remarkable talent."

"For what? Yet another way to fritter away the idle hours?" He curled a sardonic smile. "Scribbling sketches is hardly a serious sort of skill. But then, as you know, I am not much given to serious pursuits."

"On the contrary, you have proved that when you put your mind to it, you are capable of mastering a complex subject like ornithology."

"Only because you are so smart, and an excellent teacher."

"Lucas, it has been an equal exchange. You have taught me a great deal, too."

His gaze flickered, and for an instant he looked like a vulnerable boy rather than a jaded man of the town. "About what?"

"About laughter and how humor keeps the world from being too grim to bear. About spontaneous exuberance and how to enjoy each moment. About loyalty and how there is nothing so precious as love for family. About passion. And you have taught me a great deal about . . ." Her pause was almost imperceptible. "Zoology."

He blinked. "Zoology."

"The study of animal life."

"I'm aware of what the term means," said Lucas dryly. "But it's a rather broad field."

"And not one that I have studied much." On impulse, Ciara suddenly touched his shoulder. "In fact, I have a very basic question that I was hoping you might be able to answer for me."

"Which is?" His voice sounded a little odd.

"Is a man subject to the same spur-of-the-moment physical arousal as a woman?"

She saw his brows twitch. "Maybe more so," he replied. "We are far more primitive creatures."

"Ah." She fiddled with the kerchief knotted at his throat. "Interesting."

He hitched his hips back against the rock.

"Stay still, while I investigate." She slid her hand inside his shirt, savoring the tickle of hair teasing against her fingertips. She loved the feel of him—the slabs of manly muscles, the flat, pebbled nipples, the chiseling of his ribs. Drawing slow, circling strokes across the breadth of his chest, she took her time in exploring every nuance of his shape.

He closed his eyes and she heard his breath ratchet up a notch.

That she had the power to make his body respond was

exhilarating. Exciting. A glance down at his breeches showed that his cock was stiff and straining against the soft leather. Slipping her hand out of his shirt, she pressed her palm to his length.

He groaned.

Ciara rubbed the heel of her hand up and down.

"Sweet Jesus," he whispered. Bracing his elbows on the wind-carved granite, he tilted his head up to the sky.

With her thumb, Ciara fingered the outline of his cock's crested head. "A perfect specimen, I think." She worked one button open. "But to be sure I had better have a closer peek."

His teeth sunk into his lower lip.

A second fastening came undone. "Shall I go on?" she asked coyly.

"Yes," he rasped. "Unless you wish to see me throw myself off this cliff."

As the flap gave way, his shaft sprang free. *Lud, he was a magnificent, masculine creature.*

He growled and guided her hand around him. She felt him swell with life. Rocking his hips slowly, Lucas moved himself within her grip.

She dimly recalled that she had come here with every intention of putting an end to any further intimacies between them. So much for resolve and reason. Somehow Lucas reduced her mind to a quivering mass of mush.

Teasing her touch more boldly, she stroked her fingers up and down his velvety length.

"Stop."

She went very still. "Am I doing it wrong?"

"God, no." He was shaking. "It's just that in another

instant I shall spill my seed like a randy little schoolboy." He began to tuck himself back in his breeches. "I think it's time to end the lesson." But his shaft seemed to disagree. Proudly defiant, it nudged free from the flap.

"Hell," he muttered.

"Is it painful?"

A half laugh. "Exquisitely so."

"How—how do you relieve it?"

His eyes slitted half shut. "If I were in London, I would have three options. I could go home and finish what you have begun. I could go out to a gaming hell and offend everyone around me with my foul temper. Or I could visit a bordello and pay an exorbitant amount of money to have a beautiful woman bring me to a climax."

The idea of him with another woman sent a sudden wave of pure, primal passion through her. Not that she had any real right to feel possessive. She had no hold on him.

*Let it go,* she warned herself. And yet, her hands refused to heed the order. They slid across the rock.

Her body followed, sidling close to his side. "But you are not in London," she said softly.

All around them were the elemental forces of nature. Waves surged against the rocks below. Gulls swooped and shrieked with wild abandon. The very air was alive, shimmering with sunlight and the tangy scent of the sea.

"No, I am not."

"Then what do you suggest?"

He shifted against the rocks, so that his thigh was hard up against hers. "A scientist must explore all the possibilities—isn't that one of the first lessons you taught me?"

"Correct."

"Hmmm." His hand slid up under her skirts. "Let me see if I can remember what comes next."

"Empirical data," she whispered, nibbling at his earlobe. "One must always base scientific conclusions on actual experience and observation."

"Ah. Right."

"Go on, sir."

Lucas let out a husky laugh. "Are you propositioning me, Lady Sheffield?"

She ran her thumb along his lower lip. "I was rather hoping it would be the other way around, Lord Hadley."

"I should be able to figure out the basic procedure on my own." A tug lifted her gown and undergarments above her knees. The wind ruffled lace and linen, billowing the layers of fabric up to her waist. Sunlight glinted off the stones, reflecting a delicious warmth onto her legs. She stretched like a cat and purred with pleasure.

"Stay still, sweetheart." Lucas's laugh was low, lush as the ocean wave. "This is an important part of the experiment." His hands unlaced her half boots, undid her garters, and slipped off her stockings. They didn't stop there—nimble fingers removed her drawers with consummate ease. The breeze caught the delicate silk, and the garment sailed out to sea.

Ciara felt a little wicked, a little wanton, but gloriously alive. Some of her hairpins had fallen away, and her curls were blowing loose, tickling her cheeks.

He pulled her onto his lap and eased her legs apart until she was straddling his muscled thighs. The rigid length of him was like a shaft of sunlight against her flesh—sweetly sensuous heat spread to her core.

"L-Lucas."

"Yes?" he said slowly.

"I . . ." She forgot what she was going to say as the head of his cock probed at her passageway. The sound of the sea surged in her ears as he reached his large, lithe hand between her legs and guided himself inside her. She was slick and ready for him.

His finger found that perfect spot within her folds. Stroking back and forth, he thrust himself a little deeper.

*Oh, Lud, there was something to be said for sin.*

His tongue was in her mouth now, and the intimate friction of liquid flesh against flesh was intensely erotic. Now that she had a taste of rakehell revelries, she craved more. *More.* With a soft moan, she sunk a little lower, grinding against his groin.

With a growl, he grasped her bottom and lifted her up. And then let her slide down. The feel of his manhood moving inside sent another sizzle of heat through her.

"You may take charge of combining the ingredients," he said in a husky whisper.

Ciara realized she could set her own rhythm. *What a fascinating discovery.* Clenching her knees against his thighs, she set her hands on his shoulders. Each slight change in tempo or angle resulted in a heady new sensation.

Lucas looked up with a heavy-lidded smile. "I think the experiment is a success."

"One must never rush to conclusions." Despite the urgency building inside her, Ciara wished this moment might go on . . . forever.

His mouth curled up at the corners. "Oh, by all means, sweetheart, take your time."

What a delightful discovery it was that sex was more

than a rough, rapid spilling of seed. Kneading her hands along the sun-warmed muscles of his back, Ciara set a slow, sensual pace to their lovemaking, matching her rise and fall to the ebb and flow of the ocean. Water. Wind. Earth. Fire. *The elemental forces at play.* She felt in harmony with nature. With Lucas.

With herself.

A wave of joy flooded through her. There was nothing shameful or sordid in their coupling. She felt connected by far more than a length of lustful flesh.

*Love.*

Like the swirling, surging heat within her, the word rose from her core. She had never meant to make herself vulnerable to emotion again. Love was for dewy-eyed schoolgirls who were too naive to know that deceit and depravity could dress in the fancy clothes of a titled gentleman. Love was for hopeless romantics.

*Was there anything more hopelessly romantic than making love on a sun-kissed cliff overlooking the ocean?*

Laughter bubbled up inside her. Leave it to Lucas to make the experience outrageously memorable.

Beneath the curl of his lashes, his eyes were the same color as the ocean—a rich seafoam hue, unfathomable in its complexity. On the surface, he seemed her opposite, but he had far more depth to his character. He was kind, he was caring, he was compassionate.

He was wildly wonderful. And for this brief moment he was *hers*.

Elation crested inside her and then exploded into thousands of shimmering shards of sunlight.

Her cry rose on a gust of wind, followed an instant later by his hoarse shout echoing the waves bursting against

the rocks. He lifted her just enough to spill his seed on the
stone, then let her fall back against his chest.

It was all so hopelessly romantic. *Impossibly romantic.*

Ciara held him tightly, letting her breathing come back
down to earth. Tears prickled her eyes—already a sense
of loss was mingled with his essence. But she would not
spoil the moment by speaking of her feelings.

"Dear God." Lucas looked up, light and shadow playing across his handsome face. "You are so achingly beautiful," he whispered, drawing her face down for a kiss. He
tasted of sea salt and sweet wine. Of passion and tender-
ness. Of need and something she couldn't quite define.

"Lucas." With her tongue, Ciara traced the sensuous curve
of his lip. He had done this so many times, with so many
women, she reminded herself. For him, it wasn't special.

"Another day, another dalliance," she murmured, trying to strike just the right note of amused detachment.

"Aye, many shared my flesh," he said softly. "But none
has touched me like . . ." He let his words leave off to
press his mouth to the hollow of her throat.

Ciara felt her pulse quicken and thud against him.
Much as she wished to know what he was going to say,
she didn't press him. Unfinished was best for now.

His lips lingered for a moment, and then Lucas deftly
smoothed the tangle of linen and lace back into place. He
carried her to the blanket and lay down, settling her cheek
on his chest.

*Don't think,* she reminded herself. Just feel the wind
and the warmth and the sheltering circle of his arms, holding her safe. No matter that it was all too fleeting.

Lucas flexed his neck and stretched. His shoulder slid along rough stone, and his leg—his leg rubbed up against something infinitely softer.

A man could get used to awaking to the feel of Ciara's shapely derriere, he thought with a lazy smile. To the scent of her perfume. Leaning in close to her hair, he inhaled the subtle fragrance of verbena and neroli. Funny, but he had never thought of lemons and oranges as erotic. The women he consorted with wore earthy, exotic musks to arouse a man. Now, however, the beguiling hint of citrus had him recalling the tart-sweet taste of her mouth . . .

Oh, this was bad. *Bad.* He was growing hard at the mere thought of fruit.

Edging back a touch, Lucas removed his hand from the curve of her hip. Much as he wanted to wake her to another long, languid session of lovemaking, the temptation was tempered by gentlemanly scruples.

*Damnation, it was far more fun being a devil-may-care rake.*

The trouble was, he *did* care. About her and the consequences of their actions. These trysts could not continue. With a certain sort of widow, a regular assignation could be arranged. But Ciara had a young son. Lucas felt his ardor shrivel. He would not want the boy to hear nasty innuendos about his mama being a whore.

Her reputation was already slightly scandalous. Given their plans for a spectacularly public jilting, he could hardly carry on an illicit affair with any hope of it going unnoticed by the gossips. *Bloody hell.* He could just envision the boldface headlines . . .

Lucas shifted again. There appeared to be just two choices—give her up, or go through with the sham betrothal.

*Marriage.*

Strange, but the word no longer sent shivers of horror down his spine.

But as for Ciara, he wasn't quite sure how she would react to the proposal. Granted, she seemed to enjoy their physical relationship. But any suggestion of a more permanent relationship would certainly be met with skepticism. Her experiences with trusting a man to take care of her were grim, and the past performances of Mad, Bad Had-ley did not exactly inspire confidence.

Exhaling softly, Lucas watched the play of sunlight flicker over her cheek, her lashes.

"Mmmm." Ciara stirred and squinted up at the sky. "You are a very bad influence on me, Lord Hadley."

He gave a guilty start.

A sweet smile softened her chiding. "I never nap away the afternoon. It's . . . decadent."

"Disgraceful," he murmured, using humor to hide his uncertainty. "Depraved."

"Disreputable."

"I am sorry for leading you down the path to perdition," said Lucas.

Her mouth quirked. "I'm not."

"Truly?"

"Truly." Ciara looked out over the sea. "I had allowed my world to become oppressively small." She toyed with his brass spyglass and slowly snapped it open. "You have broadened my horizons, shown me new possibilities, Lucas."

*Dare he hope that she could see him in a different light?*

The lens slowly swung from the sea to shoreline. "For that I shall always be grateful—" Her words ended in an abrupt gasp. "Good God, the children!"

*"What!"* All amorous thoughts were gone in an instant, replaced by a spasm of alarm.

Lucas wrenched the glass from her hands and trained it on the spot where she had been looking. How the devil had the children been allowed to stray from the estate? The marshes were treacherous, and the cliffs posed myriad dangers for two children out wandering on their own.

But as the footpath came into focus, he realized that Peregrine and Isabella were not alone. A cloaked figure was leading the way through the twisting turns, while a second person had the children captured in his grasp.

Repressing a snarl of impotent rage, Lucas swung the spyglass in a wider arc. The search quickly revealed a small sloop at anchor in one of the small coves.

*Damn him for a fool.* While he had been preoccupied with his prick, Battersham had stolen a march on him.

"Lucas?" Ciara's voice was trembling.

"Kidnapped," he replied grimly. "Don't worry, sweetheart—I'll not let them get away." He already had his boots on. "Run home and send a servant to alert authorities—Henry will know where."

"No!" Ciara glanced at the jagged cut of rocks and set her jaw. "It will be far too late before any help can be mustered. I'm going with you."

"The way is too rough. I will be taking a shortcut."

"I can make it," she insisted.

"Be reasonable—"

"Lucas, he is my *son*."

There was no time to argue. His mouth thinned to a grim line as he took her hand. "Hold on tight. And be prepared for a rough descent."

# Chapter Twenty-three

*A* shard of stone sheared away under their steps and fell with a splash into the surging surf. Ciara stumbled, fear making her a little dizzy, but Lucas was right there to steady her footing.

She clutched at his hand, reassured by his hold. *Strong. Sure.* This was not the selfish scamp she had read about oh-so-many weeks ago. Resolve was chiseled in every taut muscle. His expression was hard as granite, reminding her of Lord Woodbridge's words in the ballroom—his scapegrace friend just needed a challenge to bring out the best in himself.

*That night seemed so very, very long ago.* Mad, Bad Had-ley had changed beyond recognition.

"Give me your hand." Lucas swung her over a deep crevasse in the rock. He paused a moment, then fisted her skirts and tore the fabric, shortening the hem by half a foot. "Take off your petticoat, as well," he ordered. "The way down from here is treacherous enough as it is—I don't want to risk losing you on an errant slip."

She obeyed in an instant. "Don't worry about me. All that matters is Perry and Isa."

His grip tightened. "You are all very dear to me. I don't intend on allowing harm to come to any of you."

Light glinted in his eyes as he glanced up, setting off a winking of sapphire ice. Ciara shivered slightly, glad she was not the enemy.

"Damn," he growled. "Come, sweetheart, we must try to move even faster."

Following his gaze, she saw the scudding storm-gray clouds moving in fast from the west. The wind was already gusting, turning the seas choppy.

"Yes," she answered, wishing they might sprout wings and swoop down upon the fleeing figures. "Let us fly."

Slipping, sliding, they descended the steep cut of rock. Her hands were soon scraped and bleeding. Briars tore at her legs; wind whipped her ragged skirts.

*Hurry, hurry.* Their progress seemed so painfully slow, and the strand still appeared miles away.

"We'll never make it in time," she gasped, her half boots nearly tripping over the uneven scree.

"Steady, sweetheart," replied Lucas firmly. "It's not as far as it looks." He angled through a cleft in the stone and led the way down a narrow ledge. "We're almost there."

The outcropping took a sharp turn, and then suddenly Lucas disappeared.

Ciara was about to cry out when she heard his voice ring out from below. "You'll have to jump. I'll catch you."

Without hesitation, she stepped off the edge. The drop was not all that great, and Lucas was there, strong and solid, to gather her in his arms.

For an instant, she was tempted to stay in the shelter of his hold.

"Brave girl," he murmured, brushing his lips to her windsnarled hair. "They will not escape us now."

Spying a footpath between the tangled thornbushes, Lucas grabbed her hand and set off at a run.

The way twisted through the coastal thickets, and the loose stones and tangled vines soon slowed their progress.

"Can't we go any faster?" she asked as Lucas paused to get his bearings.

"I dare not charge ahead too quickly," he replied. "The way turns a little treacherous up ahead, for there's a bog where the mud can be dangerous. If the kidnappers sense pursuit, they may be spooked into doing something rash."

It was, of course, a sensible reply, but Ciara couldn't help but chafe at the snail's pace. Each scrape of her half boots seemed a harsh chiding on how careless she had been to abandon herself to carnal pleasure.

"I should never have left Peregrine, knowing that he was in danger," she said aloud. "Perhaps the Sheffields are right, after all—I'm an unfit mother, a selfish strumpet who—"

Lucas whirled around and gave her shoulders a shake. "Stop it," he ordered. "You've done nothing wrong. Do *not* let their evil lies poison your life, Ciara."

She choked down a sob. "If I lose Perry—"

"You won't," he said firmly. "You must trust me on that. Now keep hold of my hand and stay silent, sweetheart. The footpath cuts in close to the sea up ahead, and there is a marsh that will slow them down."

Sure enough, on rounding a thicket of gorse, Ciara spotted the children and their captors. They had halted by the bank of a wide stream, and the two adults appeared to be engaged in an argument. Despite Lucas's warning, her breath slipped out in an audible gasp.

"Ssshhh. We must get closer before they become aware of our presence." Pointing to a sliver of space between the bushes, Lucas inched forward. "The sound of the surf will cover our approach."

The slap of the sea against the rocks echoed the churning in her chest, but she nodded, knowing he was right.

Crouching low, he picked a path down the sloping hillside, using the tussocks of salt grass to muffle their steps. The screen of thorny leaves allowed them to creep within a stone's throw of the group, and over the rushing water of the stream, Ciara could hear the babble of angry voices.

"Idiot! Why did you bring the girl?"

"I couldn't very well let her go and raise the alarm, could I?" Peeking through the branches, Ciara could see enough of the near figure to recognize Arthur Battersham. He had hold of both children, and as he spoke, he gave Isabella a nasty shake. "The little bitch bit my hand. I think it's bleeding—"

His complaint ended in a shrill curse as Peregrine kicked him in the shin. "You ought to bite your tongue, Cousin Arthur. Gentlemen aren't supposed to use bad language around ladies."

Arthur responded with a hard slap.

"Don't hit the brat. We may need him unmarked if Richard's widow insists on negotiating face-to-face."

*Lady Griselda Battersham?* Her late husband's sister had always been a spiteful, selfish creature, but how could she, a mother herself, actually be so callously cruel as to contemplate harming another woman's son?

But before she could react, Lucas slid his hand over her mouth. "Steady, sweetheart," he whispered. "Let's try to hear what they have in mind before I intervene."

"The Wicked Witch won't be in a position to dictate terms," came Arthur's sulky reply. This time he dodged Peregrine's boot and tightened his grip on the boy's collar. "You said so yourself—she'll do whatever we ask to get her whelp back."

*What did they want from her?* That she couldn't answer the question only added to her fear.

"Lud, Arthur, do I have to do all the thinking for both of us?" snapped Lady Battersham. "Try using your brain for once. Of course we're not worried about Lady Ciara. On her own, she has no influence or support in Society—a position we have taken great pains to ensure. However, this liaison with Hadley presents a potential problem."

"It's a sham," said Arthur with a malicious laugh. "He'll throw her aside as soon as he's tossed up her skirts."

In spite of the stranglehold on his collar, Peregrine managed a spirited reply. "No, he won't—Hadley isn't a filthy, rotten scoundrel like you."

"I've always known that your mother's bad blood has poisoned your veins, cousin," sneered Arthur. "You should be ashamed of yourself, siding against your father's family."

"My father was a drunk and a bully," retorted Peregrine. "And so are you."

"Shut your mouth!" Arthur let go of Isabella to slap him again when suddenly the little girl wriggled free and darted off over the rocks leading upstream.

"Damn!" bellowed Arthur.

Lady Battersham took a step and then stopped. "Bah,

let her go. It will be hours before she finds her way back to the manor house. Cousin Findley is waiting with the boat, and if we don't hurry, the tide will change."

*Thank God Isabella was free from their clutches.* Ciara bit her lip. Now, if only her son . . .

As if mocking her hopes, Arthur grabbed Peregrine with both hands and gave him a rough shove. "Don't even think of trying that trick," he warned. "And you had better hope your mama proves reasonable, cuz." His low laugh was like the rasp of rusty metal. "Sailing can be dangerous, especially in these waters. Accidents happen all the time."

A wave of cold fury washed over Ciara. For an instant, she gladly would have given the gossip columns a grain of truth by committing murder with her bare hands.

Only Lucas's strong, steady grip held her in check. "Let me handle things from here."

~

"Not so fast." Stepping out from behind the bushes, Lucas called out a warning. "I think this has gone far enough, Battersham. Let the boy go."

Arthur whirled around, his ruddy face betraying a mixture of shock and fear. "What the devil . . ."

"Trust me, you will wish that you had encountered Lucifer instead of me if you don't release Perry this instant."

"Stay out of this, Lord Hadley," said Lady Battersham. "It's a family matter that doesn't concern you."

Arthur's bravado came creeping back, encouraged by his mother's firm words and the pistol he pulled from his coat pocket. "That's right," he said. "You aren't in any position to be giving orders."

Mentally measuring the distance between himself and Arthur, Lucas slid a half step to his right. "Then let me rephrase it . . . as a request." He turned to Lady Battersham. "You are obviously intelligent, Lady Battersham. And clever enough to know that you really have no option but to negotiate." He heard Ciara move up beside him but didn't look at her. Thankfully, she seemed to sense that he wished for her to stay silent. "We are, after all, about to be related by marriage. So let us discuss this reasonably."

Lucas felt her flinch and knew the effort to remain calm must be causing her agony. *Steady, steady.* This time the warning was meant for himself. Peregrine looked so damnably vulnerable. And trusting. Though his face was pale, the boy looked up at him with a brave smile. "I knew you wouldn't let them take us, Hadley. I knew you would come to the rescue."

To Peregrine, he wasn't Mad, Bad Had-ley, the reckless rake, the wild wastrel. He was a far different man. A man worthy of admiration. His throat tightened. No one had ever expected him to be a hero. Least of all himself. But the look in the lad's eyes said otherwise.

"Isabella—" continued Peregrine.

"Yes, I will find Isabella," he said softly. "I promise you that I'll have all of you home safely soon."

Light glinted off the gun barrel. "Don't be so sure of yourself, Hadley."

"Stop waving that weapon around," said Lucas. "It might go off accidentally and actually hit something."

Arthur's face turned even redder with rage. "You won't

be sounding so cocksure when I put a bullet through your bollocks, Hadley."

"Put the pistol away, Arthur," ordered Lady Battersham. "As Lord Hadley says, there is no reason why we can't settle this once and for all."

"What is it you want?" Ciara finally tore her gaze from her son and looked up at her sister-in-law. "Money? It can't be the land, for you must know it is all entailed."

"It should belong to me," growled Arthur. "I am more a true heir to Uncle Richard than his own brat."

"True," replied Ciara with a subtle sarcasm that sailed right over Arthur's head. "However, life is often unfair, and we must learn to live with disappointment."

"Not necessarily," replied Lady Battersham with a crafty squint. "Sometimes, nature takes its own course . . . illness intervenes or accidents happen."

Ciara drew in a sharp breath.

"And sometimes, a concerted effort of cleverness can even out the vagaries of chance."

"I take it you are going to tell us what you have in mind," said Lucas.

"It's a simple exchange," explained Lady Battersham. "Lady Ciara gets the boy in return for the scientific secret that she has discovered."

"Scientific secret? I—I don't understand." Ciara gave voice to his own bafflement. "What possible interest is my work to you?"

The laugh was harsh and hard. "The fact that it's worth a fortune to the government. Even more, in fact, than your son's inheritance."

"You are gravely mistaken—" began Ciara.

"Don't try to play me for a fool." Lady Battersham

waggled her walking stick. "We've heard the talk about how Whitehall is willing to pay an astronomical price for the patent to a drug that will help protect our armies from battlefield wounds."

*Bloody hell.* Lucas felt a little sick to his stomach on recalling how he had bragged of her accomplishments to his friends at the club. "I believe that the account you heard has been exaggerated," he began to explain. "A misunderstanding—"

"And just how do you see this working?" cut in Ciara. It was her turn to be pragmatic. "I doubt that anyone would believe it for an instant if you or your family claimed credit for making the discovery."

"You are right. Which is why you will sign over the rights to the discovery to us as a gift, acknowledging that you wish to honor your late husband's wishes that his family be taken care of. My lawyers have worked out all the legalities. You have only to sign the document, which will allow us to sell it to Whitehall."

"And if I do?" asked Ciara. "You will leave me and my son alone?"

Lady Battersham smoothed at the hood of her cloak. "We would have no more reason to bear you ill will."

That was hardly a reassuring answer, thought Lucas.

Ciara, however, betrayed no hesitation. "Have you this document with you?"

"It's close. We can arrange to meet first thing in the morning."

The dowager's flash of teeth was not a very convincing smile. "Naturally, we'll have to keep the boy until the exchange is made."

"Absolutely not."

Arthur gave a snarl of laughter as he waved his weapon dangerously close to Peregrine's head. "Don't forget, dear Aunt, that you are not the one calling the shots."

"Keep quiet, Arthur," ordered his mother. "I'll handle this."

"No, actually, I will," announced Lucas. "Here is Lady Ciara's counteroffer. She—that is, I—will pay you a one-time settlement of ten thousand pounds. You are entitled to nothing, but I'm willing to be extremely generous in order to put an end to this matter. As for the boy, his release is non-negotiable. He comes with us now."

"Go to hell," cursed Arthur. "You expect us to accept a pittance when a fortune is within our grasp?"

The dowager remained silent.

"The offer is final," said Lucas. "And you have exactly thirty seconds to make up your mind."

"And after that?" sneered Arthur. Despite the show of bluster, he was sweating profusely.

"After that, you miserable muckworm, I will break every bone in your body," said Lucas calmly. He edged another half step closer to the other man. One more move should bring him near enough to lunge for the weapon before Arthur could react.

"What guarantee do we have that we can trust you?" demanded Lady Battersham.

Lucas curled a lip. "You will just have to take my word of honor as a gentleman."

The dowager appeared to be giving the ultimatum consideration.

But Arthur's gestures were becoming increasingly erratic. "We have the upper hand, Mother. Don't give in to his demands!"

"Be quiet," snapped Lady Battersham. "I need to think—"

"I won't!" cried Arthur. "I'm sick of always being ordered about, as if I am a child. We all agreed our plan is a good one, and I mean to take charge and see that we carry it through."

The pistol was now aimed at Lucas's heart.

Ciara tried to set herself as a shield, but he caught her wrists and forced her back. "Don't worry, sweetheart. Even a bacon-brained clodpole like your nephew ought to realize the consequences of pulling the trigger." He didn't take his eyes off Arthur. "And if he doesn't, perhaps his mother will explain. She, of all people, knows that murder is a hanging offense."

"Arthur!" Lady Battersham's voice was suddenly shrill. "Don't be a fool."

"Fool, am I?" The hammer cocked with an ominous click. "I'll teach you all to show me some respect!"

Ducking low, Lucas spun away and pushed Ciara out of the line of fire. The move lost him a split second, but with any luck, Arthur's reflexes would prove as slow as his wits. He saw a herky-jerky flash of steel as the gun barrel tried to draw a bead on his chest.

*Damn.* He would have to take a shot at grabbing the pistol—

*CRACK!*

From out of nowhere, a round missile whizzed through the air and struck the wavering weapon, knocking it from Arthur's hand. It flew up and then fell with a leaden splash into the water.

"A corking good throw, Isa!" cheered Peregrine. "Now hit him between the eyes!"

Lucas looked around. Sure enough, Isabella was winding up with a second rock. "It was the snooker spin pitch, sir!" cried the little girl. "I did it just like you showed me."

"It was perfect, lass. But—"

Arthur staggered back, with Peregrine still in his grasp. He slipped on the mossy stones, causing the throw to miss by a hairsbreadth.

"Call her off, call her off!" he screamed.

"That's enough, sweeting," said Lucas, scooping up the little girl and giving her a fierce hug. "You wouldn't want to risk hitting Perry."

Isabella responded with a sniff. "I was *not* aiming at Perry."

"Little hellion! No doubt you've learned your evil headstrong ways from my sister-in-law." Lady Battersham shook her stick at them. "The two of you headstrong hellions are unnatural females, I say. Unnatural! I have never seen the like of it in my life!"

"Nor have I." Lucas allowed a ghost of a grin. "My ladies are both brave and bold as Boudicca, but now, if you please . . ." He handed the girl to Ciara. "I would like a chance to don my armor and play the noble knight."

Her eyes had an odd gleam, one that seemed to come from deeper than the unshed tears clinging to her lashes. "Perry," she whispered.

Lucas stilled her quivering lips with a touch of his fingertips before turning to Arthur.

"Come now, Battersham, toss down your hand. This is no different than a gaming hell. You played your cards well, but luck was not on your side. It's time to accept defeat and settle our accounts." Much as he itched to charge in and pummel the man to a pulp, he did not wish to drive the man to a desperate act. "I am still willing to pay you something. Just let the boy go."

Arthur looked around wildly. The sky had turned gray as gunpowder, and a rumble of thunder from the approaching squall echoed the slap of the surf against the nearby cliffs.

"There is nowhere to run," added Lucas quietly.

Perhaps sparked by the word "run," Peregrine suddenly twisted and tried to bolt free.

Arthur managed to keep hold, and a blow from his meaty fist stunned the boy. "Throw down my cards? Not when I still hold an ace." He lifted a groggy Peregrine up into his arms and slid his fingers around the boy's throat. "Back off, unless you wish for it to be a spade."

Lucas looked to Lady Battersham. "Talk some sense into your son," he growled. "Listen to the seas. Your boat will have been forced to weigh anchor, and with the rising tide, there is no other way out of the cove."

"Arthur . . ."

But Battersham had already turned, Peregrine still in his arms, and bolted over the slippery path of stones that led across the stream. Pausing on the opposite bank only long enough to hurl a last curse, he then squeezed through a sliver in the rocks and disappeared.

Ciara's anguished cry echoed Arthur's shout of "Go to hell!"

"Courage, sweetheart," said Lucas. "We've no real choice—you must stay with Isa and trust Perry to me."

# Chapter Twenty-four

*L*ogic and loyalty all said Lucas was right. But at the moment, her heart had a hard time listening to reason.

Ciara hugged Isabella, willing herself not to shatter into a thousand tiny shards. Right now, Alessandra's daughter was her responsibility, and she must stand in as the little girl's mother. While Lucas played the part of Peregrine's father.

"Perry isn't in any danger." The little girl's mud-streaked face betrayed not a flicker of doubt. "Lord Hadley is a great gun. He won't let him come to any harm."

"Yes, he is."

"I hope he pounds that nasty man to a pulp," continued Isabella. She clenched her small fingers into fists. "I shall ask him to give me boxing lessons next, now that he taught me the basics of cricket."

"Look at you." Lady Battersham regarded Ciara with a basilisk stare. "You're a disgrace to Polite Society, and I see that you have poisoned yet another child."

Ciara slowly looked down at her ripped skirts, her scraped hands, her tangled hair, her friend's daughter, whose face was now scrunched in a scowl. And then she lifted her chin. "The poison flows from people like you and your son, who are overflowing with hate and greed and envy." She set Isabella down. "I am proud of who I am and what I do. And if I can encourage my son and my friend's daughter to develop their own individual spirit and to value truth over material possessions, then I shall be even prouder."

Lady Battersham gave a snort of derision. "You're a fool. You always have been."

Isabella responded by calling the dowager a name that made Ciara blink.

"Lud, where did you learn that word?" she asked.

"From Perry," admitted the little girl. "Who overheard Hadley use it when he was talking to Lord James"—she pointed a finger—"about *her*."

"It's not a term you ought to repeat," said Ciara.

"I know." Isabella did not appear at all contrite.

"I've heard quite enough. Out of my way." Lady Battersham was a big woman, and her walking stick was a stout length of hawthorn topped with a heavy brass knob. Swinging it in a menacing arc, she came at Ciara. "You may have worked your black magic to escape justice today. But don't think you have seen the last of us."

Ciara stood firm. "You are not going anywhere. This time, you will pay for your perfidy."

"And who is going to make me?" The dowager laughed. "You have no proof. It's your word against ours. We'll simply say that we stopped to visit my nephew, and as children are wont to do, the boy made up a wild story. All this will be dismissed as a mere misunderstanding."

"It's not just my word this time, Lady Battersham. Lord Hadley is a witness."

"Hadley?" The stick waggled. "Ha! As if anyone will take him seriously! Society will simply think he's up to one of his outrageous stunts."

"You might be in for a rude surprise," replied Ciara.

For a moment, there was a flicker of uncertainty in the dowager's expression. "Bah! You are bluffing." The malevolence was back in a flash. "Out of my way," she repeated. "I mean to go extricate Arthur. You see, Hadley will have no choice but to let him go. Your name can't stand another smudge of scandal."

"Only because you and your family have taken such pains to blacken it with your lies."

Lady Battersham shrugged. "I warned you long ago that it was a grave mistake to try to match wits with me." She started for the stepping stones, but Ciara moved to block her path.

"And as you see, I'm still not intimidated by your threats."

"Willful, wicked woman! I won't allow you to stand in the way of my plans. It is I and my family who deserve to benefit from my brother's estate, not you." Using her stick as a cudgel, she aimed a blow at Ciara's head.

*Spin. Twist. Flick.*

She put into motion the tactics that Lord Ghiradelli had taught her.

*Splat.* With a squeak and a squeal, the dowager fell backward, landing on her rump in the shallows of the stream.

The conte was right—when applied with textbook precision, the art of self-defense was a matter of simple physics.

Isabella's giggle was drowned out by a string of sputtering curses. For all her posturing about propriety, the dowager knew a number of highly unladylike words.

Ciara uttered her own silent oath as a new sound rose above the splashing water and gusting winds. Snatching up the fallen walking stick, she reached for Isabella's hand.

The thud of galloping hooves slowed. Branches cracked, bushes rustled. Through the gorse, she saw the shadowy shape of a horse and rider start to thread through the swampy thickets of brambles.

*"Lucas?"* called the rider.

Expelling a sigh of relief, Ciara waved the stick. "Over here, sir!" she shouted in answer. "Over here!"

A moment later, Black Jack Pierson guided his stallion down the rocky slope. His face was dark with worry, the shading accentuated by his broad-brimmed black hat and the wild tangle of rain-spattered raven hair curling down to his shoulders. With a shake of his oilskin cape, he reined to a halt. "What—"

"I'll explain later." She thrust Isabella up into his arms.

Jack fumbled to holster his cavalry pistol. "Good God! I don't know the first thing about children."

"It's simple—she is shivering. Wrap her in your cloak." Ciara stepped back from the stallion's sweating flanks. "I must go after my son and Lucas."

"No, wait! Let me go—" said Jack.

Ciara was already scrambling across the stones. "As for the Old Bat," she shouted over her shoulder, "if she so much as twitches a muscle, shoot her."

~~~

The mizzle was making the rocks more slippery by the moment. Lucas paused to pull off his boots and stockings, hoping that Arthur would show some sense of self-preservation and slow his skittering descent. Not that he cared if the dastard broke his neck, but Peregrine was also in peril.

If anything happened to the lad . . .

Ignoring the shards of slate slicing into his fingers, he swung down from the narrow ledge and dropped to another outcropping. The move helped narrow the gap between him and his quarry.

"Battersham!" he called, squinting through the swirls of fog. "Blast it, man, slow down! Your hide is not at risk from me."

Arthur answered with a shrill jeer. "You're lying!" The man sounded winded and scared.

*Bloody hell.* Exhaustion and fear did not help a man make good decisions.

Lucas tried another tack. "Look, can't you see that no boat is waiting for you in these waves? Leave the boy and go take shelter in the lee of a ledge until the storm passes. You'll be able to cross the cove at low tide. From there, it's an easy climb up a cart path to the coast road."

"Where you'll have the local magistrate waiting to arrest me!"

"Let Peregrine go and you have my word that I'll not contact the authorities."

"Ha!" A note of panic edged Arthur's voice. "Since when have you become such an honorable gentleman?"

*A good question.* Lucas began inching along a sliver of stone. It was hard to say exactly when the change had occurred. It had crept up on him gradually—a slow realization that the pursuit of pleasure was no longer of paramount importance in his life. Pleasure was fleeting, while love and family were the things that endured.

But he might as well whistle into the wind as try to explain it to the other man.

"You're right," he called. "Like you, I'm no saint. So let me put it to you as a purely pragmatic deal. Having Lady Sheffield caught up in a scandal does neither of us any good. After all, it might affect her ability to sell her discovery to Whitehall and the military. So, as her future husband, it's in my self-interest for us to cry peace for the day."

*Greed.* Now that was definitely a sentiment that Arthur Battersham should understand.

"I—I . . ."

The stuttering words were swallowed in a scream as a rock suddenly shifted beneath his feet. Arthur teetered, fighting madly for balance. He slipped again, and in twisting, he lost his hold on the still-groggy Peregrine. The boy slipped from his arms and hit the edge of the precipice, where he hung for an agonizing instant before dropping like a sack of stones into the foaming surf below.

A gust caught Arthur's billowing coat and blew him over the far side of the ledge.

Lucas was already moving—slipping, sliding, clawing his way down the rough rocks as he searched the churning waters.

"H–help me." Arthur was hanging onto a crack in the granite, his beefy body dangling over a jut in the cliffs. There was no water below him, only jagged stone yawning up like giant teeth. His face was bloodless, and his breath was a ragged gasp.

Grabbing hold of the other man's wrist, Lucas hauled him to safety.

"I think my leg is broken," whimpered Arthur through chattering teeth.

"If I don't find Perry, I swear that I shall come back and snap every other bone in your body." With that, Lucas peeled off his coat and dove headfirst into the bay.

The sea was so cold that it nearly sucked the air from his lungs. Treading water, he looked all around, trying to gauge the wind and the waves. If the lad had been caught in one of the deadly crosscurrents, there was no hope—he would be dashed to his death against the cliff.

Salt stung his eyes. "Perry!" he shouted, even though he knew it was unlikely that his voice could be heard above the crashing waves.

*"Hadley!"*

Was it only his imagination, or was there an answer? It was strange, but the sound seemed to be coming from both the sea and the sky.

"Lucas!"

He looked up to see Ciara scramble down through the steep rocks, following the same dangerous path that he had taken.

"Lucas!" she cried again, pointing frantically toward a cut in the cliff.

Wrenching his gaze around, he spotted a small blond head bobbing amid the whitecaps.

"I'm coming, lad," cried Lucas, cutting through cresting swells with powerful strokes. Thank God that as a boy he had spent countless hours swimming in the secluded coves. The currents were tricky, but he knew the dangers. He had the right angle—if only Peregrine could keep his head above water.

Kicking harder, Lucas fought through the chop. He

was now close enough to see the boy's face. Rather than appear terrified, Peregrine wore a look of fierce determination as he struggled manfully to stay afloat.

A last hard pull brought Lucas abreast of him. "Put your arms around my neck," he gasped through the swirls of salt spray. His own hands circled Peregrine's waist.

The touch of icy flesh nearly made him weep for joy.

Lud, what a sentimental sop he had become of late. His friends wouldn't recognize the sardonic, selfish Mad, Bad Had-ley of old. Perhaps because that man no longer existed.

"Don't panic, Perry. I'll get us safely ashore."

The boy's breath was warm against his wind-whipped cheek. "I'm not afraid, sir. Not with you here."

"Watch out, Lucas!" Ciara's warning cry alerted him to a new danger. He was drifting toward a shoal of rocks that guarded the narrow strip of beach.

"Stay back, sweetheart," he shouted. She had climbed down to a narrow ledge and was crouched perilously close to the surging surf. "I've got him."

But a quick glance showed the situation was serious. The cold was numbing, and Lucas could feel the strength ebbing from his arms and legs. Given the distance to shore, and the pull of the seas, it would be a close race to get both himself and the boy to shore . . .

He drew a deep breath and was about to plunge ahead when another shout rang out from the rocks above.

"Tie the end around your waist and keep hold of Peregrine!" Jack dropped a length of rope into the water. "I'll pull both of you up."

Lucas snagged the line, but his fingers were stiff with cold, and time was of the essence. "No—that's too great a weight. Just pull up the boy!" Looping it under Peregrine's arms, he managed to make a simple knot. "Haul away, Jack. I'll be fine. I'll swim for shore." Without the extra drag, he had a good chance of making it.

Jack snapped a salute and started to pull.

Slowly but surely, Peregrine rose from the waters. Ciara caught her son's collar and guided him up to the ledge.

A surge of relief swelled through his veins as Lucas watched her hug the boy to her chest with a sob of joy.

Jack was already scrambling down to meet them. At Ciara's order, he stripped off his coat and she quickly bundled her son in its warmth. She and Peregrine were in good hands now—

A vortex of swirling seas suddenly sucked him under. The churning water was black as Hades, and he felt himself sinking, sinking down into the briny darkness.

Ciara gasped in horror as Lucas disappeared beneath the surging waves. Peregrine was now safe, snugly wrapped in heavy wool. But the hero who had just risked his life to save her son was drowning!

"Mama!" Peregrine had seen it too. "Hadley is in trouble. We must help him."

*She would not—could not—lose Lucas from their lives.*

"Guard my son, Lord James." She brushed a last kiss to Peregrine's cheek and thrust him into Jack's embrace. Kicking off her half boots, Ciara spun around and dove headfirst into the water.

Her heart skipped a beat as she plunged beneath the windblown waves. Whispering a silent prayer, she groped through the murky waters, desperately hoping she wasn't too late.

Cold as ice, the currents cut against her flesh. *Too late, too late.* The roar of the surf filled her ears. And then her fingertips touched a tangle of hair. Fisting her hand, she kicked for the surface with all her might.

Gasping for breath, she opened her eyes to see Lucas's dripping face just inches from her.

"Damn it, darling," he sputtered. "You shouldn't have risked your neck in such a fool stunt."

"I—" A wave drowned the rest of her words.

He caught hold of her hand. "Follow me."

The tide was changing, and the shift in currents was just enough to smooth the waters at the opening of the cove. Lucas angled through the surf, leading the way through the shoals. The squall had just about blown over, and as they rounded the jut of rocks, the sun broke through the clouds and the sea became calm as glass.

A few more strokes and they reached the shallows. Ciara felt her feet touch the smooth stones . . .

Then, with a last lurching gasp, Lucas heaved her over his shoulder and staggered onto dry land.

Unraveling herself from a tangle of wet linen, she slid rather ungracefully to a seat in the coarse sand. Her feet were bare, her sleeves were in tatters, and her shortened skirts now revealed an indecent amount of leg.

Lucas was looking just as bedraggled, with his dripping-wet shirt and sodden breeches.

"Lud, what a scandalous picture we present," she murmured, picking a strand of seaweed from her hair.

"Scandalous." Rolling to his knees, he wrapped his arms around her. Though her body was numb with cold, she could feel the thud of his heartbeat and was filled with an inner warmth. For a moment the only sound between them was its steady pulsing, echoed by the ebb and flow of the sea.

And then a whisper of breath tickled against her throat as Lucas started laughing. "Do you think this will make the newspapers? I can just see the bold print in the gossip column—'Lord H once again in hot water!' "

"That won't do—you're shivering," said Ciara. "Perhaps the writer should consider another lead-in . . . 'Lord H submerged in a new bumblebroth with the Wicked Widow.' No, on second thought I've an even better one—'Lord H makes a new splash!' "

"You have an extraordinary talent for journalism, as well as science," he murmured, pressing a kiss to her brow. "Is there anything you can't do?"

Ciara looked up through her lashes at the chiseled contours of his face, which had become so achingly familiar. *I can't find the courage to tell you how much I love you.*

She cleared her throat with a watery sniff. "As you saw, I can't swim very well."

He grinned. "Luckily for you, I've had some practice at it."

"Yes, lucky me." Ciara tightened her hold on him, wanting to savor every last bit of this moment. All too soon, it would be gone. As would he—back to his wild life in London, while she returned to the solitude of her laboratory. Strange how a man reputed to be a devil-may-care rogue had stepped in to accept more than one role in their lives, she thought. His lighthearted laughter, his caring compassion had filled an achingly empty void . . .

"Ciara?" Lucas touched his fingertips to her cheeks. "Are you crying, sweetheart?"

"No." Her sorrow mingled with the salt of the sea. "Yes."

"The danger is over. Trust me, Sheffield's family won't ever threaten you or Perry again."

"I—I know."

"Then tell me why tears are streaming down your face, my love," he whispered.

*Love.* Her sobs grew louder.

Lucas held her tightly, stroking her hair until the snuffling subsided.

"I am sorry," she murmured, wiping her eyes. "It's just that I shall . . . miss you."

"Miss a bird-witted scoundrel like me?" He shook his head, sending a mizzle of tiny droplets through the air. "I should think you would be relieved to be rid of me."

"Please don't joke," said Ciara, unsure of how to go on. "I am trying to be serious—"

"Let me be serious too, sweeting." Lucas leaned back and lifted her chin. "I've no intention of leaving you or Perry." A hesitant smile curled at the corners of his mouth. "I am ready to take the plunge into a new life. A married life. If you will have me."

"I . . ."

"You have to admit, we get on swimmingly."

"Oh, Lucas." She dared not look him in the eye. "There is no denying the chemistry between us. But I don't want a marriage of convenience. I would want you home with me every night, not out carousing with your friends."

"No more brandy, brothels, and birds of paradise?"

She shook her head.

"I can't wait to begin my studies."

It was several long minutes before Ciara could regain possession of her mouth to speak again. "I'm not quite sure who is the teacher and who is the pupil. But regardless, we probably ought to defer further lessons until later." She fumbled with the fastenings of her bodice. "What with the children and the Battershams, poor Lord James has his hands full."

Lucas gave an evil leer. "To the devil with Sheffield's family. With any luck, Jack will break Arthur's other leg in hauling him up from the rocks." His amusement suddenly dissolved into a look of alarm. "But speaking of the others, what did he do with the dowager and Isabella while he was helping us? Surely he did not leave the little girl alone with that dangerous woman?"

"Actually, he tied Lady Battersham to a tree. As for Isa . . ." Ciara couldn't repress a chuckle. "He did the same, claiming it was the only thing he could think of to keep her from following him to the cliffs."

His brows winged up.

"Apparently she called him a number of very bad names in Italian."

Once Lucas stopping laughing, he rose and offered his hand. "We had better return the favor and go rescue Jack. By the by, how did he come to be looking for us?"

"He overheard the postboys talking when he stopped at a coaching inn on the road to London," recounted Ciara. "Battersham had tried to hire someone to abduct a child, but he could find no takers for the sum he offered. Your friend immediately turned around and was coming to warn us when he spotted Battersham's carriage pulled off to the side of the road."

Lucas pursed his lips. "You will have to tell the marchesa that Jack does have some redeeming qualities."

Ciara made a wry face. "Trussing her daughter to a tree is not one of them."

"Have pity on the poor fellow. Villains he can deal with, but Jack doesn't have much experience with children."

"All the more reason not to delay," said Ciara. "Rope, rocks, and a very large horse—I shudder to think of what Isa might do to retaliate."

His grin was no longer so smug. "You are right. We had better hurry." Pointing out an opening in the gorse, Lucas started across the strand. "Come, this way it is an easy walk back up to the top of the cliffs."

# Epilogue

$\mathcal{A}$re you sure you don't mind looking after Peregrine while we are away?" asked Ciara. "I can't help but feel a little bit guilty. It is, after all, your honeymoon, as well."

It still felt a little odd to be thinking of herself and Ariel as married ladies. The past three weeks had gone by in a blur. But somehow Lucas had managed all the dizzying details without batting an eye. He would not elaborate on how he had orchestrated the private legal negotiations with her late husband's family, save to tell her the final agreement. In return for hushing up the attempts on Peregrine's life and handing over a deed to a small tea plantation in India, Lady Battersham and Arthur were now on an East India merchant ship, sailing half a world away from London.

With the threat of public denunciation and a long prison sentence hanging over their heads, Sheffield's kin should be no further threat to her and Peregrine. To think that from now on, she could open the morning paper without fear tainting the taste of her tea.

Her lips quirked. Lucas had been equally adept at arranging the special licenses for himself and Henry, along with the perfect celebration.

Ciara rubbed at the gold ring on her finger, hardly daring to believe it was real. The double ceremony had been a quiet country service, with only their closest friends in attendance. Charlotte and Kate had hurried back from Scotland to serve as witnesses for the occasion. Their pique at missing all the excitement was quickly assuaged by seeing how blissfully happy the two new brides were with their men.

And while she had secretly worried that marriage might affect the future of the 'Sinners,' the others had all assured her that their special circle of friendship could never be broken.

*Friends. Family.* Some wild, wonderful spell had transformed the Wicked Widow of Pont Street into the luckiest woman in the world.

"Oh, pish!"

Ariel's airy dismissal drew Ciara back to the present moment.

"Go enjoy yourselves—the two of you deserve an interlude of peace and quiet together. The fortnight will likely pass more quickly than you would like."

"Don't forget that we are not likely to be engaging in nearly as many strenuous physical activities as you are," added Henry dryly. "Bird-watching can take a great deal of energy."

"So does keeping an eight-year-old out of mischief," replied Ciara as Lucas swallowed a snort of laughter.

"I am well aware of that, my dear. But after raising the hellion who is now your husband, I consider anything else mere child's play."

"You deserve a medal," she said. "Maybe two."

"Oh, come, I wasn't *that* bad," murmured Lucas with

a boyish grin. "London didn't burn to the ground. Parliament didn't explode. The Tower is still standing."

Ciara arched a brow. "Still, I shudder to think what your poor uncle endured."

Henry curled his fingers around Ariel's hand. "I think I can safely say that the lad has atoned for his youthful follies."

"Hear that, Perry?" Lucas ruffled the boy's curls. "Promise me that you will behave yourself, so that Henry doesn't regret his words."

"Yes, sir!" answered Peregrine.

"It's Lucas," he corrected. "We are family now, lad, not formal acquaintances."

*Family.* Ciara felt a welling of happiness bubble up inside her. Blinking back the prickle of tears, she watched her son look up at his new stepfather with undisguised adulation.

"Yes, Lucas."

"That's better." Lucas's expression turned impish as he regarded his uncle. "You may still have your work cut out for you, Henry. There is the matter of a little red journal that the ladies are keeping. A compendium of sorts . . . but I shall leave it to your bride to fill you in on the details."

Ariel's blush was a vivid scarlet.

"Come along, Perry. While your mama says her good-byes, perhaps you'll give me a hand with the carriage blankets and hamper for our journey—" Lucas stopped in midsentence as a large dray cart, accompanied by four burly workmen, rattled past the terrace and stopped by the garden gate. "What the devil is *that?*"

Henry shook his head in puzzlement.

"Your wedding present," replied Ciara.

The workmen untied the ropes and removed the canvas covering from the towering load.

"Why, it's . . . it's . . ." Though rarely at a loss for words, Lucas was reduced to sputtering.

"A fountain." She slanted a sidelong look at his profile. "Do you like it?"

His face went through a series of odd contortions, and then a burble of laughter slipped from his lips. "I love it."

"The far end of the rose walk looked a little bare," she explained. "So I took the liberty of commissioning a memento for all of us to enjoy. I think that it will look rather lovely there, bathed every evening in the pink and gold light of the setting sun."

Peregrine squinted, studying the decorative sculpture rising up from the stone basin. "It looks like a lady . . . and a bird."

"Yes. Leda and Zeus," murmured Ciara.

"Who occasionally appeared in the form of a swan," said Lucas.

"They are figures from classical Greek mythology," explained Ariel after a fraction of a pause. "Er, Sir Henry has some very educational books on the gods and goddesses of the ancient world. Perhaps we shall begin reading about their exploits while your mama and Lucas are on their wedding trip."

Lucas coughed. "Be careful what you teach him."

Her son grinned. "Oh, my tutor has told me a little about the myths. They are ripping good tales, especially the ones with lots of action—like flying thunderbolts, magic arrows, and the clash of the Titans and the Trojans." Grimacing, he added, "The ones about kissing are a little boring."

"When you get to be my age, you might change your mind," said Henry with a broad wink.

Peregrine looked slightly skeptical.

"Don't make a face, lad," chided Lucas. "On the whole, you'll find the stories very entertaining."

"If you say so." Her son thought for a moment. "Do I get to hear the one about Leda and the swan?"

"Maybe a little later in life," said Ciara.

"Why? Does it not have a happy ending?"

"I suppose that depends on your interpretation. As the lord of the gods, Zeus could be an arrogant, unrepentant rogue." Lucas grinned in unholy amusement as he gathered his bride in his arms and feathered a kiss to her lips. "He was certainly not a saint. But he did have some redeeming qualities to make up for his sins."

"A few," she conceded.

"So let's just say that the modern variation of the tale has a very happy ending, indeed."

She touched his cheek, reveling in the warmth of his closeness, the caress of his laughter.

"Amen to that."

Enjoy a sneak peek at
**Cara Elliott's**
sizzling new romance!

---

Please turn this page
for a preview of

*To Surrender to a Rogue*

Available in June 2010.

# Chapter One

*Y*ou tied my daughter to a *tree?*"

Rendered momentarily speechless, Alessandra della Giamatti flashed a very unladylike gesture at the gentleman who stood on the edge of the terrace, stomping great clumps of wet earth from his mud-spattered boots.

"*Si grande nero diavolo*—you big black devil!"

He stilled, and his dark face tightened in a fearsome scowl. "Damnation, it was for her own good."

"For her own good," she repeated. "*Santa cielo,* if I had a penny for every time a man said *that* to a woman, I would be richer than Croesus."

Lord James Jacquehart Pierson muttered something under his breath.

Alessandra narrowed her eyes. "I'll have you know that I am fluent in German, sir. As well as French and Russian."

"Well, it seems that your command of the English language leaves something to be desired, marchesa," he shot back. "For you don't appear to have comprehended the situation quite clearly."

Squaring his broad shoulders—which were made even

broader by the fluttering capes of his oilskin cloak—he set a hand on his hip and glowered. His olive complexion and wind-whipped tangle of raven-dark hair accentuated the shadows wreathing his chiseled features. In the fading light, his eyes appeared to be carved out of coal.

*No wonder the man was known throughout London Society as "Black Jack" Pierson.*

Alessandra did not doubt that his pose was an intentional attempt to appear intimidating. However, the man really ought to know her better by now. A delicate English rose might wilt at the first sign of masculine ire, but she was only *half* English.

As for the rest of her . . .

Meeting his gaze, she deliberately mimicked the gesture, adding one slight variation. As her shoulders weren't quite as impressive as his, she stuck out her bosom.

His dark lashes flicked up a fraction.

*Tit for tat, sir,* she thought.

After another long moment of silent standoff, he cleared his throat. "Would you rather I had let her follow me to the cliffs? It was pelting rain, the winds were blowing at gale force, and one misstep on the splintered rocks would have meant a sheer drop into the surging surf." His black brows angled to a taunting tilt. "But perhaps she is a Nereid," he continued, referring to the sea nymphs from ancient Roman mythology. "Or maybe her father was Neptune, God of the Oceans."

Alessandra sucked in her breath at the thinly veiled barb. *Men.* Most of them seemed to prefer females who were smiling, simpering—and stupid. So it was hardly a surprise that Lord James Jacquehart Pierson should choose to mock her. A noted scholar of classical archaeology, she was used to such a reaction when the opposite sex learned of her intellectual accomplishments.

And yet it still stung.

"Heaven knows," exclaimed Jack, "it would have required divine intervention to save her from certain death had she slipped."

That he was right only added an edge to Alessandra's indignation. "She said you handled her in a *very* ungentlemanly manner."

Her daughter looked up, lips quivering and a glint of tears in her eyes. *"Si."*

Alessandra recognized that look of assumed innocence all too well. She was aware that Isabella deserved a good scold for what had happened. But for the moment, she was too relieved at finding the little girl unharmed to do more than brush a soft kiss to her curls. A lecture would come later. Right now, all her fears were still fierce—and the fury of her pent-up emotions was directed at Black Jack Pierson.

"His hands were like ice against my bare skin, Mama," added her daughter in a small voice.

Jack sputtered in disbelief. "Is she . . . are you . . . accusing me of impropriety? You are mad—both of you!"

*"Va' all'inferno,"* piped up Isabella.

"I can't believe my ears," he muttered. "I'm being cursed at by a six-year-old."

"I am *eight,*" said Isabella, lifting her little nose into the air.

Alessandra winced as her daughter added several more phrases in Tuscan cant. *"Isabella!"* Forgetting her anger with Jack for the moment, she looked down in chagrin. "Those are *very* bad words. Wherever did you learn them?"

"Marco says them," murmured her daughter.

She felt a flush steal to her cheeks, well aware that Black Jack Pierson's frown had curled into a smirk. "That does *not* mean a young lady should repeat them."

"Foul language seems to run in the family," observed Jack.

It took every ounce of self-control for Alessandra to keep a rein on her tongue. She knew she was behaving badly. After all, the man *had* kept her impetuous daughter from plunging headlong into danger, however unorthodox his methods. But something about his manner set her teeth on edge. He always appeared so steely, so stiff—as if a bayonet were stuck up his . . .

*I am a lady,* she reminded herself. *And a lady ought not be thinking about certain unmentionable parts of a man's anatomy.*

Even if those parts were extremely impressive. Jack's cloak had fluttered up in a gust of wind, revealing well-muscled thighs and a solid, sculpted—

Forcing her gaze away from his lordly arse, she replied, "Italians are known for their volatile temperament, especially when upset."

"Oh, please accept my abject apologies for causing you mental distress," replied Jack with scathing politeness. He bowed. "Along with my humble regrets for keeping your daughter from smashing her skull into a thousand little pieces."

"I *did* say thank you, sir."

"It must have been in a language incomprehensible to mortal man."

*Uno, due, tre . . .* Alessandra made herself count to ten in Italian before gathering what was left of her dignity and lifting Isabella into her arms. "If you will excuse me, my daughter is shivering. I must take her inside and get her out of these wet clothes."

"Oh yes, by all means take the little cherub up to her room, give her a nice, warm bath." The flash of teeth was clearly not meant to be a smile. "And then wash her mouth out with soap."

~~~

The splash of brandy burned a trail of liquid fire down his throat. Perching a hip on the stone railing, Jack took another quick swallow from the bottle, hoping to wash the stale taste from his mouth.

*Va' all'inferno,* he repeated to himself. *Go to hell.*

Those were precisely his sentiments, he decided. The ungrateful lady and her imp of Satan could fall into the deepest hole in Hades for all he cared. This was not the first time he had offered his sword—metaphorically speaking, of course—to the marchesa. Only to have it thrust back in his arse.

So much for noblesse oblige.

To tell the truth, he wasn't feeling terribly noble at the moment. Against all reason, the thought of swords, coupled with the rapier-tongued Alessandra della Giamatti, was stirring an unwilling, unwanted physical reaction.

*That fine-boned face, exquisite in every ethereal detail . . . emerald eyes, fringed with smoky lashes that set off their inner fire . . . sculpted cheekbones that looked carved out of creamy white marble . . . a perfect nose, supremely regal in its delicate shape.*

Oh, there was no denying that the spitfire was a stunning beauty—if one could ignore The Mouth.

On second thought, that proved impossible. Jack closed his eyes for an instant, recalling the firm, full lips, the rich, rosy color, the silky, sensuous curl of its corners . . .

*No, he must not let his mind stray to forbidden territory.*

The marchesa's lovely body would tempt a saint. But her fiery temper would singe Satan himself.

Swearing under his breath, Jack took another gulp of brandy. Indeed, she was the most infuriating, exasperating woman he had ever encountered. There was no rational reason to explain why she seemed hell-bent on deliberately misinterpreting his every action. Save to say she simply disliked him.

"So don't get your hopes up," he growled, staring balefully at the growing bulge in his breeches.

What a pity that a penis did not possess a brain. Then it might comprehend how utterly absurd it was to imagine that the aloof marchesa would ever consent to a physical liaison, no matter that widows were allowed certain freedoms if they were discreet.

An intimate joining of flesh? Hah! They couldn't be further apart in temperament. It was as if they came from two different planets.

*Venus and Mars.*

An apt allusion, given her expertise in classical archaeology.

Looking up at the heavens, he let his gaze linger on the constellations. Like the ancient Greek and Roman goddesses immortalized in the stars, Alessandra della Giamatti was a force to be reckoned with. That she had a mind made for scholarship and a body made for sin was intriguing. Her aura of cool self-assurance was alluring . . .

However, every meeting between them seemed to spark nothing but thunder and lightning. It was ironic—had they dug into the subject of classical antiquities, they might have discovered that they shared some common ground.

Jack pursed his lips. Along with a taste for fine brandy and beautiful women, he also had a passion for the architecture and art of ancient Rome—though he kept it a private one, save from his closest friends. But given their most recent clash, it seemed impossible to imagine that he and this woman would *ever* reveal their most intimate secrets to each other.

Sliding across the cold stone, Jack leaned back against one of the decorative pediments and stared out into the night. A mizzle of moonlight cast a faint glow over the gardens and lawns, its glimmer reflected by silvery tendrils of mist rising up from the nearby sea. Above the chirping crickets, he could just make out the sound of the surf and its rhythmic rise and fall against the cliffs.

*Lud, what a day.*

As one of his gambling cronies was wont to say, no good deed goes unpunished. The only reason he had come to be at daggers drawn with Alessandra della Giamatti was on account of trying to help his best friend, Lucas Bingham, the Earl of Hadley—who was engaged to Lady Ciara Sheffield, the marchesa's closest confidante.

Well, not *precisely* engaged, amended Jack. But that was a whole other story . . .

He expelled a wry sigh. Hell, the next time he was tempted to play the knight in shining armor, perhaps he should think twice, rather than risk his neck trying to do something noble. Scrambling over the rocks to help rescue

Lady Sheffield's young son and the marchesa's daughter from danger had been no easy feat.

Thank God the adventure had resulted in no real harm, although there had been a few harrowing moments when his friend Lucas had been compelled to take a dive into the surging sea.

The more startling plunge had been his friend's announcement that he was, once and for all, renouncing the life of a rakehell bachelor and marrying Lady Sheffield for real.

Out of the corner of his eye, he saw the blaze of lights in the main wing of the manor house. Laughter drifted out through the diamond-paned windows, punctuated by the faint pop of champagne corks. The impending state of matrimony had set off a great deal of merriment this evening—in no small part because Lucas's elderly uncle had also become betrothed during the day.

Striking a flint, Jack lit a cheroot and drew in a mouthful of smoke. First Haddan, then Woodbridge, now Hadley . . . Was he really the only single man left from the pack of rowdy scamps who had banded together at Eton? He blew out a perfect ring and watched it dissolve in the breeze.

Shaking off his black mood, Jack took another swig of brandy, telling himself he ought to be celebrating his freedom. He was damned lucky not to be leg-shackled to a wife.

"Won't you come join us?"

Jack looked around as his friend Lucas took a seat beside him on the railing. "Thank you, but no," he replied after exhaling another mouthful of smoke. "I fear I would only put a damper on the festivities."

Lucas held up a bottle of champagne. "If you insist on drowning your sorrows alone, at least submerge yourself in a superb vintage of wine." He took a drink himself before passing it over.

With a wordless grunt, Jack downed a long swallow.

Tilting back his head, Lucas smiled up at the night sky. "Did you know that Dom Perignon, the monk who discovered the secret to champagne's sparkle, compared it to drinking the heavenly stars?"

"No," he replied, not bothering to glance up. "Only a man besotted by romance would know such drivel."

"My, my, aren't we in a prickly mood," remarked his friend. "Any specific reason?"

Jack remained silent for a moment as the effervescence of the wine danced like tiny daggers against his tongue. Then, instead of answering, he asked abruptly, "Is Lady Giamatti celebrating with you?"

"No, like you, she cried off," replied Lucas slowly. "She claimed to be exhausted from all the excitement."

"Hmmph."

"She plans to leave for London at first light," added his friend.

"As do I. So if you don't mind, I think I'll retire for the night." Jack rose and ground the butt of his cheroot beneath his boot. "And take the bottle with me for company—seeing as there are no willing wenches to warm my bed."

"Ciara sends her thanks for all your help this afternoon," said Lucas, ignoring the comment. He allowed a brief pause. "She also said to ask you not to judge Lady Giamatti too harshly. They are the best of friends, and yet she has a feeling that there is something troubling the marchesa of late. Something the lady dares not discuss with even her closest confidantes."

"Assure your future bride that she need not worry over my opinion—I have none to speak of," snapped Jack. "The marchesa and her mysteries are no concern of mine."

"Ah," murmured Lucas. "And here I thought that I had detected a glimmer of interest in your eye."

"You must have been looking through the prism of your own lovestruck gaze," muttered Jack. "Not all of us have been struck blind to reason by Cupid's damn arrow." As he turned for the terrace doors, he hesitated. "But the needling aside, I wish you happiness, Lucas."

A swirl of wind ruffled through the ivy leaves, nearly drowning out his friend's reply.

"The same to you, Jack."

He marched across the slate tiles, but as his hand touched the latch, he abruptly veered away, choosing instead to descend the side steps and take the long way around to the guest quarters. Perhaps a vigorous walk would shake off his dark mood.

*Damn.* He wasn't usually so snarly with a friend.

Lifting the bottle to his lips, Jack quaffed the rest of its contents in one long gulp. There—that ought to loosen his mood, he thought grimly, tugging at the knot of his cravat. The crunch of gravel underfoot echoed the *clink* of glass against the stones. Hopefully, Sir Henry would forgive him for the lapse of manners in littering his lovely grounds. He rounded the privet hedge and stumbled past the garden statues . . .

One of the sculpted shapes appeared to move.

Jack stopped short. Surely the wine could not have gone to his head quite so quickly.

"You need not give me that basilisk stare, sir," said the stone.

*Of all the cursed luck.* It was not a figment of his foxed imagination but Alessandra della Giamatti in the flesh.

"Lucas said you had retired for the night," he blurted out, then immediately regretted making any response.

"I decided to come outside for a breath of fresh air before seeking my bed." Her hair was unpinned and fell in soft, shimmering ebony waves over her shoulders as she stepped out from the shadows of a laughing faun. "Or is there some arcane Anglo-Saxon rule that prohibits a lady from enjoying a solitary stroll after dark?"

Her words recalled an earlier clash. "Will you never cease snapping at me for having tried to do the honorable thing, marchesa?" demanded Jack. "I have already admitted that my interference in the arcade was a mistake. How many times must I offer an apology?"

A week ago in London he had stepped in to defend her from the advances of an aggressive male. Unfortunately, the fellow in question turned out to be her cousin.

"Not that I feel I was entirely in the wrong," he couldn't help adding. "An English gentleman does not allow another male to continue haranguing a lady, especially after she has asked him to leave her alone. Code of honor, you see."

Her jaw tightened. "It was a private discussion, sir."

"Then you should not have conducted it in public," replied Jack.

Alessandra drew in a sharp breath. "That is the trouble with you Englishmen—you have such a rigid notion of honor."

"You would prefer that we act as cads?" His temper,

which was dangerously frayed to begin with, suddenly snapped. "Very well."

Two quick strides covered the distance between them.

Her lips parted in shock, but before she could make a sound, his mouth crushed down upon hers.

～⌐

For an instant Alessandra was too shocked to react. And then . . .

And then, though every brain cell was shouting at her to thrust him away, she found herself loath to listen. The taste of his mouth was intoxicating—the sweetness of the wine, the salt of the nearby sea, the smoky spice of masculine desire. Drinking it all in, she lay utterly limp in his arms, her senses overwhelmed with the different sensations.

In contrast to the searing heat of his kiss, his skin was cool and damp from the night mists. The stubbling of whiskers on his jaw prickled against her flesh, while his hair was surprisingly silky beneath her fingertips—

*Oh, Lud, were her hands really twining through the tangle of his sin-black hair?*

Alessandra choked back a moan. She had nearly forgotten how good it was to feel chiseled muscle and whipcord sinew hard against her body. The sloping stretch of Jack's shoulders—so strong, so solid—seemed to go on forever, enveloping her in a musky warmth.

A tower of strength.

*No, no, no.* What weak-willed delusion had taken hold of her? She could not be so stupid as to trust in the illusion of steadfast support. *A man to lean on?* She had been needy enough after her husband's death to reach for comfort. Only a fool made the same mistake twice.

She inhaled to protest, only to find that the earthy scent of him made her a little dizzy. Sandalwood and tobacco mixed with a dark spice that she could not quite define. Her knees buckled.

*Diavolo*—every bone in her body was suddenly soft as spaghetti.

Tightening his hold, Jack braced her against one of the decorative columns that flanked the pathway.

The initial explosion of male anger had burned down to a gentler heat. His touch left a trail of warmth along her night-chilled flesh.

Alessandra was woozily aware of his hands cupping the curves of her derriere. He pressed closer, and she felt her nipples turn to points of fire as his chest slid slowly over the peaked flesh. She found the opening of his coat, her fingertips sliding over the soft linen.

He was so big, and so . . . utterly masculine, from the darkly dangerous name—*Black Jack*—to the broad chest, tapered waist, and muscular legs that seemed to go on forever.

*Desire.* Like a serpent, it slowly uncoiled and slithered up from its place of hiding. With a liquid sigh, she opened herself to Jack's embrace, twining her tongue with his. With a rumbled groan, he thrust in deeper, filling her with his hot, hungry need.

Her pulse was now pounding out of control, but somehow, above the din in her ears, she heard the voice of reason.

*Dangerous.*

As his mouth broke away to trail a line of lapping kisses

along her throat, she finally got hold of her senses and shoved him back a fraction. Now was the moment for a scathing set-down, but strangely enough, as she searched her brain for something to say, her mind was a complete blank.

He, too, appeared paralyzed with shock. His dark lashes lay still against his olive skin, and aside from the harsh rasp of his breathing, he might have been carved out of stone. Sharpened by the slanting moonlight, the strong, chiseled lines of his face gave him the appearance of a Roman god.

Mars—the mighty, mythical warrior.

The only flaw was a tiny scar cutting just beneath his left eyebrow, a faint line nearly hidden by the raven-wing arch. *A chink in his lordly armor?* She felt an impulsive urge to trace it with her fingertip, and then touch it with her tongue . . .

A swirl of breeze tugged at the tails of his cravat, and the flutter of white finally dispelled her momentary surrender of sanity.

Twisting free of his hold, Alessandra clutched at her cloak, drawing the folds in tight to cover her night rail.

"That was unforgivable," he said softly. "I . . . I don't know what came over me—"

Mortified by her own actions—and reactions—she cut off his halting apology. "The full moon is said to stir a certain madness."

How else to explain the elemental force that had drawn them together? Without waiting for a reply, Alessandra plunged into the pooling shadows, her slippered feet nearly tripping over the uneven ground in her haste to get away.

*As if she could outrun her embarrassment.*

To her relief, Black Jack Pierson made no move to follow her.

# THE DISH

*Where authors give you the inside scoop!*

♥ ♥ ♥ ♥ ♥ ♥ ♥ ♥ ♥ ♥ ♥ ♥ ♥ ♥

*From the desk of Cara Elliott*

Dear Readers,

*Pssst.* Have you seen the morning newspaper yet? Oh, it's too delicious for words. The infamous Lord H—yes, Mad, Bad Had-ley in the flesh—has made yet another wicked splash in the gossip column. You remember last week, when his cavorting with a very luscious—and very naked—ladybird ended with a midnight swim in the Grosvenor Square fountain? Well, that was just a drop in the bucket compared to this latest *ondit*. Word has it that Hadley, the rakishly sexy hero of TO SIN WITH A SCOUNDREL (available now), has really fallen off the deep end this time. He's been spotted around Town with . . . the Wicked Widow of Pont Street.

Don't bother cleaning your spectacles—you read that right. Hadley and Lady Sheffield! The same Lady Sheffield who stirred such a scandal last year when it was whispered that she may have poisoned her husband. Yes, yes, at first blush it seems impossible. After all, they are complete opposites. The fun-loving Lord Hadley is a devil-may-care rogue, and the reclusive Lady Sheffield is a scholarly bluestocking. Why, the only thing they appear to have in common is the fact that their names show up so frequently in all the gossip columns. But appearances can be deceiving, and a friend tells me that a fundamental law of physics states that opposites attract.

Not that I would dare to wager on it. However, the betting books at all the London clubs are filled with speculation on why Hadley is paying court to the lovely widow. Some say that it's merely one of Hadley's madcap pranks. Others think that he's been bewitched by one of the potent potions that the lady brews up in her laboratory. But I'll let you in on a little secret: Whatever the reason, the combination of a scoundrel and a scientist has passion and intrigue coming to a boil!

How do I know? I'll let you in on another little secret—as the author of the book, I'm familiar with *all* the intimate details of their private lives.

So why did I choose to make my hero and heroine of TO SIN WITH A SCOUNDREL the subject of rumors and innuendos? In doing my research, I discovered that our current fascination with gossip and scandal is nothing new. Regency England reveled in "tittle-tattle," and had its own colorful scandal sheets and "paparazzi." Newspapers and pamphlets reported in lurid detail on the celebrity bad boys—and bad girls—of high society. And like today, sex, money, and politics were hot topics. As for pictures, there were, of course, no cameras, but the satirical artists of the Regency could be even more ruthless than modern-day photographers.

Hmmm, come to think of it, the hero and heroine of TO SURRENDER TO A ROGUE, the second book in the series (available June '10), are likely to generate quite a bit of gossip too. Lady Sheffield's fellow scholar, the lovely and enigmatic Lady Giamatti, finds that someone is intent on digging up dirt on her past life in Italy while she is excavating Roman antiquities in the town of Bath. That Black Jack Pierson is a member of the learned group stirs up trouble . . . Oh, but don't let me spoil the fun. You really ought to read all about it for yourself.

Now don't worry if your butler has tossed out the morning newspaper. If you hurry on over to www.caraelliott.com, you can sneak a tantalizing peek at all three books in my new Circle of Sin series.

Enjoy!

*Cara Elliott*

♥ ♥ ♥ ♥ ♥ ♥ ♥ ♥ ♥ ♥ ♥ ♥ ♥ ♥ ♥

*From the desk of Susan Kearney*

Dear Readers,

I came up with my idea for JORDAN, the third book in the Pendragon Legacy trilogy, while sipping a wine cooler in my hammock. I was rocking between two rustling queen palms when a time machine landed on my dock. And the hottest dude ever strode up the wooden stairs and pulled up a chair beside me. His eyes matched the blue of the sea and his muscles rippled in the Florida sunshine.

Jordan.

He'd arrived just as the sun was dipping into the Gulf of Mexico. And did you know that Jordan's history is as interesting as his looks?

Did I mention this guy may have looked in the prime of his life, but he's more than fifteen hundred years old? Did I mention that centuries ago he fought at King Arthur's side? And that not only is he a powerful dragon shaper but he knows secrets to save us all?

Jordan raked a hand through his hair. "Rion told me that you write love stories about the future."

"I do." Somehow, I knew this was going to be one hell of a story.

"In the future, Earth will be threatened by your greatest enemy."

My fingers shook. "Did you save my world?"

"I had help from a smart, beautiful woman."

"And you fell in love?" I guessed, always a romantic at heart.

"She was my boss." His voice lowered to a sexy murmur. "And we fought a lot in the beginning. You see, Vivianne Blackstone didn't trust me."

"So you had to win her over?"

"She's one stubborn woman." His voice rang with pride, a grin softening his tone.

Oh, this story sounded exciting. Lucan had told me how Vivianne Blackstone had funded the first spaceship mission to Pendragon. Just imagining such a strong woman with Jordan sent a delicious shiver of anticipation down my spine. "But surely Vivianne must have liked you just a little bit at first?"

"She thought I was an enemy spy." Jordan's grin widened. "And she wasn't too pleased when I stole her new spaceship . . . with her on board."

Oh, my. "I'd imagine it took her awhile to forgive you."

While Jordan was quite the man . . . still . . . he'd stolen her ship and taken her with him into space. Vivianne must have been furious. And scared. Although, the writer in me told me Jordan had been good for Vivianne. "So how long did it take her to believe you were both on the same side?"

Jordan chuckled. "It must have been after the second, no, the third time we made love."

I swallowed hard. Oh . . . my. "You made love while she believed you were enemies?"

He raised an eyebrow. "We didn't really have a choice."

I gave him a hard look. "Um, look. I'm afraid I'm going to need the details. Lots of details."

If you'd like to read the details Jordan told me, the book is in stores now. Reach me at www.susankearney.com.

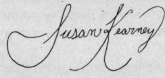

♥ ♥ ♥ ♥ ♥ ♥ ♥ ♥ ♥ ♥ ♥ ♥ ♥ ♥ ♥ ♥

*From the desk of R. C. Ryan*

Dear Reader,

Blame it on Willy Nelson. My heroes have always been cowboys.

Whether they're riding the trail in the Old West or dealing with today's problems on a modern, up-to-date ranch tricked out with all the latest high-tech gadgets, I simply can't resist loving a cowboy.

In my mind, the tall, silent hero of a Western is the equivalent of the savage, untamed Highlander. Noble, loyal, fiercely independent. Impossible for this woman to resist.

Now add to that a treasure hunt for a priceless fortune in gold nuggets, and you have a recipe for adventure, intrigue, and romance.

MONTANA LEGACY is the first book in my Fool's Gold trilogy. Three cousins, long separated, are brought together by the death of their grandfather, who has spent a lifetime searching for a lost family treasure.

Of course they can't resist taking up his search. But that's only half the story. Equally important is the love they discover on the journey. And more than love—trust. Trust in one another, and in the women who win their hearts and enrich their lives.

If you're like me and love tough, strong, fun-loving cowboys in search of a legendary treasure, come along for the adventure of a lifetime.

I enjoy hearing from my readers. Drop by my Web site and leave me a message: www.ryanlangan.com.

Happy reading!

*R. C. Ryan*

*Want to know more about romances at*
*Grand Central Publishing and Forever?*
*Get the scoop online!*

## GRAND CENTRAL PUBLISHING'S
## ROMANCE HOME PAGE

Visit us at www.hachettebookgroup.com/romance
for all the latest news, reviews, and chapter excerpts!

## NEW AND UPCOMING TITLES

Each month we feature our new titles
and reader favorites.

## CONTESTS AND GIVEAWAYS

We give away galleys, autographed copies,
and all kinds of fun stuff.

## AUTHOR INFO

You'll find bios, articles, and links to personal
Web sites for all your favorite authors—and
so much more!

## THE BUZZ

Sign up for our monthly romance newsletter,
and be the first to read all about it!